SAGE EMPRESS I

Books in the Phoenix Feather Series

Fledglings

Redbark

Firebolt

Dragon and Phoenix

Tribute

SAGE EMPRESS I

SHERWOOD SMITH

BOOK VIEW CAFE

BOOK VIEW CAFE

Published by Book View Café
304 S. Jones Blvd., Suite 2906
Las Vegas, NV 89107
www.bookviewcafe.com

ISBN: 978-1-63632-239-1

Cover Design by Victoria Davies
Interior Design by Marissa Doyle

Discover other books by Sherwood Smith at
www.Sherwoodsmith.net

ONE

IT WOULD BE DRAMATIC to say that from my earliest memory I wanted to escape the imperial palace, but that is not true. I intend to write the truth as I saw it, or I could spare myself the effort and point to the official records full of polished flatteries, or countless unctuous poems full of dramatic hyperbole. I can't resist heading my sections with some of the most egregious of these pomposities.

The truth is not dramatic, for I simply had the typical child's curiosity about the world outside the confines of the nursery. Whenever I saw a door open, I did my best to go out and explore. That curiosity is often scolded, or worse, out of small children—even for the best of reasons, as a small child does not recognize danger—but Nanny was ever patient, merely hauling me back and distracting me with a song or a toy or a story.

When I could not get through the door, I sent my imagination. My earliest memory in that regard is what I thought of as the Empire of Frogs. This was founded upon a priceless nine-fold screen called The Butterflies' Paradise. When I chanced upon it again much later, I sustained a shock of recognition in spite of how memory had distorted the actuality. As a small child, I could not see the butterflies at all. My attention, and my imagination, centered around the little frogs painted along the lower edge, among different colored pebbles and tiny pools, above which grew a forest of reeds. By the time I was tall enough to step over the threshold between rooms, I had named all those frogs after ourselves—Father, Mother, First Brother, Second Brother, Nanny and me—and I had imagined countless scenes, mostly extensions of daily life blended with Nanny's small tales from her own youth.

Once I began to be aware of palace life in its rounds of ritual and tradition, I wholly believed what everyone from the briefly glimpsed emperor to the lowest menial united in making into a truth: that palace life had existed forever, and would continue in just this way forever. Our earliest lessons were steeped in ritual and tradition, the most sacred words modified by "ancient." *It has always been done that way* was unanswerable, especially by us girls.

"The single most important lesson for a princess is deportment," my nanny repeated in admonishing me, when I was caught scrambling after my brothers over the wall to raid the peach trees. It wasn't that we were not given peaches. Oh, the beautiful fruits, there for the taking, in season—and frozen, kept in the ice houses, and made into delectable dishes out of season! But everyone knows that stolen fruit is sweeter, or so Second Brother told me. I believed everything he said until my seventh birthday, when he informed me that from now on I must wear a cow bell around my neck to frighten away demons.

"But you did not wear a cow bell when you turned seven. I remember," I said, thinking myself quite shrewd.

"That's because it's only girls the demons eat up. Here you go! Your very own." He handed me the bell.

As I had scarcely ever seen my imperial or noble cousins until then, and I had no sisters, I believed him. And the next day, when I had to go out into the garden to practice my court deportment, the cow bell clanged ridiculously as I tripped back and forth. Deportment lessons, I suppose I scarcely need to say, were tedious in the extreme, and I loathed them. The bell was a delightful distraction, and I gleefully noted that my three maidservants—scarcely older than I—were unsure what to do once I told them that Second Brother had given it to me. Whatever my brothers did was almost as sacrosanct as orders from my parents. I was highly entertained, and felt quite bold as well, imagining the demons fleeing on the wind.

Nanny had been supervising the changing of my bedding from spring to summer coverings and hangings, so at first she was not there. But when she heard the unprecedented noise, she scurried out, scandalized, words already tripping off her tongue, "Your highness, a princess is above all noiseless…" She stopped short when she saw the bell. "What is that?"

"Second Brother gave it to me for my birthday, to save me from being eaten by demons," I explained.

Gift — brothers — charms — these ideas halted Nanny's fingers in the air before they could touch the grimy cord the bell was strung with. She blinked at me. Then she turned about and vanished inside with a sway of gray robes.

Nanny was back very soon with my mother, who, even in this moment of world-trembling crisis (so it seemed to my seven-year-old self) glided toward me so smoothly that the two golden ornaments dangling on dainty chains from her hairpin scarcely trembled. "I'll take that bell, Daughter," she said, and while she lifted the bell (which smelled of cow, incidentally) up from my neck, she asked for the story that I repeated once more.

Mother's lips compressed as she glanced at the garden wall. Then her delicately plucked eyebrows lifted very slightly, and she said, "Continue your lessons. Soundlessly."

She took the bell away, which I was sad to see. Not that I feared demons. Mother's complete disinterest in Second Brother's threat had dispelled my worry on that score. I had to return to the tedium of practicing my deportment walk — this time under the stern eye of Nanny, which meant I could not conveniently forget, or lay aside, the box that I had to balance on the top of my head.

I thought no more about the bell until we were all summoned to the family's ancestral shrine at Dragon first hour, when customarily we were summoned to the evening meal.

This could only mean one thing: punishment. The forgotten cow bell came back to me, and my hands turned damp. But it was not I who was summoned before Father, and told to fetch the switch. It was Second Brother.

Father held out the cow bell.

Second Brother protested, "It was just a joke!"

"What did you say to your sister, Second Son?" Father asked sternly. He was tall, but in that room he seemed to be taller than the tallest roof of any three-tiered palace.

"It was only a joke," Second Brother mumbled, then out it came, in pieces. Every word of our exchange, after which Father turned his gaze to me. He was so tall and serious that the moment seemed terrible, and I trembled as he said, "Is Second Brother's confession accurate?"

"Yes, Father." I could barely get the two words out past my constricted throat. They came out like a mouse's squeak.

Father then turned his remote, serious gaze to Second Brother. "Your true motive? Think before you speak," he warned.

Second Brother was already pale, then he blanched to the shade of rice paper and mumbled, "I wanted the bell to make noise to disrupt our class."

"Then it was not a joke at all, but a lie in order to make your sister your tool in interrupting your education."

I remembered Mother's glance at the wall dividing the women's courtyard from the men's in our family palace. On the other side of that wall, the younger noble boys would have begun studying under the airy pavilion they would use through the summer until Harvest Festival.

"It is that lie for which you will be punished now," Father said. "After which you will copy twenty-fold Kanda's admonitions on the gift of speech. With each gift comes responsibility. Do you want to be reborn a donkey in your next life?"

From the look on Second Brother's face he would not mind that at all, if he could just leap ahead to that time and avoid the painful interlude to come. But there was no leap of time. Father administered ten swats, but at least he hadn't used the heavy cane, which was reserved for serious offenses. I had already seen that used once, an experience that so frightened me I could not bear to even look at that cane afterward, though the blood had long been cleaned off.

Second Brother was then told to kneel for the length of an incense stick to reflect on himself before commencing his copywork, after which we left, but when we got to the dining hall, Father turned to me. "I understand that you put one sensible question to your brother, but why did you not reflect on the fact that if there was any such threat, your mother or I would have warned you long before your birthday?"

There was no answer to be made. It was true. I hadn't thought past the fact that the cow bell was interesting, the lessons boring, and nobody wanted to be eaten by demons.

"You have reached an age to begin questioning irregularities," Father said to me. "If something takes you by surprise—if you suspect a hidden motive—you must begin to use your brain as well as your tongue. After the meal, you are to write out Kanda's admonition on the gift of speech, and consider every word, Daughter."

And so I did not escape entirely; though the admonition was only to be copied once, I was struggling in those days to master my writing brush, and it took a long time. I half-comprehended that I had been admonished for my credulousness, and I resolved never to believe anything Second Brother ever said, ever, ever, ever.

The next morning, the family ate together as if nothing had happened. Once remonstrances and consequences had been completed, we began anew—this was a rule in our household, though I was to discover that in other imperial households, a disgrace meant one had to earn back one's former place, which might take weeks, even months, during which everyone was supposed to diligently remind the miscreant of their disgrace. Some took great (yes, we'll call it vindictive) pleasure in these reminders, others were more earnest of intent, as our parents were always reminding us that every look, word, and gesture had consequences.

Father put on his court robe and his Censor hat, and departed for the Hall of Glorious Harmony. Mother put on one of her silken robes covered with embroidered butterflies and flowers, and departed to make her round of calls within the imperial harem. First Brother went to gather his writing case and his books for lessons, and Second Brother made to follow as I turned toward the door leading to the yard to practice deportment, before sewing and calligraphy.

Second Brother stopped me in the hall. "Sorry," he mumbled, his face, round as the moon, troubled instead of laughing-eyed with mischief. "First Brother told me you got stuck with copy work, too. I didn't think you'd get into trouble, as long as you didn't know what I really wanted to do." And he pushed into my hand his share of the sweet-cakes from breakfast, which I knew were his favorite.

My resentment vanished.

"Does it hurt much?" I asked.

Second Brother rubbed his backside. "Barely stung," he said. "Father never beats very hard." He flashed a grin. "And you ought to have seen the boys laughing behind their hands at your clanging and clanking. Everyone thought a cow got loose in the far garden. The old graybeard was furious. It was worth it," he added stoutly.

I came away from that understanding that I could ask questions, as long as these were offered respectfully (that was Mother's influence) and precisely (that was Father's).

Why are there two moons? Was Kanda a real person? I was full of questions, but rarely about what I saw before my face each day. Mostly I thought them up hoping for praise, which I got when one parent or the other deemed a question a good one. I also liked the attention, which was usually reserved for First Brother, especially these days, as he prepared for the Imperial Examination. That was of primary importance in our family, so much that Father laid aside the work he usually had with him at all times, including meals, to put questions to First Brother as we ate. First Brother's recitations were long, and mostly without flaw; Father felt Second Brother benefitted from hearing. Even I was to benefit, as helpmeet to my future husband, as yet unknown.

That summer, Mother began teaching me the game Circle, which until then I had assumed was one of the many things reserved for brothers and male cousins, like the school from which I heard the rise and fall of those boy voices as they chanted sutras. But she did not teach Circle in military terms. Instead, Mother began in one quarter of the board, with very small mathematical combinations, the moves adding or subtracting the white or black stones. Later, multiplying or dividing.

I turned eight at the beginning of the next spring. We celebrated with nut cakes and fireworks in the garden, and I was given a new ribbon for my hair and a new inkstone. A few mornings later, Mother laid down a scented message that she had received during breakfast, and told me that I had been summoned to accompany her on her visits into the imperial harem, which had recommenced with spring.

What excitement! Feeling like a paper lantern lit from within to rise toward the sky, I began to bounce, but a single reproving glance from Mother pinched out the candle.

In measured voice Mother instructed me. "You will never speak unless directly addressed. No matter what is asked, you always begin with formal thanks, and then you add 'very fine.' So. If the dowager empress were to condescend to notice you by asking if you have been a good, obedient girl, what do you say?"

"I go to the floor, and say, thanks to the infinite grace of her imperial majesty, this insignificant child is…obedient?"

"Strives to be obedient," Mother corrected. "If the empress asks if you are learning your embroidery, what do you say?"

"Thanks to the infinite grace of her imp—"

"You may address her directly, *your imperial majesty*. Only the dowager empress must be addressed indirectly, as she is too exalted for us to presume a nearer connection. It is for her to bestow the next step."

"Thanks to the infinite grace of your imperial majesty," I said, making my low curtsy to the empress, "this insignificant one—"

"—child—"

"—this insignificant child attempts to learn."

"That will do, at your age. The same pattern will serve for the elder imperial aunts, and the consorts."

"But I cannot tell them apart," I whimpered. "I might get them mixed up."

Mother gave me that look again. "Modulate your voice, Daughter. Practice, even here. I don't believe this visit will be repeated for at least a couple of years. I suspect there is some discussion about arranging your marriage, and they want a look at you first. As for the aunts and consorts, you must listen carefully to how I address each, and repeat what I say."

My joy at being included among the grownups began to give way to trepidation as I was bathed again, this time with jasmine to scent the water, and put into my festival robe of peach-colored silk, with bluebells and peonies embroidered down the front edges and along the hem. It was tied with my blue sash. My eyes watered as my maid combed my hair out again, and rebraided it very tightly, so that not a strand was out of place. My best blue ribbons tied each braid high on my head, and Nanny, overseeing this transformation, scolded me nervously not to touch them before I even lifted my hand.

We did not live within the harem, of course. Like the other lower relations of the emperor, we occupied one of the palaces surrounding the imperial garden. The trepidation had completely replaced the joy by the time I trod two steps back and to the left of Mother on her long journey to the dowager empress's palace.

That first time, everything was new, and overwhelming in

the glory of the fine statues and furnishings, the painted screens, the carved scrollwork along the beams overhead, gilt and gleaming richly. Glorious as the rooms were—very different from the relative simplicity of my home—the headdresses of the women, and their gowns and jewels, were finer still. I felt as if I moved in a painting, and I must be very careful not to put a foot wrong, or to relax my hands from their pose, neatly crossed just below the area of my navel, elbows even so that my sleeves draped smoothly.

The dowager empress did not speak to me. The empress did, but when I dared to peek at her on my rise from my curtsy, I discovered that she was not looking at me at all. Her head was turned, her gaze on one of the aunts or consorts arranged on their cushions to either side in strict rank order. My neck prickled at that look. I was glad not to be receiving it.

By the sixth palace, I began to understand why the adults only drank a single tiny porcelain cup of tea. Mother was taking in quite a lot of tea, but there would be no privy visits within the harem!

I dared to widen my scrutiny in furtive peeks, finally noting to my astonishment that I was not the only girl present. There were three others around my age, and several big girls, but all remained behind their mothers, as I did, so it was difficult to catch sight of more than the curve of head framed by shining black hair as tightly ordered as my own, and the quick flutter of gowns far more elaborate than mine. It was then that I realized I was in the presence of my distant cousins, some the descendants of grand princes—like my father was— or perhaps these might even be imperial princesses, hereto only glimpsed from a distance at the ancestral temple on the new year's first day.

I possessed myself impatiently until we got home, and then burst out with questions. Who were those girls? I would meet them soon, if I attended to lessons properly. Was I to be married? Of course—in many years still to come. Would my intended be in the school with my brothers? Probably, but not necessarily.

And, who was the empress looking at after she asked if I was attending to my lessons?

Mother hesitated, then said, "She was looking at one of the emperor's new consorts."

"Why, Mother?"

"That is the sort of question that will have to wait until you are older. However, you may have a partial answer now: the empress has dynastic concerns."

Dynastic concerns? That seemed to make sense, in a remote way, rather like the distant stars making patterns that I almost recognized, though I was told that they each had name and purpose. Above Mt. Lir, almost a square. Over the House of Eternal Peace, a kind of spear—very proper a sign to be over the place where the imperial guard lived, and guarded prisoners.

But the real meaning eluded me.

Two

Accomplished in suitable studies,
Her family modeled Kanda's example.
A proper setting for a brilliant gem…

FIRST BROTHER, TO ME, was the living image of filial piety. He could repeat without flaw endless sutras concerning truth, probity, and virtue—all the things considered the best wards against the destroying chaos of the demon world. But he had one ardent desire, which was to be the youngest to pass the Imperial Examination.

I never once saw him punished, but I did see him hurt, late the winter before I turned ten, when Father forbade him to sit for the Examination in spring. "I know you are ready," Father said. "And I know that there are several boys your age whose fathers agreed to let them test, for practice, as you say. But I have given you any number of old tests to practice with. The rest is merely sitting in an alcove and writing as graywings prowl, watching for cheaters."

"I know I could pass," First Brother whispered, his eyes sheening.

"I believe you. I think so, too," Father said. "But as yet your essays do not demonstrate the maturity necessary to win first place. To pass at the bottom or even in the middle of the ranks is to assure you an obscure first post, maybe even in some distant island, where you will be soon forgotten. It's the top ten who will gain a place under one of the ministries, and the first place is best of all, for many reasons. And to do well on your first test is considered the highest virtue, but a first test can only happen once. I do not want you to waste yours on a desire to stand out merely for being youngest, rather than most talented."

First Brother set aside his eating sticks and knelt, saying in a low voice, "This incompetent son would not dare to go against honored Father's teachings, but…could this ignorant one benefit from hearing one reason it matters if I test more than once?"

Father sighed. "Good son, you know that my generation of imperial princes did not have to test, but I insisted on it, because I wanted to serve in the government."

First Brother bowed further. "I know that my generation *must* test…"

"Yes, but you do not think yet about the why of it, how this rule affects future generations," Father said. "It's natural. You do not yet think about what being the fifth generation from a grand prince means. You are years off from marriage yet, much less considering the fact that your children will be the sixth generation—which means they could be commoners, unable to take part in governing unless they strive from the very bottom of the natural order. This is also true for you, Second Son, unless you win distinction enough to gain titles to raise your rank. Likewise, Little Sister's children will be common unless we can arrange a sufficiently prestigious marriage for her, which is the main reason why she is not yet betrothed, unlike you boys." (For nothing had come of that initial visit to the harem.) "Your wives will bring you wealth. They are noble-born. Which is all they need to be."

The boys glanced at me, as if this was the first time they'd considered what I had been hearing ever since I could remember: *You must marry well, which means perfect deportment, excellent calligraphy, impeccable knowledge of ritual…* The list was as long as my arm.

None of us, raised as we were, saw that though Father believed ardently in tradition and the ritual and order of imperial rule—especially his role as Chief Censor—it was that ardency that kept him from being showered with titles himself. Ayah! That ardency and the character of certain members of the imperial family. But I will get there.

Father continued, "I, in my arrogance, admit that I would like to see you surpass me before I leave this life. You have the talent. But it means putting you on the proper path now, a path as narrow as a sword's edge."

First Brother bowed and withdrew, and for the next stretch of days, I scarcely saw him at all except at meals, and then he always had some ancient scroll at hand—some so old they were bamboo sticks, not even paper.

Questions and instructive answers were the normal mode at mealtimes, especially in those days while the Imperial Examination loomed large in Father's mind, second only to the constant river of his censorate work. Most of the attention he could spare from that river thus went to First Brother, and sometimes to Second Brother. I was scarce noticed, unless I dreamed up questions that I thought might impress Father and Mother, even if I did not particularly care about the answer. "Why is there a red sunset on a stone day, whereas this week's stone day ended with fire across the whole sky?" I asked one morning, hoping my question would be deemed clever. I added my exact observation, which we were always exhorted to make, "Last week's fire day was gray and pouring rain. Could the stars be wrong?"

"Who is to say that there was not a fiery sunset over an island elsewhere?" Father answered. "Or for that matter, if the prognosticated fire was confined to sunsets, would not the ancients have counted fiery sunset days? The fire might indicate an auspicious day to forge metal. Or, it might be a reminder to listen for hidden fires," he added, almost under his breath, then caught one of those glances from Mother.

My parents, I had begun to notice, understood one another without speaking. They didn't even use the old-fashioned hand language, which First Brother discovered three summers before, when he tried warning an ancient gardener who seemed oblivious to a coming thunderstorm. This gardener was deaf, and First Brother was instantly intrigued to discover that this man spoke with his hands, not his tongue. Second Brother was even more intrigued. He insisted that First Brother and I learn some of this language, so that we could talk among ourselves without being discovered during long rituals. He also chivvied his friends among the schoolboys to learn it to speak behind the schoolmaster's back—until the inevitable discovery and punishment. And that ended our venture into the silent language. Though we both retained bits of it afterward.

Second Brother seemed to run into trouble with such regularity that that, too, was a part of the eternal palace life. That morning, Second Brother scoffed outright. "If all the birth lines that predicted golden dragons and roaring tigers actually came to pass, would we not have a hundred emperors? Cousin Yiuti told me one of the palace guards says that divination and charms are the doings of charlatans. Those silly maids of Little Sister's all waste what little coin they have on those ribbons with charms scribbled on them. As if those will really ward evil!"

I turned to Father. "Are auspicious and inauspicious times and days really like rainbows, which look real, but are insubstantial? Or are they like stone?"

"It would be a mistake," Father said, bestowing a frown on Second Brother, "to disregard the wisdom of our ancestors. Until I can prove or disprove any statement, I will accept it as given, and proceed as tradition dictates."

"Then those charms are real?" Second Brother asked.

"Your question is so imprecise I cannot hope to answer it, Second Son," Father said evenly.

Second Brother flushed. "I mean, do the charms truly ward evil?"

"I would have to investigate them to give you an answer," Father said in the tone that meant this was a lesson he had repeated before.

"I understand that, Father," Second Brother said quickly, to avoid a lecture on the importance of being exact in language, or in proving or disproving statements. We'd all heard those lessons, but as yet saw nothing behind them.

Father relented. "I suspect that many of those charms *are* sold by charlatans who have no true ability with infusing Essence into the ribbons. The ancients tell us that people buy them for many reasons, mostly to feel better about the future that we cannot wholly predict." He smiled. "Though the Ministry of Rites has the entire Bureau of Divination doing its best to try." This was an example of Father's rare ventures into whimsy. "But the world is wonderfully complicated, and we do not live long enough to comprehend the whole. The best the experts can do is to grasp a part."

"Then some charms do ward evil," I asked.

Father turned my way. "What do you mean by evil, Daughter?"

Second Brother made the old motion for *shut up!*

But Father was waiting for an answer, so I said, "By evil I mean things that…that make trouble."

"Ah, I will accept that, for purposes of discussion. The Essence charms put into the roof guardians have kept lightning from striking the palace for centuries. Those charms are specific. There are also charms against certain types of demons, and the fact that we hear nothing about such demons committing their depredations at least partially proves the truth of the charms' efficacy. Then there are the charms for inviting abundance, which is a very broad category. It is possible that the wider the claim, the more difficult to prove the efficacy of those. Abundance is always present in the palace, even if there is drought and famine in other islands, as tax and tribute flow in from spring to Harvest…" He glanced at Second Brother, and it seemed a lecture was coming anyway—maybe even an admonition—as Father paused to drink a little tea.

Then First Brother spoke up. "Second Brother, I can show you a scroll about the history of the Book of Wisdom. It was forbidden to the empire's subjects for at least two dynasties, and brought back for general scholars only recently. That might be why there are scant history lessons covering its correct use for those outside the Ministry of Rites."

Father was distracted by that, the admonition forgotten. "A correct observation, First Son. However, from my own experience, I can offer an observation: even if we are not initiated into the study of the cosmos, divination from casting the sticks can be quite useful in court for stimulating debate."

"How, Father?" Second Brother asked—prudently.

Father's tone eased, for he liked us to ask for teaching. "If, for example, I cast the sticks and I get the figure for 'Arrogant dragon will have cause to repent,' we must first discuss what is meant by the dragon. It could be the empire. It could be the emperor himself." Here he bowed toward the imperial throne, and we followed suit. "But that always requires very careful and precise language. It could be an actual dragon, but which kind? If the next figure is one for Wind, and it is a fire day, then we can look up the sections in the Book that discuss matters of drought, and what to do about them. Put that together with the dragon, and you can see that a serious warning is indicated, which in turn might prompt an inspection of the granaries. Do you see how such discussion can benefit the entire empire?"

We all agreed, and thanked him for his teaching.

First Brother and Father then went on to talk about how reading successful interpretations of the past can lead to enlightenment in preparing for certain eventualities. "In such a way," Father ended, looking pleased with us all, which he only did after what he deemed an educational discussion, "we come very close to *preparing* for the future if we are not actually *predicting* it."

He then praised the boys by giving them leave to curtail study that day, in order to go into the city to look for new books or scrolls on the subject—for, as he said, "A related question might be asked on the Imperial Examination."

But I had to go back to practicing my calligraphy, and then to deportment.

I was already envious of the freedom the boys had. They could run about the house (not that First Brother ever did) and the worst that happened was a laughing caution not to knock into the screens or candle trees. But if I was seen running? It was back to carving a path in the yard, doing one hundred passages of tiny gliding steps, back straight, head level, hands poised.

The boys attended lessons while I had to accompany Mother in her duty visits to the harem—something that began that spring after I turned ten, and thereafter became part of my daily life. In the afternoons, the boys went to the north court where they had lessons in martial arts suitable for their rank, and they even got to learn to ride.

I badly wanted to learn to ride. Instead, my afternoons were spent on embroidery or calligraphy, since it was deemed I had little aptitude for music. I did not have a bad voice (or a particularly good one, I discovered when I heard another girl singing), and I did very much like to listen to music, but Mother said that I was going to be too tall to draw attention to myself by playing music or dancing.

I perceived that Mother had one passion, which was letter writing. No, two, the second being reading. From earliest days I had grown used to seeing my mother discussing the testaments that Father brought to meals, before he turned his attention to First Brother preparing for the future Imperial Examination.

My parents owned many histories as well as books of philosophy. During a week of pouring rain so intense that the dowager empress sent around messengers relaxing the daily honor visit (perforce echoed by the empress and the consorts), Mother took me into the scroll room and gave me a book of Kanda's plays for children. "This was my favorite when I was your age. You'll see my practice copywork at the back. You are now old enough to read on your own, rather than merely reading the lessons I set for you. If you finish this book, you may choose something to read. These over on this shelf were my own when I was young." These were all histories, which I began dutifully to read, mostly to earn Mother's rare smiles of approval.

I began to notice that the boys' education was as repetitious as my endless deportment lessons. And, I began to understand why Second Brother was so often in trouble. His mind was quick as a hummingbird, always darting here and there, unlike Elder Brother, who was hewing a straight path in Father's shadow. Second Brother got a thing the first time, and thereafter he'd lose interest, or squirm impatiently if he was constrained to repeat it. But recitation was the foundation of education—and he had to copy out pages and pages of admonitory sutras to prove it.

THREE

THE CHANGES WERE SO gradual that as yet I had to perceive the things beneath the things beneath *those* things, like a pagoda of three stories. Perhaps the image of a pagoda is not a good symbol, except to underscore my ignorance. For example, I was given a new maid when I turned ten, though I already had the three I had been growing up with. This new one was twelve or thirteen, named Cray, which was sort of like the fish names of the maids of my generation. Mother said that Cray would be accompanying me when I began to receive invitations on my own.

And that brings me to an important incident that is in none of the official records, though perhaps it ought to be. There are far too many such, which is one of my chief motives for taking my brush in hand for this testament.

As I received training suitable for my rank, my maids received training that would prepare them for the task of serving me once I married and became the madam of a household. When I was very small I envied them for being able to chatter quietly as they worked, especially out in the garden while I had those strict deportment lessons under that loathed padded box I had to balance on my head until my neck ached.

But the maids did not get to wear silk ribbons, or embroidery—their hair ties were dull cloth, and every maid had to have her hair in the same twin corkscrews, whereas I could have braids or fox ears tied with silk ribbons, and one day, when I was older and considered of marriageable age, I'd get my first hairpin. Mother and Nanny both repeated endlessly their lessons about gifts and responsibilities: my rank was my gift, and deportment my responsibility.

I heard those words but never paused to consider their meaning. And I didn't think at all about how the world looked to Minnow, Perch, Eider, or Cray.

This particular morning it was already hot and sultry, and my head panged. My fan only moved the heavy air around. I longed to be too sick to go into the imperial harem, but I had no fever, therefore I must go.

Minnow, the maid who most often tended my hair, was combing it out when she hit a tangle that tugged painfully on an especially tender part of my scalp. All my frustrations erupted. I jerked around, grabbed the comb, and hurled it right at her. It struck her between the eyes.

She stared at me, shock-eyed, then down lowered her brows in a line of thunder as I yanked her hair, shrilling, "See how you like it!" and Minnow's hand came around in a slap. I had never before been slapped, and though it was not a hard slap, the astonishment of it struck me breathless.

Then she gasped and stumbled back as though trying to get away from me, terror replacing her anger. I pounced on her, pulling my hand back to slap her face off, but then a strong hand interspersed smoothly between us, and a hip, and both Minnow and I fell on our backsides as Cray stood between us, looking from one to the other.

I was about to order her to get out of the way when there was a whirl of Mother's favorite spring green at the corner of my eye. She said calmly, "Cray, take the rest to the back room."

The maids fled before Cray could gesture them to come, Perch at Minnow's shoulder, with a troubled glance back at me.

Then smack! That same comb bounced lightly off *my* forehead.

I stared up at Mother, who stared back. Not angry, but not remorseful.

"Mother! You *threw that* at me," I wailed.

"I meant to," Mother said. "What are you going to do about it, Daughter?"

I was so surprised I forgot my victimhood. "I..."

"You could throw it back, and then I will slap your face, or maybe bring you to the ancestors for punishment," Mother went on. "What can you do about that?"

"Nothing," I said indignantly, and burst into tears.

"Because?" Mother said, not heeding the tears.

"Because the first rule is to honor our parents," I wailed, devastated at the unfairness of everything.

"Say there was no first rule," Mother then said, surprising me even more — enough to stop weeping.

"But there is a first rule! It's always there! Father said so!"

"Then we will let that stand. Give me another reason why you can't do anything to me."

My mind worked. "Because you're bigger than I am."

"Exactly. I'm bigger, stronger, older, and my rank in the family is above yours. If I lie and say that you shoved Minnow off the roof, there would be nothing you could do, because I outrank you. How do you feel about that?"

My thoughts stuttered. I could not think at all.

"Angry, clearly. Maybe even betrayed?"

That was the word! "Yes!"

Mother then said, "How do you think Minnow feels?"

"*Minnow?*" I stared. What had that to do with anything? But right there before my eyes was Minnow's face in memory, her eyes shocked, her mouth open like the fish she was named for. "But she's a maid," I began.

"She, like you, was born naked into the world," Mother said. "Rank is like clothing, a thing we all agree to wear to hide our nakedness. To establish order and civilization. But beneath the rank and the silks, you, and I, are as naked as those girls waiting in the back room. Where I could go now and give each of them twenty beatings with the heavy stick. They are probably afraid of just that, especially Minnow, as she dared to strike you back. Do you want me to do that?"

I'd seen such a beating only once, long ago, as I mentioned before. At that time I did not understand what it was about except that it had to do with poison. But the blood was terrible, before the man went as lifeless as one of the butcher's portions of meat. First Brother had turned the color of paper, but stood fast as Second Brother ran off to be sick, and I shut my eyes.

"No, Mother," I said, rubbing my cheek. The slap had

stung a little, but already the sting was fading, whereas I knew that I'd been about to hit her with all my strength. "Don't do that."

Mother gave me a little nod, then said in a warmer voice, "I want you to remember that Minnow is human, just as you are. But she has been trained and cautioned and ordered not to strike back. She broke that rule, and I will have to punish her for it, because that is a law that they are told is inviolable. If I don't, someone else will, and probably more vigorously, for the entire household heard your noise, and every mouth is moving." She was speaking quickly, and added under her breath, "Especially those who placed her to report on every breath and bite." She closed her lips, then said in her teaching voice, "The Imperial Household Department will no doubt be hearing something before you and I finish here, which I will have to deal with. Whereas you, who threw that comb at her first, are not required to suffer the same consequence, because of your rank. Any imperial can slap or beat or starve a servant. You've probably seen it, though not in this house."

It was true. I had seen the older imperial princess slap both her maids, once for stepping on her train, and the other time for being in the way when we were all leaving the empress's palace. The maids had bowed their heads and folded their hands as if those slaps had been as light as a leaf on the wind.

This was the first time I ever considered that those girls in their plain gray gowns and their corkscrew hair-knobs might have feelings similar to my own.

"Anger and fear," Mother said, "cause scars." She tapped her heart. "You cannot see them any more than you can see feelings. But they are there. Just as scars from a scrape or a cut mark the skin. I want you to consider that as you continue your reading. Do you understand?"

"Thank you for your teaching, Mother," I quavered, my emotions a tangled knot in my heart: shame, sorrow, regret. And residual anger, though Mother's shocking act, and her words, had dissolved most of that.

"As for Minnow, she was given into your care, and in turn, she takes care of you. A good madam of rank never trespasses against the implied trust of dependents, just as a good emperor cares for his subjects, and they trust him to look out for them, to protect them from invaders, and to succor them in famine and flood. He doesn't go out shooting them or trampling their houses, though he could. And some have done. And there have been consequences, but that is one of those lessons for later, and right now the matter is you and your maids, not the welfare of the empire. When you threw that comb at Minnow's face, you broke that trust."

Maybe punishment was coming after all? To ward a possible consequence of a hundred pages of copying, I said hastily, "Kanda teaches us that trust takes time to grow, like a tree, which one thunderstrike can take down. Then the tree must take ten years, or a hundred years, to grow again. Is that what you mean, Mother?"

She smiled a little. "I probably ought to make you copy that out, but I think you've got the lesson. You're very like Second Brother that way."

Surprised, I looked back at her, and her expression changed so quickly I could not quite understand it, as she said, "I could wish Second Brother might have more of your self-discipline." And then came a smile.

I thanked her, though my heart knotted with the conviction that I did not deserve that praise. And at her gesture of dismissal, I left on wobbly legs, running as soon as I was safely out of sight. I fled in the opposite direction from my room, as I could not bear to see any of my maids at that moment. That took me to the library, thinking miserably that I wished I was like Second Brother, for he shrugged off trouble and I dreaded it. The tears started again.

I thought I would be alone, for Father would still be with the Censors and the boys at lessons. But when I got there, I found Second Brother himself. He was not at the shelves of silk-wrap-ped scrolls, each neatly labeled, or near the books that were stacked tidily and dusted every day, but over against the far wall, bent over one of the old trunks behind the desk. There were several battered trunks. This one was on top, carved with running foxes.

He looked up before I could back away, and his smile vanished, replace by the puckered forehead of concern. "Little Sister?"

"Why are you here?" I blurted out.

He jerked a shoulder up. "There was trouble. Not caused by me," he added quickly, with his quick, dimpled grin in his mooncake face like my own. "It was Them, as usual." *Them* being the two imperial grandsons. "You?"

I did not want to explain, for I could still see Minnow's face after the comb struck it. "It's nothing." I pointed to the chest.

"What's in there?"

Second Brother glanced at the door, then came the dimpled grin that meant mischief. "Gallant wanderer tales," he said.

"Oh."

"You don't like them?" he asked. "Don't tell me you're like First, your only thought duty and virtue."

I was in awe of First Brother, who—if he noticed me at all—was invariably kind. And I knew Second Brother loved him as well, though he no longer followed him like a shadow as he had when we were smaller. But it was true, First Brother was at all times sober and hard-working. I could not remember him ever given the mildest of reprimands.

"I don't think all the time about virtue and duty," I retorted—and there before my eyes was Minnow's face, staring back at me in terror. Maybe I need to, came the uneasy thought. I spoke quickly, "I like fun stories. But boring tales about outlaw men fighting and smiting one another don't sound like fun."

"Have you ever read one?"

"No." But I'd heard disparaging comments, mostly from my elders, the latest from one of the consorts, who had sighed with a languishing air, complaining that her son was always sneaking off to listen to the storytellers, whose fare was inevitably gallant wanderer tales of duels and battles, rather than some-thing enlightening.

"If Father heard you condemning anything without having read it, you'd be copying a thousand pages of Kanda a thous-and times for brandishing your ignorance like a donkey braying." As he spoke, he dug into the trunk, pulled up a grubby, much-thumbed book, and flipped through the pages with a quick and careless hand that would have earned him a clout from the schoolmaster for mistreating precious knowledge.

Except this wasn't knowledge. It was…

In triumph, he turned the book about, and held up a page for me to see.

I stared down at a drawing of a teenage girl striding…on a cloud? She held a spear in one hand, with foxtails streaming in the wind. The other hand was propped on a sword at her side. She wore an outfit that looked something like what the guards wore beneath their armor, and something like what the princes wore to their practice field. Her hair was worn high in a warrior's tail, loose with ribbons waving in the wind.

She looked right at me out of the page, her grin very much

like Second Brother's right now.

"She's a girl," I breathed, aware that was inadequate. It was like saying a phoenix rising from the midst of a fire mountain was a bird.

"That's Xue Two-Sword. She's one of Jong Siang's 110 Outlaws. They fought for justice, defeating villains in the ancient days. No man among them could beat her."

"She was a hero?" I asked. "A woman hero?"

"Not the only one. This particular book is about Lu the Poet, who used his wits rather than weapons to defeat corrupt officials. One of his companions was a girl from the lakes, part demon and part crane. She was friends with Xue Two-Sword."

"Are we permitted to read these?"

He shrugged. "They're here. No one has said not to." He added quickly, "And I've never said anything, either. We're supposed to be reading, so I figure, why not these? But I only read them at night in my bedchamber." He thrust the one about Xue Two-Sword at me. "Want to take a look?"

I took the book, saying, "Are all these trunks in this corner gallant wanderer tales?"

"No. That is, I only looked at these top ones. They're full of old copybooks and old clothes." He waved a dismissive hand as I tucked the book under my arm.

He retrieved what he'd been looking for, and we left. I returned to my room and slid the book under my *Admonitions for Girls from Kanda*. My sense of intrigue and expectation faded. A new story that did not solve my dilemma with Minnow.

My first reaction was to ask my parents to send her away, then I wouldn't have to think about her at all, except I knew that maids who got sent away were demoted to laundry and chamber pots and the like. It seemed a terrible injustice. That slap of hers had not been hard, and I had seen the terror in her face when she realized what she had done. But Mother was going to have to punish her, whereas I, who had struck her first, would not be punished.

The maids came back later, and they were silent. No chatter from the three younger ones — Cray never spoke unless she had to. I did not realize I missed their chatter until it was gone.

I said nothing until Eider took away my day's clothes to the laundry, and Perch my tea things and dishes. Cray, I knew, was outside the door in case I called, so Minnow and I were alone while I got ready for bed, and then she did my hair for sleeping. Her hand shook a little, I noticed, and when I glanced in my bronze mirror, I could see her frown of concentration below the puffy eyes of much weeping.

I turned around. "Minnow, I should not have thrown the comb at you."

She curtseyed, her face lowered. Mother had been right, whatever Minnow was thinking stayed hidden. She didn't trust me enough to resume her usual open face. She finished, laid down the comb with a kind of deliberate care, curtsied and withdrew, leaving me to climb into bed.

Alone, I retrieved the book, and let my troubles slide away as I read about the talented Xue Two-Swords, who could wield a sword by the time she got her proper teeth, and who could bound across a river and back before she was my age. She was kind to all except villains.

She never slapped maidservants, I thought as I turned the worn pages. I read until my eyes burned, then tucked the book back under my studies, and blew out my candle.

My maids were there when I woke, as always. It was uncomfortable that day, and the next, but gradually we resumed the old pattern of behavior. Eider—always cheery—was the first to comment about the weather again, and the doings of the household cats, and other little things. I found myself grateful to hear that talk, inconsequential as it was, though Minnow remained silent.

I tried to speak to them the way Mother spoke to her maids, always calmly, and clearly. To bite back my irritation, even when they were slow, and the weather was hot, and I loathed the day ahead. Eventually Minnow joined the maids' chat again, and the incident sank into the past the way leaves sink to the bottom of pools, there but unseen.

FOUR

An ornament to the court,
She illuminated the lesser lights,
With wisdom from the ancients…

THERE ARE SO MANY paintings depicting the glory of the empress's court. Poetry, too.

Mother appeared to be the meekest of the imperial court women. She never spoke, even before the lowest ranking consorts still in their teens. If addressed, Mother gave the same sort of answer that she'd trained me to give when I was eight.

The conversations followed the prescribed patterns, strictly formal, answers always expressed through gratitude and flattery of whoever we were calling on. We girls never spoke unless spoken to, nor were we offered any tea—which I was glad of, as I dreaded the scandal of having to use the privy in forbidden territory. Cray carried a flat little porcelain canteen for sips between pavilions, which eased the torment of thirst on the hottest days.

The harem court was like a painting in its beauty, but I had begun to reflect that looking like a painting at all times was not just tedious but stifling. Perhaps one only enjoyed it if one were at the center. Did the Dowager Empress enjoy sitting motionless under an elaborate golden phoenix headdress that had to press dreadfully on her neck, her face covered with such thick makeup it must itch in hot weather?

Only her eyes moved, darting lizard-like, as everyone faced her, only her. Whatever she said must be agreed with. If she, swathed in her ten or twelve layers of heavy silk and brocade, and seated in the sheltering phoenix throne, commented upon how stuffy and warm the weather was, as an icy wind whistled along the floor where we knelt shivering on our cushions in our strictly limited three layers, we must agree that it was stuffy and warm—and thank her for her graciousness and care.

The flattery, I noticed, mostly centered around beauty and youth. No consort appeared without carefully applied makeup and elaborate hairdressing. There were few like Mother who dressed modestly.

One day that autumn, I asked Mother why she only wore a single hairpin with two dangles. "You're entitled to more, as you are married to a prince. And you're as pretty as any of the others," I added, hoping to praise her.

She thanked me but in that modulated voice that meant politeness, and I understood that that praise meant little to her. She said nothing more on the subject. It was I who soon began to notice that she *never* said anything on the subject except the once, when she'd informed me that I would be too untalented for music lessons and too tall for dance lessons. When we were alone, it was my deportment Mother commented on, or my writing, or my reading. It was never my moon-round face, or my dark brown hair, my lanky limbs, or anything else about my appearance, unless I was not as tidy as her exacting eye required.

And finally, on another sultry, headachy day as summer returned, parching the world, I fussed on our way home, "If only it wasn't so tedious. Must we do this forever?"

"An empty mind finds petty things to fret about," Mother said. "A mind full of interesting matters to consider scarcely notices the passage of time."

Did that mean that Mother let her mind slip away to other things while she sat so erect on her cushion, sipping only when others sipped at their single cup of tea?

From that time, I ceased to feel guilty if my thoughts slipped away to my reading instead of remaining on the endless repetition of polite court chatter. The very next day, I called up Xue Two-Swords in mind, and relived the adventure wherein she had defeated a demon in the form of a fire-eyed bull in moonslight and a robber king when the sun shone.

Sky Wishes day arrived at last on the tenth day of the tenth Phoenix Moon month. That released us from the toil of those daily calls, requiring only a formal exchange of messages once a week over winter, except when court gathered. We were free until spring, and then the eternal round would begin again.

From earliest memory, when Mother was not seeing to household matters, she sat at her desk, her writing brush busy. For the first time, I wondered what she wrote, and to whom? When I asked, she said, "To my own mother, whom I only get to see twice a year. To my sister. I trust you'll meet her when First Brother marries, for I will be able to invite my entire family then. And to my cousin on another island."

I knew almost nothing about the Gu family, except that her father was the governor of a large city on the far side of Mt. Lir, one powerful enough to have its own army, and that Mother had been sent to the imperial city when she was small. She had been appointed to serve as a companion to one of the imperial aunts now dead, before she was deemed of marriageable age.

Now I wondered what that must have been like, but when I ventured a question, Mother invariably said, "Such matters will rest until you are older."

I was content to wait to find out about family members I might never see, especially when I had that enticing trunk to explore now that winter was here, and my mornings were for studies. If I raced through my copywork I could read!

A day or two before the end of the year, Mother and I walked in the garden while the servants began scouring out the entire palace so that everything would be fresh and new for the night the two moons met and the year turned.

Mother waited until we had crossed halfway through the garden before gesturing her maid and Cray, our always-present companions, to drop back out of earshot. "Next spring, you'll likely receive invitations to call on the imperial princesses," Mother said. "And perhaps the secondary cousins, your peers."

I should probably insert here that in those days, we were far more formal. On first meetings, and even among us children, we used the entire honorific for each cousin, plus number, adding the word *imperial* for the direct descendants of the emperor. Unless they invited us to use the general term for cousin, which was considered informal—next thing to siblings. But I will not write out Seventh-Paternal-Male-Cousin and

Nineteenth-Paternal-Female-Cousin each time, in favor of the general term "cousin."

"Why perhaps?" I asked.

Mother's footsteps covered eight paces before she said, "What have you learned about the harem visits?"

"It's always exactly as you said. We sit in rank order. No one speaks unless first spoken to by someone higher in rank. The tea arrives steaming. You must drink it before it goes cold, then we go away. Everyone tells the elders how young and beautiful they are today, and maybe they comment on the weather, or the garden blooms."

"Then everyone behaves exactly the same?" Mother's voice was even, but I sensed a question behind her question.

"Yes. That is, everyone is equally polite. They give the correct answers and bows. But..."

"Go on."

"Sometimes the empress talks to everyone except the really beautiful consort—"

"Eighteenth Imperial Consort Zenar."

"—thank you, Mother. Eighteenth Consort Zenar, who never speaks, but keeps her head low. The only ones besides the empress who dare to speak are the elder imperial aunts. And Fourteenth Imperial Consort Ye, who gets to wear a headdress with a golden two-toed phoenix."

"That is because she gave the emperor a son who is at present in favor—a warning to the Imperial Heir and his sons," Mother said.

Using their names was a privilege. We children learned everyone by title, but we had to sort ourselves out by generation, and by birth rank among our own generation. Since the emperor in particular had married young consorts over an entire generation, some of my own generation had uncles and aunts who were younger than they. This was the case with the Imperial Heir—the son of the emperor and empress—being our parents' age, but the emperor's son by Fourteenth Imperial Consort Ye was between my brothers' ages, and younger than Xianti, only son of the Imperial Heir.

"Fourteenth Imperial Consort Ye's rank among the consorts is thus the highest, except for the empress. And First Imperial Consort Chin, whose brother is a duke. You are seeing the result of court tensions," Mother said. "In part. And in part, harem tensions."

"What does that mean?"

"I will explain when you have learned the vocabulary to understand."

I said, "Has it to do with why the emperor has so many consorts, and the Imperial Heir as well?" Though I could recite everyone by title and rank order, in person I still had trouble telling them apart. It didn't help that most of those at the higher numbers, which meant lowest in rank, were exactly the same age, most under twenty. "We only visit some, but not others."

"We visit those who have given the emperor or the Imperial Heir a son," said Mother. "Even if that son is no longer alive."

"Do you ever get confused, Mother? Is that why you never speak unless asked a question, and you always give the same answer?"

"I am not confused, because I have had many years of experience that you have not, and I met each as she was introduced into the royal family. As for why I guard my tongue, it is an act of prudence. If you ask a question, many will speculate about why you ask, even if you do not get an answer. I want you to reflect on these things over the coming winter, so that you will be prepared to guard your tongue when you begin to go into company among the imperial princesses and your paternal cousins next spring. As for 'perhaps' suffice it to say that as people go in and out of favor, we might be summoned to call on them, or forbidden to. This includes the imperial descendants."

I thanked her for her teaching, though I felt I was still standing outside the gates of understanding. We reached the moon door that led to the path toward our part of the imperial palace, and so Mother fell silent, and we both shivered a little in the rising wind.

The next day the weather turned terrible, and stayed that way almost until the end of the year.

By now my lessons in Circle included the entire board, and Father sometimes watched our play, especially if Second Brother gave me a game. "Circle is more than a game," he said one rainy day, when there was little else to do but play it over and over. I lost every game that day, but Second Brother always explained why, and how I could have countered him.

"It's exercise for the mind," Father said, smiling over at Mother, who continued to embroider with exquisitely tiny, even stitches. "I lost all the time when I was young, and your brothers did as well."

Of course it would be instructive. Our lives were organized around instruction, one of the deepest of Kanda's exhortations for civilization. I found that comforting: losing became useful, rather than just dispiriting.

But Father went on. "It is also a metaphor for history."

"May this ignorant daughter inquire how, esteemed Father?" I asked.

"The board, the pieces, the rules, are constants, just as are islands, the people on them, the creatures of sea, land, and air. Our empire is the board, and the games represent the flow of history, which is like a river. Though it has its boundaries—its rules—it is never still. You strive for balance in the game, and we strive for balance in the world."

"Thank you for your teaching, Father," we all said, bowing.

He watched one more game, then returned with the quietest sigh to the never-ending pile of testaments. It did not occur to me until much later that I rarely saw Father in any context but working or teaching, except for an hour here and there. This was his form of relaxation—to sit surrounded by his family, all diligent.

Second Brother had begun teaching me the proper terms for the various common ploys in Circle, but in my mind the stones would always be seen in mathematical relations to one another, and not in military. The ploys were the steps in mathematical problems. In that way, I could see the entire board in terms of many-step calculations of wins and losses.

I finally won a game. Then another. Then three. By the time of the first melt, I'd won ten. After each, Second Brother sighed or laughed, depending on his mood, but he always gave me little gifts. "First Brother gave me candied haws and milk cakes when I learned, and I liked that, so I'll do it with you," he explained after my first wins.

After three wins in a row I was annoyed, thinking he was giving me those wins, but I began to perceive that his attention was invariably distracted, most often toward the windows. He was more like a hummingbird than ever.

There were more evenings with Father at home. Was that merely the result of winter, or had it always been that way and I had not noticed? No, I remembered how he had gone out some evenings in his fur-edged cloak to entertainments given by this prince or that marquis or another minister. Those were very rare this winter. Instead, he sat and read depositions, or else he and mother sat together, she at her embroidery—as was I, unless I got to lay it aside to play Circle, or pitch pot, but only if invited by Father or my brothers—and they talked in low voices, always about boring things, for I often heard "deposition" or "inspect-ion" or "investigation."

After so much reading about heroes who traveled about saving people, I began to perceive a little of life outside the labyrinthine world of the palace a *little* better. It was a bit like watching the rooftops and eave guardians light up to gold as the sun first peeped over the edge of the world at dawn, when silhouettes bloomed into houses, streets, carts, people.

Only this was not always a glad discovery.

I had been reading the history of the empire, and I could recite most of the dynasties' lists of emperors, and the great events of each reign. "Great" being the word the archivists used for matters that reached over many or most of the islands.

Now, the lists of who was condemned for rebellion, or for bad governing, or blamed for famine or flood in their governance, were no longer mere lists. Always remembering Mother's quick voice that day after I threw the comb at Minnow, I was beginning to glimpse the persons behind the titles and dynastic names. Specifically, how tenuous rank could be. Incidents in which this or that prince, or even higher ranks, were cast down, causing princesses to become scrub women or yard slaves overnight, because of something their father or their brother or husband did. *If* the entire family to three or even nine generations was not executed outright. It was justified as bad raising: a son in trouble was badly raised by his father, and both would suffer for it. Likewise, a father in trouble would raise only bad sons. But all of the women— grandmothers, wives, consorts, sisters, daughters—suffered too, even when they were not part of the political events that brought about ruin.

When I began to comprehend these rivers of tears below the silent women (for no archivist thought to collect *their* words, only those of the men) I found myself reading less history and more gallant wanderer tales, in which women were responsible for their own lives, bad or good.

I had loved Nanny's stories, simple as they had always been, chosen for lessons that illustrated the values of virtue and obedience. These new tales told of strange islands full of unusual birds and powerful predators and fire mountains from which glowing dragons flew, and interesting sects that women as well as men joined, becoming fearless heroes who defended the helpless, and vanquished the corrupt and the cruel. The justice of these endings delighted me as much as the intriguing details about life elsewhere.

Again, one day I found Second Brother in the library. "Did you finish reading about Kurai and the turtles?" he asked.

"Finished. How I wish I could see light skills," I said on a sigh. "Do they teach you how to leap to a roof in your training? Can you teach me?"

"No. You have to have Essence talent. I don't know if any of the guard can do it, though they are experts at all weapons. Though maybe the ferrets can. Or the Falcons."

"The Falcons?"

"Secret sect. First Brother told me once he thought we might be related to them in some way. But then he said he was wrong, and that a lot of the legends are probably exaggeration. And don't ask Father," he added quickly, "or you'll get the long teaching about investigating how many sources you are from the incident, and the ways to determine the truth. And you'll like as not get a tedious copy assignment after."

He spoke in the tone of experience. I said, "I wasn't going to say anything. But Father must know we read these. Or why would they be in this room?"

"I don't know why they are here. Perhaps Father read them when he was a boy. But he always tells First and me that willful ignorance is never countenanced, and it's better to understand what people talk about, then investigate the truth. *How* I should like to join a ship to investigate the truth of fire mountain dragons, and the land of talking turtles! Though maybe it's better not to know, if the answer will always be disappointing."

He laughed, and pointed out some others that he'd liked, and I carried them away, secreting them in my bedchamber.

FIVE

THAT WINTER IS ONE of the pleasantest that I remember.

It seemed to pass as fast as the wind until one morning, as snow battered against the oiled paper of the windows, and we all went about with hand warmers, Mother sent my maids away, and said, "You are to be included among the guests at Fire Wishes Festival at the imperial garden."

By now I knew not to bounce or squeak, but I did smile with anticipation.

Mother saw, and said, "This is why we are alone. We can still paint lanterns together and let them fly from our garden, though that might not be exciting now that you are getting older."

"I still like doing it, Mother," I protested. I had been thinking about what elements from the gallant wanderer tales I might paint on my lantern.

Mother looked pleased, then said, "Perhaps you will no longer be as excited once you've seen the imperial garden decorated with fairy lamps. It will be very beautiful, especially with the snow lit by hundreds of lanterns rising overhead. But you must not expect to be invited to light one of your own, much less paint one. We secondary families are there to watch the imperial family make theirs, unless one is singled out to be favored. You will be expected to express joy at whatever the princesses do. It is part of your social duty."

"I think it would be more fun to stay home," I said.

Mother said, "Even when conveyed verbally imperial invitations are edicts."

I suppressed a sigh, but I could not help saying, "Will there ever be any fun at court?"

"It depends on many things, including your own behavior. If the primary relations find you congenial, you will be invited to more intimate events, at which you might be granted an opportunity to participate. Perhaps, one day, that will include an invitation to the Journey to the Clouds."

I knew that was an expedition by sea with the imperial family to see the famous orchids, which required formal attire and etiquette at all times, plus competitions in poetry, calligraphy, various arts, and music for the younger generation of imperials, with everyone else watching. First Brother had remarked once that competition to be invited was intense, but to me that did not sound like fun at all.

Mother and Father had been invited twice that I remembered, each time after Father was awarded a merit by the emperor. I never understood quite what those were about, except that these were the result of much hard labor, and they achieved some change or law. The first one resulted in a new board being nailed up over the south entrance to our palace, the one only my parents used. It said Deep and Pure as Mountain Lake, and I was told that the carving was based on calligraphy made by the emperor himself.

The second time they were invited to take the Journey to the Clouds, Mother and Father had had new robes ordered. Father's Censor robe was still purple but the embroidered figure on the rank square at front and back had changed from lion to qilin, a creature whose head resembled dragons and whose body was more leonine, but with wings. I commented to Mother that I thought them less pretty than a crane in flight or a golden lion, but Mother said, "They are more rare than cranes or lions, and it is said they will sometimes speak. Their words are always wise—if you can climb high enough on a mountain to find and hear them."

"The emperor thinks Father is a qilin?" I asked.

My parents exchanged one of those glances, then Mother

said, "The crane, the qilin, the peacocks and pheasants and so on are all symbols of great virtues as are the qilins and lions and tigers for the military side of court, as well as your father's Censorate. All are not only rank markers, but also exhortations to strive for those virtues."

In other words, I thought to myself, you don't actually escape admonishments and lessons even as an adult.

My entry into the social circles of the princesses of my generation also meant having my first ceremonial robes. There were three, of sober shades—winter pool blue, the green of new peas, and pale peach, which I favored immediately—then Mother sent them off to be embroidered. "As yet Eider's embroidery is a little better than yours," Mother warned me. "But not quite ready to be seen by critical eyes. However she has been diligent in practice."

I curtseyed, thanking Mother for her teaching, and promised to do better. When I returned to my room, I told Eider what Mother had said. Eider reddened at the measured praise, and for a time after, I tried to be extra diligent about my own embroidery, though as yet a sense of competition had not awakened in me.

The briefest glance at the imperial records makes plain that my father was the fourth direct descendant, son to son, of a grand prince—the title "grand" then, as now, granted to the brothers and sisters of a reigning emperor for their lives. And sometimes their progeny, if favored.

We were the fifth generation, which as everyone knows ends consanguinity as well as imperial or noble standing, if those middle generations did not accrue merits sufficient to raise the family again. This, I quickly discovered, made a difference to my reception among the imperial princesses and cousins before I even spoke a word.

My mother's warning that my purpose was to number among the admiring audience to the imperial princesses was borne out that very first Fire Wishes Day, before winter was even over.

I was prepared to be ignored, and once I'd made my initial bows, in correct order, so I was. Only the privileged few were invited to partake of sumptuous refreshments. I did enjoy the breathtaking sight of hundreds of sky lanterns flying toward the stars from the snow-blanketed imperial garden. Why do we send lanterns to the heavens at the end of autumn and then again at the end of winter? I wondered as I tipped my head back. Perhaps our ancestors found this a way to send requests to Heaven that the coming winter would not be terrible. And that once winter had come, we'd send requests that it would end soon.

Perhaps I could ask First Brother; these days, if I asked such questions of Father or Mother, they were more likely to send me to the library to find the answer on my own, and then to report what I had learned at our next shared meal.

As I wandered about, no one asked me what I wished for, much less invited me to paint a lantern. I dutifully added my voice to the clamor of admiration for the imperial princesses' efforts, until I realized that no one paid me the least heed. Certainly not my imperial cousins.

My age fell between age groups: the smallest imperial cousins—descendants of the emperor's sisters and aunts, the grand princesses—were permitted to run along the lake watching the fireworks, as an army of nannies and graywings followed them. The teenage girls made lanterns, the boys had their own fireworks that included noise-makers, and the adults encircled the open-sided pavilion where the emperor's family sat. From that pavilion, the cadences of poetry rose and fell on the air. Thus I was the only one my age, and of no interest to the teenage cousins. That realization freed me to wander about and inspect things more closely.

I discovered that the imperial princesses' lanterns, despite the general acclaim for their talents and brilliance, were not nearly as fine as the paintings of the scribes and artists who sat at tables, warming their hands over candles when they were not painting to the wishes of roaming imperial children.

I noticed that when the teenage boys and girls came within speaking distance, voices changed. Louder, higher on the part of the girls. More laughter from the boys. And I saw First Brother among them. I had not known that he had received his own invitation from the imperial princes, but of course this would have been a yearly event for him. And yes, there was Second Brother among his schoolmates over where fireworks were being lit.

When a line of servants brought out hot wine, the youngest of us were rounded up and sent home with waiting servants. I was grouped with the babies. I did not mind. I was cold, and hungry and more than a little bored. Cray came forward with my cloak and a walking lantern. As usual, she said nothing as we crunched through the snow to the other side of the imperial garden, where hot tea and snacks and handwarmers awaited me.

Two weeks later, again exactly as Mother had predicted, my first invitation to celebrate the beginning of spring arrived. It happened to occur on the day after my eleventh birthday. I wore my new peach robe over my usual winter layers, and Mother told Minnow to braid my hair in a girl's long tail, tied by a ribbon, rather than the child's little braids or ribbon-tied fox ears, to differentiate from the serving girls' unadorned fox ear twists.

Before I left, I was given a small jade scent box. "This is for First Imperial Princess Siarti's birthday."

"Is hers today? The day after mine?"

"Hers was a few days ago," Mother said as Cray stood silently by, holding my cloak. "But the imperial family always waits until the first day of spring to summon court, as you are aware. They sometimes celebrate anniversaries or birthdays that occurred in previous days."

It went as Mother had predicted.

I was so overwhelmed by this new experience of being in company without Mother's presence that I would not have mentioned my own birthday even if I'd been asked. Imperial Princess Siarti had just turned fifteen, an advanced age to my eye. I handed off my gift in proper rank order, and watched the pumpkin-faced princess glance indifferently at it and set it aside for a servant to put in a basket with other gifts she barely noticed. She looked at me with equivalent indifference as she spoke one word of thanks, then immediately turned to praise what appeared to me to be an ordinary inkstone, stroking and patting it as if it was a piece of Heaven fallen out of the sky. She then fawned over Cousin Kuiza, who was dressed in six layers with a train nearly as long as the empress's. Worked into her loops and twists of hair, she wore a golden maiden headdress with too many dangling ornaments to count.

I stared in fascination. Cousin Kuiza was technically an aunt as she was the last of the empress's daughters still unmarried, but as she was the same age as the imperial granddaughters, they called her cousin, as they had more than thirty aunts and great-aunts. Cousin Kuiza smirked complacently as everyone flattered her, though I thought that the finest gift was a delicate, charming waist-pouch embroidered with pairs of flying geese, which had been the gift of the astonishingly beautiful Cousin Arati, elder daughter of Eighteenth Consort Zenar.

I was not the only one looking at the pouch. I caught a movement at the edge of my vision. It was none other than Consort Chin's daughter, the eleventh imperial princess Taisa, and thus second in rank after Cousin Kuiza. Cousin Taisa was more or less my height, though at least five years my senior, substantial in stature, as if her bones were choosing to go sideways rather than up. Her robe had a long train, like those of the other imperial cousins of the first rank.

I had never been so close to one of these important cousins, close enough to study her outer robe, which was covered with exquisite embroidery of sunbirds cleverly made to look iridescent, and tiny bunches of cherries amid silvery eternity knots. The sunbirds were not merely along the front edges and the hem, like mine, they were all over, including her tasseled sleeves, which were knee length.

She noticed me with no change of expression in her close-set eyes, so narrow I couldn't see their color. "Are you admiring that?" she asked in a flat tone, glancing at the flying geese pouch.

"This ignorant one thinks it is beautiful, more beautiful than any of these other things."

"Ignorant is right," the imperial princess replied, still in that flat tone, "if you think this is fine work. Look at these crooked stitches here, and here, and down here. She added more silk to hide them, but the bumps are there." Having said that, she backed away a step, and put her head a little to one side. Her braid had two ribbons, both embroidered with cherries. "Though the effect does catch the eye. Unlike these other things."

She turned away and walked off before I could answer, leaving me alone there at the gift table. The others crowded around Cousin Siarti, who had gone to a pretty desk to try out the new inkstone. I knew I ought to join them, but first I bent closer to eye the stitches. I saw what the imperial princess was talking about at once. In fact, I'd tried to hide crooked stitching the same way, though not nearly as deftly.

I joined the back of the admiring group as Cousin Siarti began demonstrating her excellent calligraphy, but my mind was on that pouch. I thought to myself that once again Mother was right. Embroidery was a valued art among the imperial cousins, and I was going to have to do better if I did not want mine to be sneered at. It was all very well to think about Xue

Two-Sword's adventures, but I would have to pay better attention to what my hands were doing.

I returned home full of observations about my first social engagement on my own, to discover that once again the auspicious time for this year's Imperial Examination had been determined, and once again Father decreed that First Brother was not ready.

First Brother had taken himself to the ancestral chamber, where he knelt before the tablets. I glanced in, and could see from the rigidity of his back that he was trying to master his disappointment. He did not argue, though; last year, what Father had predicted had come true. Only two of all the boys in First Brother's class had passed, one making it only into the sixties, and the other nearly at the bottom of the list. Both were now under-clerks somewhere outside the city.

The auspicious day for the Imperial Examinations came to pass. First Brother was silent, except in study discussions.

The second day of the examinations, as always Mother and I made our morning duty calls. We were nearly done and had reached a point on the path between two consorts' palaces when Mother's maid came up to us, Cray staying behind to watch, almost as if she were a guard rather than a companion. A quick, whispered consultation resulted in Mother turning to me.

"It seems a party of the imperial cousins is being made up to walk in the imperial garden, and the empress only agreed if it is a large party, well chaperoned."

I sensed irony in Mother's tone, and was trying to frame a question when she said, "I suppose you'll need to become aware of teenage girls' maneuverings sometime. For example, the empress is aware that her daughters are making this party to watch for the boys coming out of the examination hall."

I felt very grown up at these words, though I hadn't any idea why the empress would not want her daughters watching for the examinees coming forth. My mind leaped to the future, hoping that one day I would get to see First Brother leave the testing ground, something I would not have dared ask permission for, only because I had been told that I could not venture into the imperial garden without invitation, except on festival days.

Mother granted permission, gave Cray a nod, and the maid took her place as my shadow as we followed after the others as the girls sorted themselves into a semblance of rank order, with those Cousin Siarti favored bade to walk with her, and the rest of us walking within hearing distance, but not presuming to go closer. I lagged behind them all, knowing myself least and lowest. To my surprise, Cousins Arati and Chuti stayed at the back, too, both with heads lowered modestly.

Usually I could not see them well from my place behind Mother and their places behind their beautiful mother. But walking like this through the garden gave me the opportunity to watch them. In fact, I found that I could not take my eyes away. Both sisters were finer to look at than the finest drawings on silk. I'd overheard gossip that their oldest sister, now married, had been more beautiful still. And there were twin girls still with their nanny at their palace.

The poets talk about willow brows and almond eyes. These two sisters had the willowiest eyebrows, and the almondiest eyes. Their mouths were small and perfectly shaped, like a bud or blossom, their noses exquisitely molded. Their hairline was not straight across, like mine, but a perfect pair of arches to follow the arch of their brows, coming to a delicate point over their fine noses, and their limbs were shapely and lissome. The only feature we shared was glossy hair, pure blue-black, but while mine was braided plainly, tied with a single ribbon, they each wore a single golden hairpin, the gold glowing against their artfully twisted hair.

I sighed within, trying to imagine what it would be like to look into my bronze mirror and see one of those faces, and not my mooncake of a face bisected by a pair of thin lips that were handsome on my brothers, but plain on me, and even thinner brows. All very well for mother not to value beauty (so I thought aggrievedly) but beauty was, well, *beauty*.

We had reached the first of the pretty little arched bridges over a meandering stream when Cousin Siarti paused at the top of the bridge and looked back, saying with treacly sweetness, "But no one is half as talented as our dear cousins." She looked over heads toward the two sisters, who curtseyed and thanked her. "What are you making for Grandmother Empress's birthday?"

Arati and Chuti looked at one another, and I think each expected the other to speak. Chuti—usually so chatty—bowed her head low, as if to remind her elder that she was the youngest in age and rank between the two of them.

Arati curtseyed and said, "If it pleases our respected

cousin, we thought to make matching screens, each face of the Morning Star, as we have been told that Grandmother Empress favors that legend."

"Oh, she is sure to like that. You know she is very particular, her tastes are so elevated, but we can all be certain that you will not disappoint her," Cousin Siarti exclaimed. "But I feel so sad that in pleasing her, you neglect me, your poor, talentless cousin!"

"Oh, no, we dare not offend the exquisite taste of our imperial cousin with our poor efforts!"

"And so you dare offer those poor efforts to imperial Grand-mother? Ay, you are much braver than I!" Siarti simper-ed, then turned about and descended the other side of the bridge.

The two sisters curtseyed again and uttered thanks as Cousin Siarti vanished briefly, then reappeared at the head of a chattering group. We wound our way through the garden, which was ripe with spring fragrances and blossoms, until we reached a gazebo that overlooked an alley between a pair of enormous buildings. Here, several boys walked in ones and twos, each carrying his writing case, and all looking as if they were about five steps from falling asleep. The imperial princes would of course not be there, as they did not have to submit to the examination, so why did the princesses want to watch, whisper, and giggle behind their fans?

Eventually Cousin Siarti declared that we were all tired and thirsty, and elicited our praise and thanks for her thoughtful-ness before she sent us home. As I scampered quickly, watching to make sure no one saw me running instead of gliding with tiny steps, my hands posed properly, I thought about that walk in the garden with the older girls. I had understood every word I heard, yet I had a sense that entire worlds of meaning had slipped by me like shadows.

Six

Fond of reading,
Only books worthy and wise,
Those the teachers of kings....

A FEW DAYS LATER, the rankings for the Imperial Examination were posted, which I only knew about because First Brother was invited to attend a celebratory dinner in town for one of his school friends who had ranked twenty-second, which had garnered him a ninth-rank secretarial post in the Ministry of Justice.

I knew this much because Father praised First Brother for making valuable friends; the caution that there were bad friends out there entirely escaped me. So far, my life was involved with duty calls and my many imperial relations, none of whom had any more interest in me as a person than I had in them. I had no friends, but I had my family and my companions of legend through my reading.

The indirect warning that there were enemies also escaped me until one day as spring ripened, when First Brother came to the table with his books, as always, one cheekbone was dark with a bruise.

"What happened?" I asked.

"There was a little trouble at the practice court," First Brother said briefly.

"Not at school?" Father asked, coming to his place with a

pile of testaments.

"No, Father."

"I'm relieved to hear that. I would be distressed to discover that you were losing precious time with your masters, who are as carefully chosen as they are wise, and who could not be blamed for thinking the less of anyone who troubles study time with childish disputes."

I sidled a glance at Second Brother, who ate unflustered. He wasn't involved, I was relieved to see, and of course First Brother would not be. He must have been in the wrong place at the wrong time.

My brothers went off together, now that Second Brother had been promoted into what was called "the princes' school," meaning to study with the imperial grandsons and Cousin Guiza, the one imperial son not yet an adult. They faded from my attention when Mother said to Father, "I believe an edict will arrive later this morning."

"To us here, or in court, do you know?"

"I think to you at court."

Father frowned. "It will be the Journey, then, if the edict must be heard in public. The emperor wants a resolution to the salt trade troubles, and we are nowhere near ready. It is going to mean very late nights for the inspectors while I'm required to idle my days away aboard the imperial sampan." His frown deepened. "It will make extra cares for you," he said to Mother.

"Thanks to Mai's warning, far fewer than might be."

"Thank you for everything, my wife," Father said.

Father's servants appeared with his robe, hat, jade tablet, and other accoutrements. Mother bowed, then gestured to me to follow, for it was time to ready ourselves to attend on the dowager empress.

As soon as we began walking, I said, "Does the edict mean that you and Father will be included for the Journey to the Clouds this year?"

"It does, Daughter."

"Is there a difference between the graywings bringing the edict to our home and its being presented in public?"

"There is," Mother said, then hesitated, glancing up the tree-lined path. Fragrant fringe flowers of bright rose and blooming osmanthus rustled around us. No other people in sight besides our two maids walking behind us.

Mother said, "If the edict were to be delivered at home,

that would be an invitation for Father as Father. An invitation delivered at the Censorate is an invitation for Father as Chief Censor. It is still a merit, but in this instance it is a reminder that the emperor has certain expectations."

"About salt trade?" I asked, then said quickly, "I know that salt is precious, and important to all, and though the ocean is full of it, we cannot get that salt. We must bring it from mines. Sometimes great distances. But why would that be trouble?"

"Does the salt transport itself, Daughter?"

"No, Mother," I said, and laughed. "I've known *that* since I was little."

"You are little now, Daughter." She passed her hand over my forehead in a fleeting gesture. Affection from her was rare, and never in public, but at that moment we were secluded by two great standing stones whose irregularities were said to depict the characters for Longevity on one side, and Harmony on the other.

She tucked her hand back into her sleeve as we started up a tiny arched bridge over a bending stream. "There is labor in getting the salt, labor in transporting it, and labor in distributing it. Behind each act of labor there is a mind directing the labor. Do you understand?"

"I do. But why is that trouble?"

"Because…there are many ways to transport salt, some of which are better than others. Because there can be hidden costs. Or hidden threats."

"Threats?"

"Sometimes, there is a little salt, and a lot of something else underneath the salt in the transport ship."

"Oh, *smuggling*," I said. "Breaking the laws. That's crime!" I exclaimed, thinking myself quite wise.

"And sometimes there is crime while heeding the laws. To an extent," Mother said. "Facts can be investigated, but intent is always harder to prove." She'd lost me there, but I thanked her anyway, for we were nearly in sight of the dowager empress's pavilion.

That began the day's round, leading to the next day's round, eternal and unchanging to my impatient eye, and yet there were little differences. For example, I not only knew most of the cousins by sight, I'd begun to know them a little, at least enough to recognize whom to avoid the notice of, like Cousin Siarti, first imperial granddaughter. From her I learned that the sweetest tone and fulsomely sugary words could hide poison thorns. The term 'a rose of court' was invented for her, I think.

Also, when I caught scraps of talk among the girl cousins I began to understand more of it, though not all of it by any means. I still stood outside the gate of understanding, as I will get to soon.

I had begun a habit of walking near Cousins Arati and Chuti, just because I loved looking at them both, especially Cousin Arati. Particularly that spring, when one of the dowager's competitions was under way, as Cousin Siarti had mentioned from the top of the bridge. This particular competition was to paint a fan or screen, the best to be chosen by the empress and awarded to the dowager empress for her birthday. There were a lot of these competitions, the fiercest being the dowager empress's competition for embroidery, which she judged each Midsummer.

I was already working on my piece, diligently supervised by both Mother and Eider. The older girls seemed to like talking about their progress, though they never said exactly what they were making. It was always humble words and low glances cast modestly aside, but few of them sounded truly humble, outside of Arati. Even Chuti, I discovered, assumed a demeanor like her sister's, but her words were a little too quick and too impatient—and in spite of that humble exterior, I discovered that she was addicted to gossip. Invariably she mumbled comments to her sister as we left this or that pavilion after a tea or a poetry reading, and as rank order put me behind them, and I was entranced by Cousin Arati's pure profile and her gait like flowing water, I caught a lot of it.

I was learning by listening, though I knew Mother would disapprove. She insisted that gossip was like eavesdropping, only indulged in by thieves and spies. Mother had warned that eavesdroppers deserved what they heard, but so far it was mostly intriguing, for it had nothing to do with me. I was too unnoticed for anyone to comment on me, bad or good. For example, after Consort Chin's party for chrysanthemum viewing, Cousin Chuti observed to her sister, "Aunt Hiza's nose was red as a cherry. Only her eyes were brighter. She said it was a cold, but it has to be Cousin Yiuti again. Didn't Bream say that he—"

"Better we believe the cold," Cousin Arati said. "And scold Bream if she keeps chattering. If she's overheard, what do you think will happen to her?"

"I'll never tell on Bream," Cousin Chuti said, her fan up

before her face.

"Even if asked directly?"

Cousin Chuti fell silent, and I felt sorry for that maid.

Another time, "…do you believe Liarti? Every other word out of her mouth is a lie."

"Ignorance is safest," Cousin Arati said, barely audible. "And we all know that Cousin Yiuti is wild."

Cousin Chuti sighed. "You let Siarti and those honey-mouthed toadies walk all over you, Sister."

"Steps are easier to endure than kicks. And you ought to use honorifics, or one day that presumptuous 'Siarti' will slip out where she will hear it, and you won't be able to sit for a month. Or worse."

One day we were picking ripe strawberries in the imperial garden, and I wasn't actually following them. I just didn't avoid them, as I did the imperial granddaughters. I was caught by the very rare sound of Mother's actual name. "…Gu Fua is a devotee of Suanek, or the Snow Crane? She dresses and acts like she's ready to become a nun! But she's not *old*—no older than Mother, and she's not ugly. Not at all."

"Mother says she's deep waters…" Cousin Arati began, and then she must have sensed me, for she began to look around, but I had ducked behind a tree, burning with indignation on Mother's behalf.

That indignation stayed with me, so I brought it up with Mother. "You were right about eavesdroppers," I said, ready to be offended on her behalf as I repeated what I'd overheard. "Cousin Chuti has no sense, saying you're like a nun! You obviously don't shave your head!"

"Only some nuns and monks do that, the ones who completely abjure the world. Many serve the world, and they leave their hair as nature made it. They refrain from dressing it to attract, which is actually my own preference, as you know, when I am at home."

We had already spoken about how dress was not only a display of rank, but could be a compliment to those we visited, but Mother's preference had always for been modesty and unobtrusiveness.

I thought about those beautiful robes that the other cousins got to wear, compared to my own very modest robes. No wonder I was overlooked! In a burst of resentment, I said, "I don't see what's wrong with being beautiful. Or dressing beautifully if one isn't beautiful," I added, thinking of Siarti and Liarti, the one with a pumpkin face and jug handle ears that she covered with loops of hair and handfuls of dangling gems, the other mousy of demeanor and dull brown hair beneath all the ribbons and golden decorations. I was afraid of Siarti's caustic sweetness, but her clothes filled me with envy. "Even the dowager empress dresses beautifully, and she's *old.*"

Mother was silent for a time, and I bent over my embroidery, for we had few days left to complete our pieces. I wondered if I was about to be admonished when Mother said, "I sometimes pity the dowager empress."

"Pity?" I repeated, for I couldn't imagine anyone ever pitying her. I didn't like Cousin Siarti, but all her cutting utterances were honey and lotus blossoms compared to the dowager empress when she was in a mood. She could be scathing, and no one dared offer a word in protest. Even the favored Consort Ye had to bow and thank her after being told her face was too red, and her latest robe aged her terribly.

"Referring to the subject of beauty. I'm just old enough to remember the dowager empress when she was in looks," Mother said, her gaze distant. "She really was beautiful. Apparently she had been from the day she was born, when most babies are wizened, red little creatures only adored by their mothers. She was raised to a single purpose: to catch the imperial heir's eye during the competition for brides. Which she did. One could say that was the greatest merit of her life, a triumph, but that was accomplished at the age of seventeen, and all these long years afterward have been a fight against the effects of time. The great headdress, the thick makeup, the robes that reach to the lowest step of the dais, the heavy jewels and fabulous embroidery, are her way of hanging onto that long-ago triumph."

I did not find it in me to pity her a whit. Instead, my mind caught at the word *competition.* "The cousins say that Cousin Xianti will have a bride competition soon."

"He's a year or two from the customary age," said Mother. "I expect the summons will probably go out next year, or perhaps the year following."

I considered Cousin Xianti, whose braying laughter frightened me a little. He seemed so old to me, though he still wore his hair loose down his back the way boys did. His sleeves were the widest and his tassels the longest, swinging as he strode around, scattering lesser cousins in whatever he did. He would be married off, which meant he'd be considered a man. No more princes school for him. They would probably make him a general. I hoped so, which would mean he'd be sent off somewhere, where others would have to hear that raucous laugh.

"Did you ever have to do the bride competition? No, you were betrothed to Father, I know *that*."

Mother smiled. "I still had to answer the summons, along with all the other eligible girls."

"Even though you were betrothed to Father."

"Do you really think that if the Imperial Heir wants a certain person, that cannot be arranged?"

"Oh."

"In any case, I did not even make it through the first tier of the competition. I was adjudged too tall and too plain by the imperial aunts who conducted that round."

I had a moment to reflect that Mother did not betray a vestige of regret in either countenance or voice. In fact, I sensed more than saw a hidden smile.

Then there was noise without, and First Brother was back a little earlier than usual, bearing a scroll. He bowed, and handed the scroll to Mother, saying, "I have been summoned to accompany Master Bailu on the Journey to the Clouds."

Mother said evenly, "This is considered a great honor, to be chosen to form one of the imperial princes' study companions."

First Brother's jaw flexed. Neither spoke and once again I sensed that I stood outside in the dark, looking toward the lit windows that were covered by screens. But then First Brother bowed himself out, and nothing was said, and the days passed until Second Brother and I accompanied our parents and elder brother to the cart that would carry them to the harbor. Another cart, full of servants and trunks, followed them as they rolled away.

Second Brother and I waved until they were out of sight, then he gave me one of his grins. "Are you piled with work to be done while they're gone?"

"Yes," I said morosely. "Though I don't know when I'll have time to do it when I have to finish that piece of embroidery for her imperial majesty."

"You're too honest to leave it to your maid?" he asked, brows rising.

"Mother would know," I admitted. "She can tell my stitches from Eider's at a single glance. Do you really think that others cheat?"

"I know they do," Second Brother said as we walked through the outer court together toward the formal part of the house, where we rarely sat unless summoned. "But you also know who would get away with it."

"That is true," I said. "However, since I've got to do my own stitching, will you read to me? Mother sometimes does. It makes the time go faster."

"I'll read to you, and it won't be lessons. Unless you want them?"

"Oh, if you'd read a good tale to me, I would work twice as long!"

And so he did.

Over the next three days, as rain poured and thunder rumbled, he could not go out, and so he read the entirety of *Jong Siang and the Cricket King*, and *The Brothers Ma and the Ghost Army*. It was late at night when he finished, and I had long ago folded away my embroidery as I had made tremendous progress, but my hands ached and my eyes stung.

Second Brother carefully closed the tattered book, then said, "I just realized that that's the last of the truly good ones."

"Oh?" I said, then added, "At least I've plenty more to read. Are the rest in the trunk really that bad?"

"Not bad so much as dull, or repeats of other adventures, only with the names changed."

Thunder rumbled in the distance. We sat in the family room, both his and my servants having been dismissed. "I wonder," he began, glancing in the direction of the library. "Those other trunks. I've only taken a glance. But now that I've been through all the books and scrolls. Some several times. Maybe, since no one is around, we might go in there and take a good look through the older trunks at the back. In case there are some more of these tales?"

I leaped up, stinging eyes forgotten. "Lets!"

We each took up a lamp, and ventured across to our parents' wing as rain battered the roof and rattled the windows.

Perch appeared, yawning, drawn by the movement of our lamps, Second Brother's servant behind her. We waved them off and let ourselves into the library, where we shut the door before taking our lamps to the far corner. In the long, sharply delineated shadows, those trunks looked larger and heavier than I remembered. I hung back doubtfully, but Second

Brother put his lamp into my free hand and said, "Hold this high."

He turned to the first stack, lifted the top trunk off, grunted as he set it carefully down, then dragged the second trunk off. I set the lamps on the desk and a shelf, and opened the first trunk to dig through, holding up each book or scroll. Kanda, Kanda, Kanda, more Kanda, then a stack of Mana Ta.

I put these back, and turned to the second trunk. Some worn old clothes lay neatly folded on top. A waft of honey-locust soap tickled my nose as I lifted these out. From the size, they were children's clothing. Not babies, but for someone my size. They were plain, undecorated, the seams and hems worn.

I set those aside, wondering who had used them and why they were stored, and then forgot those as I delved into the books below . . . to find calligraphy practice in children's poems.

I put everything back as Second Brother loaded the third trunk with its items. He shook his head at my glance. "Lessons," he said. "And practice at drawing. Mostly reeds." He made a face. "Why would anyone keep these?"

I shrugged, both of us too young to ask the next question, which would not concern what was saved so much as who might have made or used the things. When the trunks were neatly stored again, Second Brother lugged them back into their pile, and we looked down at the second stack, the ones farthest in the corner.

"Shall we bother?" I asked, sneezing from dust.

"We're here. Why not? Then we'll know." He wiped his face on his sleeve. "But you might give me a hand shifting these trunks."

I took the corners of the top one as he took the other half. I barely managed my end, dropping it with a thud, and almost crushing my toes in their slippers. "Never mind," he said. "I'll tend to the trunks. You search."

More clothes, older and smaller trousers and tunics in the first one. I would have thought these clothes for servants, they were so plain, but the fabric was too fine. More children's lessons books beneath. Second Brother searched the second trunk more cursorily as I bent over the last one. More dusty papers, some brittle with age, and an old cloak, and—I reached for the bottom bundle of cloth, my fingers encountering an unexpectedly hard shape wrapped within what appeared to be another cloak, when a voice startled me, "Child?"

I jumped and looked around wildly as Second Brother flipped through three books, muttering, "If Kanda had loved family so much, why didn't he spend more time with them, instead of cursing us with so much copywork?"

"Did you hear that?" I asked.

"Hear what? The thunder? The skies have only been making war for three days now."

"I thought I heard the word…child." As I said it, I felt silly, and mumbled it.

Second Brother laughed, plunging his hand into the third trunk — then he yanked it out again. "What was that? Was that a scorpion? Some kind of biting bug?" He looked from that to my face, and he must have read his own disgust in my confused expression for he began to toss things back into the trunks. "One thing I know, there is *never* just one bug. Of any kind. I'd say we're finished. So much for more tales."

We returned everything more or less as it had been. Second Brother grunted the trunks back into their stacks, and we returned to our respective chambers. Where I climbed into bed, but could not sleep.

SEVEN

As thunder rumbled in the west,
She mastered the five virtues.
In all the empire,
Who was loyal and wise?

HAD I HEARD THAT voice or not? It had been so distinct, as if someone stood directly behind me, speaking close to my ear. I tossed restlessly on my bed, unable to sleep as I worried at the question.

The gallant wanderer tales had been filled with talking turtles, rocks, snakes, birds, dragons, lakes, and mountains. This was the first time I had ever heard of a trunk talking. Or rather, whatever might lie inside that trunk. What if there was a demon inside that trunk? An evil one? Every tale with talking objects that I'd read so far was evenly divided between good and evil intentions. But I'd know evil intentions, wouldn't I—assuming there had actually been a voice. Second Brother had definitely not heard it.

I finally decided to go back and test it. Once I'd made the decision, I slid into slumber, and woke to the milky-pale sky of late morning. No one had woken me as there was no schedule for me. By the time I was ready for the day, it was to discover that Second Brother had already gone off to the princes' school, for the masters and the fifth-rank princes and nobles' sons not invited along for the Journey to the Clouds were expected to carry on as always.

I looked over at my table, where my embroidery and copywork lay, and promised myself I'd return to it once I looked in that trunk again. Only how was I to manage those trunks on top of it? Of all my maids, Cray was definitely the biggest.

I called for her. "We're going to the library," I said, trying to sound calm and self-assured.

When we got there, I pointed at the stashed trunks, and said, "I need to get to the one at the bottom there. Help me shift the top ones." So saying, I moved to the top trunk of the stack that I needed, and braced myself. Then I looked up. Cray had not moved. She gazed at me with an expression midway between shock and disbelief.

"You can't lift these?" I asked. "I can send for one of the yard men—"

"No," Cray said. Softly, but so very definitely. Then she dropped face down to the floor. "This unworthy and useless servant begs Young Miss not to… That is… if this undeserving one may dare to put a question…"

Mother had instructed the servants while we were at home among ourselves to address us children as First Young Master, Second Young Master, and Young Miss. We were princes and princesses only when we went out.

I bit back the impulse to snap, though my curiosity had become a hunger. Ever since The Comb Incident, I had tried very hard to emulate mother in how she spoke to the servants—having noticed that her way was very different from the ways of the princess cousins, who slapped their maids as if they were dolls. Even our cook cuffed the kitchen help and the yard boys. But I'd made a promise, and I'd kept it, remembering that we were all skin under our robes.

I said, "Has Mother or Father forbidden us to touch those? If so, I never knew that."

"It is not…that is…" Cray mumbled witlessly, her forehead still to the floor.

"Cray. I want to look at something at the bottom of that one trunk. Second Brother and I went through them last night, and all we found were old clothes and a lot of copybooks. Except I think, or maybe I imagined, that something at the bottom of that trunk…*spoke* to me. I want to find out of that really happened."

Cray's head lifted. Again, she stared at me, eyes and mouth

round circles that at any other time would have prompted a laugh. It was the contrast, for though she was merely fifteen or so, she was as self-possessed as Mother. Maybe even more so. And so *silent*.

"Spoke to you?" she repeated, and forgot the honorific.

"Yes. I want to find out if that was real. Help me shift these trunks, or are you trying to say they are too heavy? We can call in someone—"

Cray rose so swiftly that I was startled. With a frown of concentration, she moved to the trunks, and though the top of her head probably came to Second Brother's chin, and she was slight, she lifted that trunk as if it was empty. And the next one.

Then she hesitated, and with slow, even reverent movements, she opened the third trunk and carefully took out the items on top of that wrapped cloak at the bottom.

She laid her hand flat on that, and looked up at me, her expression even odder.

Shrugging off that expression that was impossible to interpret, I reached in, and something hard struck against my palm. "Lift me," commanded that voice somewhere right behind my ear.

"Did you hear that?" I said to Cray, who had gone pale when the thing, whatever it was, hit my palm. "Ayah! It's heavy."

Thunk! It dropped back into the trunk.

"I heard nothing," Cray whispered.

"It said *Lift me* as clearly as you and I speak right now. But it's so heavy." I reached down, and once again the thing jumped to my fingers.

And once again I dropped it.

This time, the cloth disarranged a little, revealing the unmistakable hilt of a sword! It had some kind of stone in the hilt, white, glistening, with a hint of color.

I reached, though with the other to support my wrist, and once again the sword smacked into my hand. Cray murmured, "May this one try..." I tried to hand it to her, but the sword jerked away from her, and slammed with a thud back into the trunk.

Cray turned slowly, straightening her plain gray robe. She bowed, hands to her thighs instead of curtseying—then she quickly turned the bow into a proper curtsey, a movement so quick I almost missed the whole. Almost. "The Young Miss must inform her highness. But before then, if this one may make a suggestion, Young Miss might consider training to lift Sagacious Blade."

"Sagacious? Blade?"

"It is the name of the blade, Young Miss."

"Why?" I asked.

Cray had already spoken more in these few moments than she had since she first came to me. Her lips parted, then she dropped her head. "This slow-witted one does not know, Young Miss. All this one knows is that its presence must remain unknown to the household."

"Why?"

"Charmed weapons are forbidden by imperial edict, Young Miss," Cray said slowly and reluctantly. I got the sense that she didn't want to tell me that much, but since it had spoken to me, she must.

"Not even Second Brother can know? He'd be so surprised…" I stopped there. "Why would my parents have something that is forbidden?"

Her expression closed over, and I knew what she was going to say before she said it: "This ignorant one does not know."

"But I have to tell my parents."

"Madam Gu knows that it is there, Young Miss. It lies among her childhood things."

All that Kanda was Mother's? That I could have guessed. But not those clothes, which were unlike anything I had ever worn. Or that I could imagine her ever wearing. But I had no interest in those worn old things, and skipped to what she was willing to tell me. "You said training."

"If this unworthy one is permitted to make a suggestion," Cray said after a protracted pause, "Young Miss must first learn to lift it."

I was going to point out that that was impossible for girls, but then I remembered that Cray had just lifted those trunks. Further, she'd done it with far more ease than Second Brother had.

Slowly the truth began to percolate through me. A magic sword—like in the hero tales. And it seemed to speak to me. Me! The youngest, the least in all possible ways. I didn't know what it meant. Right then I didn't care. It had chosen me, then I had to be able to pick it up.

"Teach me," I said.

"Here is the way to learn fastest, without notice."

She dropped to the floor, her stomach down, feet together, hands flat beside her shoulders, her elbows tucked tightly against her sides. She lifted her upper body until her arms were straight, then slowly lowered herself until only her nose touched the floor. Then up again, slow and smooth.

I threw myself down, and immediately got tangled in my layers of robes. I untied those so I was only wearing my white long under trousers and undershirt. I got onto my stomach, put my hands at my shoulders, pushed…

And nothing happened.

My elbows swung out as I tried again, and Cray said, "Young Miss, to do it correctly, the arms must stay tight to the ribs."

"Why?"

"This ignorant one was told that the wrong muscles would be used, or overused, if the elbows wing out."

I accepted that and tried again, with no success. She demonstrated from the knees, which looked easier, and indeed I managed to lift myself about the width of a finger. Every muscle in my body struggled, igniting my stubbornness.

I did not know why that sword had picked me. I had no idea what I would do with it, but I was going to lift it. And if this exercise was how I'd get strong enough to lift it, then I would try it over and over until I could do it. All those endless rounds in the yard with the hated padded box balanced on my head had taught me the effectiveness of repetition.

For the rest of that day, I traded between the tasks I had been assigned and dropping to my knees. By the end of the day I was no closer to lifting my own body—and midway through the night I woke from sore muscles. But sore muscles were nothing new. My hands got sore when I stitched too long, and Perch rubbed salve into them before I slept.

I stubbornly kept at it for the next week or so, until I no longer woke sore. I was also able to get myself a hand's width off the floor going up, but coming down, I still flopped on my face. And it was stubbornness. I hated being defeated by my own body, when I could see the solution. My inability just determined me the more, both to master that exercise, and to find out what Cray knew. She continued to be silent, but when we were alone, I asked questions. "What can it do, besides talk?"

She didn't know.

"Why does it talk?"

She didn't know that, either.

"Why does Mother have a forbidden thing?"

"It was handed down through her maternal family."

"It's not a Gu charmed weapon?"

No.

"How did it get here?"

"I brought it when I was sent to my place in your chamber."

"You? Brought it? From where? Why?"

She didn't know that either.

Finally I began to suspect that she did know the answers to at least a few of my questions, but wouldn't answer, and I stopped asking. She had to have received orders to keep the secret of the sword. Even from me. That is to say, nobody had ever expected it to speak to me, so she wasn't keeping knowledge from me in specific.

The end of the second week saw the return of the imperial party. The emperor's entourage arrived first, of course. Over the next few days other ships arrived, held back by the terrible weather.

I knew better than to rush constantly to the front gate, which Mother would disapprove of. I forced myself to sit still and attend to my embroidery, with the result that by the time the cart rolled up, nearly at sundown, I actually finished it at last, two days before the festival.

"They're here," Second Brother said abruptly, bursting in through my door. "My guess is, they waited for First."

"I still don't understand why he did not join our parents on the imperial ship?"

Second rolled his eyes. "Not a chance. I don't know who invited First, but you can wager it was not Cousin Xianti. But you can also wager that Cousin Xianti made sure that First was on the last ship out."

I'd heard so much about Cousin Xianti's temper that it never occurred to ask why this petty act toward our brother. My parents had waited to board that last ship, (I understood later) in silent protest.

In the flurry of servants going back and forth fetching trunks and baskets, we managed to exchange greeting bows, Second Brother and I on our best behavior. Mother and Father both looked pleased with us as Father led the way inside, to the family's parlor.

First Brother appeared to be exactly as always, bowing himself out when Father dismissed him to rest after their long journey. Presently he went off as well, his servant bearing a load of testaments, and at last Mother and I were alone in her inner chamber.

"Mother," I said, "guess what I found! Cray calls it Sagacious Blade. And it talked to me!"

I'd expected surprise, maybe even approval, for after all the sword had chosen me. But she stared at me blankly, then her serene forehead puckered, and she said softly, "Oh, *no*."

EIGHT

Adamant as dragons in the east,
Rising on summer winds,
The comet sped across the firmament.
The world bowed, and the gods
smiled down from their jade palaces...

IN THE *CONVERSATIONS*, KANDA tells us that the stars govern the day of our birth, but once we are born, fate is balanced with all the small events and decisions that we make unthinkingly. We are to regard these as streams that feed the river of our lives. Some attribute those changes — especially the unwanted ones — to fate, and others insist that to say that is to deny the great balance between what we are given in this life, and what we make of it.

What about the great events?

"Oh, no," said my mother.

"It's fate," I insisted — uncertainly.

To which Mother retorted, "It's not fate, my child. It's an affinity. Occurred by happenstance. There are no doubt many others in the world for whom that sword will also have an affinity, and we shall find a suitable one. But that is my task, one I ought to have seen to by now. You are to forget that sword ever existed."

I burst into tears.

"Lan Renti!"

"I don't care," I whimpered. "Make me kneel before ancestors for a year—slap me a thousand times—take away everything, but I won't forget it, I can't forget. It chose me. Everybody else thinks I'm too young, too slow, too untalented, too unimportant, but that sword picked *me!*"

"Daughter," Mother said. "My decision is meant to guard your life!"

I couldn't stop sobbing.

She put her arms around me, and spoke into my hair. "Renti, my dear child, I wish you could see that I am not angry with you, I am afraid for you. To begin with, you must remember that charmed weapons are absolutely forbidden, by imperial edict. Why did you go to Cray?"

"Because she is the tallest... and oldest...and Mother, it turns out she is quite strong," I quavered.

"Heaven does have eyes." Mother closed hers for a long moment. "If you'd told anyone else. Especially the informers. I don't dare think of the result."

"I know that. I... I mean I know now that it is a secret. Cray told me, and so I didn't even tell Second Brother that I found it, though I wanted to. Does Father know?"

"He knows about the sword. I would not have tried it with your brothers without his agreement, but it was never in the house, as censors are forbidden to have weapons. We used to travel north to my family's city each year, when things were quieter. We stopped going north before you were born."

"Why is it here?" I gulped back my tears.

"There was trouble in my family's city. A rumor reached my grandmother that someone with ill intent was seeking charmed weapons, and had the power to force searches under legal pretext. She sent it to me for a time, as no one would think of searching here, under imperial eyes. Your father does not know it is here. I believe he would understand the necessity, which is part of my maternal family's responsibility as we understand it, but because of who he is, he cannot know."

I was barely able to perceive the stress of divided loyalties here, as Mother went on. "My cousin sent it along with Cray and those boxes of my old things, when Cray was brought into the palace to serve you. As expected, the gate guards gave the trunks the most cursory search when they saw that the arrival was merely a new maid, bringing old clothes and study books." She looked upward, then back at me. "I will be writing letters this very day."

"Where did it come from?"

"It came down through the silk-maker side of my family, brought by the cook's grandfather, six or seven generations ago. He turned up, scarred and crippled, after a lifetime of fighting pirates. Grandfather Cook—that's what they called him—used to sit in the sun with the sword on his knees, then one day it went to my great-great-grandfather, who was five years old at the time."

"Went?" I repeated.

"That's the story as passed down." Mother frowned slightly as she studied her lotus lamp, but I don't think she saw it. "He took to the wander when he was First Brother's age, and came back covered in merit after having defended the northwest against voracious Westerners. None of that shall happen to you, of course. Perhaps the Essence is wearing off of the sword, and it is like a guttering candle—an unpredictable flicker now and then."

"Nobody else had it talk to them?"

"Not after he died, and my great-grandfather brought it back. It was put into the hands of every boy in the family at a young age, but it stayed inert, so it rested in the ancestral hall as an artifact, testing each new boy when he was very small. It can stay in that trunk until I can get my cousin to spirit it away."

Disappointment knotted my heart so sharply that it took all my effort not to burst out bawling once again, but I knew Mother would disapprove, and there would go my chance to find out more.

"How did you find it?" she asked.

Hoping that I wasn't about to lose gallant wanderer tales as well, I told her everything, and ended, "Are those gallant wanderer books yours, too?"

She gave me a wry expression. "Can you imagine me reading such? Your father brought those in, a gift from his imperial uncle, Grand Prince Forluo, of beloved memory. Second Brother is very like him. And indeed, before he died, he gave your father those books when Second Brother was struggling to learn to read, saying that *he* didn't learn to read until he discovered forbidden fruit. I did not think that you would have a taste for such nonsense, but then you are eleven years old."

"Am I forbidden to read them?" I asked, feeling that

everything had been taken from me that mattered. Except of course for duty.

"I probably ought to, but you've had enough disappointment, I think. Many of our most venerable musical plays are just as nonsensical, if more traditional—and I don't believe silly stories do any harm. The fact that I did not know you were reading them speaks well for your self-discipline. As long as your proper studies don't suffer, you may continue to read those in the library. But if Second Brother should begin bringing, ah, romantic tales from the booksellers, as he's getting close to the age for such, I want you to show them to me first."

"Thank you, Mother," I said fervently. "As for romance, I always skip that part. All those flowery poems, it's so very boring."

Mother laughed a little, gave me a last tight squeeze, and let me go.

I trudged off to my bedchamber, where my maids awaited me. I saw four pairs of eyes study my face, which was probably as tear-blotched as it felt. No one dared ask, and I wasn't going to explain.

Was one of them a spy?

Ay! Not a spy, in the way of gallant wanderer tales, when someone infiltrates a sect in order to learn its secrets ahead of conquering them. No one would want to conquer *us*, a respectable household led by a censor! But I knew that the maids and servants not brought in from outside families were supplied by the Household Department, and they were regularly questioned for the good of the palace. I'd learned that early. For the first time I considered why I'd learned that, as part of my lessons in being circumspect, though I'd thought the context merely learning to avoid generating gossip. Now I had an actual secret to be circumspect about!

I got Cray alone the next morning. "Mother said the sword has to stay in the trunk," I said disconsolately. "I am not to have the sword. I guess I can see that. If anyone saw me, and told someone else, we might all get executed."

Cray bowed in silence, and that seemed to be the end of the matter—except that I kept doing that exercise. It gave me a tiny sense of accomplishment, even if that meant nothing much, as life returned to its daily rounds.

Mother lavished great praise on my finished embroidery, which I duly presented to the dowager empress in the garden pavilion the following week. She and the empress said many complimentary things to us all, but it was Cousin Taisa whose embroidery won the prize, which was a golden peony hairpin with dangles that ended in pearls. Cousin Taisa accepted the merit with her usual complacent demeanor, ignoring the shower of compliments we all spoke as the dowager empress fitted it into Cousin Taisa's hair, next to her golden hairpin of osmanthus blossoms. Won the previous year.

Then the empress said to Consort Zenar, "That reminds me of that cunning fan case you stitched out of silk for dear Taisa on her birthday. Alas, I wish I was as important as my sister Chin's daughter."

Beautiful Consort Zenar bowed, saying, "This untalented slow-wit would be honored to make one, if it would please her imperial majesty."

Here the dowager empress broke in, "My imperial majesty dares to observe that my favorite fan—painted by my dear husband himself, no one in all the court more talented—could really use such a silk case..."

Consort Zenar bowed her way, promised to make her one, just as Cousin Arati and her sister to a lesser extent promised to the imperial granddaughters. I'd been listening to these flattering requests for over a year, but for the first time began to wonder why the imperial elders, who surely could order whatever they wanted from the Household Department—which existed to serve them before anyone else in the palace—kept requesting things from Consort Zenar and her beautiful daughters?

On our way back, Mother said, "I was glad to observe that your embroidery looked quite well among the others, though you are the youngest."

"It wasn't the best," I admitted, after thanking her. "Though I wonder if some of the better ones were done by maids."

"At least you will have the satisfaction of knowing that yours was due to your own efforts. Especially if the empress chooses to pursue the matter."

How? Then I remembered Cousin Taisa's comments about Cousin Arati's flying geese pouch. She had known at a glance which stitches were amiss. And I could tell the difference between my own stitching and Eider's. Oh, yes, if one of the elders decided to look closely, I expect they'd be able to tell who had performed her own work.

I understood then what a close call I'd had. The imperial granddaughters would undoubtedly be excused for claiming their maids' handiwork for their own, but I wasn't so certain about anyone else. I wasn't certain of anything. Everything had been pleasant and serene to appearances, the consorts and imperial elders full of compliments and pleasant words, the atmosphere had been... sticky. Cloying, the way pumpkin-faced Cousin Siarti sounded, when she complimented beautiful Cousin Arati with that false smile and those malicious eyes.

It struck me then that Cousin Siarti was mimicking the empress and the dowager empress, and I turned to Mother. "Their imperial majesties both talked about Consort Zenar's clever sewing, but why..."

Though I'd looked around, and no one was on the path before or behind us, Mother laid her finger on my wrist. Then she murmured, "Look at her hands next time she is asked to serve the tea."

Look at her hands? Eighteenth Consort Zenar always hid her hands. I'd noticed that before. Unlike some of the others, who flaunted gold and jade rings. What would be wrong with... "Ayah."

I glanced down at my own fingers and thumb, covered with healing pinpricks. Once again it was like that sunrise reaching the tops of the roofs and turning silhouettes into tiles and walls and doors with calligraphy down the sides. If the consort's hands looked anything like mine from those constant labors in making tiny, clever things and embroidering them, only to be asked for another and another...

"Why?" I asked uneasily.

Mother took her time in answering. When she was satisfied that we were truly alone, she said, "Many reasons. I do not pretend to know the insides of minds or hearts. But I can guess: because she is beautiful. Because she only gave the Imperial Crown Prince five daughters, and no son. Because she was barely seventeen when she caught his eye, and he made her the center of court, leaping her past everyone above her in rank—which ended the day the dowager empress insisted that he marry in a new consort who might birth sons."

I considered that briefly. Then said, "Is it odd, that there are so many consorts and not that many boy cousins? Or girl cousins, though more of them?"

I thought my observation quite grown up, but Mother gave

me one of those looks that meant I was not going to hear any more on that subject. She said, "It is a matter better left undiscussed, lest speculation be overheard. As I was saying, at seventeen some believe their triumph is eternal, and she was not very generous. When she was set aside in favor of a new consort, those who had been slighted or overlooked began to treat her as you see now. Do you understand, a little, why I encourage you to learn to be prudent?"

"I think so." Every meridian in my body chilled as I began to comprehend that smiling, deliberate slow torture.

"People caged up together for their entire lives can regard the smallest error as vast as a war," Mother said. "Don't forget that."

NINE

Graceful as a reed in a spring breeze,
She mastered all arts,
Gaze never wavering,
As she followed the moons into the great future.

SUMMER BEGAN TO RIPEN at last.

Our world inside the imperial palace enjoyed warm days of fragrant breezes, the flowers more plentiful and intensely hued than ever after so much rain. Consequently, there were more gatherings out of doors: poetry reading in the pavilions, paint-ing sessions alongside the canals, and the sedate games that did not jar anyone's headdress or wrinkle long silken sleeves. The dowager empress also continued to host contests to gauge our calligraphy, embroidery, and the older girls' ability to respond to one another with poetry invented on the spot. None of the imperial elders favored vigorous games like pitch pot, or board games such as Circle, so we never played those except at home.

I tried not to think about the sword. I was kept busy enough that I had little time to brood, other than imagining myself and the talking sword in place of this or that hero in the gallant wanderer tales that I rationed out for myself.

One afternoon, Mother and I left the last consort's palace, and to my surprise, there was our family cart waiting. Knowing that she believed walking was a virtue, unlike calling out several servants and two horses just to carry the two of us a short distance, I looked at her in surprise. Then upward, expecting to see dragon-clouds tumbling fast and shooting lightning over the sky. But the azure sea of air beneath the heavens was innocent of threat.

Mother said in the hearing of a pair of passing guards and of the consort's maids who had accompanied us out, "Thinking ahead to imperial birthdays, Daughter, we might give their imperial majesties and your imperial cousins silver fur caps, as I overheard the empress extolling the one she possessed as a girl. The best furs come from the north, and it's always better to examine them ourselves."

I knew that finding the correct gifts for people who had everything was a continual worry in the court. I did not see why I had to accompany Mother, but I was not being asked for my opinion, and Mother's forehead was tight, her mouth set.

This did not seem to be the moment to exult in the fact that we were about to leave the palace for my very first time. I was vitally interested in everything: the Imperial Guards in gold and crimson at the gate, Mother handing her jade tally to her maid to hold out to the guards, and then being waved through as men bearing great spears with wicked curved tips saluted briefly as we rode through.

My first glimpse of the street was disappointing, for the buildings were much like those in the palace, only not as fine. These seemed an artless jumble, some with double roofs, some with only one, structured at different heights. Most had oiled paper windows, as usual, pushed out by a stick. People wander-ed everywhere, and once I turned my attention to them, I was fascinated.

Not that I got to stare long. When we were clear of the magnificent stone qilin, wings outstretched, who guarded the gates, Mother said, "I have done everything I can to prepare you for a tranquil life, my daughter. But it seems I erred in trying to keep you free of the burden of secrets."

I managed not to respond that I *loved* knowing secrets!

Mother continued, "We may always speak freely before Gui, Bao, Mai, and Cray."

Mai was the maid mother took with her when she left our palace, just as Cray invariably accompanied me. Gui, driving the cart, and Bao were yard men—doing whatever jobs required strong men. They also prowled around at night, chasing off any rats the cats missed, and generally watching over things, as the Imperial Guard paced the tiled paths between palaces.

Mother went on, "These servants are known to my family, and are trustworthy. Among our house servants, Fern, Dai, and Eider must be regarded as informants."

"Eider!" She was so cheerful. If I were to choose someone as a likely spy slinking about sinisterly, Eider would be among the very last I'd consider.

"It is the duty she was raised to," Mother said. "Your behavior must never vary, and prudence must be your byword."

"*I* know *that*, Mother," I said, hoping to stave off having to copy out *Kanda Addresses the Little Girl Searching for Treasure in the Bamboo Forest* yet again, warning how words are the true treasure, and every one spoken is forever spent—as I am certain you all are aware, the longest and wordiest among all the cautionary tales.

Happily, Mother seemed to have other things on her mind. "You will be meeting my cousin, whom you'll address simply as Gu Auntie. She travels as a silk merchant."

The car slowed before an emporium, and we descended, Gui going to the horses' heads as Cray and Mai put the step back on the cart and followed us sedately.

The shop contained shelves and shelves of fabrics of all kinds, and in a back area, costly furs. Mother allowed the proprietor to steer us toward the costliest, and after a short time bargaining, Mai carried our purchases as we left.

As soon as we got outside, Mother glanced around, then her eyes widened in shock for less than a heartbeat. If I had not been watching her for clues to what we were to do next, I might have missed it.

She said calmly, "Mai, put the packages in the cart. Daughter, would you like a candy rabbit?"

I loathed sugar desserts, and Mother knew that, but her tone, and the way she glanced at a white-haired old woman in threadbare gray clothes, made me hesitate. The woman held a frame filled with hardened sugar shaped like Suanek and the Morningstar God in both faces and lucky animals and other auspicious symbols. She stood in front of a booth whose front table displayed more elaborate candies.

In any case, Mother did not wait for an answer, but closed her fingers around my wrist and pulled me toward the booth.

"Candy, candy!" the old woman called out in a cracked voice. And as we approached, "Come inside, madam! We have better shapes inside the booth, where the flies won't bother them."

We followed her into the booth, which was stiflingly hot, and smelled strongly of honey and sweet spices.

The old woman turned around, scowled, and said, "Gu Fua, where have your wits fled?"

My wits fled when Mother dropped to her knees, head bowed. "Grandmother, peace and long life be yours."

"Peace indeed!" The old woman's whisper was all the more fierce for being hissed under her breath. "Don't you start in with the flowers and airs, you wretched girl, making me have to come all this way!"

"Honored grandmother," my mother began.

"Do you really want to keep this girl of yours ignorant in *these* times? Especially if the sword has chosen her? We know it has chosen girls before. Grandfather Cook was quite specific about that. And I told you, you were tested along with both your cousins."

"It is precisely these times that moved me to be rid of it as soon as—"

"I suppose you can be forgiven for forgetting what you heard when you were small. It's true we taught you little more about Sagacious Blade when we discovered that you were summoned to court. But surely someone must have told you when you brought your boys that the sword takes care of itself. Also. Whoever it has chosen has lived a very long life. *If* the sword stays with them."

"If someone told me, this dull-witted one did forget."

"Don't give me that courtly talk! It roils my spleen. It was probably our error anyway, when you brought your boys up to us, knowing you had to return to this pit of hissers. Ayoh! Never mind. Is this your girl?"

Black eyes swept me from braids to dusty slippers, and I hastily made a deep curtsey, then sidled a look Mother's way for a hint on proper address, for this was obviously not Gu Auntie.

"Very proper and modest," this venerable and surprising woman said briskly. Imagine anyone calling Mother 'Gu Fua' as if she were a ten-year-old yard sweeper caught pinching milk cakes! The grandmother wasn't all that much taller than I, but her presence seemed to fill that booth. "Tell me exactly what happened with Sagacious Blade."

I turned to Mother, who nodded, and so, in as low a voice

as I could, I outlined my discovery once more.

"Succinctly and clearly told, child. Bodes well. And you thought to get my fourth grandniece...what are you calling her? Cray? To go with you? Good instincts, or Suanek is watching over you. Pay attention to what you're told, and work hard, and you'll come out all right. Though maybe not as a duke's wife strutting about with her eyes above her head, as your mother hoped."

I curtseyed, too intimidated to point out that the advice to work hard was what I heard every day of my life, but I had never heard anyone call my mother to task for her ambitions.

The grandmother did not wait for me to answer. She pushed a hardened candy figure of Suanek on the fish into my fingers and said, "Go stand out there and lick that, while I have a word with your mother. Fua," the grandmother said, turning away from me, "I will preface with praise. I'm very pleased with Fourth Grandniece's progress. Gui says she is diligent in daily practice, and is learning apace..."

I went out into the street. I strained to hear, but the booth muffled whispers. Giving up, I pretended to lick that treat as I watched guards march by in cadence, weapons and armor jingling. Street vendors wandered by, selling all manner of things, and people wearing clothing of a sort I'd never seen before entered and left stores. Down the street, music drifted out of a decorated emporium called the Garden of Heaven. I glimpsed young men and women laughing and calling to passers-by, inviting them in.

My attention did not linger on adults. I was more interested in anyone my size or younger, so when I saw a furtive small figure lurking beyond a sign for a tea emporium, I turned to find a child with two round eyes peering out of a dirty face. The child's clothes were dirt-colored rags, and I could smell that beggar from where I stood.

When I saw the child's gaze go from me to the candy in my hand, I held it out. The beggar hesitated, poised to run. "Take it," I whispered — I did not want to be thought ungrateful if the grandmother came out to see her gift handed off.

When I glanced at the booth door, the beggar lunged, snatched the candy, and sped off so fast it was almost as if no one had been there. Except I was rid of the thing. I turned away, looking up the street at a cavalcade of mounted individuals with bright red, conical hats tied under the chin with embroidered blue ribbons. All the men except the youngest had beards, but the most interesting was a girl who appeared to be not a lot older than I, riding behind the leader. Her hair was all done in long braids with beads worked into them. She wore a red jacket over dark riding trousers. Her jacket was worked with luck signs, many of which I'd seen in gallant wanderer tales. She gave me a grin and they vanished into the crowd.

I was afraid to move from where I stood until Mother emerged, and though she wore her usual calm expression, I sensed worry.

The grandmother was talking. "…and now I must spend the remainder of the day selling here, as I promised. Never mind! It's diverting enough, watching the world pass by. Go."

"Mother," I said, when the grandmother had gone back into the booth to bring out more candies for the table, "look there."

For I had caught sight of that same beggar, or perhaps another the same age and size. There was no sign of the candy Suanek. Instead, the beggar had brought a host of other children, all ragged and dirty, flies buzzing around them.

"Shoo! G'wan!" another vendor called. "Your filthy dust will get on my skewers!"

"Those children look so hungry," I said. "Do we have something to give them?"

Mother sighed. "I will take care of it. Get in the cart."

She pressed something into Gui's hand as I climbed in. As soon as he got the cart moving, he threw a handful of coins across the road, and the children scrambled to get them, struggling wildly.

Mother saw me watching through the window. "It is a good gesture, but I am afraid it is merely a drop in the ocean."

"At least these ones will eat today, that's what Xue Two-Shoes says. There are beggars in the gallant wanderer tales," I explained. "But never more than one or two, except in towns where there is an evil and greedy governor. Or after a war. Mostly it's one, and they are the Morningstar God or the White Crane in disguise, or a fairy or a demon. The other ones end up plump with plenty once the hero gives their things back."

"These ones are real. They are children just like you. Far too many of them."

"You sound angry, Mother."

"I am. Not at them. I feel certain none would beg if they did not have to. I know that they are an annoyance to the vendors, because they will steal if they get a chance. I had Gui fling the coins away from us while we moved, or they might have over-whelmed us in their desperation. The disgrace belongs to those so high they do not see it. Or will not," she added under her breath. "But that is not your concern. You met my grandmother today. She walks a different life path than I, but she has convinced me that you must learn a little about defending yourself, which will mean more work for you, Daughter."

"Not sword fighting?" I asked.

Her brows drew down. "No. I remain a firm believer that there would be fewer problems in the world if we used the wits the gods gave us to solve our troubles, rather than fighting. But learning how to defend yourself long enough to slip away, that was something I was taught, before I was sent as a hostage to the palace. Those are my practice clothes in the trunks."

"Hostage?" I repeated.

"All of that will become clearer when you get older," was the hated answer.

As always.

Cray approached me that evening, when she had the nighttime duty, after I'd dismissed the other maids and I was in my night things. Though I was yawning after the long, hot day, the instant she entered, my sleepiness fled.

"Cray!" As soon as I said her name, I recollected a stray fact: if that grandmother was my great-grandmother, then Cray was some degree of cousin. I stared at her uncertainly.

But she was not uncertain. With her usual blank face, she said, "I am to instruct Young Miss in the fundamentals of dance."

"Dance?" I repeated. "Aren't I going to be too tall?"

Cray's expression remained as blank as a ghost mask. "I am to say that the new training is dance training."

"Oh-h-h-h-h."

"But first, Madam Gu says that Young Miss is to handle it this one time, in hopes it will impart precious wisdom."

It—Sagacious Blade!

My maids had been sent to other errands. Cray and I went to the library, where all was exactly as it had been. As it must be, this being Father's principal room during daylight hours. First Brother as well.

This time I helped Cray shift the trunks—though I was

vastly disappointed to discover that they were just as heavy as I'd remembered. My labors had not strengthened me as much as I'd hoped.

My disappointment vanished when we reached the bottom of the trunk, and I closed my hand around the hilt of Sagacious Blade. "Bu! There you are," it said, right behind my ear. "Lift me."

"Bu?" I asked Cray, disappointment surging. "I'm wrong after all…"

"No, it sometimes calls people that, I was to remind you," Cray informed me.

In the cart, Mother had quickly outlined the sword's history as the grandmother told her. This history had apparently been written on very old rice paper ages ago, and bound into the hilt. Mother's great-grandfather had read the disintegrating paper, finding that it had listed a lot of people in an unknown family, beginning with someone with the odd name 'Bu' — which really didn't tell anyone much of anything.

After the Bu people, there was a list of merits after each name (Mother called it boasting) among gallant wanderers and the like. Because of this less-than-respectable legacy, no one had recopied the list before it disintegrated except for the warning that those whose hearts knotted with greed would lose the sword.

I unwrapped the blade with shaking fingers. It was beautiful, a rich bronze with overlapping scales worked into the blade. The white stone glittered in the candle light.

I lifted the sword with a grunt, feeling my muscles pull from my back to my wrist. At least I *could* lift it, but there was no chance I'd be able to wave it about like Xue Two-Shoes.

A sense of satisfaction that was not my own flooded me. "You know my rules, child. Work and learn, work and learn," Sagacious Blade said to me. And there was this sense of being patted on the head.

Then the voice fell silent, and my arm was straining. At a gesture from Cray, I lowered the sword to the wrappings. "It told me to work and learn, and that's its rules. Can you lift it?" I asked Cray.

She slowly — hesitantly — touched it, then held it up.

"Do you hear anything?" I asked.

"No." Her voice was flat, but I sensed disappointment. "It lets me lift it. Or, it's inert." She drew a breath. "It knows I'm not trying to take it away from you."

There was nothing to say to that. She was older, and trained, and a cousin, but here she was my maid. Had the sword really chosen me because my birth rank was higher? If so, what about Grandfather Cook?

I said none of this to Cray. Together we tied it up again, then replaced it, and loaded in all the other things, and last, the trunks.

We went back to my room. With the door shut, Cray said, "First, I am to teach you to learn to fall properly."

"Fall?" I repeated.

"Dance begins with knowing how to fall. May this one demonstrate?"

She tumbled to the floor, fluid as water. Then rolled to her feet again, smoothly and deftly.

I saw the utility at once. In winter, if the ground was icy, I often slipped, and had fallen painfully several times. Especially if I was hurrying.

"If Young Miss would try?" Once again she demonstrated, looking like a leaf drifting down. Surprised, I tried, and barked both elbows and a knee.

Cray gestured for me to mimic her, moving more slowly. She seemed to roll to the ground, then back up again, unlike me, who went to hands and knees, backside in the air. But I knew by now that many repetitions lay ahead of me, and again I made a challenge of it.

Morning brought the old aches, just as if I'd never done the other thing, but this was nothing new. Remembering how much my arm and back had strained just to lift the sword that had spoken to me, I added falling and rising to my up-and-downs when I was alone.

TEN

The Circle board is the world;
the points are the stars.
They said white and black are fighting,
She saw them living and laughing.
Circle games and human life…

DAYS PASSED. MY BODY twinged when I first rose in the morning, and hunger gnawed at me after my practice, which kept me thinking about those beggars, and what Mother had said. What could I do? Even if I had any coins of my own, which I did not, I was not permitted to go outside the palace gates.

It was comforting when I was achy and sore to play Circle with Second Brother. If I thought in terms of armies, I nearly always lost. Various military terms made little sense to me. Second Brother's favorite gambits flung squares of armies this way and that in order to make charges that would sweep me from the board in a reckless squandering of markers. My strategies—if they could even be called that—required balance of gain and loss all across the board, and if I built a strong enough structure of gain, I could consolidate my wealth while tricking him into having to spend his, and drive him off the board. Whether those little black or white markers represented a warrior or a coin, I hated losing a single one so much that Second Brother deemed my play stodgy and cautious.

"Stodgy," I repeated once, resentful. "At least you're not calling my strategy girl play. First Brother is just as careful. I've watched him."

To my surprise, Second Brother said, "He's stodgy, too. Anyway, Siarti and Liarti both are more reckless than I am. If they played a real game, they would always lose, but the boys always let them win, especially Siarti. Yiuti wins, but he cheats. The best of all the cousins is Cousin Taisa. She beats everyone."

I noticed that the only one he used 'cousin' toward was Cousin Taisa, she of the perfect embroidery. "Even the imperial princes?"

"Especially them," Second Brother gloated, his curving grin making his dimple leap out. "Xianti can't play half a game without thunder and lightning if he thinks he might lose, and Kianti just does what Xianti tells him to do. Even if it's stupid."

Second Brother knew them all well. I only knew them by sight, not that I desired proximity to Imperial Prince Xianti, son of the Imperial Heir, whose temper got whispered about most. I wondered when—perhaps if—I would stop being regarded as one of the babies, and receive an invitation to the gatherings where girls mixed with boys.

Ayah! Being considered too young was not new, and I didn't really mind being called stodgy. Circle was merely a game, and nothing came of wins or losses. It was the calculation of costs that interested me. And irked me, if I lay awake in my warm bed on achy nights, trying to imagine how many coins it would take to buy food for beggars. I knew this was a useless exercise due to my ignorance about how many there were, what foods cost in different seasons, and the like, but my mind kept going back to those dirty faces.

Two days later, I was still aching when the first cold rain struck, blowing petals from the roses, which scattered across our path. We pulled our cloaks closer, and I shrugged my neck down so mine covered my ears and nose as my mind went back to those beggar children.

We had just come out of Consort Zenar's. I was beginning to understand that the morning calls were summonses issued by the dowager empress. Sometimes by the empress. But the invitations for gatherings at which we heard poetry, or music, or they watched as we girls displayed our talents so that the imperial elders could judge, might be issued by favored consorts like First Consort Chin, and Consort Ye.

At gatherings given by the girls, the adults were not present, and if there were snacks, we could eat them. But at the adult gatherings, unless specifically invited, we young ones stood behind our mothers, as we did in the morning calls. Except, of course, when the dowager empress would favor some girl or other (nearly always her granddaughters) by inviting them to sit by her and choose snacks. She might even bestow the highest accolade, which was to use her own golden eating sticks to choose a delicacy and put it on the favored one's plate, as all of us watched, our mouths watering. Though I noticed that Cousin Siarti invariably waited for someone else to eat a snack before she would try it. It didn't occur to me to ask why. I had no wish to emulate her.

We almost never were invited to Consort Zenar's. Today had been different.

"Mother, I know that these invitations have to be approved by the dowager empress."

"As head of the harem, yes."

"Are they favors or punishments? My apology, this ignorant daughter spoke inexactly. Are the consorts instructed when to have one, or do they choose to have one?"

"Ah," said Mother, and though I'd made certain no one was near, she glanced around before saying, "that depends."

"I was right, sometimes they are told to hold one?"

"Yes."

"What is the difference?"

"When the dowager empress favors someone, she sends her graywings to do the work, and the imperial kitchens provide the delicacies. If the host is not in favor, she must provide from her own household allowance, or her own wherewithal."

"There was so much food at Consort Zenar's," I burst out as the wind tried to tear my words away. "I wish we could take all those dishes that no one even looked at, and give it to the beggars. Why doesn't anyone think of that?"

"Are you asking a real question, or fretting because you are not invited to sit with your elders to eat?"

I thought of the way the consorts each watched the others, and remembered little comments after such gatherings about how sad it was that this consort was partial to cooling foods that aged her ten years, or that consort certainly adored her warming foods (in other words, greedy), and hungry as I might be, I didn't think I would ever be hungry enough to want to eat under all those watching eyes.

"I truly don't mind. I noticed the little twins didn't get to have any either. I know I can always get snacks at home. What I really want to know is why no one thinks of sending all those untouched plates to the beggars."

"I can't say what is in anyone's mind," Mother reminded me. After I apologized, she said, "You seem to be implying that the food will go to waste. I feel very certain that at this moment Consort Zenar's daughters are all eating the best meal they've had in days. And what they don't eat, the servants will finish. Or they might even all eat together; I do not know how the consort runs her household."

I was beginning to learn something about household accounts. In our palace, Mother gave the cook specific orders rarely, mostly different dishes to tempt Father to eat more, or the very rare times he gave a banquet. Otherwise, our food was what I had discovered was regarded as plain fare, lots of vegetable dishes cooked with a variety of spices, dumplings, noodles or rice. We did have meat, though rarely; it was mostly fish, caught off the shore and brought in daily.

I'd learned through listening to Perch's chatter that in some high-ranking households, the madam ordered the servants to have one diet, and the family another—the servant diet being (according to Perch) next thing to temple fare. Or plainer.

Mother continued, "I do know, and I tell you this because I trust your discretion, that the dowager empress constantly finds reasons to dock Consort Zenar's household allowance. As for other households, *in general*," she emphasized the words in a way that suggested she was thinking of the exceptions, "I believe there is very little waste in the palace. The household stewards are vigilant in the areas they can control."

"Oh." There I was, chastened yet again by the realization that I'd not looked past appearances. Mother seemed to sense my disappointment in myself for she said, "Daughter, you were supposed to assume that Consort Zenar's household is as wealthy as the other consorts'. Consort Zenar wishes to save face just as anyone does."

We bent into the wind, which tore through my clothes to chill my flesh as if I wore the lightest gauze.

"Secondly," Mother said. "For someone like me, or one of the consorts not in favor, to put forward suggestions about sending food could be seen as arrogance or presumption, telling the emperor or empress what to do. It can also be seen as indirect criticism of their rule. Most people pretend that those refugees don't exist, but that doesn't mean everyone is indifferent to their plight. It's a matter of not knowing what to do to mend matters."

The chill increased inside me. "I did not think of that."

Mother drew a deep breath. "However. If you are quite serious about this desire of yours to feed the hungry, I believe I can find a way."

"Please tell me," I said eagerly.

"This is something I used to do regularly, before I was married, and had to assume the duties of a wife of a censor. What you do not know yet, perhaps, is that all the temples regularly find ways to hand out food to the hungry. It would not be appropriate for you to go to the monks, of course, but the nuns at Suanek's temple would welcome another person handing out the baskets of pancakes that they make for the purpose."

"I'll do it," I said eagerly, thinking of that exciting street, and the satisfaction of seeing those thin figures getting something inside them. Also, I very much liked the inward image of myself dispensing all this largesse without having to scrounge coins, or try to cook. I loved the image of those tattered girls my age welcoming the sight of me and my basket of good things.

"We shall see how long your enthusiasm lasts," Mother murmured.

It was a relief to get back inside where it was warm, and for a few days, nothing happened. Mother's habit had always been to go to the temple on new moon days, unless there was special cause; if Father prayed, which was rare, it was always in the ancestral hall. My aches diminished as—slowly—my body learned the falling leaf skill, and by the time Mother summoned me to go to the temple with her, I discovered that I enjoyed tumbling about and rolling up to my toes, over and over.

Mother and I lit incense, bowed three times, and we prayed silently—me for a chance to hand out food to the beggars— then Mother took me to the chief nun, and said that I would like to volunteer at the relief table.

This venerable woman explained to me that between all the temples, and the donations from the palace that came through now and then (mostly, I got the impression, when this or that member of the imperial family or noble needed all the nuns to pray for them, and gave donations in order to catch the benevolent eyes of Heaven, and improve their good luck), they had all the days of a week covered. I was to join them on each third morning at dawn, accompanied by Cray and one or other of the drivers. Mother would not be there. This was to be my own merit.

The first time, I was so excited I didn't sleep. As sometimes happens, the reality was far less exciting than my imagination. I had seen myself the recipient of grateful thanks and smiles. And I did get a few, but those were pretty much all from mothers. Most of the children my age either ignored me completely, their attention entirely on the food in the basket, or their gazes were indifferent. Several even glared resentfully at me, but they said nothing. Dirty hands snatched the pancakes as if I'd snatch them back.

Even so, when our baskets were empty and we returned to the cart for the journey back inside the palace, I did feel a sense of accomplishment. With the addition of my pair of hands, the food got distributed that much faster. Thus I felt good about myself when I returned and changed out of my yard practice clothes into my nice robes for the harem visit.

The next week I was there again, and the next, and the next, though that day it was raining hard. But Cray held my umbrella over my head—and the refugees were right there in line, absolutely sodden. No hanging back for better weather for them, even though they had no other clothes to change to. At least they smelled less.

Several days before Harvest Festival, summer vanished before cold winds and whispering leaves. Cray came in late one night carrying two fans. She handed one to me. It was plain, the ribs quite sturdy unlike the fragile ones I was used to. Handling a fan properly had been one of my earliest lessons. But this one felt so different, I looked at it as if I'd never seen a fan before.

Then Cray gestured for me to bring it down, as if the fan were a stick of some sort. And when I did, she stepped close, and used her fan to deflect it while she twirled out of range. Intrigued, I waited, and when she motioned for me to strike at her, she demonstrated again—this time faster. Then it was my turn to raise my fan, deflect, and turn. She shook her head and positioned my hand: I was not to strike with it, but bring it up in a circle, deflect her strike, then twirl out of reach. Again and again.

Once I got it, she added proper stances, moving slowly, like leaves falling just as I'd learned in the fall-and-rise. The slow, deliberate grace of her movement was very much like a sedate sort of dance, but the intent was very different. I was not fluttering my fan at some watcher. I was using it to keep another fan—or sword—away, and once again, the slowness and deliberation of the movements pulled at my muscles as if I were beginning all over again. But by now I knew the pattern: each new thing was going to bring on the aches until I'd done it enough times to make it as natural as walking. I was never going to be another Xue Two-Shoes, leaping to roofs the first time she was taught light skills, and swinging a sword expertly by age ten. I was two years past that, coming up on thirteen, and I was only able to lift that sword.

However, it had chosen me. Why, I had not begun to question. For now, the thought that a charmed sword had picked me over everybody else never failed to lift my spirits.

Cray practiced with me now and then. We never spoke. That is, she would always respond politely to me, in as few words as possible, if I asked questions. She never offered a word on her own. If words were her treasure, I thought early the morning of Sky Wishes Day, after an entire practice with no word spoken, she surely had preserved enough to buy Mt. Lir.

Practice and studies had to be done early because we had been invited to attend on the imperial family's gathering in the imperial garden to celebrate the day, and rumor had gone round that this year, the weather being clement, the emperor would grace the gathering.

I put on my best rose robe. As I did, I noticed that it barely brushed over the tops of my slippers. I hadn't even noticed that I was growing until that moment.

Though much of harvest month had been cold and rainy, the festival day remained clear and balmy. The imperial family were seated under the three-tiered pavilion in the middle of the lake. Everyone had to go over one of the arched bridges in order to make their bows, then leave by the other bridge. The gliding, silk-glistening progress was a splendid sight as we approached, the pavilion lit by moon lanterns hung in the trees and all along the eaves of the lowest tier, and the rise and fall of autumnal music drifted over the placid lake waters, played by musicians seated along the far edge of the pavilion, away from the throne.

The rest of the pavilion held more of the imperial family than I'd ever seen before. I knew all the imperial consorts by sight except for the foreign-born, seldom seen grand princess, wife of the much-admired but blind First Imperial Grand Prince Miluo. He sat next to his brother the emperor on his throne, swathed in costly brocade, an imposing figure in girth as well as height. I peeked at them all from behind Mother's shoulder. The grand prince appeared to my eye to be much younger than his nephew, Imperial Crown Prince Jiarza, though he was actually only a year younger.

"How was he blinded?" I whispered to Second Brother.

"Winning the War of the Eastern Sea," Second Brother said—which I already knew, but he was too busy peering surreptitiously himself to give me details. "Ayah, the grand princess is the one next to him, but Vaha didn't come. As usual."

Vaha being the grand princess's daughter by the defeated prince who'd started the war. This adopted princess was First Brother's age. I'd heard her referred to now and then, but nobody ever seemed to see her. Nor did they use her courtesy name—Princess Meiti—as much as they used her birth name, Vaha.

Mother pressed a warning hand to our shoulders, and we fell silent as we passed the guards on duty before the pavilion. We made our bows, Father was invited by the emperor with a gesture to join the ministers gathered along one side, mother was then invited by the empress in a twin gesture to join the women along the other side.

We three passed over the second bridge, and were free.

ELEVEN

Who better knew the law of civilization?
'Tween father and child,
'Tween husband and wife,
The older brother guides
The younger brother follows;
The old preceding young;
Friends deferring politely;
A ruler who heeds his ministers;
Ministers who heed the people:
She grew by these ten right conducts…

I WAS PREPARED TO wander around unnoticed as usual, but to my vast surprise, who should emerge from the gliding dance of bowing and greeting but Cousin Chuti, the gossipy younger sister of Cousin Arati of the beautiful face.

"Cousin Renti! You are always like a shadow. Just like your admired mother, who everyone says is the most modest in the entire palace, saving only the Elder Grand Princess."

Was she really speaking to me? I looked to either side. She was!

"Do you have a lantern to paint?"

Of course I didn't. We'd released ours right before leaving, but before I could say that I did not, she tugged my sleeve and towed me through the swarms of teenagers to a bower of osmanthus in bloom. That heavenly fragrance blended with the sweet bite of chrysanthemum, whose shrubs framed a crescent of little tables overlooking the lake. The imperial granddaughters' tables were central, though with space between, which accommodated two separate crowds.

Like Cousins Arati and Chuti, the imperial princesses were also about the same age, though unlike the beautiful pair, those princesses always seemed to be watching each other as well as the company. I'd noticed that in gatherings, they did not walk together unless there was rank order.

Servants waited at both tables, ready to do the painting and calligraphy, or to bring more warm rice wine, or whatever they desired. Cousin Siarti's honeyed voice rose as she gestured imperiously with her fan at her small court, which was mostly made of well-dressed boys, their long sleeves glimmering in the lantern light, tassels dancing as they fanned themselves. They laughed on command. I wondered if I was seeing flirting. Though surely (I thought) they had to know that when the emperor picked a husband for her, it would not be from among them. It would be some foreign prince or king.

Chuti guided me away from where neither of us would be especially welcome, and we crossed to the far end of the crescent, where sat Cousin Arati, surrounded by a lot more teenage boys as she carefully painted a flying swan on a lantern. With a little jolt, I noticed that First Brother had joined them; I was so used to my brothers having a completely different life from mine that it surprised me to encounter them socially.

Cousin Chuti drew me to her elder sister's table, saying, "We have lanterns here. Choose one!"

First Brother noticed me then, and smiled my way. "Renti! You've come to paint another lantern?"

Cousin Chuti grabbed my wrist and swung our arms back and forth. "Little Sister Renti is so shy, Cousin Yanti, she's as invisible as a ghost. But we will watch out for her, won't we, Arati?"

I ought probably to insert here, in case things have greatly changed, that in addition to siblings addressing one another as Elder or Younger, or by their numbers if there was more than one, 'Sister' or 'Brother' was also used to imply a relationship that was as close as siblings, but no closer. Girls called one another 'sister' and boys 'brother' but across genders it was only permitted between betrothed couples.

I knew all of that in the way that I knew that I breathed,

but I never thought about it. I was so surprised to find myself addressed as 'Little Sister' by Cousin Chuti that I was unaware of much else.

Cousin Arati looked up from her painting, smiled my way, then glanced quickly toward the boys. No, by the way her gaze caught on First Brother's, she was looking at *him*. Were they friends? I didn't know anything about my brothers' friends. Then she returned to painting.

I sat down with Cousin Chuti and we began to paint an unadorned lantern as she chattered on, pausing every so often to praise my entirely unpraiseworthy effort at making a rabbit. I was self-conscious, though the others pretty much ignored me after that initial greeting. They were more interested in what Cousin Arati was making, especially that group of boys.

"What are you going to wish?" someone asked.

"Or, who?" a girl said behind her fan, amid much laughter.

"I will send it up to Heaven with a suitable thought," Cousin Arati said as she laid down her brush. She had put osmanthus blossoms in her pure black hair. The way she did it, sweeping from over her ear up toward the top of her head, was more simple than elaborate hairpins with dangles, but graceful. It reminded me of swans' wings—much like her lantern.

"What are you going to write?" asked that same girl.

At once all the boys began offering quotations.

"Our schoolmaster is always saying, 'He who asks a question might be a fool for half an incense stick, but he who doesn't ask a question remains a fool forever.'"

"Here's my military brother's favorite: You can't keep the birds of sorrow from flying over your head, but you can keep them from building nests in your hair."

"No, nothing about military wisdom," a voice rose above the clamor. "What has a fairy from heaven to do with swords and generals?"

First Brother spoke up, only once. "Good deeds pay with good results and the evil pays back with evil."

"That's *just* what a censor's son would say! B-r-r-r," another boy scoffed, causing laughter.

Then another called, "Ayah, you scholars, enough with your wisdom! Or do you really dare to offer Heaven good advice? Write about romance! 'In the eyes of an admirer, the plainest is the Morningstar God.'"

"My mother says that living *with* love is happy, but living *for* love is foolish," someone else offered.

A honeyed voice cut in, barely hiding its imperious tone, and Cousin Siarti approached as everyone deferred. "Cousin Arati, I suggest you write something like 'Different flowers match different eyes.' It's short."

Cousin Arati had stood when Imperial Princess Siarti walked through with her long sleeves brushing the autumn grasses, and her train keeping everyone at a distance lest they step on it. Cousin Arati bowed, then sat down and began writing *different flowers* on the lantern.

The imperial princess swept her fan in a circle and faced the boys. "My imperial elder brother says that he's starting some fireworks over by the lake. The reflection should be beautiful. Send those lanterns to Heaven and come along!"

Those who had been lingering lit the candles inside their lanterns and released them to the sky. I followed suit, without writing anything under my badly painted bunny. As I stood I happened to look Cousin Arati's way in time to see her add in quick characters…*pays back with evil,* and with even quicker motions, she released her lantern.

Then she stood there, her profile outlined against the glow from the braziers warming the imperial elders some fifty steps away. She was such a lovely sight I wished I could paint with any degree of success, then she stilled, and once again I saw her gaze catch First Brother's.

Cousin Chuti tugged my sleeve again, and when I turned back, First Brother had gone off with the rest. Cousin Arati's voice rose from the head of the group, exclaiming in delight as fireworks hissed into the air and burst into glories of sparkling color that reflected in upturned faces.

Central among those setting off the fireworks were the two imperial grandsons, Cousins Xianti and Kianti.

Here were two more I seldom saw, though again I heard a lot. I'd been told they were twins, but they did not look at all alike. Cousin Xianti was much bigger and louder. Cousin Kianti looked frail, laughing in delight when his brother lit bangbangs.

I loathe bangbangs. I did not at all understand what joy boys got in loud noise, though my brothers had always liked them—especially Second Brother. The loud bang hurt my ears and made me jump, my nerves and meridians disturbed. And, being the smallest and youngest and least important, I was very soon dodging swinging sleeves and elbows and sweeping, clapping fans as the warm rice wine made its rounds, brought at the snap of imperious fingers by Cousin Xianti.

As soon as Cousin Chuti let go of my sleeve, which she soon did, I walked down the path toward the climbing roses, so that I could see the reflection of the fireworks in the lake, and get a distance from the boom and crack of the bangbangs. My gaze remained upward, or toward the lake, so I was only vaguely aware of the swarm of teenagers gradually separating into competing groups.

My moment of notice was over. The warm evening, the proximity of laughing eyes over fans and the graceful frame of drifting hair and beautiful clothes, intoxicated the two groups at least as much as the rice wine. Glances and soft words and occasional gusts of laughter rose, the interactions too quick for me to catch. I divided my time between watching the light reflections, and staying well away from Cousin Yiuti, who I knew from Second Brother's occasional tales was often in trouble, if not looking for it. He was so often compared to a sneaky fox that I had fully expected him to look like the slim, sinuous drawings of foxy characters in the gallant wanderer tales, but Cousin Yiuti was actually short and chunky, fond of very bright and elaborate embroidery, with extra panels swinging with every movement.

The other I remained wary of I could always locate by his loud voice: Cousin Xianti, the imperial first grandson, tall and bony—his features not quite fitting together, but somehow he wasn't ugly.

I was looking straight at him when he straightened up and stilled, turning his head sharply a heartbeat before everyone else. This was when a pure, sweet-sharp sound resonated over the water, utterly compelling, but quite unlike anything I had ever heard before.

At once the fireworks were abandoned, as everyone converged as if drawn by invisible strings toward the imperial pavilion, where, I heard on whispers around me, it seemed the emperor had requested the grand princess to play.

I caught up with Second Brother. "What is that sound?"

"That's the crystal armonia from the Cinnabar People," he whispered back. "The grand princess brought it with her when the grand prince brought her back."

That song, almost too sweet to be endured, and oddly penetrating for so delicate a sound, wove itself in and around the pure notes of a flute. As the teenagers ranked in a tight circle, deferring to rank (which kept me firmly in the back), I hopped up and down, then finally retreated some ten or twenty paces to climb up on a boulder.

The low, carved rail of the open pavilion kept me from seeing much. I made out a figure whose dressed hair glowed with brassy highlights below her elaborate phoenix headdress as she used a tiny crystal hammer to strike an odd instrument that looked at this distance like a tree made of crystal bubbles.

Next to her stood the oddest figure: a girl around Cousin Arati's age, her hair completely loose, hanging down her back. Its color was even brassier than that of the grand princess: I was seeing my first actual person with red hair. The Princess Vaha wore a plain dress with no ornamentation on the long sleeves, nor was there anything in that oddly colored hair. She stood next to her mother, playing the flute, a light, fluttering melody complementing that strange tinkling sound. Her playing was skillful enough; as someone whispered about but never seen, she was an interesting figure.

When they finished their song, everyone clapped, and one of the consorts was then prevailed upon to play the erhu, and another to accompany her on the zither. The court remained gathered, all but Princess Vaha, who bowed to the emperor and then walked away, the crowd parting like wind-blown reeds to let her pass.

She looked neither right nor left as many whispered, and more watched, including the usually loud, bold First Imperial Prince Xianti. Especially First Imperial Prince Xianti. He watched her all the way until she vanished beyond the inner palace.

The day following Sky Wishes Day, we woke up to another sleeting cataract. The dowager empress released us from daily harem calls for the winter, and a woman arrived whom Mother introduced as a dance teacher. These lessons were the same sort of dance lessons the other imperial cousins got. My maids saw me learning to flutter a fan and twirl around, but mornings and nights, I practiced with Cray's fan.

The first snow arrived.

It looked beautiful, but I soon came to understand how

bleak that white purity could be for people constantly seeking warmth. The pancakes lost their warmth almost as soon as the nuns took them out of the ovens to slide into the baskets, and my fingers hurt as I passed them out. I kept sticking one hand then the other into my armpits, the basket bumping my hip as I passed it from one elbow to the other.

On New Year's Two Moons, we received a great load of palace donations, most likely left-over food from the many banquets. These foods, some dried out from sitting overnight, or stale, were still received with enthusiasm.

When I got home, it was in time for breakfast, at which Father said, "In Spring, First Son, you will take the Imperial Examination. You are ready."

First Brother flushed, then smiled so brilliantly, for the first time I didn't just see First Brother, I saw the boy that some of the imperial girl cousins included when they discussed who was handsome and who not. Though I still found those interminable discussions both boring and pointless, as the elders would choose whom we'd marry. Both my brothers had future wives. I had no future husband as yet, for which I was just as glad.

"I will bring out the celebratory wine," Mother said.

"Once you're a famous scholar, you can sneak me in," Second Brother crowed. "Get me an under-secretary position that will take me out to the harbor. Remember that!"

First Brother stood there looking dazed, until Mother herself carried in the fragrant wine made of haws, honey, and rice made from her family's recipe. Our butler brought in the best porcelain, only used for great occasions, the cups shaped like lilies, with gold edging. We toasted First Brother, whose face reddened to the ears. "I shall do my best not to disappoint my family," he said, his voice husky.

I had thought that First Brother was diligent before, but that was laziness itself to the way he threw himself into his studies now. Before I slept at night, I always saw his windows glowing on the male side of the family courtyard, and there was still light when I woke in the mornings. He put questions to Father at meals—and if Father was not there, he drafted Second Brother into checking his answers in the books as he went through each question in the stacks of old examinations that Father had provided him with.

But now that First Brother was to take the examination, he was excused afternoons from the princes' school to study, which meant Second Brother could not be there. I offered to help First Brother to study. And when he hesitated, I said indignantly, "I'm *nearly thirteen* now, not three!"

"My apologies, Little Sister. If you can find the references, I would be honored, but don't you have your own lessons?"

"Nothing that I can't do when Father and Second Brother are home."

First Brother doubted that I would be able to understand his references, but once he explained his way of marking them, it made perfect sense: next to each question, he had noted the source, the page—or if it was an old scroll, the ribbon marking—and the column.

When he saw how quickly I could find references, even though I understood very little of what was there, I at least could read it back to him, and prompt him as he shut his eyes and recited.

As winter blew its cold winds and snow flurries, my fan lessons went on as usual, and each third day Cray and I rode the cart to the temple. Though I hated going out in the cold, I kept thinking that if the refugees (or beggars, as they were more frequently referred to) came, and the nuns kept baking the pancakes to give out, I ought to be there to dispense them faster. But some days were more difficult than others, as we huddled in our layers, no one lifting their face lest frost sear eyes and noses.

At least for me there was always hot soup with internally warming and invigorating ingredients waiting on our return, and tea.

TWELVE

Admired and emulated
For her benevolence…

HELPING FIRST BROTHER STUDY was our first duty.

I discovered something odd about how memory is not the same for different people, even within the same family. Second Brother and I traded off practicing with First Brother. We all knew that Father preferred Second Brother to do most of this practice, because for him it was vital to learn the same material, but when he was at the princes' school or at the practice court, and Mother tended to all household matters as well as reading the endless river of testaments that Father brought back so that they could discuss them, it fell to me to be First Brother's study partner.

Over time, I was able to recite passages back to First Brother, once I comprehended how they fit into a whole. In fact, the more I perceived that whole, the easier it was to understand that flow of words, which seemed in its very repetition to make it easier to fit together.

But it was the repetition that defeated and wearied Second Brother. It wasn't that he didn't understand. He did. He could sum it all up, usually with a succinct image, and he was usually right. However even well-described images are not acceptable in the Imperial Examination. Precise quotation is. Also, and this we all found odd, Second Brother could invariably recollect *where* a bit was cited. "It's in a scroll, about this far in," he said once, pointing to his other fingertip and drawing a line to halfway along his forearm. "Halfway down the column." And he was often right—but could he remember the precise word-ing? Almost never. Repetition made him restless, and he could not concentrate.

My being able to recite back meant that I could begin early on the embroidery competition, which kept my hands busy as First Brother read long, long passages to me, sometimes several times through, so that they remained firm in memory.

Winter passed. The moons began to separate on their monthly rounds, the sun strengthened, snow melted. Plum blossoms appeared first, and Earth Wishes Festival approached, when we cleaned the ancestral hall and prayed for those gone before. Spring was coming. My thirteenth birthday passed, then the dowager empress sent graywings around to inform us that she awaited us for the first greeting of spring.

Mother and I attended harem court as always.

The day after that, Cousin Siarti celebrated her birthday, which had fallen some days before. As always, we girls in the primary and secondary families were invited, in addition to a very few favored ducal or ministerial girls.

And ayah! I discovered what a double-edged blade being noticed could be.

I put on my new robe, having grown out of my previous ones. The new ones were pretty much like the old ones, well made, with modest embroidery. I found myself secretly wishing for something really pretty, a guilty wish that went unexpressed because it was unfilial. Even my maids noticed how plain the new robes were, for Perch exclaimed as she twitched the new one into hanging correctly, "Oh, Young Miss. I can hardly wait until you are married, and you can wear vermilion, with blue and green embroidery!"

I kept my face blank, though inwardly I longed for a robe of summer sky blue or spring green, embroidered with iridescent hummingbirds all over it, between peach blossom clusters.

Cray presented herself, Mother gave me the fur hat present, and I set off for the granddaughters' wing of the empress's palace.

Would Cousin Chuti speak to me again? I did not spot either Cousin Arati or her chatty younger sister among the other guests. I laid the fur hat on the pile of gifts, and, resigning myself to dullness, turned to admire the fog-gray silk robe of a duke's daughter, embroidered with spring green twists of budding vines between the two moons.

Then Cousin Siarti's imperious voice ordered all the servants out except her two maids, who always stood in the background until given a command. There was no falsely honeyed tone, this time.

The guests' maids bowed themselves out, Cray lingering uncertainly. "Out!" the princess snapped at Cray, who curtseyed, and followed the rest.

That sharp yet syrupy voice never failed to urge me to put space between myself and her, but to my surprise, as the door slid shut, the gathering of girls parted like water as Siarti advanced in my direction. When she had advanced within a step or two, she raised her arm and swung her palm right at my face.

After half a year of daily practice, I slid aside as her palm passed my ear, my mind stuttering with shock.

She snapped, "Hold her still!"

The two maids seized me by the upper arms. Cousin Siarti's hand came around and dealt me a ringing slap as she shrilled something at me. I was so shocked that I lost the sense of her words, and I would have fallen had not the two maids held me. As it was, they both staggered a little, and my head rocked, wrenching my neck. I barely had time to draw in a shuddering breath when she slapped me again. "Who do you think you are, fifth-rank worm, with eyes above your head!"

I heard the words, but they still made no sense. My lips were so numb I couldn't get words passed them, and she raised her arm to hit me again. My tear-blurred eyes saw a flash of crimson. Then Cousin Siarti gasped, her pumpkin-round face bright red.

I blinked the tears away to find Cousin Taisa's hand in its crimson sleeve pressing down on Cousin Siarti's arm in its celestial blue silk. "Siarti. If I am expected to witness such an offensive spectacle, I will first understand the reason."

All the other girls stood in a circle, shock in most faces, and in some fear, excepting only Cousin Liarti, mousy younger sister to Cousin Siarti. She stood in a meek pose, her lips parted, eyes avid.

Cousin Siarti confronted Cousin Taisa, her face mottled to those jug-handled ears she hid behind braids and golden dangles. My face throbbed in time to the slam of my heart against my ribs, and my knees trembled so badly that if were not for the bruising grip of the two maids, I would have dropped to the floor.

"You heard," Cousin Siarti shrieked. "We *all* heard, *over and over*, how the Minister of Justice ranted before the entire court about the meritorious Chief Censor's little daughter who selflessly dedicates herself to relieving the plight of the filthy beggars clogging the streets." Cousin Siarti rounded on me, eyes glaring. "A presumptuous, arrogant little donkey whose pretense at modesty is forcing *us* to sew those *wretched* lengths of cloth because *she* wants to parade her name before all the court. What do you have to say for yourself, donkey?" She snatched her hand away from Cousin Taisa, and raised it again.

I could only stare as I mumbled through rapidly swelling lips, "Don' unnerstand."

Cousin Taisa lifted her brows slightly. "Siarti, halt. I strongly suspect this girl has no idea what you are talking about."

Cousin Siarti narrowed her eyes at me. "Have you or have you not been going to the temple to feed beggars?"

Before I could get out a *Yes, but*, Cousin Taisa's flat, somewhat ironic voice cut in, "Did you know about the speech made by the Minister of Justice that mentioned you and your elder brother by name?"

"This one did not," I said, my voice sounding a distance away as my ears still rang from the blows.

"You lie," Cousin Siarti exploded.

Cousin Taisa said, still in that flat voice, "Think a moment, Siarti. You yourself have made game of the Chief Censor's wife ever since I can remember, calling her a nun, and the like. Do you think either she or the Chief Censor would repeat such acclaim before their children?"

"I did not know," I said, still stunned.

"As expected," Cousin Taisa said.

Cousin Siarti, spun around to glare at her younger sister. "It was *you* who said she was swanking all over last autumn, arm in arm with that beggar Chuti as she bragged about her meritorious deeds."

"I might have misheard," Cousin Liarti said in her sweet, mousy lisp, but her gaze on me was so cold that my meridians chilled to my toes. "Didn't I overhear you telling Chuti all about it?"

This was the very first time Cousin Liarti had ever addressed me. As I stared at those unblinking eyes, I began to understand that loud, irritable, hot-tempered Cousin Siarti was not the greater danger, in the sense that one could always hear the crashing gallop of a charging beast of prey. The true danger had always been the younger sister, not much older than I, and slithery as a poisonous snake.

She was waiting for me to assent, I could see it. I also knew that if I did, we would be complicit together in that lie. And being bound together with her in a lie could not possibly be a good thing.

"I don't know what you heard, but it could not have been me," I said. "I don't think I said anything, except that I would try to paint a bunny on a lantern. I never told anyone what I was doing."

"Then why did you do it?" Cousin Siarti demanded. "Ah, of course, you were told to. So your Father could lead his faction against my uncle in court, and sound so modest doing it."

I must have looked as bewildered as I felt, because Cousin Siarti whirled, and this time that striking hand dealt a hard slap to her younger sister's face. Cousin Liarti staggered back, and the rage in her glare hit me an invisible blow. Because it was me she aimed it at, not her sister.

Cousin Taisa sighed. "Siarti, this is your birthday fête, but if you wish to celebrate it by handing out slaps to everybody, I'm going straight back to the palace."

"No, no, it was all a misunderstanding," Cousin Siarti said in a wheedling voice. "Dear, sensitive Sister Taisa, please take the seat of honor." Cousin Siarti guided the unresisting Taisa right past Cousin Kuiza, who was usually the center of attention.

Cousin Kuiza flushed, but took the next seat down. I think everyone was still somewhat shocked by that outburst. They hastily took their seats, leaving me to the last, alone with my throbbing cheek.

Voices rang high and false as they conspired with all their might to pretend nothing had happened. They laughed at every one of Cousin Siarti's utterances, and loud was the praise of Cousin Siarti as she went through the gifts, how beautiful she would look, how clever she was to inspire such delights, how sublime her taste was. Even the fur cap was praised, until Cousin Siarti figured out it was from me. She tossed it aside, but I saw her gaze follow it, and I knew that Mother had chosen well.

I managed to keep my head up and my voice steady until time for departure. As soon as I reached the outer court where Cray waited, my throat began to close up. Cray saw me, and her straight brows drew together. "What happened, Young Miss?"

My jaw locked. I knew that if I tried to speak I'd disgrace myself before all those passing servants and guards. I said nothing at all as we paced back through the budding imperial garden, me aware that my throbbing cheek was red as a beacon.

At last we reached home, and safety. As soon as Mother saw me, her eyes widened, and she came forward, arms outstretched, and I lost my very tenuous control as she held me to her and led me to her room, sending all the servants out.

Once I'd cried myself out, I blubbered out my tale of woe, and at the end, Mother frowned. "Daughter, I am sorry I did not foresee this."

"Cousin Liarti lied about me. Why? Why would she hate me? We never even spoke before that, and the way she glared at me, I was afraid she would put poison in my tea."

"I will not assume anything about how the imperial children are raised. I can only say that in other situations, where perhaps there is very strict punishment at times, that punishment might get repeated as normal behavior by everyone."

I thought back to that awful experience with Minnow and the comb. By now Minnow seemed not to remember it, but I could not forget.

"I can tell you very definitely that it hurts one's hand to slap that hard, almost as much as it hurts the person slapped. Only someone who slaps a great deal can become inured to the sting. For someone younger, who is too small to escape, lying might become a defense. But that is merely an observation about persons elsewhere, when I was your age."

"I was afraid of her. But I was also afraid to lie and say that I had talked about going to the temple to Cousin Chuti."

"Staying with the truth," Mother said, "is the best response."

"I don't understand why what I'm doing would even matter to them," I whimpered.

"It has to do with faction fights in court. Specifically, what to do about the refugee problem—and who should be responsible. Whatever is decided, there will be a not insignificant cost, at a time when the treasury can ill afford it. But that is not your trouble to fret over. More to the point here, I suspect that someone in the imperial family decided that the imperial granddaughters must earn merits. That would explain the plain sewing, which ordinarily is the type of thing given as a task to those confined in the cold palace."

"I don't know why you and Father did not tell me," I said.

"We discussed that," Mother said, and held me away from her, searching my eyes. "But we decided you did not need to hear tainted praise."

"Tainted because..."

"For political emphasis," Mother said. "This was not true praise. Your name was not the only one mentioned. Your First Brother was praised for being one of the top students at the princes' school, who modestly remained back last year, when the other top students sat the Imperial Examination. All this was to flatter your Father through his methods of raising his children, in a politically motivated speech."

"Oh." My emotions were in too much turmoil for me to understand my reaction, except a vast sense of unfairness at my being slapped for something going on in court that I had nothing to do with.

"I didn't even know anyone knew," I ventured.

Mother said seriously, "I have told you before, and will repeat it now, somebody is always watching. Always. Do you wish to continue your efforts? You needn't answer now. You may take as much time as you need to consider."

I shook my head, then winced and fingered my cheek, a pulse of anger knotting my heart. "I will. I like doing something, even if it's small. And I won't let those imperial cousins ruin a thing that I like doing, that doesn't hurt anybody."

Mother nodded. "Very well. Continue or cease as you think best. It is good for you to learn to make decisions for yourself, and to think ahead to all possible consequences. I expect Mai is supervising Perch in overseeing a fresh decoction, which ought to help soothe your nerves, and I will fetch my special salve made from century ginseng root. We'll put it on your cheek now." She shook her head. "I am going to give Cray direct orders never to leave you alone again. If either of those two attempt to send her away, you must think up a polite excuse and leave yourself. At last resort, you can always claim stomach trouble and run, but do not let yourself get mired in imperial matters."

"I will."

Mother permitted me to stay home the following day. I do not know if the dowager empress or the empress asked about me. I expect they did not. I was too insignificant. As for the grand princesses and the consorts, I wondered what, if anything, they saw when my mother appeared alone.

Mother's salve soothed the swelling, leaving my cheek still reddened. The following day, I had to go make my bows— "We will go on as if nothing happened," Mother said—but before we left, Mother dusted my other cheek with a little rouge.

I ignored the imperial princesses. They ignored me. No one said anything to my face, though I did catch Cousin Chuti staring, and I think she was going to come to me when we left the empress, but her sister twitched at her sleeve, and they walked apart, as always, staying close to their mother. I walked close to mine, and resolved to go on as if it hadn't happened.

And the following week, I was at the temple as usual.

The auspicious day for the Imperial Examination came at last. We breakfasted before dawn, then Mother and I went to light incense and pray for First Brother as Father and Second Brother walked him to the grand court between two of the government buildings, which had been cleared out, and rows of small booths set up. Women were not permitted over there, of course, but Second Brother described it all to me when he returned, Father having had to go straight to court.

Mother and I hastened off to call on the dowager empress. When we left, and passed betneath an arched bower of budding roses, I found Cousin Chuti next to me. "Cousin Renti," she said. "Forgive me for troubling you with a question, but did we hear that Cousin Yanti is included among those at the Imperial Examination?" Her elder sister stood a few steps behind, hiding her needle-pricked fingers as usual, her gaze down so that her long eyelashes brushed her cheeks.

Surprised, I curtseyed.

"My sister and I will light incense for him," Cousin Chuti said eagerly. I looked from her to Cousin Arati, whose delicate coloring glowed beneath her almond eyes. If anything, this year she was even more beautiful. "As we do for all our cousins each year," she added.

I curtseyed again, and thanked her on First Brother's behalf, then she stepped close and whispered, "Why do you go to the temple yourself instead of sending things by a servant?"

Was she implying that I wanted to be seen? Except that if someone was watching my cart go to the temple, then they'd also see any of our servants carrying things, and it would be easy enough to find out what they carried. This conversation, short as it was, reminded me of what Mother had said: not only was everything watched, but gossip was like rain, impossible to halt.

I said only, "I did nothing wrong," and hurried to catch up with Mother.

First Brother was not home when Mother and I returned. The dance teacher arrived, and between my lessons in the complicated patterns of fluttering sleeves and flower postures, my whirling and snapping through my fan "dances" with Cray, and my embroidery, I filled the time that had fallen to studies with First Brother.

He returned the next day, looking exhausted, but beneath the marks under his eyes there was a hint of a smile, like the sun behind the clouds. First Brother said little until Father returned. Then all he said was, "I knew all the questions."

Father put his hands together. "We shall see."

Thirteen

*…she learned very early
the truth about polished jade
flaunted to make men covet:
It's the thief who gains most…*

"Who is Lan Yanti?"

"Elder son of the Chief Censor."

"Oh-h-h-h-h, of course such a one would rank first…."

A wind of whispers rustled around Second Brother and me. Mother had permitted him to accompany me to the grand buildings where the postings for the Imperial Examination had been made. And there, to our immense satisfaction, ranked first on the list, was First Brother's name.

I stared at it to make certain the characters would not vanish like some charmed words in a hero tale, or transform to the characters for another Lan and another Yan with the generation name "ti" added. But it remained as written, in scholarly calligraphy, and we stood there with happy smiles as around us people hunted for other names, speculated, wondered, and gossiped.

"…his father will surely receive a hundred letters by tomorrow, offering their daughters in marriage."

"Oh, those princes' boys are all already promised, you can be certain of *that*."

I was startled to realize that these gossipers were referring to First Brother.

Second Brother gave me a rueful glance. "When they start naming his children, which they will probably start next, it's time to go home."

A few days later, at an auspicious hour, those who led the list in both civil and military examinations assembled at the temple to ride in triumphant parade all down the main street to appear before the emperor at court and receive their first posting.

We heard them first. Bawling horn trumpets competed with screeling gourd pipes, followed by two drummers and a youth not much older than me banging away at a brass gong. Behind them, the scholars.

Accompanied by an honor guard, they rode wearing their new blue robes of the ninth and lowest rank, the second and third with a single peacock "eye" feather in his new hat, and our brother with two feathers, the "two eyes." They would only wear these badges of their triumph on this day. Their hats would be plain tomorrow. But the distinction would follow them forever.

Mother had agreed to permit Second Brother to bring me to the palace gates so that we could watch First Brother's triumphant ride. We stood near the stone qilin who protected the world with a paw as other palace teens emerged through the palace gates, and mixed in with city people.

First Brother rode at the head of the parade. It was a bright morning. We spotted him far in the distance. He really did look handsome. The crowd thought so too, especially a lot of teenage girls who were lined along the street, some veiled, others in groups. Many threw flowers, and a few shrilled blessings at him, though he did not look right or left.

"Look how popular he is," I said to Second Brother. "I understand cheering because he looks very impressive in his new hat and robe, and the double-eyes feathers, but those with baskets of petals, they had to know he was coming in this long parade? How would they know that?"

Second Brother cast me a tolerant grin. "As you'll no doubt discover one of these days, there are certain bookstores that do a steady business in selling pictures of handsome scholars or beautiful girls, court or common. They're called flower boys and girls. The pictures are very artful, and all with suitable adages written down the side, to give them a semblance of learning. Our First Brother has been a popular flower boy for a couple of years."

"Does he know that?"

"I wouldn't dare tell him," Second Brother said with a chuckle under his breath. "If I did, he'd be sure to ask why I was wasting precious time loitering about when I ought to be studying. Unanswerable!"

"Anyone else I know in those pictures?"

"I'm not sure who you know. You certainly don't know the popular dancers at the entertainment houses. Among court girls, Arati leads the list, as you'd expect."

"First Brother a flower boy," I said, trying to get the two ideas to form a single image, and failing.

"Ah, not for long. Once he marries, he'll no longer be one. It'll be my turn." Here, Second Brother wiggled his eyebrows as he looked down in pretended modesty. "By then, you'll be old enough for Mother to let you buy suitable books, and you can buy a few of the best pictures of me, if you can smuggle them past Mother's dragonish eye."

I had to laugh at him then.

"Ah, here he comes. Let's see if he notices us."

A pair of graywings accompanying the honor guard tossed brass coins to either side. People scrambled to catch these. I saw the flash of rags, and noted younger refugees eeling through the crowd, pacing the graywings in hopes of gleaning more coins. The competition was fierce.

Second Brother and I began cheering along with the crowd as the horses clopped a few paces away. Now that he was close enough to see, I noticed that First Brother was at his best because he looked fully rested for the first time in memory, not quite smiling, but we who knew him detected the joy in the very subtle narrowing of his dark eyes.

It was then that a small hand tugged at my wrist, and here was Cousin Chuti. "Sister's and my prayers were answered," she said, giggling as if she were my age, and not a few years older.

Beyond her, Cousin Arati bowed politely to me from her position half-hidden beyond the other stone qilin. Her bow was the polite, respectful one, as if I were older, and I bowed back the same way. She wore a huge hat with a veil, but I discerned her exquisite profile within that veil, then turned my attention back to Cousin Chuti, who called congratulations at First Brother. I doubted that their prayers, however enthu-siastic, were more responsible for First Brother's success than all those many many days of grinding hard work, but it seemed ungracious to say that.

Anyway, I was distracted by the tilt to Cousin Arati's head as she watched First Brother's horse approach. A breeze wafted her veil aside, which she did not appear to notice, so intense was her gaze upward. Was it just her bloom? For at eighteen or nineteen (I was not certain which as the sisters were among the many who celebrated their birthdays, if at all, at home—as did we) she was more arresting than the famous paintings of legendary beauties I'd seen here and there in palaces. Though it could be that their expressions were invariably vapid, whereas I could see a fixed question, or perhaps yearning, in Cousin Arati's perfect heart-shaped face.

I don't what prompted me to look First Brother's way, but I did, to catch a fast glance at her. It was only for a heartbeat, then they both looked away. Cousin Chuti remained at my side, speculating about what position he'd be granted in court.

"... maybe even a secretary position? Though isn't it usually older men in their twenties and even graybeards who get those places? But a First Rank, he can do anything. I'd want the Treasury, I think. There's sure to be extra money lying about here and there. Or perhaps the Ministry of Rites, one of the Entertainment departments. It would be fun to pick plays..."

She scarcely paused for breath, and certainly did not wait for me to answer, so I didn't have to keep silent about what First Brother really wanted, which was to work in Father's Censorate.

First Brother's horse passed us as he rode through the gates, and Cousin Arati glanced at her sister, making a quick gesture beckoning her. Their maid was right there with Cousin Arati.

Cousin Chuti sighed, patted my hand, and whispered, "We'll invite you over after. You can tell us all the details!" And then they were gone.

"Not good, not good," Second Brother muttered.

I turned to find him looking in the other direction, beyond the imperial guards who stood with halberds, where Imperial Prince Xianti stood alone, space respectfully cleared around him as people cheered for First Brother. For once I had not heard the imperial prince's loud voice. His having arrived without my noticing unsettled me, or perhaps it was the cold hatred tightening his face all the way back to the muscles of his jaw as he watched First Brother disappear up the grand path toward the Hall of Glorious Harmony, at the center of the government buildings.

Once the procession vanished inside the gates, the crowd dissolved, city people going about their business, and palace people following more slowly inside the gates. We joined them. When we were somewhat clear of the press, I said, "It looked to me like the imperial prince was glaring at First Brother."

"Glaring! I'd call that what that old poet Mek Mak calls shooting eye-arrows at him. Poisoned arrows," Second Brother said.

"Why? First Brother doesn't have enemies, does he? How could he? He never does anything wrong—ever."

"That's the problem," Second Brother said. "It's been that way ever since I can remember. Maybe it was fated. Or maybe Xianti just hates First because First doesn't get into trouble."

"Why would anyone hate First Brother?"

"Why does anyone hate? But he really hates First Brother." He walked a few steps, tossing his belt tassel on his fingers, then said, "I'm not good at recollecting exact words. You know that. But I do remember Mana Ta saying that for some, seeking justice is an ever-burning torch." He patted his chest. "Here. "

"You're thinking of First Brother? I can't see Cousin Xianti that way," I said.

"Oh, but the torch in his chest burns just as bright. Brighter. First, like Father, is unwilling to believe a thing until it has been proven. Xianti is equally passionate in his belief that justice is whatever he points at. Because one day, after his grandfather and father are dead, he will be the emperor. And then whatever he points at *will* be the truth. So, why not begin now?" Second Brother patted my shoulder, looking rueful. "I hope by the time he sits in the dragon throne you and I are living somewhere far, far away. But First will stand right up to him. Jong Siang and his 110 couldn't measure up to First when he sees an injustice."

"Ah," I said. "First Brother is very much like Father."

"Yes. No flattery for either of them. They'd rather fall into a cesspit than to utter a single face-saving falsity. When we were small, when one or another of the imperial princes said or did something stupid, First wouldn't look the other way. Though the rest of us usually did." Second Brother shrugged. "In large matters, I think it's right to speak up. In small things, why?

Judgment is always going to go their way, as sure as the sun will go east to west. We expect it. There's comfort in that. Even when the sun burns hot in summer, we know how to avoid the worst of it, if you understand me."

"I do. It's the way that I have to always watch out for Cousin Siarti, and especially Cousin Liarti. I didn't do anything wrong, but if they do anything wrong to me, it'll be my fault."

"You said it right." Second Brother looked pained, his smile lop-sided. "Father insists that justice eventually catches up even with them. But he is so long-sighted that he might be talking about their progeny five generations from now. Or their next lifetime."

"I have another question," I said as we entered the outer area of the garden, on our way home.

"And I am your sage? I like that!"

"I don't think I can ask First Brother. At least, I'm not certain I'd understand his answer. If he answered."

"Go on, now I'm intrigued, little sister."

"It was the way he looked at Cousin Arati. Was that...flirting? It couldn't be. They weren't laughing. They weren't even talking."

"Oho! You're waking up to that, eh?"

"'That' what?"

Second Brother gave me his lopsided not-quite smile again. "How much do you know?"

"About what?"

"Where flirting leads, I guess is the best way to begin."

I sighed. "You're the one who gave me books with romance in them. And I've seen a little of that at imperial gatherings. All the fan waving, and little poems that make others go, *Ah-h-h-h, I know what that means*, and flowers. And in the books, jugs of tears, or else drowning themselves if they don't get to marry. Mostly it's the maidens who do the drowning, though every so often it's a handsome scholar. I always skip that part. It's so dreary."

Second Brother's smile had faded, leaving him looking a lot like First Brother, with no humor in his face at all. "I'll just say this. First and Arati like each other. They always have. Ever since he first fixed her pinwheel after Xianti smashed it. It was at the emperor's birthday around the time I lost my front teeth."

"Do they want to *marry?*" I wrinkled my nose.

"Why not? We're five generations apart."

"But First Brother is betrothed. Oh, but boys can marry more than one wife. Unlike us. Though I don't know what anyone would want with more than one husband. Is it that, too, besides justice? But why would Cousin Xianti care? *He* can't marry Cousin Arati."

"Xianti doesn't want anyone but Miracle Vaha, if you ask me. He just wants to get in First's way."

To be expected if he hated our brother. My mind caught on "Miracle Vaha." I'd heard the word once or twice before, but no one had ever explained why the foreign princess would be called "miracle" unless it had to do with the cinnabar in their blood to cause those skin blotches called freckles, and that bronze-colored hair. Cinnabar is poisonous, and yet there they were.

"Why do they say Miracle? Is it her hair?"

"Her hair?" Second Brother repeated, then he looked up, and away, and at me, and finally said, "I wasn't there. Father and Mother both would set me to copying a thousand pages of Kanda if I were to repeat hearsay."

That came far too easily. "I'll ask Cousin Chuti," I grumped.

"Do that." He grinned, his tone very much like one setting down a very difficult, noisome problem. Then he added, "I'm glad to see you friends with Chuti. Xianti and Siarti seldom get along, from what I've seen, but they unite in one thing, having scared off all those who used to be friends with Arati and Chuti."

"Do you know why?"

"Jealousy." Second Brother shrugged. "As long as I can remember, Arati always got all the attention that Siarti thought ought to be hers as First Imperial Princess. But that's my guess. Mother would point out that my only proof is witnessed behavior, and Siarti rants and stamps enough even when she isn't jealous. Anyway, you asked about First and beautiful Cousin Arati. Look, small one, this is only my guess, but I'm saying it so you won't ask and loose a shaft of arrows. You know how private First is."

Finally I was getting *some* answers. "I won't ask, if I understand what not to ask."

"I believe that some of that fire burning inside First is because he hopes to earn rank and merit enough to win Arati as a second wife. He's already betrothed to Mu Lakanda, who is good friends with Arati. She won't mind, if it happens. You'll like her. Mother and Father are certain to be giving a betrothal banquet soon, though Father won't let them marry until First has been at his place at least a year. He'll want First to put all his mind to getting a good start at wherever the emperor puts him."

That certainly made sense.

"Arati has not been betrothed yet, some think because the Emperor listens to the Imperial Crown Prince, who still loves Consort Zenar, though the empress and the dowager empress both hate her. He might be fond enough to let them choose who they want to marry, though there are some who think that Arati is too much of a prize. Which makes First want to work harder."

I half-heard all that about consorts. My mind dashed down an entirely different path. "Maybe that's why Cousin Chuti talks to me, because she wants to please First Brother?"

Second Brother lifted a shoulder. "Might have begun that way. Chuti is like a puppy. She likes everyone who likes her. Just don't trust her with anything you don't want repeated, because she's like a pup who can't stop chewing everything in sight. But if you're friendly to her, she's friendly back. Like me. Would rather step around trouble if we can. Unlike First, who will trample a straight line right through the midden if he sees the truth ahead."

We were nearing our palace by then. By mutual agreement we let the matter rest, and joined Mother to wait for Father and First Brother to return. They soon did, arriving together, a singular event that, like the wearing of the peacock "eyes" feathers, would only occur once.

First Brother, for all his scholarship, was still a youth in the eyes of the court, and so he was not even made a censor under one of the departments, but an investigative official.

"I'm to work under the Court of Surveillance," First Brother told us. I'd thought he looked quite fine riding on the horse in his new robe, but now it was as if a sun had been lit inside him. "We work alongside the Emperor's Own, or to put it better, in tandem with them, on matters of state. They must share their findings with us if their orders impinge on any of the six ministries."

"They could not have chosen a better man," Second Brother said as Mother poured out the celebrative wine with her own hands. "You're like those dogs who take one whiff of a scent, and cross ten islands, then burrow down into the deepest mine to dig up a hidden gem."

First Brother grinned as if this was the most hilarious of jests. "It is just what I hoped," he said. "I'm to accompany a senior brother—the agents call one another brother—for a time, then I'll get my first orders."

I'd never seen him this excited. We toasted him, then Father said, "Remember caution and patience. Many eyes will be scrutinizing you for the least presumption, to bring against me. While I can and will bear that, I fear only that such an occurrence will contrive to hold your advancement back."

First Brother clasped his hands so tightly that the tendons stood out as he said, "Thank you for your teaching, Father."

And the next day, at breakfast, he appeared in his new uniform, a belted jacket with long flaps cut for riding, over dark trousers and boots. All his hair had been tied up neatly in the man's topknot, a plain dark-stained wooden hairclip fitted over it, and on that a plain loaf hat. But he wore that more proudly than a prince his gold and pearls, because it was part of his uniform. It all made him seem years older, the bones of his face sharper.

"I have exchanged letters with Madam Mu," Mother said. "The third day of the new month has been deemed an auspicious day for family matters, so your betrothal banquet will be held then."

He left after eating no more than half a biscuit, and Father rose soon after, saying little, but we all detected the proud smile on his customarily somber face. He, too, departed for morning court, and the rest of us went to our regular day.

The rest of the month passed swiftly, the morning round of bows to the imperial elders improved by Cousin Chuti seeking me out to walk and chat, once the imperial princesses were either gone or far ahead. I had never had any friends, because I had been kept at home. But I knew from reading what friends were, and I thought that this, too, required practice, as anything did. Luckily, I soon found that Cousin Chuti asked fewer questions after it was plain that I had little to say, and those words chosen cautiously. She was content to talk, and my part was to listen, though I discovered that what made her happiest was being asked questions.

And so, one day when I was invited to paint peach blossoms with the sisters and a few of their mother's relations, I sat with Cousin Chuti under a shady tree, and while the others plied their brushes, I said, "Do you know why Princess Vaha is called 'Miracle'?"

Cousin Chuti's eyes widened, and her finger went to her lips. She looked around with a kind of hidden glee, then said, "Let's take a walk to the stream to wash our hands."

Intrigued, I agreed, Cray following at a distance, out of hearing but not out of sight.

"I barely remember it," Cousin Chuti said. "And I didn't see everything. The elders don't want anyone talking about it," she added with a grin. "But you know how that merely makes it more interesting."

"Oh?" I prompted.

"It was all Xianti's fault. Of course," she said, with a scowl in the direction of the great palace of the emperor, beyond which lay the Crown Prince's palace nearly as large. In there dwelt the father of the four imperial grandchildren, and his sons. "He was not supposed to be lighting bangbangs and risking his precious self." Her nose wrinkled on the word precious. "But he'd stolen rice wine, or made his servant fetch it, though we were not supposed to touch that until given leave."

I already knew that the dowager empress, a very abstemious woman, forbade palace women from drinking any wine, at least in her presence. It did not surprise me that she had issued a command forbidding it to the grandchildren.

"He got careless, and set a tree on fire. Grandfather prized that redbark tree, which was said to be brought all the way from Kanda's island, and so very auspicious. While the servants were putting out that fire, Xianti decided to light bangbangs on a bridge. I saw him there, and I saw the graywing grandmother sent to tell him to stop. He was no older than my age. Me now, not then. He got angry, and started laughing. I remember that. When he laughs like that, we try to run." Cousin Chuti's eyes widened, and she looked around before continuing. "Do you know what graywings are?"

"Servants," I said.

"No, I mean their…" Her hand drifted down her robe below her waist. "Nature."

"Oh, something about neither sun nor moons," I said, impatient for her to get back to the story.

"That means neither male nor female, though we say he and she, as they choose. But they aren't he and she, not really, you see." She stopped there, and when I shrugged, she said quickly, "Xianti said something about how he wanted to really see that there was nothing under their robes. He threw a string of bangbangs at the graywing's feet between one step and another, and they went off, and suddenly Cedar gave a terrible cry."

Cousin Chuti's pretty face sobered. "That I remember well, that cry. It was the most horrible sound I ever heard. His clothes were aflame, and Xianti was just laughing, but then quite suddenly Vaha was there. Running barefoot. She often does that, goes without shoes, which no one else would ever do. Liarti is always saying she doesn't arrange that poison-colored hair because it's hopeless, unless she were to begin by pouring ink over her head, but *we* think it's fine, in a strange sort of way. Like flowers are different colors, so why can't hair grow in different colors, too? I lost myself. No, I didn't. She ran up, and then there was a golden light."

Cousin Chuti's hands came apart, her sleeves swinging wide, and I saw that her under robe within that silk sleeve was worn thin as a beggar's covering, except it was clean.

"Arati insists that the Morningstar God appeared next to Vaha, in her goddess form. You know of course that the Morningstar God is the graywings' god."

Mother had taught me that the Morningstar God is the god of beauty, having two faces, and dual natures. But we'd never had much to do with any of that god's festivals or symbols.

"*I* saw no god or demon or dragon, only a bright glow, almost like a beeswax candle, but brighter, as Vaha put her hands on Graywing Cedar's legs, and then he stilled, and his legs…" She leaned down and patted her calf. "Were red, but the burn was gone."

"It was a miracle healing?" I asked. "Why is that some sort of secret? Is it not meritorious?"

"Because Imperial Grandmother would have it stay a secret," Cousin Chuti said. "Sister and I think it was because Xianti would lose face before everyone, so cruel a deed, and against a defenseless graywing. But perhaps it was also because Vaha fell right down on the grass next to the graywing, and we all thought she was dead, but she was stunned. They might not want the easterners to find that out, and think that we did something to her, and that war is to be fought all over again."

She spread her hands wide. "When she woke she said she

remembered nothing, and she has never been trained by Essence Healers, who are very rare, you know." When I nodded, she shrugged. "Only a few of us saw it happen, and we were all small. And all saw something a little different, I guess depending where we were. Imperial Grandmother was very angry with Xianti, and passed an edict about it to be unspoken of. So the elders never talk about it. The graywings are *always* as silent as a tomb. Vaha never did anything like it again. But she's so very *odd*."

"She plays the flute well," I said.

"She plays the crystal armonia even better. When she plays, you can hear it all over the palace. Yiuti has tried to get her to play for us, but she seldom comes out of Grand Uncle's wing, and we're forbidden to go there. Come! If we don't return, someone is sure to seek us, and demand to know what we spoke about. Ayah! I meant to say that Xianti is fascinated by her. He thinks she has powers but hides them. But if she had powers, why would she not fly right back to the east? Everybody knows that she and her mother are really hostages. Anyway, now you know!"

We walked back and returned to our painting, Arati's gaze following us with a kind of longing in her face. I suspect now that she wanted to glean from me everything she could about First Brother, but was unwilling to do it, while her younger sister had no such qualms.

I had plenty of time now to concentrate on my embroidery, an intricate design of eternity knots interwoven with longevity stars, and in the center, chrysanthemum petals all in satin stitch. When I looked over each star I could recollect what First Brother had been studying at the time. The whole looked very fine, I thought as I carefully stitched the last set of leaves.

However, at the dowager empress's gathering, she scarcely glanced at my offering over which I had labored so long and hard. As always, it was Cousin Taisa's work that won the accolade, and when I looked at it, I could see how superior it was to mine in every way. She had executed graceful heron wings with the complicated herringbone feather stitch, and worked longevity symbols in intricate chain stitch that caused everyone to exclaim in admiration.

She accepted the praise as her due, and when others held out their work to her, trying to elicit admiration, she was precise in her criticism and very qualified in her approval. I did not ask for her opinion of mine. I thought it would be too dispiriting to hear it.

On the way back home, I wrung my hands—for I'd undone and redone several sections the previous night, burning through two candles—and said to Cray, "Do you think my fan exercises are ruining my fingers? I can't seem to get as fine a stitch in any sense."

Cray gave her head a shake. "If this one is permitted to observe, Young Miss has not seen the imperial princess's mistakes."

"Very true."

I didn't have long to stew in my disappointment. I had to help Mother to execute all the many small tasks that must be done at the last moment before the banquet at which we would be receiving the Mu family. Our hall had to have all the furnishings taken out so that the floor could be well scrubbed, though it was swept each day, then it was reset with the best cushions and little banquet tables in two rows perpendicular to the modest dais on which the two sets of parents, and the betrothed couple, would sit.

All the best porcelain dishes had to be arranged precisely, and on the day, I was dispatched with Minnow and Perch to pick baskets of flowers from our own garden, while Eider helped with all the clothing.

When the palace gong rang first dragon hour, we were all lined up at the south door to welcome the Mu family. I had a role for this, my first banquet; in the past, during our very rare banquets, I had been confined to my room, hearing the music and occasional laughter or hubbub of voices from a distance. My role was to entertain the Mu daughters, of which there were four, all with "Kanda" as a generation name, Lakanda being the third.

She and her sisters had never been inside the palace before, and had a lot of questions. They were easy to talk to. They had come meaning to be pleased. They were all tall and thin, and used to wealth, judging by the manner in which they wore their jade rings and hair ornaments worked in gold. We, being girls, sat at the very end of the long row on the women's side, which meant our conversation was little heard by the head tables.

Lakanda turned out to be even more of an eager reader of gallant wanderer stories than I, and had a lot of suggestions for new authors to try. As for romance, if there was any, I saw no sign of it. Other than her polite bow to First Brother on entry, that was the last time she looked his way, or he hers. You would not even know that they were old playfellows.

After the two fathers toasted one another and made the announcement that the wedding would be set on an auspicious day in a year, Lakanda rejoined her sisters and me, and huffed a sigh of relief. "It can wait two years, or three. I don't care if I'm almost twenty when I marry. I am in no hurry to become a madam locked behind doors. I mean to see every play, and dance at every festival, before then. Once your mother lets you go outside into the city, you must come with us, Sister Renti."

It seemed that all our lives thus were laid out before us.

FOURTEEN

FIRST BROTHER HAD BEEN at his new work for ten or fifteen days. He was rarely back in time for the evening meal, returning far later than Father. If anything, the emperor seemed to be releasing the court earlier than I remembered.

Our harem visit on this particular day passed exactly like all those before, as if nothing in the world existed outside of the dowager empress's domain and interests. When we arrived home, Second Brother's manner reminded me of a few years ago, when he was always a heartbeat away from jumping up to fly a kite, or throw sticks for the yard dogs. He said little at dinner, for Father's brow was tight.

Something had happened in the world outside the confines of the harem, but I'd learned that if our parents wanted to discuss it, they would tell us. Instead, they were notably silent, their expressions reserved, though conversation was conducted with calm politeness as ever.

Second Brother must have seen my question in my face, for once the meal was over, he turned up at my room, a rare enough occurrence that he surprised me in the middle of my evening fan practice.

"What's that you're doing? It almost looks martial," he exclaimed, after pushing his way past my maids. Since I'd never given any orders to keep anyone out—I'd never needed to, as only mother and my maids entered—they stood about uncertainly.

I gave them the wave that released them to go about their duties. Second Brother flopped down at my writing table and picked up my writing brush. "I suppose all warmups look alike, for you have to build strength in the same muscles, whether you're dancing or swinging a sword. Anyway, the news is, the emperor summoned Xianti before the court, and awarded him his first task, the one he's begged for since last year—"

"What would he beg for, except to be appointed a general?"

"Close enough. He said he would address the refugee problem. Yiuti insists that there was a lot of arguing in the palace, as The Perfect Guiza also put forward ideas." Cousin Guiza, who I'd only glimpsed among the primary imperial family, was the youngest of our generation—the son of the emperor's favored Fourteenth Consort Ye, who was only outranked in the harem by First Consort Chin.

Second Brother went on, "Son against grandson, as usual. This time the grandson won. The emperor took the entire family to the hall of ancestors, had Xianti light incense and pray to the ancestors as a man, and then took him to court and bestowed an imperial tally on him. And jumped him to second rank, behind the imperial elders."

I could not imagine Xianti, loud and always rampaging about, standing still and silent in court, wearing the purple robe of a high-ranking statesmen.

"…which means he can command the imperial guard, and demand gold from the treasury. Of course we don't know how long he's been harassing his father to beg the emperor, but it finally succeeded. Xianti must have boiled his spleen at the thought of First getting a hat while he was still prancing around with his hair hanging down his back like a boy with his first rattle, ha ha!" Second Brother began tossing my writing brush on his palm the way he tossed his belt tassel.

"Has First Brother said anything?"

"He won't, except to hope that the problem will be well solved. You know what he's like. However, you can wager he'll be on the watch, whatever his current orders are. And he won't be the only one." Second Brother picked up my court fan and eyed it critically. "My friend Ban says that his brother, who's now a secretary in the scribes, was on duty in court, and *he* said Old Yiulo was looking like thunder, but that wily Uncle Koza grinned like a death's head. It must have been he who prevailed on the emperor."

Second Brother knew all these imperial uncles either by sight, or from talk in the princes' practice court, but I had to mentally reach, recognizing "Old Yiulo" as Elder Grand Prince Yiulo, the son of Grand Prince Lunshar, brother to the Emperor Yanshar who died before I was born. Wild Cousin Yiuti was the grandson of Old Yiulo, who had commanded the army in several defenses, about which I knew little, battles not deemed necessary for girls' education. Uncle Koza being Father's fourth cousin, said to be Cousin Xianti's favorite among all the uncles. Not that there were many left alive.

"What are you thinking?" Second Brother asked, leaning on his elbows as he played with my fan. "Should I not say, 'death's head'? Are you worried about inauspicious words?"

"I was thinking that there are not very many uncles except the old ones. Or aunts, except the old ones. Or cousins, really, when you consider how *very* many consorts there are. I wonder why that is."

"You do go to the root of things, Little Sister." His eyebrows shot up his forehead.

"I ask what I want to learn," I said, removing my fan from his impatient fingers and setting it aside.

He picked up my writing brush again. "Learning is good—that's almost the first sentence we hear, besides *do not touch the fire*—but I think you're getting to the age when some questions can catapult you onto the bridge of knives without your knowing it. Like *that* one."

"What subject? Why we have few uncles and aunts?"

"Yes, which is related to so few imperial births." He tossed the writing brush from hand to hand.

It occurred to me then that Second Brother enjoyed being questioned, and talking, as much as Cousin Chuti. In spite of the fact that our upbringing emphasized prudent silence and few words. "What has that to do with few cousins?"

"To begin with, some of those deaths were mysterious illnesses." He pointed the writing brush at me.

"Mysterious…in the stories that usually means poison."

"Yes." He tossed my writing brush higher, to spin in the

air. "It's probably time for you to find out that sometimes those stories are about things going on now, but the writer sets it in the past, with legendary figures, to sidestep imperial displeasure. It's a sly way of criticizing goings-on in court."

Instantly I wanted to know what was real and what not.

He went on, "'Mysterious illness' is what is said in court, usually by the imperial physicians. But anyone else bringing it up is sure to be confined to their palace for introspection, if not worse." The writing brush missed his fingers and clattered to the floor. I swooped down to pick it up and replaced it on its stand.

He said with an apologetic smile, "That brings us to why there are there not that many male cousins in our generation. That is an imperial concern of nearly every dynasty, you'll find, if you start reading imperial history."

"Has someone been poisoning them all?"

"It's the rare imperial relative who gets away with more than one poisoning. But there are exceptions. However, with us, there's another reason."

"Which is?"

"Before you were born, Father told First and me, an old monk—or someone dressed as an old monk—appeared at the Ghost Moon temple, selling pills that would guarantee the birth of boys. Expensive pills. He insisted that was because the herbs were all century herbs, and further had been blessed with Essence by a qilin atop a mountain all the way in the south. A pregnant woman due very soon who said she'd only had girls bought his pills, and within a week came back to the temple to show everyone her new baby boy, and he sold a lot of pills. He was brought before the emperor, who paid gold for all his pills. The man said he would bring more if the emperor would furnish him with a ship for the long journey to visit the qilin."

"What did the imperial physicians say?"

"They were skeptical, but the emperor liked the flavor, and insisted he felt stronger." Second Brother shrugged. "Maybe he did. He ate the pills every day, even doubling the amount the monk had prescribed. So did the Crown Prince—and some of the imperial uncles. By the time the physicians were able to determine that besides ingredients like bitter melon and ground papaya seed, which were known to work *against* fertility, and some herbs that, ah, make men feel stronger in the bedroom, there was some sort of poison in the pills. This poison destroyed their fertility. At first the consorts were blamed. I vaguely remember a lot of marriages, which explains all the younger consorts. Consort Zenar was the only one who got with child, the little twin girls were born, and there were no more imperial children."

That explained my being the only one my age among the imperial children—which I had wondered about once or twice. I'd assumed it was fate. All the other small ones younger than I were descendants of imperial aunts, out of the line of succession.

"Did the monk come back? It seems a very bold charlatan who would swindle an emperor!"

"Bold, or hired. Father said that the investigators both in the Censorate and among the imperial ferrets were very suspicious. Especially when they discovered that he took the ship and sailed north, not south! But not far enough. The ferrets tracked down the monk, who was no monk. He took poison before they could get out of him who he was running to, or who had sent him. But within a year the uncles who had not taken the pills didn't survive their mysterious illnesses."

My nerves chilled. "That's frightening."

"And stupid," Second Brother said, lowering his voice. "Father says, this is exactly why you must always investigate all claims. Now you know why it is not a subject to raise before any of the imperial family."

He soon left, and I sat down, my exercise forgotten. All of a sudden the quest for knowledge, which had seemed so pure and good, seemed to be a road with many hidden pitfalls. That determined me even more to begin reading the history scrolls so that I could answer dangerous questions for myself. Because that wall of scrolls was written to educate future scholars and government officials, all of whom were men, I had avoided it, assuming it was Father's and my brothers' preserve. But nothing had happened when I coached First Brother in his studies. And we were permitted to read anything.

I began that very night. It always seemed prudent to begin at the beginning, so I went to the shelves with the oldest bagged scrolls, and picked out the first one.

Reading it was tremendously difficult. Those scrolls, written on bound bamboo sticks, contained oddly shaped characters that were the harder to parse because the ink had faded. I ended up making a chart of old and new characters once I'd puzzled out the meaning of a sentence. It was slow going, and exasperating—and I think I would have given up entirely, had not Father, or perhaps one of Father's ancestors, often added tiny notations on strips of paper that were bound into the scrolls. By checking these, I was able to correct my equivalency chart. This was my very own investigative task, and I got the same sense of challenge that I did when trying to master exercises, and embroidery.

More days passed.

We almost never saw First Brother. Father also returned later, and his face was so stern that I dared not speak first during meals.

I was barely a third of the way into the first scroll, which seemed to be all legends, or lists, when a palace graywing brought an edict inviting us to attend the Journey to the Clouds.

Us.

All of us. The edict included a lot of flattering language which claimed that my brothers and I were all so diligent, knowledgeable, modest, and loyal that the imperial grandchildren had specifically requested us as models to inspire them. I thought immediately of Cousin Siarti slapping my face, and figured that some scribe must have written that, because *she* surely wouldn't!

The following day, during a boating party on the lake, I felt it was safe to ask Cousin Chuti about what to expect.

She sucked in a breath of pleasure. "It'll be jolly to have you with us! You will like the orchids, I think. Do bring your favorite writing and drawing things, as we always have lessons. Ah, and don't feel intimidated. There is a vast train of sampans, with the court ones far from the favored part of the imperial family at the very front, and their particular guests. Which is invariably visiting princes during the time they were marrying off all the older girls. Or someone the emperor is paying particular attention to."

She looked rueful, and though I was sad for their plight (I knew that they didn't number among the favored part of the imperial family), I was helpless to do anything about it. I left for home after the gathering far less worried than when I'd gone.

First Brother was not pleased. His expression closed off, making him look very like Father when Father went to court, and he didn't speak at all. All my parents said to Second Brother and me was to repeat, several times, that we must watch our manners waking and sleeping. And my maids were so intimidated by the prospect that when we were told we could only bring one servant, who would tend us personally, as everything else would be provided, Perch and Eider turned to Minnow, who paled, until I explained what Cousin Chuti had told me. Then she brightened, and I told Eider and Perch that they would go together to help at the temple in my place, accompanied by Cray. "And since I won't be here, and there will be little to do, I'll tell the drivers that whoever is on duty is to let you have time to visit the street. Would you like that?"

They would, and thus we were all excited at the prospect of something new when dawned the day deemed auspicious for safe travel, and my family left the palace for the first time in my memory.

I had been on boats in the lake now and then, but never in a ship. My body was uneasy at first, especially when I ventured into the cabin, which made the omnipresent shifting of the floor feel like vertigo. Minnow was so ill that Mai, Mother's trusted maid, put her to bed with ginger candies to suck on, while I lay on my bunk as Mother read poetry to me in a soft, soothing voice.

About the time my body adjusted to the motions, we arrived at the harbor at which the journey commences. Framed by great, rocky palisades, it was filled with ships, banners flying. Huge warships, elegant yachts, and between them small boats going back and forth. In the distance a sudden great shout rose, accompanied by the roar of hundreds of weapons banging on shields. Seabirds rocketed skyward.

"What is that noise?" someone asked, as we passengers stood about on deck. "Is that an accolade for the emperor?"

A minister said, "No. The emperor has probably already been greeted, with gongs and trumpets. I expect that's for General of the West Ran Ymek."

Second Brother said behind his hand to me, "Recently cleared the encroaching westerners out of the entire sunset archipelago."

I hadn't even known that there was a problem so far to the west, where Kanda had legendarily lived before beginning his wanderings.

We could see nothing but ships as our vessel glided slowly toward the pier. When I was small, Mother had showed me a map, teaching me the difference between a river, which divided pieces of the same island, and a passage, which divided two islands. Rivers were fresh water, fed by streams from the mountains that ridge most islands. Passages were salt, and inhabited by sea creatures. There was rumor of a great kraken that ruled the Sea of Heaven's Peace, which was where the Journey to the Clouds turned about. The passage was this kraken's pathway, or so Second Brother told me: if we were lucky, we might get to glimpse it. I was not certain that I wished to see a great kraken.

My attention was drawn to the fabulously long sampans flying the crimson and gold Lan Banner. The two greatest, even longer than the warships, their banners decorated with golden streamers, had to be for the emperor and his family.

Once we walked down the ramp from our ship to the pier, Father and Mother turned away from the grand sampans toward the more modest ones in both size and the number of banners. But we had not gone ten steps before a graywing hurried up, bowed low, and said, "His imperial majesty requests that Chief Censor Lan and his august family honor the imperial family with their company."

Father's eyelids lifted, betraying a flicker of surprise, but he bowed slightly to the graywing, saying, "His imperial majesty does us too much honor," and after a couple of similar exchanges, we were led to the first sampan, where the imperial family had gathered on an enormous foredeck that was half the size of the entire ship we had just sailed on. Here was a magnificent pavilion built to ward the sun, open on all sides to the breeze and the view.

We followed a general, who was dressed in elaborate armor that clattered with every step as he approached the throne. Everyone was staring at him as he dropped to one knee, armored fist pressed to his heart. I glimpsed a scarred, bearded face as he and the emperor exchanged greetings. The general had a loud, rumbling rasp of a voice, as if it had been roughened by years of yelling.

A third voice joined—that was blind Grand Uncle Miluo, who I'd never heard speak before. This uncle, who had been General of the East before winning the last battle despite being blinded, turned his face from side to side as if trying to see as he said, "Ymek! Come, sit beside me. I've lit incense every day for you…" Their voices died down to murmurs as graywings brought a cushion up to make space for the scarred, bearded general beside Grand Uncle Miluo. Grand Uncle Miluo's foreign wife was not there. I looked around, having barely a chance to notice no brass-colored hair among the various dark heads of the imperial offspring over on the far side before it was our turn.

This was the closest I had ever been to the emperor. In previous encounters, he had been at least twenty or thirty paces away, and up on a higher dais. The dais here was a mere step, and we were a mere ten paces before it, close enough so that I could see the emperor's pouchy eyes taking in every detail of us as I stole glimpses at him from behind Mother's shoulder.

We made a full obeisance, were told to rise by the emperor, who welcomed Father with a cascade of compliments on his wisdom, loyalty, and merit, then indicated for Father and Mother to sit at one side of the dais, as the three of us children made our bows to the empress (the dowager empress was also absent), and then to the Crown Prince.

This imperial uncle I had only seen once or twice in my life, and each time, he was ruddy-faced with drink. It was so now. I caught a whiff of aromatic rice wine as my brothers and I bowed to him, and to his Crown Princess, who never spoke during harem gatherings, and was largely ignored by the empress and the dowager empress, and then we bowed to the favored consorts of both emperor and Crown Prince.

Having successfully navigated this ordeal, we were passed by a hovering graywing down to the far end of the pavilion, and there were the cousins, arranged strictly in rank order.

Cousin Xianti, as first son of the Crown Prince, led the line. He grinned, bony face shifting into smiling lines that on someone I distrusted and feared less might be considered appealing. "Yanti," he said to First Brother. "Banti." A brief glance at Second Brother. Then he nodded at me, but he didn't address me—I was clearly too young, or too insignificant, to trouble himself with. "We've put you in with my sisters and Yiuti. You ought to enjoy that." Cousin Xianti waved toward where Cousins Arati, Chuti, and their little sisters stood.

The words were friendly, the gesture that accompanied them broad and open, but maybe it was just habit, how his voice made everything ironic, even slightly sinister. Or was that merely my trepidation? Because my heart was pounding fit to leap out from between my ribs.

First Brother flushed as he bowed, his expression easing after we passed by to make way for the next guests. My brothers' manners were too well-trained for any overt expression to escape them, but I sensed their total bewilderment at this utterly unexpected treatment. However, there at the end of the imperial row stood Cousin Arati, more beautiful than ever as she curtseyed to us, her gaze lifting to First Brother's face. For that moment, clearly, all those two saw was one another.

Second Brother fitted himself in with stocky Cousin Yiuti, he with the personality of a bangbang. Cousin Yiuti stood with some more distant cousins and dukes' sons. Second Brother knew that knot of boys, having gone to school with them since he was small, and they were soon laughing and joking.

As for me, Cousin Siarti gave me an indifferent nod, her gaze going immediately elsewhere. But Cousin Liarti smiled as she made a tiny bow. And though I—having since witnessed, and survived, the smoldering glow of fire in a demon's eyes— am very careful with such expressions, I can remember clearly how Cousin Liarti's eyes glittered with malice.

FIFTEEN

...and saw when the gauze sleeves stir sweet incense,
And peach blossoms swirl upward, lissome and coy,
Soft clouds upon the mountain rise and tower,
Their wind sweeps the petals. Gone, gone.

MOTHER AND FATHER WERE in the emperor's great sampan, along with the other honored guests and the primary imperial family. We children were assigned to the second of the great bannered sampans, with the less favored imperial family. I was grateful to be in a different vessel from the imperial grandchildren.

I had a snug cabin directly next to Chuti's, Arati on her other side—closer to the imperial sampan, therefore a degree higher in rank. We girls had the south side of the sampan, the boys the north. Minnow was in a windowless closet with the other personal servants down the middle.

Minnow was still tottery, so that first night I readied myself, which did not take very long. This was one benefit of modest style. Mother's maid Mai inspected me before we gathered for the emperor to pass alongside the sampans in order to officially welcome all the Journey guests, and to receive their bows.

He began with us, as from both sides of the harbor,

hundreds of lanterns decorated with auspicious characters and symbols rose toward a sky shading toward sunset.

The imperial family made an impressive display in their gorgeous silks and jewels as they slowly slid by, the glowing lanterns high above them. They looked like a painting, all except for that martial general with beard and armor. He was quite a contrast.

We bowed down to the mat-covered deck, and once the emperor had safely passed me, I lifted my head to take in the sight. The imperial family truly were like an elaborate painting, though I noticed that the emperor's complexion was very yellow, and wondered if that was an effect of the golden silk he wore, alone of the entire court.

With the emperor bestowed in his sampan at the front, we were free to gather on our own foredeck, which afforded a wide view of the rocky cliffs to either side; sometime or other we had begun moving, which I had not even been aware of, so slowly did the polers cause us to glide along.

Narrow boats with gracefully arched swan prows conveyed people back and forth among the sampans, propelled by muscular polers. We younger generation were summoned to join the imperial family for the evening banquet, held in a pavilion with sliding doors open at either side to afford us a view of the passing cliffs. The boys sat behind Father and I behind Mother, but at this, my first imperial banquet, I felt too close to the dais for my comfort. Father was very near that dais, with only that rough-faced general higher.

Second Brother observed to me on the swan boat back to our sampan, "General Ran Ymek was definitely the target of the toasts and boasts."

"He didn't say much, but he certainly can hold his drink," Cousin Oraiti said with admiration. Our rarely-seen cousin sat with Second Brother; Uncle Torza, his father and our paternal uncle, was governor of Benevolent Winds, an important island up north somewhere. Uncle Torza turned up once or twice a year if summoned, always alone until this year. Seated there next to Second Brother as he was, Oraiti resembled Second Brother more than did First Brother, though his features were blunter, his mouth broader, made to laugh. I think it was the mirth they both barely contained.

"I noticed. Not a scrap of a poem out of him, either."

"Not much came out, but a lot went in. I wonder if they all eat that hearty in the army. Maybe I should've asked my father to send me," Oraiti said.

"Except between meals, what would you be doing? Marching in rain and sleet? That's when you're not dodging arrows and swords."

"There's that. But he brought that entire army through the western war safely—the harbor was full of them cheering him. Did you hear it?" Oraiti asked.

"He's popular," Second Brother said appreciatively.

"Maybe too popular," Oraiti said, with a quick look back, but the others sat in a clump at the front end of the swan boat.

"Too?" I repeated. "How can anyone be too popular?"

Oraiti glanced at the silent poler behind us, then leaned toward me and murmured, "Have you read Ar Laq's poem to the indigo plant?"

I'd ready plenty of Ar Laq's poetry—or so I'd thought. But then I recollected a line from the warrior poet in one of the gallant wanderer tales, about a "dye bluer than the indigo plant itself."

In other words, it's seldom a good thing when someone is more popular than the host.

In this case the emperor.

My expression must have shown my sudden comprehension, for Second Brother said, "Sixty ships waiting in the harbor guarantee everyone's safety and peace."

"In honor of the general and of course of his imperial majesty, whose grace and benevolence shower upon the general," Oraiti added in the same soulful tone Second Brother had always used when covering up mischief.

We reached our sampan then, and stepped from the swan vessel to ours, and the polers glided silently away, giving no sign whether or not they'd been listening.

We had been taken to the foredeck, which was a broad, inviting space under a fringed canopy. We were alone right then; Oraiti grinned and hitched a leg over the low rail, leaning back against one of the canopy's carved poles. "My father says that this entire journey is going to be a river of honey before..." The tassel at the end of his silken sleeve flashed as he jerked a thumb backward. "... the hunter puts the bow away as fast as he can once the wolf is gone."

I went off to retire, proud of having understood the bow reference to mean that the emperor would want to send the general away as quickly as possible, now that the war was over. Which made sense. As that same warrior poet in the gallant wanderer tale had said, "Armies are trained to make war. If they don't have one, they tend to find one. And popular generals have a habit of becoming kings."

Or emperors?

We woke to thick fog. A vague sense of music persisted, dissipating with my dream.

I realized someone was knocking when an impatient rap at my door caused me to sit up in bed.

Cousin Chuti opened the door and entered, saying, "You're still abed? Did you hear the sunrise hymn? I know the singer. Aunt Chin often has him over. His voice is so beautiful."

I looked out the window, then back at her. "Did I miss the orchids, then? Are they behind this fog?"

Cousin Chuti gave the somewhat complacent, reassuring laugh of experience before the beginner. "No, no, they are coming. You will not miss the orchids! But we have to gather for morning school." Her expression turned wry. "The demon pair will be joining us, and you won't want to give Siarti, or Tutor Garnet, the excuse to shame you for sloth." She made a warding sign with her hands out. "He *always* favors *them*."

"No indeed," I said, throwing aside the covers.

Three of the imperial grandchildren gathered with us on the foredeck, which had been set up with fine little writing tables and silk-covered cushions. It was a relief to see that Cousin Xianti was not there. First Brother showed no expression, looking odd there wearing his hat, a reminder that he was no longer a student, but a man with an imperially appointed position.

That gave him rank over all the boys but Cousin Kianti, a thin, even frail boy with the same bony, oddly-put-together features as his twin Xianti, but his face was so much thinner, and his expression so different. Sleepy. Dreamy is a better way to put it. Or maybe it was just short-sightedness, for when he dipped his brush to write, he lowered his head closer to the paper. There was nothing alarming about him, except perhaps the way he always followed Xianti and did whatever he asked.

Tutor Garnet was a short graywing with thin, grizzled gray hair escaping from his broad-winged cap. "This morning's challenge will be in Shen-style poetry, upon the topic of the filial virtues. Those three whose poems best reflect the topic will receive a golden longevity knot for your belt jades."

He smiled and bowed toward the imperial grandchildren, and I thought, three prizes, three imperial grandchildren—or else the three children of the emperor.

I was wrong.

I have never been any good at poetry. I did not even try, as it takes me days to produce something barely adequate. Assuming that even if Xianti and his siblings scribbled ink on their papers they would win the accolade, I wrote out a poem I had written (and rewritten) for Mother a year or two before. By the time she pronounced it passable, I had replaced nearly every word.

Second Brother did not even try—he wrote out a very old poem by one of Kanda's followers that surely the graywing tutor would know, but at the end, this Tutor Garnet smiled and praised Second Brother, saying smoothly, "The ancients are truly the best, are they not? Always wise to emulate them."

And then he indicated First Brother and me as Second Brother stared, his mouth slightly open. "And here are two examples for us all. Very well written, very well indeed. In fact, I believe that you two shall carry the honor of choosing first among the prizes."

First Brother remained like stone as he accepted a golden knot. I bowed and thanked the tutor, but as I went to choose mine, I caught Second Brother's eye. He gave his head the slightest shake—as if I needed warning to be wary.

Then a loud, brassy gong echoed down the sampans from ahead. Those of us with manners hesitated, looking to the tutor as Cousin Siarti lunged up, and crossed to the front rail.

Cousin Liarti remained behind, her face a picture of modest retirement until the graywing said, "We are finished for today. Tomorrow, we will work on calligraphy. Enjoy the Cascades from Heaven!" He opened his hands outward, dismissing us.

Cousin Liarti scampered after her sister. I stayed where I was, unwilling to go anywhere near those two. It was far too easy to imagine one or the other pushing me over the rail into the waters—that kraken was never far from my mind—and claiming it was my own stumble.

As it was, I could see just fine from where I sat as we began to glide past a thundering fall. Spray hung in the air, a scintillating mist, throwing rainbow after rainbow. As soon as we passed that one, music greeted us! Giddy with delight, I looked around.

Second Brother pointed to a cliff above, where we could make out the tops of the heads of musicians and singers giving us a beautiful ballad in the round, which replicated musical cascades of sound.

And once we passed them, here was another tremendous fall on the other side!

That one gave way to more and more waterfalls, the air filled with a continuous, exhilarating rush and rumble of sound. I forgot the rest of the world as I gazed continuously back and forth as the rest of the cousins looked and talked and laughed, wonder and delight the main emotion in all of us who were seeing this splendor for the first time. Even Siarti and Liarti failed to scorn or threaten us, but stared and stared, whispering quietly. Except for one or two glances back at quiet, studious Cousin Arati, who alone sat sewing, occasionally darting a glance to either side.

That set the tone over the next days, which blended together. When the great cascades gave way, we rounded a wind-carved cliff atop which someone had built a small pagoda, and the rocky palisades gave way to terraced slopes on which grew orchids of every hue. The scent was intense, but never overpowering. The breezes were too strong for that. The sound of the water, the color-drenched scenery, and the fragrances elated me, and my brothers' and Cousin Oraiti's presences kept me from worrying about what the imperial granddaughters might do.

But they were only with us for morning school, during which they stayed away from me, ignoring me as if I was not even there. If I was supposed to feel insulted, they failed utterly. They also left Cousin Arati alone, which was even more surprising. Cousin Chuti noticed as well, and whispered to me as we climbed into the swan boat the second night, to be carried to the imperial sampan for the evening meal, "Those two must have been told by someone to leave us be. All I've overheard from them is gloating about how uncouth and savage and bloody the General of the West is. Mother told us that some people always need to be looking down on someone."

They left in the swan boat, along with the empress's daughter Kuiza, and First Consort Chin's daughter Taisa, to go forward and make their bows to their grandmother the empress, upon whom Mother and the other women had to wait all day. I thought about poor Consort Zenar from time to time, but I suspect Mother at least sat with her, as their respective ranks would put them near one another.

The emperor did not seem to require his youngest son or his grandsons to wait on him all day, so they stayed with us on the second sampan. With Siarti and Liarti gone, and Cousin Kianti apparently content to sit in the sun and read (I never ventured close enough to find out what he was reading), no one else appeared to notice as gradually First Brother and Cousin Arati drifted closer and closer together as the beautiful days blended into starry nights as any bad weather held off. They were always in company with the rest of us. First Brother was far too scrupulous to go off alone with a girl to whom he was not related. And Cousin Arati was too wary, for while First Brother never looked about him, perhaps knowing himself to be well within the dictates of propriety, Cousin Arati invariably cast quick looks about with a slightly hunted expression, which would clear as soon as she saw no danger.

And so they would talk, or to read to one another, as the others played endless games of Circle, or drew from the spectacular scenery, and a couple of times Cousin Guiza brought out a guqin and played softly. To my surprise, wild Cousin Yiuti once appeared with a flute, with which he played duets with Cousin Guiza. Otherwise Yiuti was the center of the Circle games, often trying to get the others to lay wagers, or he'd elbow Second Brother and Oraiti into playing pitch pot at the back deck.

When he didn't practice his music, Cousin Guiza, the one the imperial granddaughters disparagingly referred to (when he was not by) as The Perfect Guiza, sat alone studying, ignoring the scenery—which he must have seen every year since small—copying out texts, or writing, or talking to Tutor Garnet. Cousin Kuiza played with her bracelets and yawned.

Each morning there was imperial school. We did calligraphy, and then drawing, and then recited poetry. The tutor praised my brothers and me for our efforts. That, and the stunning scenery, and the countless dishes of foods that I had never tasted before, would have added up to the best experience of my life, except for the smirks on the faces of the two imperial granddaughters. But they kept their distance, and I wondered if it was because of Cousin Taisa's presence; she and Kuiza of the elaborate clothes and golden hairpins were our age, but they still belonged to the generation above, and I had seen that willful as the imperial granddaughters were, they deferred to and flattered that pair of aunts addressed as "cousin".

Especially around Taisa, whose flat manner had put me off in our early days. That, and her serene confidence when she won all the embroidery competitions, and most of the drawing contests. But she had brought that same serene confidence to my defense that terrible day when the First Imperial Princess decided to punish me for my temple contributions. And it was in that same blunt, flat tone that she uttered her observations, which I had begun to perceive were fair as well as astute.

And so, though I'd not asked her opinion of my overlooked efforts in embroidery, on the third day, right after morning school, as a brief rainstorm obscured the beauties of the mountains, I brought out my embroidery. When she shook out her robe, and happened to glance my way, I gathered my courage and said, "Cousin Taisa, could I trouble you to cast your expert eye over my poor attempt?"

"Poor?" she repeated, brows raised, and I remembered that she disliked mendacious humbleness, though she said nothing in the presence of the elders, who required it after lifetimes of hearing and speaking it.

"I expect it's poor, though I try as hard as I can," I said.

"Mmm." She waved off the other imperial daughters. "I'll take the next boat."

Liarti sneered my way, but the pair said nothing as they followed Kuiza onto the swan boat, which was ours exclusively.

Cousin Taisa bent over my frame, then pointed to a cluster of chain-embroidered vines worked into longevity knots, and touched the nearest corner, into which I'd begun to add finches, the empress's favorite bird. "Your stitches are much improved, but you still do not see the whole."

I looked at her in puzzlement, because I could see the whole very clearly. I even slipped the cloth out of the frame and spread it on the writing desk. "In this corner, the longevity knots in the star jasmine vines, because the empress likes auspicious symbols and her favorite scent is jasmine. And over here..."

"I see what you are doing, young cousin," she replied. "But you are adding in all these common items because you are told that they are propitious. Because they are favorites. But there is no harmony with the whole. You crowd them all in, showing off your stitchwork. Can't you see how congested it is? How much all this needs a far larger background so as not to exhaust the eye?"

She went to Tutor Garnet with the confidence of one who would never be scolded for presumption. He bowed, and she brought back a sheet of paper, poured a splash of water and ground the inkstone a few quick rounds, then dipped a brush. "You begin with a design..."

With a deft stroke, she sketched a branch going from the southeast corner to the northeast, then added branches in quick, graceful flicks. "Then perhaps some peach blossoms. Everything properly auspicious. But do you see that this fits the frame of the paper? Stand back. Don't speak. Look."

I did. Her branch made an austere design, but it drew the eye in the correct direction. Then she held up my unfinished cloth. It seemed to sag in the corner where I'd finished the vines, and even with the half-done hummingbird, I could see it was a snarl of shapes.

"I do see it," I said, overcome with dismay. "Thank you for your teaching."

My deep chagrin must have been obvious, for she laid both down, then said, "You were not taught by an artist."

"My mother taught me."

She was silent a moment, then said, "And I believe your excellent mother taught you to the best of her ability, but I suspect she also was not taught by an artist."

"She said that such things are frivolous. For one in my position," I added quickly. "That I will never be called upon in such a regard. I must learn enough to not shame myself, and I'm better employing my time in studies."

"A scholarly attitude indeed, most commendable. I'd let the matter drop if you seemed to be indifferent to art. For those who'll never know anything better, nor will they care. But I've seen you closely examining fine work, or watching a beautiful scene. I think you are responsive to the arts of nature as well as of making."

Not knowing what to say, and uneasy at the reminder that indeed we are always watched by someone, I put my hands together and bowed.

She said, "I was taught by dear, sorely missed Aunt Yeluo that art is one of the best of our human endeavors. And that we ought to be taught by the best, to hone our eye just as other skills are honed." She patted my hand. "That's what I have to say." And as the swan boat slid back, the midday gong echoed off the rocky cliffs, "I must go." She walked to the boat, my stuttered words of thanks following her.

Aunt Yeluo, I remembered, was sent to marry an eastern prince after Uncle Miluo's peace. What must her life be like among all those foreign cinnabar people, I wondered as I looked down at my partially finished embroidery. I was reluctant to throw it away, as I had already put a great deal of work into it. I know. I would make it into a cushion for my own chamber, as a reminder of this lesson.

The day after that, the sampans emerged into the Sea of Heaven's Peace, into which poured the most magnificent of all the waterfalls, a crescent of frothing waters that created a mist so dense that the snow-crowned peaks far to the west, which fed those mighty waters, seemed to float in the sky.

The sampans now floated, guided by the men who had exchanged their poles for long oars that dipped and rose in slow rhythm. We drifted by, then rounded an island on which stood a nine-story pagoda. We glimpsed nuns and monks working and praying, heeding us less than the birds wheeling and diving about the waves rippling along the rocks below the lowest level.

"This is halfway," Cousin Chuti said as we stood at the rail. "The grand banquet in honor of the General of the West will be tonight. And we of the younger generation who know music or dance are to provide the entertainment."

"I look forward to seeing it," I said.

"Ayah, none of us are very good, truth to tell. Taisa is stiff as a tree. Kuiza is even worse, though not as terrible as Liarti, who is always wrong-footed, and blames us. Siarti, too. The empress told them not to dance at all, which is an unlooked-for blessing. As for me, no matter how mightily I throw those sleeves, I can see everyone's eye on my sister. Ayah, when she marries, it will be my turn to be the admired one!"

She cast a glance in the direction of First Brother, sitting with Cousins Guiza and Lianti as he read from an old text. "I'm sorry that Vaha isn't with us. I do so love it when she plays that armonia of hers. I could almost wish to go east, if they play those every day." She sighed, smiling. "We're doing our Willows Brush the River dance. Which we did for the dowager empress's birthday last year. We're lucky that the empress told us to bring our water-sleeve robes. I *do* wish you could dance with us," she added generously. "It's such fun."

"Thank you for the thought," I said politely, instinctively certain that Mother would not approve. Though I still did not fully understand why she had changed her mind about my learning to dance. "But you know I only began learning, and I'm such a stumbler, I'd ruin it, even if it was only a dance with fans, and not those impossible gauze sleeves."

"But that's what's so fun," she protested. "Making the shapes in the air! Arati's in her room practicing now. She can snap out the characters for 'peace' and 'love' but I can't yet. Kuiza and Taisa can't, either. I wish the Mu girls had been invited. Parkanda can do five characters. She's the best dancer of our two generations!"

She brought me in to look at her robe, which was dyed a soft green, pale from neck to waist, and slowly deepening to forest green at the gauzy, drifting hem. She held the robe up to herself, smiling. Tiny gems winked and glittered here and there, in the curve of the neckline, at the waist, lower down on the opposite side, and scattered along the hem.

"What do you wear beneath it?" I asked, noticing how I could see her favorite hummingbird robe through it.

"A silk robe of silver," she said. "It's very beautiful. And we'll have orchids in our hair."

It did sound very fine, too fine and fragile to wear to the banquet; Chuti wore her much-seen peony robe, carrying the green dancing dress in a bag. After several days in the august company of the imperial family, I had accustomed myself enough to be able to eat without worrying over every bite.

Until now, the imperial musicians and dancers had provided entertainment. Once the food had been brought out, the emperor toasted his guests, turning most often to the general, who sat between him and the empress, a rare honor. "Tonight, we have reached the turning point, and in celebration, I have requested my own family to offer their poor efforts for entertainment," the emperor said.

"Thank you, thank you," the general replied, and of course matched the emperor drink for drink. Both were already flushed, the emperor quite mottled in his golden robes. "My son Guiza will offer a tune on the guqin," the emperor said to the general.

Cousin Guiza played with skillful vigor, but from the vague way the general nodded and smiled as the empress herself refilled his cup, he probably could not tell good from bad.

After that, Cousin Yiuti joined Guiza in a duet between flute and guqin. Cousin Kuiza proclaimed a poem. Then even frail Kianti was brought a drum, so that he would not have to rise, and the imperial granddaughters joined the three, singing a duet as Cousins Guiza, Kianti, and Yiuti played their instruments. I so disliked Siarti and Liarti that I found myself meanly wishing they would sing poorly, but they were too well-trained for that. In fact, Liarti, whose voice could get so shrill in sarcasm, was high and clear, if somewhat weak in volume.

There were a few more songs, and then the girls came forward in their dancing robes. They took up a position below the dais as the imperial musicians played for them, a beguiling melody above the syncopated tap and thrum of drums.

Cousin Chuti's evaluation seemed to be the general thought, for Cousin Arati danced in the middle, the other girls around her as she twirled and leaped and posed, the green gauze floating about her, obscuring and revealing how the silver silk rippled over her shape. They danced barefoot, with orchids in their hair, their hair loose as shadowy waterfalls down to the backs of their knees. Cousin Arati, dancing, lost all her melancholy and wariness. Even her needle-pricked fingers were hidden as she snapped the sleeves into the air in dramatically sudden lines, floating arcs, and deft zigzags. I could see how much she enjoyed dancing by the happy smile parting her rouged lips, and the very natural color in her cheeks.

Before the dance ended, I sensed how silent the watchers had gone, my eye straying to the general, who had forgotten his cup as he gazed unblinking. The dance was a triumph, at least for Cousin Arati; I glanced belatedly at the others, Taisa indeed walking through it stiffly rather than the graceful sways and lissome curving poses that Arati did so well. Cousin Kuiza seemed to always be a heartbeat behind, stumbling a bit to catch up, and Cousin Chuti was crimson-faced as she danced with all her might, when softness might have done better.

But Cousin Arati was good, at least as good as those dancers we'd seen earlier. Maybe it was her beauty, and her clear pleasure in the dance. I thought it splendid, but why did I sense ripples beneath the surface? Maybe it was the fixed gaze on that general's face.

At the end, as they bowed, the emperor leaned toward the general, whispering, one hand turned toward the girls, and the empress leaned in, too, smiling and smiling as she spoke.

The general bowed awkwardly to both, and the emperor let out a great laugh and slammed his palm on the table, making the golden dishes jump. "My honored guests," he said. "This is indeed a day of celebration! Before you all, I am passing an edict bestowing the General of the West Ran Ymek as Prince of Ran. He shall take up residence in the island he so ably liberated from the western invaders, which henceforth shall be renamed Ran. And I shall honor him with my own granddaughter Arati in marriage, as Princess of Ran. We will hold the wedding tomorrow, at an auspicious hour, once we reach the orchids!"

Shock rang through me, shared by those girls standing below me. Poor Arati staggered, as Chuti and Taisa sprang to her side. I turned my gaze to the dais, where the emperor beamed, the general laughed with drunken mirth, and the empress smiled with the exact same malice I sometimes saw in her granddaughter Liarti. The imperial crown prince stared as if it was a pet bird being handed off, and not his daughter. The imperial crown princess was even more wooden of countenance—but after all, it was not her daughter being given away.

Cousin Arati heaved in a great breath, and it's difficult to say what might have occurred next, when the empress said in that poison-sweet voice that never failed to lash our nerves, "Daughter, you are so surprised by your good fortune that you forget your manners."

I saw Taisa dig her fingers hard into Arati's arm. Chuti's jaw jutted, but she, too forced her sister into a bow, awkward as a wooden doll. Then Cousin Arati said in a trembling voice, "I thank your imperial majesties..." That was all she could get out.

The empress shot a look at Consort Zenar, who had half-risen, then said, "My dears, take her to the guest room in my wing. There is much to be done by tomorrow, so we had better begin now, don't you think?"

As the girls led Arati away, I looked across the room at First Brother, who had gone rigid. Before him sat Father, whose expression had also gone stony. Had he known about First Brother's hopes? I had thought not. Father always seemed above such things as flirtation and the like, so concerned was he with law and state.

More toasts were drunk. I could scarcely bear to look at Cousins Siarti and Liarti past a single glance that revealed no surprise whatever. This plot had been arranged between them, and maybe even Xianti was in on it. Why else would he invite First Brother, except to hurt him publicly?

In the swan boat on our way back to the second sampan, Cousin Chuti wept in rage. Cousin Taisa came back with us—she who had freedom of movement, to an extent. "I'm sorry, Chu," she said over and over. "I really had no idea that this was going to happen. If I had, I'd have refused to be part of that demon-cursed dance. Except they would have found another way."

"I'll go in her place," Chuti said fiercely. "I can bear it. I can bear anything. But she is so delicate…"

Cousin Taisa sighed. "I expect she's being kept under the empress's eye to prevent just such an occurrence."

"They'll gloat at her all night long," Chuti replied fiercely. "Ayah! I want to *kill* Liarti! She gloated! *How* she gloated!"

"Let's not talk wildly," Cousin Taisa said, with a meaning glance at the polers. Who were no doubt chosen from the imperial ferrets, for all I knew. "Remember, Liarti will relish every tear you drop. Every sign of fury. If you want to frustrate her even a little, tomorrow, you must pretend to be happy for your sister. After all, it truly is an advantageous elevation. She is going to be a true princess. With her own court."

"But with *him*. A barbarian! They never stopped complaining about how uncouth he is—"

"And now you know why. He surely cannot be as bad as they made out. For one thing, Uncle Miluo values him, and he is the very best of the uncles."

"He's military. I'm sure he values him for killing enemies," Cousin Chuti muttered, and a fresh sob seized her.

The rest of the evening went on like that; when a maid was sent summoning Cousin Taisa, she had to leave, proving that even she had limitations on her. It was I who sat with Chuti as she paced between her own cabin and Arati's empty one next door. She veered between crying and uttering threats that I was glad no one could hear but us.

It was late at the end of the dragon hours when she towed me back into her sister's empty room once again, the candle in her hand flaring wildly, and flung herself down by a trunk.

She dug feverishly inside, then pulled out a slim silken pouch, exquisitely stitched, and embroidered with two swans with necks entwined.

This pouch she opened, and withdrew some wrinkled leaves. Their scent drifted on the warm air as she held them out to me with shaking fingers. I took them, and saw that characters had been written on them in a fine, small hand. First Brother's hand. He had inscribed poems.

"Promise me to get these to Arati," Chuti said to me in a low voice. "I know they won't let me anywhere near her. But you could get your mother to give them to my mother? Even the empress won't keep a mother and daughter from saying goodbye."

"I'll do it," I promised, taking the leaves.

Finally, after vowing to find a way to break up that wedding, she fell into an exhausted sleep.

But break it up she could not do. More proof, if it was even needed, that the empress at the least had been planning this all along was the fact that bride and groom were decked out in fabulous gold-embroidered clothes in the crimson of the auspicious wedding. The sampans had all been decorated in red bunting through the night, giving the sampans a festive air. The new Prince of Ran received as a wedding gift from the empress a precious cup that the famed military leader Liad II had once drunk from. All which attested to careful planning.

I had worried all night about how to get those leaves to Mother, but after all it turned out to be very easy. Mother didn't even say a word, just took them, and presently I saw her walking with Consort Zenar as they filed into the banquet chamber.

Poor Cousin Arati looked very much like a heroine from a ballad in her wedding clothes and golden phoenix headdress, for not even sorrow could touch that beauty of hers. I'd begun to hope that that general would wake from his drunken evening and think again about a sudden marriage thrust upon him, but one look at that besotted face, and it was clear that he would have no problem obeying the imperial edict.

As for First Brother, he moved about like someone who had been gutted by a dull sword, whose body had not yet realized it was dead. He never spoke, and after the wedding, he stayed in his cabin. Not even Second Brother was allowed in.

I worried that he might never come out, but when we docked a few days later, he did emerge, noticeably thinner, but very much in command of himself. We were in time to see the new Prince and Princess of Ran disembark from the imperial sampan, Consort Zenar walking at her daughter's side in support until they reached the ramp of the army flagship.

Cannon then went off, with thunderous booms that echoed off the hills, and then all those ships in the harbor erupted in clashings of shields and banging of swords, as crimson and gold banners were let down from atop sails, tangling in the wind with ribbons carrying auspicious signs.

Once we were on board our ship, Father and Mother went alone to their cabin, Father absolutely gray-faced.

To my surprise, First Brother stayed with us, looking exhausted.

"You've got to eat," Second Brother said. "That white-eyed wolf Xianti will no doubt come to the harbor to see us arrive, and gloat."

"I know," First Brother said, his voice low and tired. "I will."

"It won't be so bad," Second Brother said. "Oraiti insists that the general is genuinely popular with his men. That means he isn't likely to be a tyrant."

"I know," First Brother said again. "It's the one thing I have to hold onto, that he knows how to be decent to raw recruits. I have to assume he will bring that decency to marriage, even if she's reluctant." He glanced up at us. "I will join you for breakfast on the morrow. But this night, I'd as soon be alone."

We watched him go off to his cabin, and when the door was shut, I said, "He looks just like Father. It's like he aged twenty years in those few days."

"He'll improve once he eats a meal." Second Brother patted my shoulder.

"What surprises me is Father," I said. "I didn't think he knew about their...about them. Cousin Arati and First Brother, I mean. He looks as sad as First Brother!"

Second Brother's expression changed. First a wince, no a flinch, then an uncharacteristic anger. Then he walked about the little parlor off which all the cabins opened, before he turned. "I'm not sure if I ought to say anything..."

Indignance flared through me. "You can't possibly dangle that in front of me, and then not say! And if you come out with I'm too young, I'll...I'll poke you with my embroidery needle when you least expect it."

Second Brother uttered a strangled laugh, but then he said, "Little Sister, this concerns you. Father's worry is all about you."

"Me? Why?"

"Don't you see it yet? This whole thing was planned..."

"I got that much. Those two villains Siarti and Liarti gloated the entire way back."

"Yes, about Arati and First. But Father wasn't worried about them. I don't think he even knew about them. He would have disapproved strongly if he had known. It was the emperor who invited all of us, don't you remember?"

"Oh yes, all that honey about my talents and modesty," I said with all my sarcasm.

Second Brother sighed again. "Don't you see? It all was a reminder. To Father. That the emperor can marry *you* off just as fast. To anyone he wants. The invitation, the Journey, was an assassin's knife sheathed in jade. A threat."

Sixteen

POOR MINNOW WAS EVEN more ill on the return journey due to a series of storms that rocked the ship unmercifully.

Minnow was not the only one who suffered from the tumultuous sea. An indefinable but unpleasant tinge to the hot summer air wafted through the ship, and Second Brother and I spent as much time outside as we could. We talked a lot about the Journey to the Clouds, once we'd both slandered our imperial elders long enough to ease the anger in our spleens, safe in the awareness of our words being dispersed over the water by the chasing wind imps.

"Try to think of advantages," Second Brother finally said. "It's the only way I've found to endure what can't be avoided."

"There isn't any advantage," I complained, my gaze straying in the direction of our cabins, and First Brother.

"Surely there is one," Second Brother said. "Ran is an enormous island. Far from here. The empress can't harry her anymore."

"That is true," I conceded. "She will never have to sew for them, ever again. And yet there's the fact that her life has been abruptly uprooted, with as little apparent thought as one uproots a plant to put in a pot. We don't hear about men being awarded as prizes to women."

Second Brother laughed. "What an odd notion! And yet, if

the woman was as beautiful as Arati, I can think of few who'd not welcome being her prize. But go on. Think of advantages for Arati."

"Ahhh…she will never have to shiver under the dowager empress's frown."

"Yes!"

"Or see Siarti again. Or her malevolent sister."

"Now you've got the idea. Don't you feel a bit better?"

I breathed in the briny ocean wind, hot and warm by turns as yet a new tumble of thunderclouds rapidly approached. "Yes. Almost yes."

"What now? Tell the wind," he encouraged. "It's always worked for me."

I eyed him. "Why would you have to tell the wind anything? Oh, I know you used to get into mischief, but that was when you were small."

His crooked smile and a raised shoulder preceded, "Right now we're letting the wind cure you."

Obediently, I said, "I am ignorant. I know I am, in so many ways, but Father's worry, and what you said about the emperor. I've managed to live this long without understanding that 'court politics' doesn't simply concern all those unseen subjects out there." I waved a hand around me, toward the hundreds of islands of the empire. Some claimed we ruled at least a thousand, and thus the name in the emperor's many titles: Heaven's Chosen Ruler of the Empire of a Thousand Islands. "It can affect *me*."

"That's what politics *is*," Second Brother said. "Why do you think I want an appointment that will take me far from court?"

I tried to see all this new information in the light of a Circle board onto which someone had suddenly dropped fistfuls of markers. "I am to understand that there are ways in which the emperor, or someone, wishes to counter Father."

"Counter the Censorate. But also Father."

I accepted that, but my thoughts remained on my own potential plight. "It must be Father in specific, as the Censorate knows nothing about me. No one there would care if I was married off tomorrow to the Demon of Blue Ghost Isle. But Father is so very scrupulous. Why would anyone wish to go against him?"

"Isn't the answer obvious? Those without scruples."

"Are there such among the ministers? I thought they were

chosen for meritorious contributions!"

Second Brother sighed. "I don't know a lot of it myself. You know Father only discusses court memoranda with Mother. Perhaps Father's being unwilling to change his mind once he has reached judgment might make enemies of those who are like the weathervanes, smiling wherever the most influential wind blows."

I thought immediately of Siarti and Liarti and their flattery of the cousins the generation ahead—Kuiza and Taisa in specific—and from them it was an easy reach to the endless petty tortures of the empress. Suddenly drained, and overwhelmed because I couldn't see what these court matters *were* that might threaten my life with sudden change, I turned my back. "The sun is much too hot. I think I want to sit under the pavilion."

"Not enough wind there for me," Second Brother said, and he trotted toward the stern of the ship, where the wind was freshest.

We had sighted land, and drifted into the harbor at the imperial capital the next morning under a summer-bright blue sky, though the season was supposed to be ripening spring.

Minnow looked so wretched that I said to Mother, "May we take Minnow into the cart with us? I don't think she ought to be under the sun in the baggage wagon." I pointed to the weary-looking servants readying the bags and boxes and baskets to be carried down the ramp to the waiting wagons.

"I was going to suggest that myself," Mother said, with a sober look toward Minnow, who was being held up by Mai— whose face was drawn as well.

Minnow crowded into the cart with Mother and me and Second Brother; Father had another cart, which would take him straight to the Censorate. Because there were only three benches, I took Minnow onto mine with me, as she was my maid. The heat from her body made the already oppressive air nearly intolerable. Fanning myself only seemed to push the sluggishly humid air around without the least relief.

I threw back the curtain, even though girls were not supposed to be seen, but Mother said nothing. She sat with her eyes closed. Even Second Brother was limp, his forehead shiny.

I forced my attention outward. The trip through the main street to the gates seemed different in a way I could not quite define, but I attributed it to that odd feeling that the ground was still moving, even though it wasn't.

When we reached the welcome sight of our palace, my other three maids awaited me in my room. "Did you go to the temple?" I asked as I sank gratefully onto my cushion.

Eider and Perch exchanged glances as they curtseyed, then Perch said, "We did! That is, Young Miss, we tried, the second week. But the nuns sent us back again, saying that the refugees were gone, and so they were not giving out food anymore. There was no need."

"What? How? What happened to them?"

This time it was puzzled glances, then both apologized for not knowing. Cray stood behind them. She had—as usual—not spoken, but a slight tick of her chin upward made me think she knew something. I sent the two to settle Minnow, and to unpack my travel things. "What do you know?" I asked Cray when we were alone.

"Nothing that I witnessed, Young Miss," she said with her usual care. "But one of the nuns was up one night during the first storm. She had a bad stomach, and on her way to the privy, she heard a great many horse hooves. Barely discernable above the rain. She was afraid. She was going to peek at the wall. But Mother Abbess told her to go back and stay indoors, that the Imperial Army was out there in force. It seemed they had a great many prisoners, and it was safer inside. The next day, they discovered that all the refugees were gone."

"Where?"

"I do not know."

"They wouldn't put them in prison, surely?"

"I do not know."

That ended the subject. She asked if I'd remembered to do my fan exercises. I said I had, and demonstrated, and she had many critical remarks to make about my having begun bad habits. I had to go back and do the exercises one move at a time to correct myself, and then it was late.

The following day, we were expected to wait upon the dowager empress, as always. Her room was stiflingly hot, with two censers burning her favorite incense. After so many days away, she looked even more wizened and stick-like under her many layers of face paint and silk than ever, almost like one of those demon-warding figures set up in certain shops who followed northern gods and rituals. Only her eyes moved, glittering.

But everything was exactly as ever. I mean exactly. Neither the dowager empress or the empress acknowledged by word or look Cousin Arati's absence. The empress brought up the latest competition, which this year would be painted screens at the side of the lake. As Mother and I left, our maids holding sun umbrellas over our sweat-damp heads, I tried to moisten my dry mouth before I said, "Mother, is it a good or a bad thing that the refugees were taken away in a night?"

"How did you hear about that?"

I told her, and she said, "I cannot answer that. But I will remind you that this is a subject not to be raised outside our home." Her voice was low and intense, and my head, already panging from the fierce sun and the heat, throbbed more.

When I got back, I said, "Where is Minnow?" when only Eider appeared. We were on firm ground now. She ought to have recovered.

Eider curtseyed very low, which the maids did when they knew I was not going to like what I was about to hear, and as she came up, her honest eyes under their straight brows now round with fright, she whispered, "Minnow has come out with fire dragon fever." She whispered as if some demon attending on fire dragons might hear, and smite her with fever.

I gritted my teeth hard, for I had been longing to have my hair brushed out again, which always soothed me, and my brow cooled with lemon balm. My spurt of anger was unreasonable, I scolded myself. No one likes to be feverish, and Minnow's favorite scent was lemon balm. She'd often said she liked the scent, and the feel of the cloth as she wiped my brow. She had to be feeling quite sick.

"Have they given her willow bark?"

"Oh, yes, Madam did herself."

"Good," I said. "She should rest. And stay abed until she is feeling better, which means the illness has left her, and cannot jump to the rest of us."

Eider bowed her agreement and I sent her off. Though her embroidery was now nearly as clever as Taisa's, she had a heavy hand with the hair brush, and my head throbbed too much to tolerate it.

I ought to be working. I turned my dry, aching eyes to those old scrolls. A fine idea, to learn history, but of what use was it to toil over the origins of the Golden Dragon Dynasty in our distant past when I needed to understand why the emperor had showered Father with special treatment, compliments, and smiles in order to make a threat without actually ordering it? This was a perfect illustration of tending the peach tree to wither the apple tree. Except, according to the gallant wanderer tales, that was something people did to influence those in power over them. And who had more power than the emperor? No one in this world!

Did that mean the emperor thought Father had commensurate power? Impossible. Or was he aware of doing something that the Censor might censor?

My head panged more, and I thought impatiently that I was foolish to stand about asking myself all these questions I could not answer. I had heard the commotion that meant Father had been dismissed early from court. I must try to catch him before he settled in to his work, and would not want to be disturbed.

I did not cross the courtyard, where the sun glared so bright it hurt my eyes to look at the tiles. Instead, I took the long way round, which at least was under eaves. I halted when I heard voices emanating through the paper windows: Father's and First Brother's.

Lest you think me unfilial enough to spy on my own elders, especially at so young an age, I want to point out that first, I was suffering from an increasingly intense headache. And second, I was hearing some of the very same words that I had been perplexed about. My instinct was to lean against the wall long enough to understand my own dilemma, and then either announce myself, or go away.

"...understand that it was an edict presented before the court, but Xianti swept them away in so furtive a manner that it requires at least a cursory investigation!"

"The emperor approved," Father said heavily. "You heard his own words today."

"This is Xianti," First Brother said in so strained a voice it cracked. "However, he did it will have surely been criminal, if done by anyone else."

"But it was not done by anyone else," Father retorted. "He had been granted the tally, and the wherewithal. He accomplished what the emperor tasked him with."

"Driving them out in the night, with no warning. An initial inquiry at the coroners' indicates there were more unexplained dead than can be accounted for by age or mischance at the harbor, or the occasional fight at the gambling houses. Xianti leaving corpses in his wake is so characteristic," First Brother stated. "And yet he stood there in court in that purple robe, smirking right behind Uncle Koza, like a pair of fox-demons.

All I ask is permission to investigate on my own time. I promise I will not slack a moment in my given tasks."

"And what then?" Father asked.

"What do you mean, what then? If I discover maneuvering outside the laws, I will present my testament before the court. According to proper ritual and law, of course."

"Except that it appears your intent is to question Xianti's promotion—a promotion granted today by the emperor—and not his work."

"But..."

"We both know what Xianti is. But we both know that your intent amounts to an attack on the emperor's grandson, which the emperor—and a good part of the court, who sincerely applauded the news that the troublesome matter has been resolved—will take as an attack on imperial authority. We have to investigate *actions*, not individuals, unless so ordered."

"But we both know that the emperors have always passed edicts to investigate..." First Brother halted. "Yes, I see it: it is the emperor's prerogative."

"My good son, if Xianti flouted his orders in any way, you would have a case, but so far, you do not, do you? He executed his orders."

First Brother muttered, "It's the method that stinks, and I mean to find out how, where, and..." Then his voice heated. "When I remember him standing up there, two steps from the throne, and that *leer*—"

"Two steps from the throne, precisely. My good and dutiful son, your passion is leading you astray, or I have been remiss as a father."

"Never. This son is stupid and unfilial—"

"Now, now, my point is, in the Censorate, our first rule must always be to investigate the action, not the person making the action. No matter how despicable we find that person; even those we like least can, and do, perform their duty as they perceive correct, and we must always leave the road open for their next action to be beneficial and wise."

"Thank you for your teaching, Father."

"Reflect, if it can afford you a modicum of comfort, that the emperor surely has his own plans. He has postponed promoting Xianti until now, which indicates to me at least that he might have his own qualms. In any case, we are not tasked with speculating on imperial motives. There is already enough scrutiny on us over the transport issue, the possible corruption down at White Jade harbor..."

I really was eavesdropping now. Though Father had finally named two court issues—transport and corruption—I still knew absolutely nothing about how these were problems. And surely, interrupting so heated an exchange was not a good idea. Especially when I was so *tired*.

I backed away, longing only for my own room, which unaccountably seemed so far away. Very far away. I remembered then that I had refused breakfast, as the sight and smell of congee had made my stomach churn.

The light had turned white, leaching all color. I tried to shrug off my outer robe but my fingers had turned to sausages. I bumped against walls as I stumbled past mother's rooms and reached the hallway leading to my rooms when sunset dissolved the light around me, and I crumpled to the floor.

I woke with heavy, gummy eyelids, my entire body on fire with pain. Mother sat anxiously by my bed, her eyes heavy and horrified, Cray standing behind her, equally horrified.

I discovered that I lay on my side, my arms curled around something long and thin and ungiving:

It was Sagacious Blade.

SEVENTEEN

Great was her foresight,
That infamous summer,
And swift her leadership…

"Why… bring…" I tried to say, but discovered that my throat was so raw I could not speak. Only a whisper came out.

Mother also whispered, "No. It just came." She glanced up at Cray, then back at me. "We shall be the only ones to nurse you."

I was too sick to ask why. My senses had stretched to their limits, each sound too sharp, the light so bright that every detail down to the weave of fabric scraped my aching eyes. A vile taste in my mouth and the sense that my sheets had turned to rose thorns made me whimper with misery. I tried to thank Mother, to apologize for being so unfilial as to disturb her, but I was too weak. I closed my eyes and slid into fever dreams.

When I woke again, I was on fire from within. Everything hurt even more than before. The sword was gone (actually, hidden at the foot of my bed, as they'd tried twice to remove it, but somehow it found its way back, Cray told me much later) and an unfamiliar figure bent over me, a candle flaring wildly behind his white-frosted head.

This was my first sight of an imperial physician, called by Father.

He laid my wrist down gently. "She has the fire dragon

fever, as you suspected."

Mother turned to the servants crowding behind. "You must tell the Chief Censor and First Young Master to leave the house at once, and not to neglect walking in zigzag to confuse the fever-bringing imps. Every servant who has not had contact with Minnow or my daughter must move to the far side of the court. All who have been face to face long enough for an imp to leap from her remain on this side. At once."

No one would question that. Everyone knew that demons traveled in straight lines. The rustle of movement scratched at my sensitive ears as the Imperial Physician breathed a sigh that fluttered the veil he wore over his lower face. All I saw were his eyes below his white hair, and his physicians' hat. "Poor little soul!" he said. "I do hate to see the young afflicted so." He shook his head, his kindly eyes reflecting the flame of the candle that Cray held near. "I could petition the imperial household for a share of ice, to help bring the fever down, and perhaps a small dose of precious kingsilver. Two doses would empty her body of all foul matter left by the fever imps."

Mother bowed, saying, "I thank you for your generosity. We would be grateful if some ice can be spared, but as for the kingsilver, it is far too precious, especially if the imperial household is also threatened. It would be undutiful to presume. My own family's nostrum for combating fevers has been willowbark tea. It ought to suffice?"

The imperial physician said, "This is good, this is good. It exhibits a long history for its curative values." Then he raised a gnarled forefinger. "However, no more than a dose at sunrise, and one at sunset. Willowbark tea does scour the filth of fever out of the afflicted, but it also scours the stomach, especially in the young, whose flesh is so tender. If she thirsts, plain boiled water will suffice, as much as you can get into her."

Mother bowed, thanking him. He closed up his case, ending with, "I will write out a prescription for restorative medicine, once the fever abates. It should be given to any in the household who are afflicted by the fever, as it will restore blood and the balance of the meridians."

As he went away, so did my preternatural awareness. I slept.

All too soon they roused me, and bade me drink willowbark tea, and I whined and moaned because trying to swallow it flayed my throat. That bitterness seemed the last betrayal.

But then an old voice spoke somewhere behind my head, "Ah, my Bu. Bodies, bodies, bodies. You are making me feel the aches again! You are to drink your medicine. And you are to drink water. Do you wash dirty clothes in a cupful? No, you need a river to carry away the dirt pounded out. You listen to your Granny Zim. You can only pound out that fever with a river."

It was the sword! The old voice in the sword. My grandmother. I had a new grandmother. Everything made sense to my fever-addled mind now. The sword had chosen me because my grandmother was in it. But why did she call me Bu? I stopped pushing the cup away, and forced myself to take tiny sips, though each one caused a fresh surge of fire. But when I lay back, the pain began to recede a tiny bit with each breath, and I slept.

Then the dreams came.

At first I fought them fretfully, for the dreams made no sense, filled as they were with people I did not know, wearing clothes that looked strange, and speaking in odd accents. But when I heard my grandmother's voice, I relaxed. She was familiar. She was looking out for me. She was *teaching* me. I let the dreams come, for at least I did not have to do anything but float there, listening.

The initial dreams brought me music. Granny Zim taught me, explaining terms I'd never heard before, and my mind strove mightily until it made sense of the jumble, because there was one constant in my life: lessons.

The music dreams gave way to other dreams, filled with new people, in new places. Once a deep forest, as Granny said, "You must learn the fundaments well, then everything builds on that..." as someone wielded the sword. I recognized the sword by the beautiful overlapping scales on the blade, and the wink and gleam of the opalescent stone in the hilt. I also recognized one or two of the fan exercise movements. More lessons! I had to learn those, and once again I strained and struggled to comprehend as Granny Zim repeated, exhorted, and at last praised me for my diligence, and I slept. Then I'd rouse, and there was more water to drink, or bitter willowbark, and here would be a new dream.

That meant a new lesson. I didn't have to know who anyone was, or where I was, I reasoned, for while I was in the grip of fever, this was a clear and logical line. All I had to do was learn the lesson my grandmother wished me to learn.

These went on and on, punctuated by moments of half-awareness as I obediently slurped a river of hot water.

The last dream surrounded me in hot desert winds, sand striking me in gritty stings. There was no ground beneath me! "No, you must balance…" but I was suspended in the air, turning over and falling, falling. I landed with a jolt strong enough to rouse me out of the dream, but as it began to unravel, there was Granny Zim's last exhortation, "You must first learn balance on three bamboos tied together…"

And I was awake. Truly awake, sodden with sweat as Mother, with exhaustion rings around her eyes, sponged me off. "The fever has gone, my good child," she murmured.

The shards of dream withered away. "Mother…" My voice was feeble, but it was at least a voice, and not a painful husk.

"I am putting you in fresh clothes and bedding once you are clean, so that these can have the fever washed out of them." She pointed to a waiting basket hung round with charms to keep the fever imps from escaping into the room again.

A short, uncomfortable struggle—I was weak and limp—then I lay on cool sheets, my damp hair spread over the pillow. "*You* must sleep, Mother," I said, my anxious eyes on her tired face. Remorse made me fretful; I sensed it had been a very long time.

She stroked my forehead reassuringly. "I shall. Now that the fever has left you. But first, you must try to get some congee into you. It is very thin. Try to swallow."

I smelled the congee, and my appetite woke at last. Five or six sips filled me, and I lay back, wearied by my efforts. My reward was to see a real smile from her as she glided out in her small, graceful court steps.

When I woke next, the sword was completely gone. The top of Cray's untidy head lay at the edge of my bed, pillowed on her forearm as she slept deeply. I sat up slowly, careful not to disturb where she sat at my bedside. The world swam unpleasantly for a moment, then righted more or less, though I felt odd, as though my head wobbled on a reed.

I crawled to the end of the bed and eased out, sliding my feet into my house shoes waiting there. Cray didn't stir. I remembered her there at Mother's side, and wondered how long since she had had a proper rest. Where was everyone else?

I crossed my room. I still hadn't much strength. Out in the hall, I met Minnow, who looked as peaked as I probably did.

She dropped a slight curtsey. I saw the effort it took. "What can you tell me?" I whispered.

"The Madam has the fever," Minnow responded, equally low. "Mai won't let anyone near. Second Young Master, as well, and Koi." That being Second Brother's servant.

"Who is tending him?"

"We all try to, Cray going between you and him."

"I will help to tend Second Brother," I said, and shuffled my way to the kitchen.

That was my life for the next stretch of days. Our household comprised the entire world during that time. At first I had to rest between each journey to the kitchen and back. But I rapidly recovered my usual strength, and so I sat longer by Second Brother, who muttered disjointedly until the night when his fever finally broke, and he recognized me.

His upper lip lengthened, and he said in a thread of a voice, "Mother still did not come."

"She is very ill," I said, surprised at his tone, which was unfamiliar, almost a tone of loss.

His expression cleared, then he looked away. "I'm sorry, Little Sister."

"Why?" And when he didn't answer, but rubbed a finger over his gummy eyelids, I said, "Once the fever leaves, we've been sponging people off and changing them so that the fever imps can't jump back into them. I'll fetch Croaker to tend you," I said, naming the cook's youngest boy.

"Is Koi also sick? Is he all right?" And on my reassurance that Koi was weak but fever free — and had been asking about him — he said, "Can you send Bao in, or did it get him, too?"

"He is off serving Father and First Brother at the Censorate," I explained.

Second Brother grunted as he sat up. "I'll wash myself." He looked around, his sweaty, tangled hair hanging down in long worms. "Take away that basin, Little Sister. I'm for a bath. In cold water. It's still blazing hot."

"I'll fix you some congee, with currants in," I said, knowing that that was the way he liked it. "And the medicine the imperial physician prescribed."

He turned up, bony and thin, but clean, at the same moment I was carrying a tray toward his chamber. I sat with him while he ate it, and watched as he began to regain a little color with each bite.

When he was done, I gathered the dishes, and paused.

"Why did you say that about Mother?"

"Say what?"

"That Mother still did not come."

His face reddened. "It was merely fever blabber. From stupid dreams." He looked away, and I knew that he would say nothing more on the subject.

"I'm going to go check on her," I said, and he went to visit Koi, his servant.

Mother was still whispering feverishly, Mai vigilant at her side, two maids standing by ready to spring at Mai's command. I heard my name, went in to reassure Mother that I was there, then I saw that I was merely an unwanted extra in that hot room, and retreated to my own.

Cray did not catch the fever, but she looked ill and tired from days and nights of nursing; it was she who had sat up night after night by Second Brother's side, while I slept to recover my strength.

"You ought to rest," I said. "It might get you now."

"I had dragon fire fever when I was small," she said, then rubbed her temples.

I felt very much like Mother as I said, "Cray, everyone is resting, or recovering. And Second Brother is well enough now. He wants to tend himself and Koi."

She bowed and withdrew, even from the back looking like she carried a weight of chains.

The next day, once Minnow had dressed me and I'd gone to the kitchen to eat, as Perch was still recovering, I remembered the world outside our palace. I went to Mother's room, and found Mai bringing out a basin and cup. "Am I to go alone to call upon the imperial elders?"

Mai curtseyed to me, saying, "They did not tell you, Young Miss? The imperial palace is in deep mourning. The dowager empress is no longer with us. She died the night the fever took you. The Crown Prince died three days after. The emperor is still ill, from what we have heard."

She went on to the kitchen, neither of us reacting much. My mind went immediately to the requirements of deep mourning for imperials. It meant undyed cloth worn over all, and festival events suspended until after her funeral. Even court would be suspended for ten days, which would conclude at the third call for her soul to return.

I retreated back to my room, aware that my mind had gone first to the trouble the news would bring, and not to any regret over their deaths. No, to speak truly, I was relieved at the death of the dowager empress, though I knew that I ought not, and I would never say so out loud. It would be criminally unfilial. And yet I could not be the only one hiding this reaction. How many felt the same? I wondered as I went to my room, and for the first time in days, picked up my fan.

It was good to move again, though I did not perform with much strength.

Mother's fever broke that night. After that, Mai permitted us to take turns bringing her meals and strengthening tea. Mai never did fall sick, whether due to the charms she wore inside her garments and out, or to her having suffered and vanquished the fever once before. Slowly the household began to return to normal.

With court still suspended, Father and First Brother returned with Bao and their own personal servants. Before their arrival the household had been turned out and scrubbed by all those recovered enough to do it. Then we hung fresh charms everywhere, after lighting incense to the kitchen god in hopes that our fire would remain clean of fever imps.

Even with this preparation, that very night, Father fell sick, and Mother—still too weak to do much more than sit up—sent me to warn First Brother to go straight back to the Censorate.

I crossed over to the men's side of the courtyard. I was so used by now to going in and out of sick people's doors without knocking, I opened First Brother's bedroom door. The boys' rooms were like mine, except that instead of instructive or inspiring pictures hung on the walls, they hung either exhortations in calligraphy or martial things like bows, and each had a sword on a rack. I had never seen either brother so much as touch a sword, though I knew they trained.

I found First Brother at his desk, his lips curled in a smile I had not seen for ages as his brush moved rapidly over a paper.

"...incontrovertible?" Second Brother was saying as he lounged on the bed. "Little Sister!"

His greeting clashed with First Brother saying, "Absolutely incontrovertible proof." Then he hesitated, seeing me.

Second Brother waved a hand. "Go on. She knows everything."

First Brother sent him a reproving look, at which Second Brother said unrepentantly, "*Mother* knows everything, at Father's behest. We all grew up with that. And it's she who taught Little Sister."

First Brother cast me a doubtful glance, looking tired, but triumphant. I think his triumph overcame his habitual respect for the letter of propriety, for he said, "It took *three* of us to track down what happened to the refugees. The women, children, and old men are established at an old outpost and a village that had been abandoned, as was reported to court."

"And?"

"It was Han Xin who uncovered the proof."

"Han Xin," Second Brother said. "Isn't he…"

"Cousin to the Graywing Cedar, who Xianti burned," First Brother said with a flick toward me, and when I did not react, he went on, intent on his report. "Found that the men of those villages were taken aboard ships bought by Uncle Koza, under the guise of trade ships. It was said they 'volunteered'."

Second Brother pursed his lips. "Then…that proves Uncle Koza is building a private army, does it not?"

"And Xianti is deep in the treason."

"A private army, like our grandfather up north?" I asked, wondering why that was treason.

Both brothers glanced at me as if they'd forgotten I was there. I still had not delivered my message, because I was finally learning something about current affairs! At last!

Second Brother said to me, "Our Gu grandfather's army is not private in the sense that First means. Grandfather Gu has a tally from the emperor himself for a defensive garrison, as do all the governors. Private armies, unless on orders from the emperor, are strictly forbidden."

"I've got to inform the court," First Brother said, looking down at his half-written paper. "And the emperor, while he is still…" He stopped, casting me another doubtful look.

"According to Yiuti, the emperor's raving," Second Brother said to me. "The fire dragon fever got its teeth in him, and not even double doses of kingsilver is curing it." He grinned. "But First, as I was saying before Sister came in, you can take your time. Talk to Father about the best approach. Xianti isn't going to be rampaging over the imperial island with his pet imperials any time soon, whether or not the emperor wakes up and summons court."

First Brother looked sharply his way, his brush suspended in the air. "Why not? He doesn't have the fever, does he?"

"Worse luck, no. According to Yiuti. But, as I was about to tell you, Yiuti nipped his tally."

First Brother gasped. "That's a killing offense."

Second Brother patted the air soothingly. "Ay, he knows that. He's not crazy—"

"Touching that tally is the definition of crazy. I always told you not to consort with him. He can get away with madness because of who his grandfather is, but you can't."

"*I'm* not touching anything," Second Brother said, his empty hands held up palm out. "And Yiuti promised that he'll put it under a cushion or in the privy or somewhere, once he's had some fun watching Xianti run around like a rabbit chased by a scorpion."

First Brother hissed a sigh, then turned a reproachful glance to me. "Why are you here anyway? You ought not to be. You're too old to be in this wing, for propriety's sake."

Affronted, I repeated my message. Then, reflecting that First Brother was doing his best to get himself directly back to the Censorate with whatever he was writing, I opened the door to leave, and nearly ran into Eider standing right outside with a tray.

"Eider?" I exclaimed.

She backed a step and curtseyed, apologizing. "I was sent with this medicine for First Young Master to drink. To ward fever imps," she said after.

Second Brother appeared at my shoulder. "How long were you out there?"

Eider blinked at him as she curtseyed again. "I just got here, Second Young Master, and was about to scratch at the door."

"I'll take that," Second Brother said, reaching for the tray. "Pass the word to Mother that First Young Master will be on his way in a moment."

"I'll do it at once," she said, curtseyed again, and sped away.

I watched her go, recollecting then that sweet, honest Eider was a Household Department spy. I ran after her, and caught up just outside Mother's room. That was good, then, I reasoned. If she'd run in any other direction, I would have been more concerned. But what exactly could I do?

I said, "Eider, anything you might have overheard is just Second Brother joking around. You know that, don't you? He's always joking. It's better not to disturb Mother, or Father, or *anyone*, especially now that we are in deep mourning, by repeating his nonsense. You must stay in the palace…we don't want to risk any more fever imps coming or going," I added, reflecting that I was not supposed to know she was a planted spy.

Eider cast down her eyes and curtseyed. "Yes, Young Miss."

I watched uncertainly as she scratched at Mother's door and was let in, then I sighed. Really, there wasn't anything more I could do, and anyway, she did say she had just arrived. I could not confine her to the servants' wing, or even question her, without revealing what I knew.

All the same, as much as I could, I kept an eye on Eider for the remainder of the day. She remained right in the palace, going about her duties—and Second Brother didn't seem worried when we two dined alone that evening, and I whispered my concern.

He whispered back, laughing, "The house is full of spies. But she said she didn't hear, and anyway, *I* didn't do anything. The trouble—if there's going to be trouble—will be Yiuti's. *He's* the fox among the chickens."

"If you are not concerned, I won't be."

"You're as diligent as First," Second Brother said approvingly. "It's good that two of us have a proper sense of duty. Ayoh, there is trouble enough. The emperor out of his mind from fever, the ministers up in arms about whether or not the dragon fire fever is going to cause a drought, or if there is some other cause, because different rituals are demanded to propitiate the Heavens for different cases. Cook tells me that while you and I were raving with fever, there was any amount of thunder, but not a drop of rain. Very bad for spring planting."

"Will they do rituals during deep mourning?"

"I think there are rituals especially for deep mourning," he said. "Making me very glad I'm not a candidate for the Ministry of Rites, for those boys have got to be climbing into mildewed and dusty archives searching for those rituals. I must be a demon changeling, for you look as serious as First, and no doubt Father will as well when the fever leaves him, but I think it's all pretty funny."

We talked on about grand rituals within memory until we'd eaten, then we both went to greet Mother, and to inquire about Father's state, which was no better. Then we separated off, me to my rooms to toil away at that old bamboo scroll as I tried to decode the ancient language.

I'd gone to sleep on top of my bed, wearing my lightest

wrap in the heavy, sultry air, when I heard my door slide open. I was sleeping very lightly, and sat up instantly. "Who is there," I whispered.

"Me," Second Brother said, a shadow briefly lit by moonslight between the slats of my window. "Where is your night maid?"

"Cray is tending Perch," I said. "I told Minnow to sleep with Eider." Not adding that I hadn't wanted to keep Eider in with me because she snored.

"Good. Perfect. Renti, you've got to get into Father's room and find me money while I pack a few things."

"What?"

He glanced over his shoulder, then came up to my bedside, saying softly, "I have to run. The imperial guard will be turning up. They have to find the house asleep and me gone."

Despite the sultry air, chill gripped me. "I don't understand."

"And I don't have time to say any more than this: my friend Lui sent a message to warn me. Xianti is putting the blame on me for the stolen tally."

"But you—"

"It doesn't matter that I didn't. The empress just issued an edict in the emperor's name, with Liarti as witness to my having done it. There is no defending myself against *them*. Though," he added in an uncharacteristic, savage hiss, "Liarti is going to discover sooner than later that sharing a lie with Xianti is never going to benefit her. Go! Please. Get me whatever you can."

The urgency in his face, lit by Phoenix Moon, overcame my shock. "I can't go in there, even if I knew where to look. No one will let me by. But Mother can."

"No. *Don't* tell Mother." And forestalling my indignant *why not*, he swiped a hand as if batting aside my question, glanced back once more, then said, "I love Mother. We all do. But I'm very certain that she will insist I do my duty and turn myself in. Give me a long lecture about justice, when there is no justice with Xianti in league with Uncle Koza. She'll probably even lecture me for my friendship with Yiuti, though I don't believe he would betray me unless something very bad has happened."

"I don't think..."

He cocked his head, listening not to me, but somewhere beyond my rooms, then muttered, "No, can't wait for you to argue. Do you have money? Of course you don't, you're never allowed out." A last glance of mute appeal, the moonlight reflected in his eyes, and then he swung about and was gone in a few steps.

I looked for Cray—who of course was not there. All I could think was that I had failed him. I ran to Mother's chamber, and to the drowsy maid on duty, said, "I must speak to Mother alone."

Mother sat up in bed. "Renti?"

I leaned toward her, smelling the lemon balm Mai had used to brush her hair, and whispered the entire story in a tumble of words. Before I finished, Mother got up, and in her nightgown, with bare feet, sped swiftly through the house, looking into empty rooms for Second Brother. But he was nowhere in the palace.

Before she crossed the courtyard back toward our wing, the flare of many torches glowed above the gate wall, so like a sudden fire it startled us both. Then the loud rap of an armored fist on the gate, followed by another more vehement one.

Mother darted back into her chamber to snatch up her summer chamber robe. By that time the yard men had wakened, and Bao was there, looking to Mother for orders.

"This is the imperial guard, with an edict to apprehend the criminal Lan Banti! Open at once!"

Mother's hand shook as she gestured.

The moment Bao slid the wooden bolt back, the gate banged open, and imperial guards streamed in. They wore full armor, swords at the ready, as if we were an invading family, and not a girl and a woman in night clothes. They dashed past us to disperse in all directions as their captain approached Mother, moonlight gleaming in the feather on his hat that proclaimed his rank.

"May I see this edict?" Mother asked in a strained voice. "This is a house of illness still, and we were all abed."

The captain held out his imperial tally, which meant he was under orders from the emperor.

Mother fell silent, arms tightly crossed. Guards began to reappear. As they passed the captain, they shook their heads or said, "Nothing," and the last one muttered—though I heard it clearly—"The Censor is delirious, afire with fever. I did not want to go into the chamber. The servant swears no one came in."

"That'll do for now," the captain said curtly. He tapped his armored chest in salute to Mother, and the guards streamed out.

Two heartbeats later it was as if they'd never been there, except for the open gate, and the way Mother sank down to her knees, her face covering her hands. "My fault, my fault, my fault," she sobbed into her hands.

"Mother," I exclaimed, dropping down beside her. "How can you be at fault? It's Liarti's lying—and also, where is Eider," I snapped, as servants began approaching with cautious steps. For everyone was awake now. Desperate anger surged in me; I intended to slap her, hard, for betraying us.

"She's gone, Young Miss," Minnow said in a small voice. "Someone summoned her away just before turtle first hour."

Mother sighed. "I hope it was the Household Department. If it was someone from the palace, she will be floating in the sea now, weighted down by stones."

Those blunt words, said in a whisper of utter regret, shocked me cold. "Go back to bed. All of you. There is nothing to be done," Mother ordered, and perforce they all had to retreat, though with the exchanged glances and lagging steps of persons full of questions that were already breeding more questions.

Mother sat where she was, a bowed figure on the tiles in the middle of the yard, tears moonlit on her wan face. "It is all my fault," she whispered.

"Nothing is your fault, Mother," I said, catching her hands, which were clammy. "Or, it was Eider, though I ordered her to stay in the palace—"

"She no doubt reported to someone else here. Any number of people eager for promotion," Mother said. "First Son will do anything to stop Xianti taking the throne, and Xianti, I suspect, will do anything to halt that testament from coming before the ministers until he, or Koja, are sure of their grip on power. But using Banti as his scapegoat...and Banti not wanting you to come to me...it is my fault. I never let him play... I never knew how to play." Her whisper was quick, low, and desolate.

"Mother, I don't understand!"

"I hope that you never will. That when you have children, you will do better, and not leave one to his brother so that you can shape the one most like you... Ayah! If he had come to me I would have bundled him into one of my robes, or Mai's— she's taller—and given him coins. Now he has nothing...he will not know how to..." She bowed her head, and sobbed noiselessly into her hands, her shoulders shaking.

I looked up at the moon, stunned and sick. Vivid as a knife cut, there was Second Brother's face before the eye of memory as he begged me. I thought: there is one thing I can do, and that is to find him. Bring him back, and let Mother find a way. She always finds a way.

Mai appeared then, going straight to Mother. I ran inside and to my room, where I flung on the first day robe I could find. Cray appeared, leaning in the doorway. Whatever she'd said about how well she was, it was clear she wasn't altogether recovered. "Where are you going?"

"To find my brother."

"You cannot—"

"Don't say it. I won't listen. I know where he'd go. I *know* where he'd go," I repeated, thinking of his occasional, idle wishes about getting on a ship and sailing away. "But I have to run fast."

Cray nodded sharply. "I'll get my shoes."

EIGHTEEN

…with knotted heart and sorrowing brow,
She anguished over loyalty's unjust reward.
For secret and seen, if there's no harm,
Then pure loyalty is a silken bond…

MY FIRST MISTAKE WOULD have been attempting to leave by the front gate.

Cray shook her head. "There is surely one of the searchers left behind on watch," she said, and led me to the yard wall that gave onto the garden where the young boys' study pavilion lay, where so long ago Second Brother had laughed as the cow bell clanged around my neck.

We climbed over, and then she pushed me behind her. Thoroughly intimidated, I raised no protest, but bent over, though running like that became steadily more painful after some twenty or thirty steps.

When we reached the other end of the garden, she looked about carefully. "Did he say where he would go, Young Miss?"

"He didn't, but he's always talked about taking a ship and going to explore," I answered impatiently. Each heartbeat carried him away another step. "I want to search the harbor. Surely we can catch up with him if we are fast."

Cray bit her lip, her eyes shadowed in the sinking light of Phoenix Moon. Ghost Moon was barely rising right then. "This way."

I began to doubt my first, determined impulse. My original thought had been to run as fast as I could along the paths I knew to the palace gates, and thence up the main street to the harbor, looking into every face of any male I encountered, until I caught him. Simple. But the reality was not simple. First of all, there were patrols roaming everywhere. We had to run and duck. Run and duck.

"Always in line of sight, but not at every point unless they get reinforcements," Cray explained to me. "So far, they're following the protocol for night patterns."

I remained silent, aware of my own profound ignorance. Second Brother had been training with the princes and nobles. Surely, surely, he would know that? They would have heard about such things?

I was gasping for breath before we even got outside of the imperial garden. A sharp pain stabbed my side, and I had to walk as I fought to breathe. Cray led me to a night soil gate, and bade me crouch in a shrub while she checked. I pushed my nose into my armpit, my eyes watering. At least I could catch my breath, even if each made me want to choke.

Presently she returned. "No alarm out yet, Young Miss," she said. "The guards are sparser here. No one likes the smell, especially in summer. We'll be able to get outside the palace without being seen."

She spoke the truth. There was no sign of a patrol. We slipped out, picking our way along the edge of the path, and she led me by narrow alleys and streets until we began smelling brine. "How do you know all this?" I whispered presently.

"Training, Young Miss."

We finally reached the harbor, and once again she took the lead as we moved from deep shadow to deep shadow, always avoiding light, and hiding every time there was a noise. It was a nerve-shattering sort of a chase. No, not a chase. It was a blind search. We made it from one end of the harbor to the other, twice. By then, the last tiger hour was passing. Phoenix Moon had completely vanished, and Ghost Moon rested above the roof guardians of a row of silent, dark houses.

"He might already be on a ship, Young Miss," Cray said at last, though her tone expressed my own doubt. "Morning is nigh, and laborers are coming to work." She indicated bulky figures heading toward the harbor. "Soon it will be swarming. You won't find anything in that crowd. We ought to return. As it is, Madam will be both anxious and angry that we left without permission. She will surely have sent Bao and Koi, and others who know Second Young Master, to comb all the places Second Young Master visits."

I could not argue with these sensible words. I knew I had utterly failed, and my eyes stung. "Mother will understand, won't she? I had to try to find him. I had to."

Cray lifted a shoulder. "We ought not to have gone." She said it low, as if talking to herself.

We found the night-soil gate as empty of people as before, and slipped inside, to retrace our steps. Once we had made our way through the imperial garden, the shadows had begun to lift a little, and Cray moved faster. She kept peering in one direction, and turning her head from side to side.

Presently she said, "Young Miss, I think something is wrong. The patrol pattern is off. That happens if patrols are pulled from less important areas to reinforce another area..." She peered intently eastward.

Was that ruddy glow morning? It seemed very localized. "Please stay here, Young Miss. I can move faster on my own. I think I need to scout ahead."

I was so tired that I did not argue, but sank down gratefully on the spring grass. I was actually nodding off when Cray was back, breathing fast. "The palace has been cordoned off," she said abruptly. "I climbed a tree. I saw..." She looked away, then back, her face in the dim light of the sinking Ghost Moon blanched and strained. "I saw them being lined up in the courtyard. Chains on their hands."

I started upright with a wail. "No! I have to..."

"You mustn't," Cray snapped—no *Young Miss*. "Listen!"

"Mother can't lose two of us—"

"Madam was out there, too," Cray said, low and rough.

I sucked in a breath to scream, and she clapped a hand over my mouth, hard. "Don't. Don't. Don't. Get hold of yourself. Don't scream. Are you going to listen to me?" she asked as I tried to pry her fingers off, but she was far stronger.

I jerked a nod.

Cray lifted her hand, and said, "I apologize, Young Miss. But you must think about it. Madam's great pride is *you*. Just as First Young Master is the Chief Censor's pride. It would kill her if you walked up there only to be clapped in chains with everybody else. She has to know exactly why you left. She will be watching. If she doesn't see you, it will be the one hope she has. You *have* to see it is true, Young Miss. Think!"

I knew she was right, though agony made me want to shriek at the injustice. "They didn't do anything wrong!"

"We both know that, Young Miss. We cannot fix whatever is going on. We *can* get away. Madam would want that. Chief Censor, too."

"But…where? Do we keep searching for my brother?"

Cray knuckled her forehead with both hands. "We might continue to evade the imperials, especially if you and I are not a priority. But, if the ferrets are sent to search, neither you or Second Young Master will be able to evade them. Second Young Master is somewhere out there. He might be with one of his many friends. If so, then he might have a chance. You, at least, I can keep safe. If you do not arrive at the prison, Madam will have hope. Yes. I think that's right. That's in keeping with my promise to keep you safe."

"But…" I tried to figure out what was the filial thing to do, and utterly failed. Because Cray was right. The way Mother had swiftly outlined a plan for Second Brother to disguise himself to get away had made me see that to her, her family came before imperial demands.

Then Cray said, "Young Miss, do you not believe, as I do, that Second Imperial Princess Liarti will do anything she can to make you suffer, if you are in prison?"

Liarti! Busy lying for her horrible brother. Convinced at last, I sat back down abruptly. "Where to go?"

"I have a place, Young Miss. But we need to get out again, and the sun is going to be up soon, and a search on. It might already be happening. They will be looking for a girl, maybe two girls, if they count to see who is missing. I know where I can get clothes, if you stay right here." She started up, then whirled around. "The sword! They mustn't find it."

"Sagacious Blade?" I exclaimed. I had completely forgotten it. "But what use is it to us? I can't fight anybody with it."

"If they discover a charmed sword, it will certainly be held against Chief Censor, as they are quite forbidden. You have to call it, Young Miss."

"Call it? What does that even mean?" I asked. "I've only touched it once or twice…" As I spoke, distorted memories of my illness returned. "During the fever. Mother said…"

"You called it, Young Miss. Or it came," Cray stated. "When the fever struck. You heard a voice, you said once?"

"Yes…"

"Speak to that voice, Young Miss. No, not aloud. Close your eyes. Call in your mind. Who is it who spoke to you?"

"Grandmother Zim," I said. "That's her name. She calls me Bu."

"Call her, Young Miss. Tell her it's Bu, and you are in danger."

I tried to do that, but my thoughts leaped about like frightened crickets. I did try, but with no conviction. I did not believe anyone, or anything, could hear me outside of my head.

Except that the sword had spoken to me without a voice.

"I'll try," I said.

"Very good, Young Miss. Call that sword," Cray said. "I'll be right back. Stay here, and think about the sword. See it. Remember Grandmother Zim speaking to you. What did she say to you last? Give her an answer. Tell her what happened to your parents…"

Cray flitted off.

I struggled, trying to think at the sword, but it felt like trying to shout into a wind, only with no voice. I couldn't believe it would be the least use. But I had to try. I knew that sword was forbidden, and it had become my responsibility. I could not let it get Mother killed! Or Father and the rest of our family!

The shocking image of my parents with chains on their wrists stabbed right through me. Words failed me, but memory images, sharp as knives, rose before my inner eye, and with them all the emotions I had tried to fight. I sobbed—and then staggered as something hard whapped straight into my chest. My arms closed around…the sword.

I lay back on the ground, shivering, with the sword in my arms.

"Oh, well done, Young Miss, well done," Cray breathed, reappearing with an armload of clothing. "Now, Young Miss, you must put these on."

"I need to go to the privy," I whined beneath my breath.

"Do it in the grass, Young Miss, but we must be swift!"

Though I was still Young Miss, it was very much Cray who was giving the orders. I pulled off my clothes, acutely uncomfortable at doing so in the open air. But we were surrounded by shrubs, and Cray was busy changing, too. I discovered that she had brought me yard boy shirt and trousers and straw shoes. These were horrible, scratchy, and altogether wrong—both too short in the toes and too wide.

"Sit," Cray said, pointing to the ground. "I need to wind up your hair in a topknot."

While I struggled with the twisted straw cords that held the shoes together, her fingers tugged and yanked at my hair. The straw scraped my hands unmercifully, and I bit my lip to keep from crying out. She tied a rough topknot on my head with a bit of straw, and then reached to bind her own hair up. In the weak light, her contours changed, with those rough clothes on, and her hair skinned up to the top of her head—she looked in the fading moonlight like a boy.

She swept our robes into a bundle, used that to pick up the sword, then tied the corners into a knot before slipping the bundle over one shoulder. "I will lead the way, Young Miss."

I kept stumbling in the straw shoes as we slunk back from shrub to shrub, until we reached the night soil door. We hid for a short time; already there were carts coming out, and empty ones going in.

Cray held us back until one cart was well through, and another coming up the path, the two pulling it walking head down. "We must not run, Young Miss, for it will draw notice. We should walk slowly, as if we've been emptying chamber pots all night."

We slipped out as the sun topped the eastern roofs, and this time we dived immediately into the first alley we came to. We walked rapidly as she kept looking about her for smaller, older alleys. Then, when the three-tiered heaven-turned roof corners of Suanek's temple appeared off to our right, the tension in her face relaxed a little. "Not far now."

I walked with my head down, my neck tingling as if enemy eyes already searched for me. I did not want anyone looking at my face.

It must have been second horse hour when we entered the yard of a dyers. Strong smells rose on the hot wind, mixing into a fetor that made me cough. We crossed a long yard past rows and rows of long lengths of cloth of every hue drying in the sun, and then ducked into a building.

A young woman saw us. Her eyes widened, and she gestured for us to follow her. I was thankful when the narrow corridor led to a stone stair, and we descended into the relative coolness of a basement, where barrels were stacked and stored. We squeezed past these to a warren of small rooms.

"Water," Cray croaked.

The young woman vanished, then came back with a jug of water so cold it numbed my teeth. I gulped and gulped, holding out my cup before she finished pouring some for Cray.

Once we'd slaked our thirst, another young woman, who resembled the first, brought steamed buns, and we devoured those. As we finished, the two were joined by a sun-browned man who appeared to be Father's age. His thinning hair showed bits of frost at the temples, beneath his headband.

"Watcher," Cray exclaimed, standing to clasp her hands in a circle, fist inside palm.

I realized I was seeing the gallant wanderer salute as the man she'd called Watcher said, "What is your report, Fourteenth Young Sister—"

"I'm Cray now," Cray said. "I know it's a palace name for my generation's servants, but a cray is not a fish, and I've made it my own. I—I like hearing it." To my astonishment, the silent, somber Cray reddened.

The Watcher said, "A new era traditionally requires a new name. It is well, Cray. Now, is your arriving here with this … young person …" He glanced at me more closely, his high brow furrowing in confusion, and it struck me that he was trying to decide who I was. No, he thought I was a boy!

"This is Young Miss," Cray said, and hefted the heavy bundle that she had carried all this way. "The Young Miss claimed by Sagacious Blade."

Everyone stared at me.

"I would like to hear that story," the Watcher said, "but urgency requires us to understand one another first. This search going on is for a young man, I thought somewhat older than, ah, Young Miss?"

"It's for Second Young Master," Cray said. "He dared to go against the imperial family. I can make a sketch, if you will send scouts out to look for him. He got out ahead of the family being arrested. We think they were arrested."

And during the time one of the women went to fetch ink and paper and brush, Cray quickly outlined our actions since leaving the palace.

"An imperial search," the Watcher said. "It might even come to house to house. We will be safe enough here."

The elder of the two women said, "No one but the family and the ribbon-weaver and the shoemaker on either side know about the pool down here, as our three houses are built directly over it. It's a generational secret."

"But that is not a solution for long, unless we wish to abide here," the Watcher said. "Go ahead with your sketch, Cray, if your Young Miss here will tell me a little about this brother? It will help our scouts, perhaps."

Words spilled out of me as I tried to describe Second Brother, but I kept correcting myself, and then dashing down paths of anecdote, then catching myself to explain. It was a dreadful recitation. I began to feel that it was useless, and frustrated myself. All my training had been toward explicating ideas, preferably with references to the sages and to traditions, in poetic terms.

I halted in the middle of an impossible sentence full of backtracking and glanced down at the drawing emerging from Cray's brush. I gasped. "That's him! That's my brother. That's his mischief smile!" I looked at Cray in wonder. "You are a very good drawer."

She blushed to the ears, avoiding everyone's eyes.

"I will give this to Grandfather To show the scouts," the Watcher said. "I suggest the two of you get some rest. We will leave once it's dark, and there are no patrols in the area."

"Leave?" I repeated. "Where?"

"Did you have a destination, Young Miss?" one of the women asked.

"I...didn't...but wouldn't it be wrong to..." I was going to say *just leave them*. It was then that I truly understood that there was nothing I could do to aid my parents, except to go die with them, but Cray was right. It truly would be more unfilial to force my mother to watch helplessly as the imperial granddaughters gloated, or worse, than to go to the prison just to reunite with my family. But it did not feel right. Sorrow began to rise, crowding my chest, and I breathed hard as I said, "Go to my Gu family?"

"They will be watching the road for exactly that," the Watcher said with sympathy. "We will go in another direction entirely."

I swallowed, and swallowed again, the knot in my heart swelling to my throat. We were led to some beds laid on a carpet in an alcove in that stone cavern, above a small pool, and I curled around the sword that Cray quietly laid next to me. I covered my face with my hands, and let the grief come.

I finally slept, but it seemed only moments before I woke with aching eyes and head, and I got my first lesson in the true meaning of loss of rank.

My mother was not born a princess. Though she married a prince, he was so low in the orders of imperial rank that he was a single step from the dividing line to mere nobility. I have tried to demonstrate how they tried to raise their children with an awareness of shared humanity with all: Father, impatient of such distinctions except as they contributed to an orderly ranking at court, and Mother, always mindful that anything put at a vaulting height has a corresponding crushing drop if knocked down. And everything, save only mountains, came down eventually.

Even so, when we woke and were summoned to eat, the young women served Cray first, as she was known to them. It was she, and not me, whom they asked first if she wanted more, if she needed anything. I sat there in common clothing, my hair a snarled ball on top of my head. *We were all born naked*, Mother had said. My once being a princess was akin to us watching players who came to enact one of the old dramas based on Kanda's conversations, in which we pretended those on the stage were truly scholars and kings and demons of the ancient past. For me, the play had ended. But I was still alive. Mother would want that. She would take comfort in that.

I took a determined bite, and another, and another.

After that meal, the Watcher joined us, holding out two sturdy carryalls, with sword loops sewn in. "Each of you will put belongings in your own carryall. Yes, you will now carry your own sword, for it is your responsibility."

"But it is heavy," I said. Actually, I whined.

"You will gain strength the faster as you carry it," was the response. "You are no longer a Young Miss. You are now Ran, which is a popular name for common boys as candles, so expensive, are considered auspicious. Wherever we encounter suspicion, we will claim to be traveling to the next town, where the two of you are to be enrolled in the local school to begin your studies for the Imperial Examination. But I am teaching you self-defense along the way." He indicated Sagacious Blade. "Before we leave, you are to cover that hilt with paint and soil, making it look unsavory. Cheap. Nothing that would interest an avaricious interrogator."

While we'd slept, the people of the house had washed out our robes, dyed them the dull blue and brown of common clothes, and once they had mostly dried in the intense heat, they cut them up, making them over into garments fit for young boys. As they finished sewing these sloppy garments,

Cray had been weaving straw hats for her and me. I used the smelly paint they offered me, streaked with dye, and a kind of nut oil, to smear and dull Sagacious Blade's hilt, so that it, sticking up from the dull, cracked sheath, looked old and worn. Then I slid it into the loops on the carryall.

Cray and I slung these carryalls over our shoulders. I tried to shrug the unaccustomed weight into place as Cray bowed and thanked them. I hastily followed her example. They gave us a flask apiece, a couple of apples, shallow dishes of plain clay, a short pair of eating sticks, some jerky, and a couple of buns.

Then, with no guards or servants or fanfare of any kind, not even sun umbrellas, we set out under the rising Phoenix Moon. The heat was still emanating from the ground as we moved from deep shadow to deep shadow, stopping often so that Watcher could listen and scan.

All three of us breathed somewhat easier when the buildings became farther apart, and then gave way to gently rising countryside.

We walked swiftly that night, making me glad that Mother and I had had a habit of walking everywhere, though never as long. I was stumbling with tiredness when the sinking Ghost Moon signaled the coming dawn, and Watcher found us a grassy knoll at the bend of a wandering stream.

And that became the new pattern for two nights, then at last the Watcher said we could travel by day and sleep at night. I learned during those days that grief does not abate after one paroxysm of wild crying. It comes in waves. Strong. Relentless, remorseless. And it gains one exactly nothing, after leaving one limp and drained.

We slept outside, which turned out to be far more comfortable than beds inside a stuffy room while the hot, clear weather persisted. When we woke, we scavenged for food. If we were lucky, we found a stream to camp by, and fish to catch and cook. But more and more we were unlucky, finding only mud or dried silt where streams usually ran. Greens were already turning summer yellow, even brown. Flowers hung limp and withered.

I went back to my old court days of taking a sip of water from my flask, and holding it in my mouth as long as I could before swallowing it. That old trick served me during those early days as we climbed up and up.

I was always tired, at first. Toward the end of a day, that

gnawing exhaustion would turn to agony, and the only thought that kept me from demanding a stop was the image of Liarti (for I no longer thought of her as "cousin") smirking at me from outside a prison cell.

After a few days, once we woke, the Watcher bade us perform what he called "seeds," as he scouted and scavenged. That meant doing a few falls, then balancing on forearms, and then doing the fan dance. No, the fan *form*, as Cray called it now. There was no fluttering or posing or sweeping sleeves coyly. Cray explained the second morning of that practice that women in entertainment houses, as well as many sects, used fans with steel tips as self-defense. We sped up the form, and I began to see how the sweeps and strikes might actually be lethal, had I any strength or speed behind them.

After another four days passed, Watcher decided we were to swing our swords and do the beginning four steps of the fan form after all the rest. I pulled Sagacious Blade for the first time, to discover that it had become noticeably lighter. I caught the others watching me more or less covertly. I felt very self-conscious that the secret had had to be kept for so long.

Cray asked one morning a few days later, "Is the sword speaking?"

"No, it is silent."

"Let's get going, my boys," the Watcher said.

That afternoon, as we toiled up a steep path past stands of shadeless bamboo, the lowering clouds deepened, and in doing so, turned the color of a bruise. Used as we were to thunder and maybe a few splats of rain, if that, we kept on until lightning struck up the hill from us, a sudden, blue-white leaching of color, and as thunder clapped right overhead, down came the deluge that the water dragons had been saving up all these weeks.

At first it felt unspeakably wonderful, but that changed abruptly when hail began to cut at us. We sheltered miserably under a thrashing oak, Cray shivering as much as me.

It was a long, wretched night, but the next day, all the springs and waterfalls had come alive again, though running brown before they were safe to sink our empty flasks into. By then, of course, we had long eaten the apples meant to be saved for last, just for the moisture.

Whenever there was cover, and Watcher heard the approach of horse hooves or people walking, Cray and I hid. But twice we were crossing broad plateaus, with no cover in either direction. We met other travelers both times, who asked idle questions. One shared tea, which Watcher accepted, but sniffed carefully before he brewed it. He told our story while Cray and I looked down, then—wishing one another fair journeys—we went our separate ways, me with pounding heart, though no one so much as glanced at me.

We also spotted the occasional village, mostly nestled in little valleys, surrounded by citrus and jujube orchards, gingko, and parasol trees, with the occasional redbark sentinel on cliff tops, or shading pools in rarely glimpsed chasms. Often the enticing smells of their cook fires wafted to us before we sighted rooftops, but Watcher had us avoid them all, until after that deluge. That time, he told us to wash out our clothes and spread them to dry in the sun—it cleared to hot weather that next day—while he went off alone to a village, and came back that evening with a basket of food, and news.

"Village rumors are always to be little trusted," he warned. "Exaggeration is the rule, but what I gleaned was that there is a new emperor, and at least one prince fighting to claim the throne."

"Did they say anything about…executions?" I dared a question.

He gave me a glance, his expression somewhat pained, before he said, "There are always such rumors. People often delight in rivers of blood—as long as someone else is shedding it. Do not regard any of it as truth, except this: the possibility of marauding bands of imperials dashing this way and that as they hunt each other becomes more of a possibility. The sooner we reach our scrape, the better for us all."

"Scrape?" I repeated, and then I remembered that the word had at least another meaning besides using an edge to run over something. Falcon nests were called scrapes.

And Cray smiled a little, saying. "The Falcons' home."

I bit back the question *How far*. The answer would be meaningless. I was afraid this hard climb, the rocky ground, the insects, being dirty and grimy and hot and hungry was to go on forever. Though I was slowly becoming so inured that the agony had dropped away, leaving only wretchedly tired muscles by the time we stopped.

In any case, two weeks of climbing, three thunderstorms, a dozen or so avoided travelers (including a caravan that had rather a lot of guards riding the pack animals), and seven villages later, we began going downhill more than uphill. Now the surroundings differed subtly; there was more ginseng, and reedy banks on slower winding streams, for the land was higher, the slope more gradual. Fewer rocks and more growing things. We were able to scavenge early berries of several kinds, and fish again.

Five mornings after that, the Watcher said, "We're here."

NINETEEN

*Out in the world, all saw just empty clouds and
mountains.
Not guessing that this secret dwelt right at
hand...*

I WAS TOO INTIMIDATED to ask Watcher any questions, but
when he bade us wait on a ridge while he scouted ahead, I said
to Cray, "Who are the Falcons? Is Watcher their chief?"

"Watcher is a scout," Cray said, peering intently—
hungrily—down into that little valley. "And sometimes a
guide. He will probably go back down the mountain tomorrow
or the next day. Or to somewhere else. Once he talks to the
Falcon Chief. As for the Falcons..." Her chin lifted. "The
Falcon sect are protectors. Many in your mother's mother's
family are among us. Madam asked for someone to be sent for
you. They chose me."

"They," I repeated, remembering that surprising day with
Mother's grandmother. I also remembered thinking that
Mother didn't quite approve of her cousin's life. Or her
grandmother's. Would Mother want me here? Better than
prison.

The familiar grief-knot tightened in my heart. In an effort
to distract myself, I looked down at conical roofs surrounding
a practice field, where a group of youths trotted out, spaced
themselves, and began doing a form with long sticks. Behind

the largest cottages lay terraced vegetable gardens, jujube trees thick all along the south-facing ridge. Lower down, where the sizable stream widened into a pool before tumbling away northwards, rice grew. I had seen pictures of rice in the gallant wanderer stories. Now I was actually in a gallant wanderer village. I tried to find excitement in that, but stronger was the urge to tell Second Brother, and there was the knot, tighter. Was he alive? I wanted Mother to know I was safe, but was she alive to care?

My eyes had begun stinging when there was a rustle, and Watcher was back. "Child," he said to me, "Chief Rain wants to interview you first. You will be safe here, whatever is decided."

Cray clasped her hands, bowed to Watcher, then without a word, she bolted down the narrow path.

"She seeks family here," the Watcher explained to me as he took off his straw sun hat, tugged the skewed kerchief tied around his forehead, and replaced the hat. "Come along. I'll explain a few things as we go."

I tried clasping my hands the way Cray had. "Thank you for your teaching. And for bringing me safely."

He patted the top of my grimy, untidy head with a callused hand. "You're a good child. But I expect life will be very different, here. Those born and raised here accept everyone fairly easily, but not all share that, especially in their early days. Understand that some come from troubles, just as you did."

I looked back at him in question.

"Once the chief accepts someone, then that person begins a new life. It is not done to query into pasts. Though some talk freely." His eyes strayed to Sagacious Blade, sitting at my feet, and he said, "I suggest you learn its ways as soon as you can."

With that, he led the way down the narrow path.

Everywhere, people were busy, some weaving, others working bamboo. Small children scampered up to one of the terraced vegetable plots to weed. Dogs chased around, plumed tails beating the air, tongues lolling. I glimpsed a white-haired figure through an open window, bent over a pair of sturdy sandals.

Central to all that lay the practice field, where those with the long sticks whirled and clashed, whirled and clashed, shouting in cadence. I didn't see where Cray had gone, as Watcher led me to the largest building, which was built in the familiar U under a peaked tile roof, with tilted eaves on the south side.

We entered a dim room, and Watcher turned to the right, sliding his feet out of his shoes. There were no house slippers waiting, of course. Just a basin of cloudy water to dunk one's feet into, and a mat to rub one's soles along, before treading beyond a screen so old it was difficult to make out the figures on it, to a room with cushions all around the walls.

At the far end sat two elders, a silver-haired grandmother wearing an eyepatch and a monk in undyed cloth, with shaved head and wrinkled face. He had one of those sanded, smooth long sticks leaning against the wall behind his mat.

They turned. I halted, unsure what to do; in the palace I'd go to the floor, but that was an imperial prerogative, or reserved for one's elders in the family. Or for a master. Would not it be presumptuous to do that here?

Then I remembered the fist in clasped hand bow, and self-consciously performed it.

"Come forward, child." The one-eyed chief had a mild, reedy voice. "Where I can see you."

I did so.

The monk rose to his feet, sketched a blessing in the air, picked up his staff, and departed with a kindly smile in my direction. He joined Watcher, and the two left together, talking in low voices.

"Are you well? Do you need to eat?"

I was hungry, but I had been trained over the past days not to expect someone to run to the kitchen and produce succulent fruits or tasty little cakes whenever I wanted a snack. Surely there would be mealtimes here, and I had learned to wait. "I am well, thank you."

"You do have a look of Madam Gu," Chief Rain said to me. "Watcher described what he knows of the imperial troubles, which might very well follow you up here. There are two things that keep me from sending you on your way with a wish for good luck. One is that your great-grandmother was my sword-sister, back when the Falcons were all women. The other is that Sagacious Blade chose you, so there must be something to you that the demon in the sword thinks worthy."

"Grandmother," I said without thinking. "Not a demon. It's Grandmother Zim inside the sword."

"Oh? I had not heard that the rumor of its speech had been true."

I flushed, and curtseyed, uttering a formal apology for speaking out of turn.

"Never mind that honey-tongued court talk," she responded, wiggling her fingers at me. "As often as not uttered with hatred in the heart. I've seen the results. *You* have seen the results, I believe, or you would not be here."

She turned her head so that her good eye could study me. "You're probably too young to have a goal, except for revenge, revenge, revenge, I suppose."

"I had not thought about revenge. Justice, that is different, and I do so want that for my family, who did nothing wrong." My eyes were stinging again. "I just wish that I'd—"

"No use in wishing," she interrupted, though mildly. "The arrow never returns to the bow, no matter how hard we wish it would. What do you intend going forward?"

"I don't know," I admitted. "I only wanted to get away before the imperial guard could put me in chains, too. Cray showed me to where the Watcher lived, and he said we would come here, and here I am."

"Good enough. What is your age?"

"Thirteen."

"And what shall we call you?"

Watcher had called me 'Ran' and I'd posed as a boy, but that had only been convincing if I didn't speak or move, Cray had said. If I took off the generation name Ti, and altered the tone of the name my parents gave me—which seemed more precious now—it would be written differently. Giving it the most common pronunciation, "Ren," I said.

"Ren, we can try you for a season, then revisit the matter, if there is no danger resulting from your appearance." Chief Rain drank some tea, then clapped a hand to her knee. "Ordinarily we would test you to see where you stand, but Watcher says that you're a very beginner. We will start you with the little ones, and go from there." She wiggled her fingers at me again, as though shooing an insect. "Go find Young Four—that is, Cray. By now she will have greeted those she remembers. She will get you settled."

I clasped my hands to her and backed out, unconsciously falling into court mode, as I had been trained to do since I could walk. Once I stepped out into the bright sun again, blinking after the dimness inside, I found Cray waiting for me.

"Were you born here?" I asked.

"I was born in a village on another island. Brought here

before I walked," she said with a distinct tone of pride, and I noticed the absence of the honorific, modest as "Young Miss" was in the imperial hierarchy.

Was there no hierarchy beyond Chief Rain here? I wondered, but I would soon discover that there is always hierarchy with humankind, always. It remains only to discover how that is defined.

She showed me to a square hut indistinguishable from the others, except for the word "Work" painted in red on either side of the door. All the cottages had similar names: Virtue, Strength, Truth, Peace. The floor was swept clean, outside shoes in a rack inside the door, bedding rolled up on a shelf. A sleeping platform extended down one side. Cubbies for belongings on the other. Cray told me what to expect, and I was able to set down my carryall at last. With my shoulders considerably lightened, I followed her out.

Someone rang a gong. It was noon. Meals were eaten on low, square platforms on which sat low tables, set outside Chief Rain's building. We sat on the bare boards. Cray led the way to where a lot of children sat with those under sixteen or so. We joined them, and Cray introduced me simply as Ren, then gave me a rapid series of names that I had no hope of remembering.

If I shut my eyes, it was almost like an imperial picnic once the adults were at a distance, voices mixing freely, but without the courtly cadences. Some stared openly at me. They ate quickly, then it was time for more lessons.

Cray said, "You'll go with the small ones." She ran off to join the older group.

The children began by running over, above, and under a series of obstacles. I believed myself to be quite hardy after walking up a mountain. I expect I was. But I had never in my life been permitted to run, much less climb, once I'd reached the age of six or seven, and so I was miserably behind children half my size.

At the end of the day, the girls from Work cottage went together to bathe, and I had to figure out how to wash my own hair, and comb it. I was still at that chore when most of the others had gone to sleep, but I felt a small sense of triumph (and a great smarting of scalp) when it was done at last. I braided my hair tightly, grateful that at least I knew how to do that.

The following morning, the entire sect rose together at a

gong, washed out our mouths with a sip of stale tea, dressed, and gathered in the field to do the seed forms together, experts in front, and ranks according to ability, all the way to the little ones at the back. Where I was set with them.

After "seeding the sun" as they called it, we dispersed to our respective chores or classes in the martial arts, until noon, and so on.

And that set the schedule for the following week or two as summer ripened in that high mountain valley. There were no lessons in calligraphy, or painting. There were no courtly conversations, with musicians playing gently in the background. It was hard training, from morning until night, when I fell asleep the moment I wrapped myself in my bedding. I slept so hard that the grief did not torment me as badly as it had.

The only time we did not train was when we took turns weeding, pulling or picking vegetables, cooking, and washing and setting out laundry. Everyone was my teacher. I seemed to be regarded with the sort of tolerant patience that those of ages four and five got as they struggled with their lessons.

There was only one task at which I proved myself adept: that was mending. Embroidery was easy to adapt to mending, for it seemed easy and sensible to me to use silk stitch, or even braided chain. My stitches were regarded as tidier (and prettier) than anyone's, with the result that a great portion of the mending was handed over to me. That freed me from harvesting, which I found exhausting.

Sagacious Blade remained under my second garments on my shelf, untouched: the beginners used wooden weapons only. But there came a day nearing midsummer, when the moons were farthest apart in the night sky, when I realized that I had caught up with those my age in the obstacle course. And the most basic seeds, or fundamental steps, had become rote. At least my practice in my room at home had done that much to prepare me for this sharp turn in my life.

One afternoon I was directed to a pile of mending, which I could do without much thought as I sat under a parasol tree, watching the older Falcons at archery over at the targets. A group of those nearer my age began doing a sword form, and I realized that I was anticipating each step, each twist, thrust, recoil, lunge. It was then that I remembered those dreams during my fever, sent by Granny Zim in the sword.

I *knew* that form. I knew how to balance between hip and

shoulder. I found my shoulder twisting as I imagined that high block, and the reverse backhand stroke made faster by a shift of one hip.

My body twitched and jerked, until I set aside the mending, ran back to Work cottage, and fetched Sagacious Blade from where it had lain since I first put it down. No one was around, everyone at various classes or tasks. I retreated to a little secluded glade, and put myself through the form.

It took a few tries before I got my body to match the dream. But it did not take long. I sensed a quiet hum of approval, and for the very first time since the troubles began, a tentative sense of exhilaration stole through me when I was able to do the form correctly all the way through. I did it a few more times, until my blood sang in my veins. I was scarcely even breathless.

I decided that I'd continue doing that, whenever I was alone, just as I had at home.

You might notice that I have not yet introduced any of those I had come among, some of whom became famous (or infamous) later on. It is well to remember that I had never learned to interact with others except within court. Mother had exhorted me to keep my thoughts to myself, and to never ask questions except under safe circumstances. I thought myself sinking safely to the background, as I had been in court. An uninteresting nonentity, my strongest shield.

My day, mostly spent among those ten and younger except when I had mending, which I did alone, was spent at different ends of the valley from Cray, and sometimes I watched her from a distance. She had spent most of her time when within my visual range standing patiently. When we had to speak, she had been just as chary of spending words as I'd been cautioned to be, if not more. Raised as I was not to indulge in gossip, especially with the servants, I had never thought about where they came from, or what they wanted when they were not standing by with quiet demeanor, waiting for orders.

Little as I knew Cray, I could see in every line of her body how happy she was as she strove at her weapons, and when those older teens and the adults played hunt-and-catch games, she was invariably selected a leader among those around fifteen.

The days gathered into weeks, as summer in the mountains ripened in the bright sunlight, broken only by the occasional fast-moving storm. Hungry Ghost Month waxed and waned, with a festival gathering around a great fire in the center field.

I wandered alone, as I had at court gatherings, fighting against the usual onslaught of homesickness as the adults drank and laughed, silhouettes dancing with abandon around the fire. The children ate the treats we'd made ourselves. They played games, none known to me other than pitch pot, their variation to toss an arrow into the vase, rather than an enameled rod. I looked on, assuming myself all but invisible.

As the sun slanted toward Harvest Month, we got many more cold days, and out came winter clothing, which I did not have, of course. I caught Cray one day as she returned from staff practice. "How do we get winter things?" I asked, shivering in a wind that seemed to come straight from the breath of an ice dragon.

Cray looked at me with a quick flash of surprise. "You did not ask?"

"I don't know whom I ought to ask," I replied. "I did put my question to Little Finch, in my cottage, but she said her mother saw to that." Little Finch's mother being one of the archery instructors.

Cray looked away for a time, and I wondered why so simple a matter required so much thought. But then she turned back to me. "There isn't anything in the rag basket?"

"I know every piece in there," I said. "It's all summer cloth. I think the heavy cloth gets passed down until it's worn thin."

Cray blinked at me from those wide-set eyes. "That's right, you've been doing the mending for those who're all thumbs." She frowned at the ground, then looked up at me after another of those lengthy pauses. "I'm told that someone will be coming from the imperial city very soon. They bring winter stores. And swap scouts and watchers out. The dyers will send cloth."

I was going to ask the difference between scouts and watchers, but she was hailed by one of the older girls, and walked off with an abruptness that never failed to remind me that court politesse had no place here.

Harvest Festival came and went, with celebration of singing, dancing, games, and good food, the rest of the harvest being dried or pickled and put up in jars and baskets. I had never before understood how much work went into preparing for winter, a time when one could not go up into the garden, or to the jujube orchard, and pick what looked ripe, as we'd been doing since my arrival.

Sky Wishes Day came, but without the setting off of sky

lanterns. I ventured to ask eleven-year-old Little Finch, who slept on my other side (I was against a wall), "Why is no one making sky lanterns?"

She gave me an incredulous look. "And give any enemy a pointer to where we are?"

"There is no celebrating, then?"

Her superior expression eased. "We have our own way. You'll see. It's fun!"

Many had hoarded broad leaves fallen during the past days, carefully pressing them flat. These were brought out and shared around with those who had none. A tiny fragment of wick was pressed in a bit of beeswax brought down from the hives way up the mountain, and each lit a leaf lamp, then set it into the water of the stream. We soon had a river of winking golden light carried toward the falls.

As the other children around me set theirs on the rilling water, they whispered their wishes with a prayer, instead of writing it on their leaf. I would have liked to write mine. It seemed more earnest, a stronger exhortation to Heaven for the safety of my family, but I had nothing to write with, and though there was ink in the main house, reticence kept me from doing something that the others didn't do.

Was Heaven listening, beyond that sky brushed with wispy clouds showing the last ruddy edge of color from the vanished sun? I watched my leaf bump along, the little flame flickering, until it mingled with the others. Then my eyes blurred and stung, but I was getting better at breathing through the ache and sting of sorrow. My heart was still knotted, but I was growing accustomed, reminding myself of what Watcher had said: most there had come from troubles. I was not alone in that.

The next day, life returned to the usual pattern in the Falcons' valley.

Then, six days later, ahead of the first snowstorm, one of the lookouts posted on the promontories ran down to report, "The wagon is here! The wagon is here!"

It was just after the midday meal, and people swarmed about getting ready for afternoon activities. Nearly everyone turned toward the south rim of the valley where the road emerged. A woman and a girl in a really ugly undyed, stained robe walked at the halters of a pair of donkeys pulling a loaded wagon.

They started down the path. The donkeys' ears flicked as

they smelled something familiar, and they began to trot, the wagon bumping and shaking until a swarm of Falcons raced up to surround it, and take over drawing it, a couple of ten-year-olds unhitching the animals and leading them to water.

It was another cold day, and I stood with my arms gripped against my sides, hoping that that promised sturdy cloth would be brought forth from the wagon.

Willing hands unloaded sacks and baskets of dried seaweed, salted fish, lychee nuts, and other commodities to help get the community through the winter, then came rolls of cloth dyed mostly in the blues, greens, and browns of common life. There was one of a warm, soft yellow, and another of black.

Once the wagon was empty, some of the adult Falcons lingered around the driver, all talking at once. The girl in the stained robe stood by, looking uncertain as she gazed around.

My attentions snagged on that uncertainty. Then on her face, which was familiar. A hard, sharp jolt in my heart at the sight of those straight eyebrows beneath a high forehead. Eider? Anger roused, then died. It was not Eider, who had been tall—my height—but this girl was at least a hand taller. Eider could not have grown that much since that terrible day. And those eyebrows were too thick. Also, this girl did not have Eider's pointed chin, but a squarer jaw with a chin dimple…

I looked past the braids. "Koi?"

I only realized I spoke when the "girl" turned her head. It was definitely Second Brother's personal servant Koi, dressed in the braids and the badly-made robe of a yard drudge.

My heart banged painfully and I began to run, all the questions that had tormented me for weeks forming up behind my lips, but then the driver looked Koi's way and said urgently, "Koi."

Koi caught himself, standing stiffly. I knew instantly that he'd been reminded not to fall into the habits of the palace. He stared at me as if it took a moment or two to recognize me. When was the last time I'd spoken to him? I could not remember, we had so little to do with one another, though we lived in the same palace.

I had one distinct memory of us all playing with a host of fuzzy ducklings by the pond in the yard after a spring rain, when I was quite small. We were all there, both my brothers, their servants, and at the time I'd only had Minnow, who was learning to pick up my things. First Brother had been showing us to be very careful with the tiny little balls of fuzz so as not to hurt them, when shadows fell over us, and adults swooped down, separating us all from one another. My next memory was commencing those long, straight lines, with a bolster on my head, as I began training in court movement, my ears ringing with exhortations about speaking only when spoken to, and never with the servant boys.

I scarcely saw Koi after that until the fire dragon illness, and while I had carried food and water to him, I don't remember speaking to him at all. I'd never before seen that resemblance to Eider in the upper part of their faces. The anger against Eider pulsed again as Koi remained stiff and uncertain.

I closed the distance between us, and whispered, "Did you find Second Brother? Is he alive?"

The moment the words were out, I saw my answer in the way he closed his eyes, his expression anguished, "No, Young…"

I put up a hand. "I am Ren here."

"Ren," he repeated, with a jerky nod, as if his body wanted to bow, and he had to fight the prompt of habit. "I hoped to find him here," he admitted, low with regret.

"Koi," called the scout who had brought him. "Come meet Chief Rain."

I had to bite my lip hard at this interruption, yet another small reminder that I had no rank. My wishes did not supersede those of anyone older, nor could I give orders.

I formed a question. "May we talk when you are free?"

Once again his head began to dip in a bow, but he stopped. "Yes," he said, and followed the scout, leaving me standing alone.

Cray dashed up to him before he'd gone ten steps, and he began speaking to her in a low, rapid voice, both easy with long familiarity. I was already cold, but a sudden chill seized my nerves and made me shiver when I saw the light gather in Cray's eyes, before she swiped her sleeve across her face to dash the tears away.

TWENTY

*Within this valley, she knew not the fate of those
she loved —
Out in the world, the world gripped by storm
clouds and flying dragons.*

THE GOODS FROM THE wagon were immediately distributed, the new cloth offered first to the elders and to the Falcons who had outgrown last year's clothes. They passed those to the older teens, and so on down to the current guardians of the small ones. I, who had grown up seeing my family every day, was surprised to discover that many parents or older siblings of the small ones were on the wander, which was what the gallant wanderers called their journeyings. They were all used to families being separate then coming together; Cray was one who looked forward to spring, which might bring back her mother from far islands.

A basket of unwanted garments—Koi's robe among them—reached us at Work cottage very soon, after which the older girls were permitted to choose first. PanPan, the tallest of us, turned to me, holding off the smaller girls, saying, "Ren, you don't have any winter things, I notice. You ought to have this tunic." She held up something brown, with very long sleeves, long in the body, cut up the sides for riding. I noticed gaps near the hem, as if cut by a knife. Or a sword. Two patches elsewhere.

"That's Master Sima's," Little Finch wailed. "I wanted it!"

"You've got two good woolens! Two!"

"But I wanted *his* tunic. He's such a hero—here—who wants a wool robe so I can..."

PanPan snorted. "You know very well all the heroism goes right with him. It doesn't stay in his clothes. And any luck that might have clung was well beaten out on the rocks when it got washed. Do you want to find Ren's frozen body lying next to you, once winter sets in, her ghost sitting on your chest?"

"No," Little Finch said with a quick gesture warding bad luck, then she turned to me. "Will you take this blue wool in trade? See, it's very thick. My Grandmother Ki made it. I'll be your donkey in your next ten lives if you let me have Master Sima's tunic, please, Ren?"

The others were all staring at me as Little Finch lowered her voice. "Everyone knows he was wearing that when he shot Rireg Blood Hand through a gap like *that*." Two fingers parted the measure of a thumb's width. "And when he took on the six shadow guards of that pirate who tried to take over Jasmine Island up at the Dogleg!"

"I don't mind," I said. "I just need something warm."

PanPan looked at me uncertainly, then scowled at Little Finch. "You know you're not to badger people."

"I truly don't mind," I said. "That blue one looks thick, and I'm not used to how cold it is here in the mountains." I cut myself short. Had I said too much?

But no one was thinking of imperial courts. "Oh-h-h, a southerner," one of the other girls said on a long note, as if everything was now clear. "Everyone knows it's always hot down there."

Little Finch took the brown robe, hugging it to herself, then she pulled it on. And stared down at the holes near the hem as everyone laughed. It was enormous on her. "I'll grow," she stated, but fingered the holes.

"I can stitch those up," I said. And, because the robe did look terrible, "I could embroider a bit to hide the puckers..." I stopped, wondering if there might be a rule against embroidery here, for I'd seen none.

Little Finch's eyes widened. "Would you?"

"Certainly."

She slipped out of the brown one and handed it back to me as the meal gong reverberated brassily. The others had quietly distributed the rest of the clothes, and I took the ugly stained one, for it was clean, and it could be worn beneath the blue one for added warmth. I noticed that I was still getting sideways glances as they packed up or put on the new things, then ran for Chief Rain's.

I sighed as I followed more slowly. I tried my mightiest to be quiet, and to do what I perceived to be duty, and yet I was still getting *looks*. I was apprehensive that these stares might result in my being told to go away. I was terrified of that, for after those weeks traveling to the mountains, I knew myself unprepared for the wander. In fact, I had seen enough on the journey with Cray and Watcher to suspect that I would soon be very like those poor refugees I'd handed buns to, last year.

At the midday meal, I spotted Koi, sitting with Cray and the other mid-teens. Relieved at the sight of him, I watched from my quiet corner, longing to question him. But when the meal ended, he was drawn off to be tested, something I'd forgotten about.

I fully expected him to be as ignorant as I was, but to my astonishment, he picked up a staff, swung it around a time or two, as if warming his wrists, shook out his hands, then took up the proper stance as one who knows it well. One of the young men who taught us beginners set to with him. Koi defended himself with quick, sure clacks and taps and whirls, looking quite expert to my still-ignorant eye, and I thought, of course he would know these things. I'd forgotten that my brothers had trained at the Princes' Court, and who but Koi would practice with Second Brother? For preference, study was First Brother's choice between lessons or duties.

I found myself rejoicing at every successful defense on Koi's part, because if Koi was good at defense, surely Second Brother would be, too. And that argued for his being somewhere and safe after all. *He* could defend himself, unlike me.

I turned away to obey the inward prod of work, determined to complete the task I'd promised Little Finch. As I looked at those patches and the gaps that had to have been cut by a sword, I considered embroidery images.

Little Finch and the others had not objected to my offer, which argued that embroidery was not forbidden. But what would be acceptable images? I was used to embroidering court images. Phoenix was for the empress; the idea of stitching this beautiful bird made me shudder at the context. The same with lotus and peony, peach blossoms and hummingbirds.

Image aside, I remembered that I would be limited in

quantity as well as color. I could pick apart rags so that the threads could be reused. I'd seen an old yellow thing in the rag basket, the fabric far too worn to be mended.

When my gaze roamed the rim of the valley, taking in the mostly-bare trees, I returned to the jujube. How about jujube blossoms? They were considered common, but what of that here? I could braid chain stitch along the cuts, and then embroider a row of jujube blossoms, whose shape, with the harmonious balance of five large petals with five smalls ones between, reminded me of stars. Yellow would be a cheery color against brown.

I carefully cut a length of the yellow, found a place sheltered from the wind from which I could watch Koi in the practice field, and began my task. The weave in the much-washed rag was easy to pick apart. Braided chain stitch to mend each hole, stem stitch to outline the five petals, satin-stitch for the petals, knot stitch for the five smaller petals, with chain stitch to connect the knots to the flower. I kept the flowers tiny, lest I run out of yellow thread.

I was halfway through my second mended tear when Koi finished with sword, listened to the instructor say something, then waved a dismissal. I started up, ready to run down the trail from my spot under the sheltering redbark tree, when Cray emerged from out of Virtue cottage, and joined him. They began talking. I lost sight of them as I rounded between two cottages, then I caught up and they both looked my way.

I don't know what they saw in my face, but Cray looked around furtively, then said, "There was no sign of him dead."

The two joined me, and we walked back up the trail to sit under the tree. I was aware that I would have liked to have Koi to myself so that I could ask all the questions I had suppressed within me, but there was no sending Cray away anymore. Besides, they clearly were so familiar with one another that there was none of the awkwardness I felt when I had to think out everything I said, lest it come out in the wrong mode of address and tone. Or lest my questions give rise to dangerous assumptions as to motive for asking.

"Tell her," Cray urged Koi. "From when she and I left to search."

Koi said, "Madam Gu sent Gui and Kwan and me to find Ban—Second Young Master—"

"You can use his name," Cray said, her fingers gripped together. "Truly, she won't object."

"Cray is right," I breathed, my mind buzzing with all the revelations of these simple words: that when alone, my second brother had let his servant use his personal name, in spite of family rules. That Cray knew that. That perhaps she had even used it, though the female and male servants were strictly required to stay in their own wing.

But Koi was speaking. "Madam told us to first take robes from Mai. Braid our hair like girls. Fetch baskets, and go as maidservants. To pass the imperial guard. It did get us past the guards. Right before they were summoned to search the palace. And arrest the family. We did not know that at the time."

He stopped, his gaze distant, and I suspect he looked within himself at bleak memories.

"We separated. I found no sign of him. The light was coming up, I thought of going over to the scribes' wing on the east side, when Little Pig pelted along the street, looking everywhere. I stopped him, and he said the imperial guard had broken down the gate. Torches everywhere. He was afraid they had set fire to the palace."

I realized I sat there with the needle suspended over the cloth, and began working again as I said, "Did you see anything?"

"Yes. I only half-believed him, as Little Pig's known for, ayah, telling stories."

"He's a liar," Cray stated.

"Yes, though he's not wicked," Koi countered. "His lies are exaggerations. Gui said he'd make a storyteller one day…" His head dropped, his mouth downturned, then he sighed and resumed. "He was so frightened that I mostly believed him, enough to take the long way, up through the stench gate and down through the young masters' schoolyard, to the boundary trees along the Cloud Canal. From the branches we saw the Chief with a wooden yoke around his neck, and chains on his wrists and feet. He was not able to stand."

"The chief Censor was full of fever," Cray said softly.

"Yes." Koi glanced her way. "Bao and Fumek had to hold him up. Madam was next. Mai tried to fight them away when they came to put chains on her, but a guard knocked her down, and Madam said to stop. We could barely hear their voices. First Young Master turned up then, dragged by guards, and Kwan was also dragged in. He'd gotten rid of Mai's robe, and loosened his hair. I think changing out of the robe got him caught. First Young Master was beaten and kicked before they threw him into a barred criminal cart."

"What?" I protested. I'd only seen one of those once, when I was small. The prisoner in the cart had been raving as he attacked the wooden bars of the cart, blood flying off his hands, which he didn't seem to heed. "First Brother would never fight."

"No. He didn't do anything when they kicked him, and once he was in the cart, he sat upright, hands on his thighs, as though sitting before the throne," Koi said dully.

Cray murmured, "It's to be humiliating."

I understood that immediately, but I also knew, though I did not quite have the words then to express it, that First Brother, knowing himself having done no wrong, would never feel the humiliation. Only the pain, and he'd hide that for the sake of our parents.

My throat closed up yet again as helpless anger burned through me, but I did not tell Koi to stop talking, hurtful as it was.

He went on. "The guards banged and crashed through the palace. We could hear them throwing things about and kicking through the sliding doors all the way from the trees."

"Searching for Second Brother and me?" I asked.

"I think so," Koi said, with a sober glance my way. "They all came back empty-handed. By then they had finished chaining the servants. They marched them out, toward the Path of Heaven. To make a spectacle of them, Gui said later, when we met up."

Cray muttered, "They could have gone by the inner paths. It's crueler this way."

"It is so," Koi said. "Little Pig was crying by then, and I did not know what to do with him. He's not yet eight! But they had chained the two little kitchen boys younger than Little Pig. I was trying to decide whether to go back to my search, or to find somewhere safe for Little Pig, only where, when the air filled with the strangest sound, as though heaven had opened and the immortals sang. It was so sad, and yet so piercing, that I was afraid."

"There is only one sound like that. The crystal armonia?" Cray asked, eyes round.

"Yes."

"How could that sound reach the palace from such a distance? Surely the foreign princess could not have taken that delicate instrument into the Path of Heaven?"

"I don't know," Koi said. "But I jumped down from the tree, and ran to the willow clump—"

"Where you can see the bend in the Path of Heaven, toward the garrison side?" Cray said. "I know that clump."

Koi sighed. "I got there well ahead, as the procession was going so very slowly. The first imperial prince had joined it at the front, on horseback. Only his horse sidled and fretted, and he fought hard to control his mount, who clearly was bothered by the sound of the crystal armonia, which seemed to come from everywhere."

"You can see the west tower of Water Dragon Palace from there," Cray observed. "The Path turns below it before heading toward the prison."

"Yes. From those trees I could just make out the Cinnabar Princess high on that tower, the morning light catching in the crystals as she played," Koi said. "The light shone full on that cinnabar head of hers, making it almost look like a crown. By then a great crowd had gathered, guards and servants and ministers' servants and even some ministers, but no one jeered. No one moved. They were all silent as that sound reached out over the entire palace. First Imperial Prince Xianti looked up at the Cinnabar Princess, who played and played as if no one was there, and she kept playing that forlorn song until the last of the prisoners vanished through the gate. I followed, running parallel to the path. I saw them taken inside. Then, as the gate closed, the music suddenly stopped, and the silence was like the sky closing, bang." He clapped his hands lightly. "Everyone very quickly dispersed. I did, as well, not knowing what to do with Little Pig. But when I reached our shortcut back of the empty palace of Old Uncle, I found Gui waiting."

Koi rubbed his hands over his knees as a cold wind rattled the few remaining leaves above us. "Gui said to take Little Pig to Aunt Ar, and when I told him I'd meant to go over to the scribes to see if Second was hiding with his friends there, he said he'd just returned, having seen imperials go in. He retreated fast."

"Then they were already questioning Banti's friends?" Cray asked, her hands clasped so tightly her knuckles whitened. It was strange to hear her use my brother's name, a familiarity that was forbidden servants. But I suspected Second Brother shrugged that rule off when alone.

"Yes. At least the ones they know. I don't think the first

imperial prince knows how many friends Second Young Master has. He would never count those among the servants."

Cray said, "It is so." Her slightly easier tone matched my own weak glimmer of hope.

"I took Little Pig through the back gate where the nightsoil cart was waiting. Aunt Ar was there, and took him. She told me they had Eider." A quick glance toward me, and my expression must have reflected the flare of anger that hearing her name brought up, when he rose, looking about, and then dropped to his knees before me.

"Don't," I protested, trying to catch his hands. "Don't—"

"Cousin Eider begged me to make a full bow begging forgiveness if I was to see any of the family again," Koi said.

I tried to stop him, saying, "You did nothing wrong. Please don't bow, please don't."

"Eider is my cousin, and I made a promise," Koi said, laying his hands precisely on the ground, and his forehead to the tops of his fingers. Three times, he bowed, then rose, and as he wiped the sleeve of his robe across his forehead to remove the trace of mud, he added, "She wanted to throw herself in the sea. She tried, but my mother as well as Aunt Ar stopped her. She fought them."

"She is your cousin, and I perhaps ought not to say, but she *spied* on us. And repeated everything she heard," I said bitterly. "As far as I'm concerned, she ought to be in prison with the rest. No, she ought to fling herself into the sea. I'd watch, and not light a single incense stick for her soul. It can wander forever," I added even more bitterly.

"She acted under orders," Koi said evenly, avoiding my gaze. "I won't say she was right or wrong. I'm telling you what she thought. First, that because Second Young Master had made it clear he had not stolen the jade command tally from the first imperial prince, she was certain he'd be perfectly safe. And First Young Master had nothing at all to do with any of it. He only listened, so he would be safe."

"She'd have to know that Cousin Xianti would use anything against us," I retorted.

"But she did not know that," Koi responded. "My cousin is not the cleverest person, but she has a good heart. Surely you know that."

"I'd thought so," I admitted in a surly voice.

"But she also had ambition, and her mother has even more ambition. The Household Department always wants to know what happens inside the palaces. Eider was told to be a listener. There were several."

As my mother had warned me.

Cray said to me, "The Household Department tries to protect the servants as they can. So many went into the imperial palace and only came out lengthwise, wrapped in white. They don't even get a proper burial, unless one of the Household happens to see the cart before they are dumped into the sea."

"True." Koi nodded her way.

"Go on about Eider," I said, falling into the old habit of orders.

"She longed to be promoted to the embroidery department. Every year that passed without that promotion made it more likely that even if it happened, she would be kept in the low ranks, embroidering the same figures over and over on the fronts of ministers' robes, or on the guards' cloaks. To get the training for the highest levels—to do the embroidery for the imperial temples and inner chambers—the training must begin no later than twelve, and this year she's twelve."

I had not known any of that. Further, Koi spoke in a tone not of instruction but of reminder, as if I'd known all of these things, but had forgotten.

But I did not know. Mother had taught me to use my servants kindly, but at the same time I had been trained never to chatter with them, which too quickly turned to gossip. Always dangerous. My maids had chattered in my presence, but they'd never discussed ambitions or hopes before me, I understood now. I'd assumed that they had none, other than being my maids for the rest of our lives.

I looked from one to the other of these two former servants, both older than I, who previously had never been permitted to speak without first having been spoken to. It was quite clear that while most of my life had been visible to them, theirs had been entirely invisible to me. And it had never occurred to me to question that, much as I'd prided myself on my clever questions about other aspects of the world.

With that unsettling sense that I had ignorantly done wrong, I said, "Where is Eider now?"

"She insisted on staying in hiding, though it means living among the chickens most of the time."

I had learned, through tending the Falcons' chickens (a chore I hated almost as much as I had harvesting) that these are very messy birds, though they are amusing to watch.

"She won't leave until a way is found to rescue the Chief Censor's family," Koi said. "I left, though I still had the fever, for I only added danger. I spent a number of days searching for Banti, both Gui and I. That included going to the cold-storage houses behind the city justice courts to check the fresh corpses. He was never among those." Koi rubbed his knees again, then said, "We slept on the beach, or in alleys, or on roofs. We begged at the temples for food. We lived like that, still seeking Second Young Master Banti. I stayed away from the Household Department, but Gui, I found out, has a watcher friend among the scribe servants. He brought news that the first imperial prince had ordered a city-wide house-to-house search for the missing Lan family 'criminals' and anyone associated with them."

Criminals. How I hated hearing that! "My family? Is there any word of them?" I could not quite get out the words *Are they alive?*

I was not even certain I'd wish them alive, if they were being tormented for the entertainment of the imperial grandchildren.

Koi said, "No one among those I know has seen anything of them, but word did come from some connected through the Household to the kitchen staff in the prison: it seems that the first imperial prince had changed his initial orders, to keep them imprisoned until such time as they could stand trial."

"But no trial?"

"Not before I left," Koi responded, looking down at the muddy ground. "Gui said the servants are all convinced that Prince Xianti's afraid of the Cinnabar Princess Vaha, and that the new emperor is afraid to act against the Chief Censor, as all the ministers are angry as bees in a hive under attack."

"New emperor?" I asked.

"Ah, I did not tell you that Grand Prince Yiulo disappeared the night that Prince Koza declared himself emperor."

Grand Prince Yiulo, brother to the former emperor and grandfather to that troublesome Yiuti, was once important in the military. Prince Koza was the next youngest surviving brother to the former Imperial Crown Prince—neither of these men was familiar to me, except as distantly glimpsed figures in fabulously embroidered silk robes, jade, and tassels, at imperial family gatherings.

Koi went on, "Grand Prince Yiulo vanished with his entire family, and a good part of the imperial guard. Word through the Household was, the new emperor was in a rage, and issued orders for purges of all suspected palace spies. That means graywings and servants. The new Crown Prince Xianti ordered a house-to-house search for Prince Yiuti, who'd vanished with his grandfather."

"So the matter of the missing tally no longer matters?"

"No longer," repeated Koi, "as Crown Prince Xianti now commands the imperial guard. What's left of them. Gui told me that the Falcon watchers were sending up the winter stores, and that I could go with them in my guise as baker's laundry girl, to help manage the donkeys. Scout Trogon and I were sent off before the search reached much past the Street of Gongs. Gui remains behind, to stay on watch for Banti."

More questions streamed through my mind, but the sun was almost gone. They noticed, too. Cray said to Koi, "We've got to get you settled in with the boys before nightfall."

She got up and started down the path. Koi, from habit, backed a step away from me, his long hands uncertain, but he caught the bow before making it. Then he followed Cray, his crow-black braids swinging. By the next day, those had transformed to a tidy topknot like the rest of the boys.

But first, the next morning, when those of us in Work cottage woke, I handed the mended, embroidered brown garment to Little Finch, finished the night before. She shook it out, and fingered the tiny yellow jujube blossoms, her eyes widening. "These are so *pretty!* It's like what a *princess* would wear," she breathed.

Too vividly I imagined Siarti's sneer, and Taisa's judicious scorn for my crooked stitches, for I had no proper embroidery frame, and no silk thread, just what I had unpicked from the rag basket. When I blinked away that horrible inward image, I found a couple of the other girls edging toward me, as everyone else looked on, even PanPan.

"Can you do that for me?" one of the girls asked—someone who had never spoken to me once since my arrival.

"I can, and I will," I said, "but there is little extra thread among this valley's supplies. I have to unpick rags, and until I can find a way to dye those threads, which I've never done before, I'd be limited to whatever color the rags are."

The others accepted that with serious looks and went off talking, as Little Finch stroked her new robe proudly. Over the course of the day one or two others approached me to ask about embroidery, and I gave the same answer. After the evening meal, when one of Cray's friends appeared before me, holding out a scrap of deep blue-violet, and said, "Can you make embroidery out of this?" and I responded in the affirmative, she went away and I heard whispering outside the door.

When I emerged, I found a group of four standing in a circle. At my appearance they broke away, except for the one who'd spoken to me. I recognized her as one of the ones who was fiercest with the double-stick. She said quickly, "I'll fetch my robe," and whisked herself off toward Virtue, where the older girls stayed.

I saw Cray coming out with Koi. When they saw me, they approached, and Cray said, "You look lost. It's Koi here who is new!"

Koi glanced at her, and from his manner, I guessed that he was still perturbed by the relaxing of the protocols that had governed our lives so strictly. More was to come; I said, "I guess there is no rule against embroidering things, but some are acting as if they'd never seen it before."

"No," Cray said, "they've seen it, though few know how. It isn't taught, unless someone offers. You could. Mostly they are surprised that you would offer."

"Me?" I repeated. "Why me? That is, I do my best to do my duty and keep quiet, for I don't wish to cause trouble."

Koi and Cray exchanged looks. Koi dropped his gaze, but Cray chuckled. "Ren, I guess you have no notion what you look like to the other Falcons."

"Ignorant, I know," I said, my face heating up. "I'm trying to learn the seeds as quickly as I can."

I was about to mention my practice with Sagacious Blade, when she uttered a short, snorting laugh. "You swan about," she said, "even when you sit down to eat. It's that imperial court glide, the phoenix among the chickens." And when I recoiled, the laughter faded from her face. "It's not an accusation. I've begun to realize you can't help it. All those years of training out in the courtyard. But you don't talk to anyone, and you have that blank face most of the time, so no one knows what you think. You surround yourself with an invisible wall. So you caught the little girls by surprise, making those blossoms on Little Finch's robe."

Thus a painful lesson in learning that the way we perceive ourselves is often not what others see.

TWENTY-ONE

*Proof she was Heaven's Chosen
by effortless mastery of all she surveyed...*

WHEN I WOKE UP on mornings, my breath clouding as I emerged from my cocoon of blankets and the icy world outside glittering coldly, I was glad to have that thick woolen robe and the ugly one beneath it, over my underthings. This valley seemed so much colder than the palace had been, but as the Falcons' invariable cure for chill was to work hard at practice, there was no use in complaining. I was also grateful for thick stockings, and the equally thick woven bamboo shoes that some wore instead of boots. I found that if I warmed my toes before I put them into the socks and shoes, they stayed warm for most of the day, as long as I did not let any snow fall inside my shoes and wet my feet.

There was practice of some sort every day, and when I was free, I found it very soothing to take up Sagacious Blade to do the sword form, which I was getting quite fast at.

The Falcons readied for the turn of the year.

Several wanted embroidery. Three wanted to learn it, two smaller girls and a boy Koi's age. I found myself a teacher in this one thing, instead of always being the last and lowest of students. Tay, the boy, had the artist's eye like Cousin Taisa's. He grasped at once the idea of using stitching to make patterns, and with only three stitches, he made really handsome interwoven patterns along the edges of robes and hems.

New Year's Two Moons arrived.

The celebration again was unlike palace customs, though we all cleaned thoroughly before the year ended in order to scour out the last of the year's bad luck. New signs went up on the door frames, this year sayings related to skill. We lit incense to the Heavens and bowed in all directions. Some prayed and others went out to toast the skies with hot rice wine the moment the moons touched. The feasting was held in Chief Rain's place, as were all meals that could not be eaten on the outside platform. There was singing and dancing, and games. Someone even unearthed a battered Circle board from somewhere, after which Koi and I swept the field, then played one another. He won all three games, to my disgust. He'd learned all Second Brother's extravagant strategies, but he was never wild. He did not spend counters recklessly, thus chiseling relentlessly at my hoarded forces. Against this player, I needed a new strategy, I saw, but I'd only developed the one.

The boys in his cottage whooped and shouted for joy, especially those who had laid wagers, and the girls in my cottage groaned and sighed and rolled their eyes at the boys, especially those who had lost wagers. Though I noticed that Koi's smiles of good nature seemed forced, and I wondered if he was missing Second Brother, too. Every sudden, sweeping move seemed to evoke his laughing presence.

It was very late when we all shuffled (or staggered) off to bed.

After that, for the first five days, no one swept, lest we sweep out any good luck that had been drawn in with the year turning.

On the sixth day of the new year, after we cleaned out the kitchen god's hearth and laid it anew, Grandfather Healer tapped the shoulders of the two girls I'd taught to embroider, then he came to me. "You three and young Tay have learned to ply needles with precision, I'm told," he rumbled. "Come learn something about healing with needles. I will need an apprentice one day, and even if it is none of you, the others you travel with can always use even simple healer skills."

With that, he took us to his little hut, which was appended to Chief Rain's house, and sat us down before a drawing of the human body. All the meridians had been sketched, with their names, and the important clusters.

We stared, too intimidated to speak. But the longer I stared, the more I realized I knew what would come next. I was familiar with them all: an unpleasant flash of memory accompanied this awareness, my skin sensitive to the touch, my muscles aching, as I'd struggled with the dreams.

We were told to memorize the names of the fourteen meridian channels, and a single point along each, by morning. Then we had to go to our other practices.

That night, Tay joined the three of us girls in crouching over the old, crackling drawing. The more I looked, the more I recollected, though I was afraid to say anything until I was certain.

The next day, Grandfather Healer summoned us, and the others did their best. Hua identified eight meridians, and five or six points. Tiger Moth, a year older than I, successfully named twelve, Tay thirteen, faltering on the second heel vessel. I began timidly, but as Grandfather Healer pointed to each meridian, there was its name in my mind, and I spoke them with increasing steadiness as he passed from those to nerve clusters, and thence to specific points.

He finally stopped, and put his head to one side, mirth in those dark eyes under his frosty white brows. "Modesty is all very well, Ren, but you might have informed us you've been tutored."

What could I say, that it was buried in fever dreams? "I was afraid I remembered wrong," I said, bowing in apology before I caught myself.

"Do you wish to become a healer?" he asked.

"I don't know, Grandfather Healer," I admitted.

He laughed a little. "There is time, there is time. But we will have to study apart from these learners."

Hua, the one who only had achieved eight, said, "I don't think I want to learn this. It's too hard, and I want to do more embroidery."

Tiger Moth, the other girl, remained silent, but as soon as Grandfather Healer dismissed us, she said abruptly to me, "Will you practice with me?"

Tay flashed a grin. "I was going to say the same."

By now I'd come to understand that what I took as indifference in others, or even aloofness, could be uncertainty or shyness. I assured them both that we could figure out how to study together—something very new for me, but which Second Brother could have taught me. Ah, would I never cease getting that stab of grief and regret and fury whenever I thought of him?

The three of us began meeting at night, sitting near the cottage door, as boys were not allowed in Work. We recited, one or another tapping their body until PanPan insisted Tay go away and we put out the lamps and sleep. Tiger Moth had dropped embroidery for this new thing. I found I could stitch and study; going over the points with them reinforced what I had been given in the dreams, though I found that—like Second Brother—I remembered what I'd heard.

I now had to learn what each meridian and its corollaries controlled with respect to the five essences and four elements, and as we were martial artists, along with lessons in freeing meridians came lessons in disrupting the harmonious whole: various poisons and how to counter them.

This in turn loosened the bindings of my third fever memory: hand to hand grappling. Each memory stemmed from an expert who had wielded Sagacious Blade, I had begun to realize. The sword master had been a man. So, too, the healer. But the grappling expert had been a woman, her accent very garbled the way they spoke in the far north. The trend of her lessons was escape for a small woman; she emphasized using her thumbs or knuckles at certain spots, which I recognized as meridian clusters. If pressed hard enough, these froze an opponent, though a needle was better.

And Essence affected it all.

Grappling was the winter sport when even the hardiest could not practice outside. We unrolled mats stuffed with old armor quilting over the floor in the great dining hall, and Chief Rain and one of the men, named Bem the Horse, oversaw the hand-to-hand combat. He taught the art of the fist, and she taught the art of the fan. Which Cray had given me the basics of, so for once I was not the lowest in that. As for the fist, my use of pressure points made my opponents wary, though I was terrible at the actual fighting.

Afternoons were for sparring or for other pursuits. Grandfather Healer continued to teach the three of us. One blizzardy day he set down his precious, worn book of herbs and medicines. "There is an old scroll called *The Five Essences*," he said. "I am primarily an herbalist. I understand the essences of the human body, and how to correct them, but detecting Essence in its pure form is not given to me, so I did not pursue studies in that direction. My Herbal is my guide." He patted his book, the work of a lifetime. "However, I would not be a good teacher unless I recited *The Five Essences* introduction, which we had to learn by heart. *The divine world is connected to the world of living things. If a seeker understands the affinities between stone, fire, tree, water, metal, and the sixth being the stars, the seeker begins to perceive that the world is not chaotic, but ordered in patterns. Comprehending the events of the stars reveals clear connections between all the living things of Earth, visible and invisible. To reach harmony, the seeker must understand balance as well as affinity, the equal pull between all things.*"

He stopped to regard us. Tiger Moth's gaze had wandered to the chart of herb categories. Tay picked absently at a scab on his hand from a small cut gotten in a practice scrap.

Visible and invisible. My head reverberated as though an invisible gong had been rung inside it.

Grandfather Healer gave a quiet laugh, and said, "It seems the three of you are much like me. Perhaps it is well."

I understood then that I had hidden my reaction without meaning to. How to express what I felt? These words had granted me a single glimpse of the way everything was tied together. Everything, from these lessons, to the striving of defense and offense, to the design of an embroidered screen as I caught an echo of Cousin Taisa's dry voice. I turned to Grandfather Healer, who was already moving on to the properties of ginseng. He had just said that he had little more to teach about the invisible world: that of Essence.

When we left that day, racing from eave to eave to escape the sleet, Tay shrugged off Grandfather Healer's *Five Essences*, saying, "What's the use in theories? I don't see Essence, I don't feel it."

"Nor I," Tiger Moth said. "Whereas I can see, and feel, a difference if I place my needle correctly."

More and more as winter prisoned the valley, my interest strayed toward the puzzling, vexing, fascinating realm of Essence, whereas Tay's attention shifted toward herbs and medicines, and Tiger Moth toward healing the ills of the body.

My problem was a sense of vertigo, as if one eye saw one thing and the other saw something else. I could not quite reconcile it all. But by now I was so very used to being the ignorant beginner in each new thing, with yet a new upward path to climb, that I considered resolving this double vision as yet another mountain.

By midway through the second month, Tay and Tiger

Moth were so enthusiastic that they wanted to forge ahead of Grandfather Healer's very slow, repetitive pace. I was used to repetition from years of lessons in Kanda's thoughts and ways, in which repetition, shaped by the elegant balance of a point reframed two ways, drove home the lesson. This plus that sense that a cloud of Essence was *there*, just out of reach, made me lag behind the others in putting it all together effectively.

We practiced on ourselves before we practiced on one another. These experiments often produced weird effects, like being stung by invisible insects, but sometimes it hurt sharply if we were wrong, and on one horrible occasion, Tay's eyes rolled right up and he passed out when Tiger Moth ventured to sedate him by draining his Metal vitality through Earth points.

Tiger Moth and I did not breathe until he stirred, turned green, and we got a pan under him just in time before he lost his last meal.

"Aie! That was...not the right acupoint," he said, rubbing his chest through his clothes.

"No more experimenting ahead," we all agreed fervently — a secret relief to me, the slowest.

More time passed, then the upper slopes began to thaw, and for a time everywhere water dripped, trickled, rushed and tumbled, as snow gave way to rain. Sentinels once again climbed the promontories to watch the various roads in the distance—and right about the time the first travelers of the year were reported, the people in the tiny, hidden hut villages farther up the mountain came down, many needing supplies after being sequestered over winter. Some were young couples, bringing new babies to introduce to the community; I'd learned without much interest that when the valley gallant wanderers paired off, they were offered a winter up in these cottages. Most of the permanent residents in those tiny high villages were weavers, bringing good woolen cloth from the sheep that roamed the slopes during summer. This cloth was shared out to make new winter clothing.

Presently I woke up with the smell of spring in the air wafting through the open windows in our cottage. The day came when I sat up on a clear, starlit spring morning, aware that I was now fourteen. I told no one. I'd seen by now that birthdays were mainly matters for families or for lovers or for shield brothers and sisters, little gifts made by the givers. It seemed less awkward not to say anything.

Instead, I began, for the first time, to think of the season ahead, then the year ahead…and beyond.

The light was still dim, the rising sun beyond the white-topped mountain to the east. I dressed swiftly, took my sword, and slipped out. Once I reached my grove, I sat on a boulder with the sword across my knees, and laid my hand on it.

"Grandmother Zim?" I asked. "Are you there? Why did you choose me?"

"You are ready to ask me that, my Bu? It is well. It is well."

"Thank you, I am grateful," I said, bowing, though I was not at all certain she would know that. It is often said that swords do not have eyes. Does that not include charmed swords?

"I sought a Bu who touched me with no greed in heart and mind, and no burning anger. But with that deep pool of ambition, as had my own Bu."

Second Brother had no greed in heart and mind, that I was confident about. If he'd had burning anger, it was so well hidden that I never saw a hint of it. But…

"Ambition?" I repeated. "I must confess I don't have ambition."

"The pool is there. Ayah, a lake! But you've yet to bend to drink."

"Oh." That was a relief—something that would come with age. I was not aware of any ambition, except to stay alive. And to free my family, if it was at all possible, but mostly that urge was compounded by frustration at my helplessness.

"But you must in the fullness of time do something for me," Granny Zim said.

"What is it?"

"You will take me to the mountain."

"Which mountain?"

"Where YinYin dwells."

"YinYin?"

"In the fullness of time, my Bu. In the fullness of time."

And I sensed a silence in that strange place behind my ear. I was far too intimidated—and too respectful of my elders—to demand she remain to answer my questions. Oh, *so* many questions. It was clear enough that I must find them out for myself. And that had to begin with unraveling, much as I teased apart the threads in rags, those dreams she had given me.

My sword form, I knew, was ready for testing. This testing

would begin as soon as the practice field dried again. But there were those other dreams.

The last snowmelt held, and the youngest of the children ran out each morning, shrilling with vigor, to test the practice field. At last this was deemed dry enough, with a fuzz of green sprouts along the perimeter. That initiated a complexity of tests and new groupings and new lessons. Some of us beginners were told that we were going to practice with steel for the first time, so those who had been given swords were to bring them.

It was time for Sagacious Blade to make an appearance. I cleaned off all the stains and accretions that had dulled the hilt, and polished the blade until the bronze shone richly. Tall PanPan, who had taken from her shelf a sword handed down from someone in her family, proudly buffed its plain sheath with the edge of her sleeve, then glanced at the old, cracked sheath that housed Sagacious Blade. But when she saw the blade in my hands, she whooped in surprise.

"I thought yours was an old foot warrior blade, from the dirty hilt and that old sheath. But that stone in the hilt—and those scales! *Where* did *that* come from? It looks like something from either a king or a pirate."

Everyone in Work paused in dressing and readying to stare from her to me to the sword in my hands. PanPan's exclamation revealed to me that while some, such as Chief Rain, and also Cray, knew Sagacious Blade's history, not everyone did. I could tell that history, except that it was connected to the Gu family.

Gossip, for most of my life, had been the great enemy. I'd since learned that there were worse enemies, but old teaching still had its grip on me, and I thought immediately of rumors flying about once people began traveling again. Would word of this blade—that someone had been searching for—connect to my family, and thus bring danger to the Falcons?

A secret only remained a secret if no one knew it.

Or if it was disguised.

Therefore I'd lie, as a way of keeping them all safe, without anyone having the burden of a secret.

I reached for a likely animal with scales. "This is my pangolin blade," I said.

"Pangolin!"

"Is there demon blood in your family?" someone else asked.

"That's a terrible thing to say," began PanPan.

"No, I meant only in the way Sun has, that her father could turn into a crane. Only demons, the good demons, can take the shapes of animals. And humans." Sun was one of the older girls, a slim, graceful person who rarely talked, but she had lightning reflexes.

"Oh-h-h," said the youngest ones.

PanPan pursed her lips skeptically. "I'll believe Sun can be a crane if I *see* it. But of course there are good demons," she hastened to add, with a quick look upward and out the window, while making a warding sign. And when nothing happened, "You just don't hear about them much. The way you don't hear about all good people in the world, only the wicked." She turned to me, her expression earnest under winged brows. "Is that true? Your pangolins are good demons?"

I considered her words, relieved that she had not said the word 'family'. Though it was implied. This implied lie hurts no one, I thought rapidly, and I clasped my hands in the gallant wanderer salute, as I couldn't quite bring myself to say yes.

By then everyone was ready. We ran out in a group, and assembled in our rows. I went straight to the back, as always.

The instructor, the same Master Sima whom Little Finch and the other youths venerated for his heroism, called, "Let's warm up with Seed One."

We warmed up through the seeds, and then he said, "Now, show me what you've practiced, or didn't practice, over winter. Give me your latest form." A few groaned. More laughed.

The older, skilled Falcons were first. I watched carefully, recognizing my own form done by the second person. I listened as Master Sima corrected the line of the boy's arm in one stance, and whacked a hip back into alignment with the flat of his blade. Otherwise, it matched what I had been doing.

Down through the ranks until the youngsters in my group did their shorter forms, then it was my turn. My heart thundered against my ribs, and I had to pause and breathe calm through myself before I walked to the center of the practice field. I took up my stance, leveled Sagacious Blade, and swung and slashed through the long form that I had learned through that unknown teacher whose memories Grandmother Zim had offered me. Sagacious Blade hummed in my hand as I whirled through the form, the tails of my robe snapping.

When I finished, returning to my starting position, point down, I thought happily that the blade was no longer heavy or a strain. It felt more like an extension of my arm.

Only everyone was staring.

Master Sima stepped in front of me, bent to put his hands on his knees, and peered humorously into my face. "No one told me we had an apprentice from Sky Island here," he said, straightening up and addressing the others. "That is pure Ze Bek form. Really pure. I can almost see his bald head from the drawings in the ancient manual," he exclaimed, and the others laughed, but it was not cruel laughter. It was appreciation, and amazement. "Did you cultivate with the disciples of Ze Bek, Young Ren?"

Hua, eleven years old, piped up, "Ren is from *pangolins!* See the pangolin scales on her sword?"

"My teacher was Granny Zim," I said quickly. While it was fine if the others were busy putting together a history for me, I realized I'd have to remember it. Better to stick close to the truth. "Then things happened, and, well, it's the only form I know."

"And you hid it until you were sure of yourself among us," Master Sima said. He was a tall, rangy martial artist, his thinning hair worn up high in a tail. "That is prudent. So, young Ren, you trust us now?" He chuckled. "As it happens, with that form learned, you really don't need the others. It's an excellent foundation. You really ought to be sparring before you start on the more arcane forms."

"Sparring?" I repeated, appalled.

He squinted at me. "Let's show you what the form is for, and incidentally give the others a treat. Go through the form again. I'm going to mirror it."

I began again, my heart beating rapidly. He began the form a few steps away; when I lunged he blocked, tapping lightly enough to sting my hand through my grip on Sagacious Blade. I regripped the hilt, and then it was my turn—there was his blade coming at me, but my arm came down in the long-practiced block, and whirled toward his neck. Clang! Feint—

lunge—stab—clash! I began to understand the rhythm, and so, when he said, "Again! This time, with some force," I put my entire body into it, until the effect of the crashing blades reverberated down my arm to my body, thence to my planted foot.

It was exhilarating, and demanding on my joints. I also understood why most wore headbands, as sweat ran down my forehead to sting my eyes.

He stopped, then said, "I think for you, taking the form apart in pieces, and working on the alternative attacks and retreats as well as plenty of sparring, will get you caught up with your peers. Even put you well into competition. If you work at it."

Then it was the turn of the last two ten-year-olds, while I stood by in a daze, considering all that I had just learned. My hands throbbed a bit from the new experience of hard contact with weapons, but Master Sima had skillfully limited the strength of his blows. I must get more strengthening, I mused, absently rubbing at my lower belly, which had been rumbling uneasily since I woke. I'd assumed it was nerves, as there was no bad taste in my mouth, which would come of eating something that disagreed with my digestion.

I thought, still, I must get to the privy, when I discovered a very uncomfortable sensation down there; the gong for midday rang then, and everyone began to disperse for the meal, as Sima finished evaluating the last of the children.

I ran for the privy, Sagacious Blade still clasped in my hand. When I got there, I discovered a stain of red in my underclothes. Shock rang through me. I knew what it was. Mother had explained what was to come when I turned ten. But I'd always thought that she would be there when it finally happened.

"Ayah," said Grandmother Zim behind my head. "This Bu is a girl? Bodies, bodies, bodies. You've enough Essence to ward the Phoenix moon time comfortably, my Bu."

"I thought I was supposed to drink ginseng and willow bark tea," I whispered. And get soft pads. No, there were no servants. I'd have to make one, no, two, at least. "Oh-h-h-h."

Another girl on the other side of the low modesty panel said, "What?"

"Nothing," I yelped—as Granny Zim said, "That is the usual remedy for the cramps, but one of my Bu girls understood matters of Essence. I learned so much from her!

You have so much Essence within you, the talisman charm will be far more comfortable..."

Granny Zim's long-ago "Bu" spoke a charm that I was to perform with a talisman sign, an image of her long-ago hand sketching it out. And that was how I learned that I did truly have an Essence talent, though I still was unable to do anything much with it. Maybe it came with age, I thought as I left. At least I had this new method to deal with the moon blood that was far better than ginseng and bitter tea and washing pads.

After the meal I was summoned to begin sparring.

I hated it.

Sparring, at least for a beginner, is the very opposite of order. The beauty and strength of the forms I had practiced were deeply satisfying in part because I knew them so well. The problem was, though my arms and legs had been trained to respond in the correct manner, that knowledge was always a heartbeat too late when I perceived a weapon doing its best to stab me in various places. My defense was always late, wild, and ineffective.

Which *hurt*.

Small cuts and bruises were a regular thing among the others, that I had already seen. It was now my turn to experience them, and I loathed it. I kept wanting to put down the weapon and use reason whenever I faced a sparring partner. My lips shaped words, and I had to smother that instinct and pay attention to my blade. The only time that instinct proved useful was for distracting an opponent. A fair tactic, though it usually only worked once, if at all.

My knowledge, the skilled warriors explained in their various ways, was lopsided. I ought to have learned that form while practicing each of its moves over and over in sparring bouts. Now I had to catch up.

And so the days sped by, mornings and early afternoons taken up with sword, staff, archery (I was dreadful there), double-stick, and hand-to-hand grappling. Afternoons with Grandfather Healer. Some days we spent roaming the hillsides in the balmy spring breezes, bent over as we searched for and identified wild herbs that could be used to counter various ailments or poultice wounds. Then Tiger Moth and I chanted the long lists of meridians and herb specifics, as I did my share of the mending, and embroidered when someone wanted something, and had located some thread.

I knew it might be useful someday, but Tiger Moth's whole face shone with her enthusiasm, and I invariably wanted to quit long before she did. I yearned for books to read. Even old scrolls. But books there were few in the valley, and paper very scarce. There was only the herbal, which I studied with a ferocious intensity.

My only break in the measure of those days was when I was teamed with another my age to climb up to one of the promontories to watch the roads for a day. The rule was, until you turned eighteen, you watched in twos. Cray was my partner my first time. We had to rise before dawn, and toil up a narrow path to a high cliff, and sit screened by flowering wild roses. We carried food for the day in a basket, and there was a waterfall nearby, though the water was icy.

A spectacular vista lit gradually as the sun rose, the greens of spring contrasted with the wind-scattered last peach blossoms, and clumps of early bright pink peonies. I discovered that I did not like heights when I tried leaning out to see directly below.

I sat back, keeping my gaze on the distance and the winding roads as I mentally reviewed Grandfather Healer's latest lessons from his herbal. We had a slate and chalk for keeping track of travelers going either way. Cray kept that. I could see her drawing, but at first she wouldn't let me see what she made before she scribbled it out, glanced my way a time or two, then started over.

We did not talk much, but the silence was companionable enough. The sun rose, diminishing the shadows. They had shrunk to puddles beneath the tree branches overhead when Cray started up to her feet, peering under her hand toward the south. "I think I saw someone," she said, leaning out as if that little bit would get her closer to the unknown travelers.

I began to scramble to my feet, catching sight of the slate and the chalk that she had cast aside. I glanced down, surprised to see…me. No, it was sort of me, but the nose was wrong, the neck too thick. It looked more like Second Brother, really. Was she missing him, too? I had not known they had broken the family rule and become friends, but then he made friends with so many people.

I decided to let her talk about it or not as I tried to peer beyond the haze. The dot gradually split into two, then resolved into a pair of travelers, both with packs on their backs, one walking with a staff. They disappeared beyond the ridge, and a while later appeared again on the curving fold of road that followed one of the lower hills along the river. They vanished again, then reappeared far below as the shadows lengthened.

We watched them wade into the shallows of the river, then climb out and continue on, until they were gone altogether, and Cray turned away, silent, drooping. Who'd said her mother was in a faraway island? She was watching for her mother to return.

When I glanced next at the slate, there was nothing but a smear, except for a "2" and the word "peddlers."

When the sun rimmed the western mountains, we began our climb down. Ought I to say anything? Her manner was so very closed in. Oh, I was still so ignorant about what to say to people outside of ritual! I decided that since she had said nothing, it would be intrusive to put questions, and thrust sympathy on her that she had not indicated she wanted.

When we got to the valley, I offered to take the slate to the chief, and Cray ran off into the darkness.

TWENTY-TWO

She walked in the footprints of far-off times,
her lofty thoughts on tales of glory…

THE FOLLOWING DAY, CRAY behaved in her accustomed calm, silent manner, making me wonder if I had imagined those emotions just because I was feeling them. Reminders of my family were akin to the blows in sparring when I was too slow or made a false move. No, more akin to a needle in the wrong spot; Grandfather Healer permitted Tiger Moth to try the needles, but only in certain acupoints that would cause no distress if the needle was not correctly placed. Tay and I, he said, still needed more time.

I was content with that. The needles intimidated me, whereas using a knuckle or thumb was far less alarming. And my interests pulled me in another direction, though there was scarce time to ponder that, as my days were busy with training, sparring, and mending, in addition to taking my turn at weeding, harvesting vegetables, and serving at one of the watch posts.

Competition day! The girls in Work had anticipated these endlessly. My bouts were over fairly early. I was promoted beyond the beginners to the lowest rank of the middle. Cray remained a step ahead of me in all the martial arts. Koi was promoted to the bottom of the highest group in hand-to-hand fighting and in double-stick, and well in the middle of the older teens with all the others, which was visual proof of all the practice my brothers had had. They'd just never talked about it in our family, where only scholarship was prized.

The days sped by, the only change being that PanPan was told she would move to another cottage with the older girls come the new year, and the woman in charge of the kitchen would be adding her ten-year-old daughter to Work cottage. This got me to consider the question of my future. I could not think past my family unjustly imprisoned. I knew I could do nothing, but my sense of duty cried against that very frequently, especially in dreams.

There arrived a summer day when someone shouted from the ridge, "Two spotted from the south!"

Those words sailed through the open windows of Grandfather Healer's hut, but it would never do to interrupt him lecturing on the properties of stingflower. Once the lesson finished, I slipped out to find Cray and Koi coming from different directions.

"It's Watcher," fluted a small child, running downhill. "With a grandmother!"

The impossible remained impossible—it was not Second Brother.

I made myself turn away, for I was supposed to be wiping down the mats and airing them in the midday sun. News would be told to everyone, I reminded myself. There was no hurry. I saw Koi going with lagging steps off to where the young men were passing out the staffs. Cray had vanished entirely.

We'd almost finished dragging the mats out to air when Little Finch bolted from the main wing, "Ren! Chief Rain wants you." She ran back to the kitchen.

My heart crowded my throat as I started up, then looking toward the leader of the work party. She waved a hand, releasing me, and I shot across the courtyard to the door, slid my shoes off, and advanced…to discover Chief Rain sitting with another white-haired woman.

The interior was dim after the bright sunshine of outside, but there was something familiar about that small, upright figure next to the chief. Recognition lanced through me. She was Mother's grandmother, the one who had spoken to me about Sagacious Blade so long ago!

"Shut the door, child," Chief Rain said. "I think this conversation is best held without interruption."

I sprang to do so, and as I sat down, the chief turned her head to sweep her single eye over me, then smiled. "You see, Sister Ou? She flourishes."

"I do, Sister Rain. You make me very happy indeed. Come here, Renti. No, you are Ren, at present. It will do. Sit beside me. I once told your mother to send you up here one day. I regret how it came about. Ayoh! You are getting tall and strong. What are you learning?"

I described my typical day, then bowed from my seat, saying, "Great-grandmother Ou—"

"Granny Ou will do, child. I am proud of being a granny. Great-Grandmother is a mouthful, and smacks of court perfumes."

"Granny Ou, may this anxious daughter ask if my honored ancestor brings any news from the capital about my mother?"

Chief Rain sniffed. "You see, we still have not trained the court out of her."

Granny Ou leaned back as she chuckled. "It's to be expected. One year here to ten or twelve years in that stifling atmosphere."

Thirteen, I thought, but all thirteen of those years constrained me from correcting an elder.

"How is the experiment going?" she added.

"Well enough," Chief Rain said. "It's to be expected. The boys and men we brought into the Falcons all being our own brothers and sons, or friends of same."

Granny Ou gave a grunt. "I did not believe having men join the Falcons would do us any good, but from what I saw on my walk in, things have not changed greatly."

"Everything changes." Though Chief Rain chuckled, I sensed resignation.

"True, sister, true."

"But these men understand that the Falcons will always have a woman as chief, and if they accept that, they are welcome to contribute. And they do contribute. Sima and Ho brought their skills to sharpen ours. *That* is a constant labor," Chief Rain said, lifting her voice to cheer again. "The best sword in the world still requires the occasional application of the whetstone."

"Speaking of swords," Granny Ou said, turning to me. "I trust you have been training with Sagacious Blade?"

"Yes," I said. "I think Grandmother Zim likes my being here in the valley. The sword hums, sometimes, when I am exercising."

"Granny Zim?"

"That's who is in the sword."

"So it does talk to you! Has it taught you to fly?"

"Fly?" I repeated, astounded.

"The stories about it were consistent: it spoke, though only the wielder could hear, and it has the charm for flying on it."

I was about to deny that, but from my memory of the fever dreams arose that strange, unsettling, vivid sense of being in the air. A sense that I loathed; I did not even like sentinel duty up on the cliff.

"I can't fly," I said.

"Hmmm." Her brows drew down. "Perhaps the Essence is fading. It's to be expected, I suppose. That sword is very old. Have you told others about it?"

"No," I said.

Chief Rain gestured toward me. "She made up a history for it. It's known as the pangolin sword."

Granny Ou hmmmed again, considering me. "That seems a clever lie. Not a family trait," she observed.

This was more neutrally said than scoldingly, but I was so very much my parents' daughter that a sense of blame dealt a blow to my heart, and fire burned up into my face. "I...I let the others make up the story. Though I did say that the scales were pangolin scales, and implied that we had—"

"Demon blood," Chief Rain stated. "I thought it well done. Any snip of gossip that escapes, and you know it will..."

"I see," Granny Ou said. "Yes, I agree. If that sword is thought to have pangolin scales, rather than dragon scales, it becomes less interesting. Referring to dragons is rarely good for anyone but kings and emperors and those who want to flatter them. Ay! The demon blood is true enough," Granny Ou added calmly, taking me very much by surprise. "Much as my prudent, orderly granddaughter wished to deny it. It is not in the Gu family at all. It is in ours, daughter to daughter. A point of pride with my own grandmother. But your mother's way of addressing change was always to cling to what she perceived as order."

Here at last was my opening to put my question again. Though I knew she did not want courtly talk, I could find no other way to draw the conversation back to what I craved most. "This anxious daughter hopes that there might be news of her mother..."

Granny Ou looked away through the window as she rubbed gnarled hands. "There is, though I expect you will not like hearing it. No, no, they are still alive. That cold snake Koza is too shrewd to take steps against them. He knows that he cannot keep news from leaking, especially after that wretch of a nephew paraded them so publicly before all the court before prisoning them on specious charges last year. Koza does not want Governor Gu coming over the mountains with his entire army, which he knows would happen if someone kills his favorite daughter."

Favorite daughter?

Granny Ou studied me. "How old are you, exactly?"

"Fourteen."

"Mph. A year after I first took to the wander. Though we had to. But I learned. And survived."

At that moment, someone tapped at the door, and Granny Ou rose with a grunt of effort. "Don't send them off, Sister Rain. I'll take her away to talk. Ay! It's been a very long road. But though the tree wants rest, the wind never stops. Come along, my girl."

"Should I get Cray?" I had remembered that Cray was also related to Granny Ou.

"I just finished speaking to her before we sent for you," was the answer—and there was the jolt. I had no rank! I must not expect to be told first. Granny Ou went on, "I brought her paper, and she's no doubt off scribbling until it's time to leave."

"Leave? You and—"

"Fourth Grandniece, that is, Cray, and you. And I think I had better take that boy who was raised with your mother's second boy."

"Koi?"

"That's the one. The fact is, that nephew of Koja's, what was his name, Xianti, that was it! He's on his way north with half an army."

"North—here?"

"Not here specifically, I trust. But there is no doubt that at least some of them will pass through, because he is sweeping the island for the grand prince's boy in your generation—"

"Yiuti?"

"That's the one. The matter is, this wretched Xianti will no doubt be on the watch, and you children all have that Lan jaw. You and young Banti got your mother's eyes with that heavy eyelash fringe. Distinctive family features both. Ay, my girl, you will never be pretty, not with that Lan jaw and that thin mouth, but you'll be handsome until you're older than I am. More to the point, that white-eyed wolf Xianti would know you at a glance even if it was midnight on Ghost Night. Aye! I took one look at you just now, in that room kept dim as night to preserve Rain's one good eye, and it was your father I saw, until you turned your head, and there was your mother's profile. No doubt he knows that boy of Banti's, Koi? Koi, by sight, as well. They have to be a week behind me, but even so, I told Rain not to be caught napping. Scouts can range days ahead, especially on a search."

"What happened? Why is he searching?"

"I expect the true reason is to get rid of him for a time, but Koja is also worried, because he knows the grand prince has painted a target on his back. Ay! The more I think about it, the more I expect scouts to be beating every tree between the palace and the mountains, and beyond, to see if any dates fall. If I know my Sword-Sister Rain, she will have this valley turned into a sheep farm by Ghost Night."

The fifteenth day of the sixth month, the first night the moons are farthest apart—four days off! "A sheep farm?"

"It is how the Falcons hid in plain sight for generations, when necessary. Those ladders for repairing the roofs? Turn them on their sides, get them into the ground, and the practice field we all sweated on as girls makes a sheep pen. She'll have girls running up the mountain right now to round up a flock for the pen. And all the boys are probably packing now, to go over the hill to the monastery to join the monks for the summer, which will keep them out of being forced into that wretch's army." She spat onto the dusty ground. "That's why we brought in the boys in the first place. Once that fool of an emperor got rid of the last of the old military families, making the way for the bullies and honey-tongues who wanted to climb by being generals, there went the old traditions of army life."

We had gone out the back door to the kitchen garden. On coming around the side of the building, we discovered the entire valley busy as a hive that's been struck by a stick. Granny Ou told me to fetch my things and meet her right on that spot.

I ran to Work, to find Tiger Moth stitching madly. "We just heard your grandmother came to fetch you. There you are," she wailed, and then sighed. "Can't be helped. Here." Two last, rapid stitches, then she bit off her thread.

With both hands, she held out a hemp-woven…harness. A sword harness, I realized when I looked at it wonderingly. At one end was embroidered an oddly shaped animal.

Tiger Moth said shyly, "I meant to embroider pangolins all across, but this was to be a gift for next spring. You know how slow I am at embroidery now." She shifted from foot to foot, eyeing me uncertainly.

I realized I was staring. "Tiger Moth, this is so kind! So generous…I don't know what to say! I've never had a gift before. I mean, from outside my family."

She blushed dark red, but I sensed she was pleased. "You taught me to embroider. Then you've been helping us. Tay and me, I mean. Though we can tell you aren't really wanting to be a healer."

"It—I—don't have a gift for you," I exclaimed in dismay.

"Don't you see? Every day you've given us a gift. This is my return." She jerked up her hands in the gallant wanderer bow, and then hastened out the door.

"Don't fret. She's shy. Always has been. They'll put her to work fast enough. Here, let's show you how this works," PanPan said practically. "Have you ever worn a sword harness? No? I thought not."

With some shrugging and tugging and adjusting, we got the harness set over my shoulders, so that Sagacious Blade rested against my back, in reach of my right hand.

"You'll have to practice pulling it from that angle. But you'll get it. And you'll even learn to resheath it without stabbing yourself. Just remember to practice twenty times on rising and before you sleep. And when you have a moment. Also good for the arms."

"Good luck," Little Finch said, the other girls echoing.

I packed up my things, then Koi, Cray, and I met Granny Ou at Chief Rain's building. Granny Ou wore a broad straw sun hat, even broader than the ones Cray and I still had from our journey last year.

We made our bows, and Chief Rain said, "We always tell our wanderers before they depart about the Falcon markings, if you find yourself in a city, without wherewithal."

Cray didn't look surprised, but Koi mirrored my own puzzlement.

"I'll instruct them on the road," Granny Ou said.

Chief Rain clasped her hands to Granny Ou, and we began our journey, Granny Ou using her walking stick as we climbed the back path up through the wild mulberry and hemp, toward the northern ridge. I stopped once to glance back. Everyone was busy, no one paying any attention to us. That was the gallant wanderer way, coming and going freely, so very different from the deliberate pageantry of court, and being watched and evaluated at all times.

It was warm, and getting warmer, especially as we snaked our way single file up the goat and sheep trails. But eventually there was a welcome downward slope, with water at the bottom of it. When we stopped to drink, and refill our flasks, I said to Granny Ou, "What did Chief Rain mean by Falcon markings?"

Granny Ou smiled at Cray. "Can you tell them?"

Cray's chin lifted proudly. By now I knew who among those in the valley regarded the Falcons as family, aside from blood relation. Cray was one.

"The Falcons are very old. They began as nuns following Suanek. They learned to defend themselves and their temple, though some say it was girls sold as entertainers who ran away together, then joined the temple."

"Good enough," said Granny Ou. "Go on."

"There are many branches. They all vow to save women and those who cannot help themselves. The seeds include using the fan as a weapon, though there are a couple of sects, women all, who also fight with fans."

"Assassins," Koi said. "I heard that the Falcons were assassins."

"They were not assassins," Cray retorted, sending him a cold look.

Both turned to Granny Ou, who said calmly, "There was a branch who did hire themselves out as assassins, specifically targeting evil men who beat their wives to death, or did other such terrible things. But that branch was eventually disavowed when they got involved in imperial politics. Go on to the wings."

Cray shot another glance at Koi, as if waiting for argument, but he merely walked along, peering northward. She said, "In many cities there might be a place, usually some sort of inn. It'll have some reference to birds in its name, and on the wall left of the door, low down, a scratched wing sign." She sketched an arc with three slanting lines coming down from it.

"If you see that, it means that a Falcon watcher or scout is in residence. You'll need to have something with the same sign if you go to one and want to stay without paying, and to hear any Falcon news."

Here, Cray turned over the bottom corner of her summer tunic, disclosing an embroidered arc with the three lines. "It can be scratched, or drawn, or carved. The watcher sees it, knows you for a Falcon. You can stay, and you'll hear Falcon news."

"Try to reserve this privilege for times when you have no other wherewithal," Granny Ou said. "Otherwise, well done, grandniece." She said to Koi and me, "If you decide to claim kinship with the Falcons by using the wing sign, that means abiding by Falcon rules. There aren't many besides what is sensible: you keep to yourself what you're told, unless carrying a message, and if they ask you to work, you do what's asked in return for shelter and food."

Koi said, "I noticed no one has a tattoo." His eyes strayed to my sword in its harness, but he did not ask.

Granny Ou said, "Our grandmother ancestors' view was, such things are necessary for men. Women do not generally require the letting of blood to bind one to her word. There is enough blood-letting in the world." She chuckled. "Go ahead. Say it: it sounds arrogant."

Red stained the ridges of Koi's cheeks, but he did not deny that she had summed up his reaction.

"Consider this. In fights, everything else being equal, it's usually the biggest and strongest who prevails. The biggest is very seldom the woman. Also, while history is packed with scrolls about wars between men, I invite you to find one in which women go marauding just to be marauding. When women fight, it has usually been because it's that or annihilation."

"I'm not arguing about that," Koi said. "My mother said much the same. She also had a lot to say about sects. My aunt, too. Though," he said in haste, "I didn't find what they warned about here." He gestured back toward the valley.

"If you remain long enough, you'll probably find Falcons who are arrogant, secretive, and everything else that you've been warned about," Granny Ou said, thumping her walking stick into the dust. "Generally speaking, the Falcons resolve matters among themselves by avoiding one who has proved untrustworthy. Word spreads fast."

She pointed the stick northward, and we peered through the late afternoon haze toward the river, which lay gray and gleaming like an unsheathed sword in the distance. Straw hats bobbed about, tiny dots of yellow, along the undulating rows of rice paddies alongside a great bend in the river. "We've done well for a first day. I suggest we camp up here. We won't need a fire, so no need to hide. We'll face a somewhat treacherous descent with morning light. It is going to get very steep, which is why travelers don't come this way. But it cuts as much as three days off the journey by the trade road."

She spied a leaf-sheltered knoll before we did, a spot near a little fall from a rocky outcropping that fed the wild mulberry growing all over. It was good to slide the harness off my shoulders, and drop my carryall and sword to the grass beside me.

Cray and Koi each pulled a steamed bun out, but though I was hungry, I looked at my things to consider where to embroider the wing sign. Why not on my outer robe sleeve, inside the hem? I bared that, and had pulled out the pouch I'd made in which to keep the needles I'd been given, and the various lengths of thread that I'd carefully wrapped and stowed, when Cray paused with her half-eaten bun in one hand.

"What are you doing?" she asked.

"Embroidering the wing sign," I said, surprised. "While we still have light."

"Shouldn't you think about it first?" she said. Her voice was even, as it nearly always was, but I still felt that I had taken a misstep.

Granny Ou said, "I believe that Renti, young as she is, understands discretion."

"Discretion doesn't make anyone a Falcon," Cray replied, looking down at her bun. "Any more than does convenience."

The exchange was easy, and that was the end of it, but still I sensed that I had erred somehow. Or rather, that Cray believed I had erred. I decided to consider the matter, and tucked the needle pouch away, picked up my flask, and picked my way down to the waterfall to drink away my thirst, then dump out the last of the water in the flask, which had gone stale on the long walk. I rinsed and refilled it, then washed my face and hands before climbing back up to rejoin the others.

No one spoke much. I badly wanted to ask Granny Ou more about what she'd gleaned of news. The words *There is, though I expect you will not like hearing it,* had been echoing in my head during the long trek up the mountain.

I wanted to ask, but I was afraid of the answer. She'd said they were alive, which I did want to hear, so… that led to increasingly bleak suppositions beginning with *"How* alive?"

In early days I would have scolded myself for imagining a tabby into a tiger, except terrible things had happened already. I wanted badly to speak to Granny Ou without the others present as I feared what I would hear. But the problem resolved itself as Koi stretched out and was soon boneless in deep sleep. Cray fell asleep soon after, and I knew the sound of her sleep breathing.

Granny Ou was still sitting up, her eyes gleaming in the starlight. I tiptoed around the others to her side, and was formulating a question when she said softly, "I wondered what was on your mind."

"You said they—my family in the prison—are alive, but that I would not like what I hear."

"It is so. And yet you wish to hear it anyway?"

"Yes."

"Very well. But remember: you can do nothing. It is done. And giving yourself pain, any kind of pain, will not help your family in the least."

My stomach roiled at this.

"It could be worse," Granny Ou said quickly. "Though it's bad enough. It's mostly the new imperial Crown Prince and his two sisters. Those girls got into the habit of going to the prison to taunt them. Then one of them got the idea of forcing your mother out into a courtyard, still loaded with chains, to clean the chamber pots."

"Mother wouldn't care," I muttered. "I mean, she would." Vivid was the image of my fastidious mother. "But I know what she would say, that it was honest work. That someone had to do it. And if fate had put her there to do it, she would do it well."

"So it was," Granny Ou said. "So it was. Those two princesses were denied the evidence of the humiliation they sought, and things might have worsened, but apparently word reached Koza, and he chased them out again. He threatened them before the entire prison staff, saying that if Governor Gu came over the mountain with an army to free his favorite daughter, those two would be staked out as targets, and they were forbidden to set foot there unless they wanted to take up residence in a cell."

A hot, fierce spurt of triumph shot through my vitals—though I was instantly sorry for it. I knew what Mother would say to that. It was a struggle to regret whatever had occurred to make those two that way.

Granny Ou sighed. "There is no easy way to put this, but that foul Xianti went to question your brother when Koza was elsewhere, and started in with torture. He'd broken the bones in his writing hand, and put out his eyes before that northern princess appeared suddenly."

Gone was the pity in an instant. Shock burned through me and I choked down a scream of rage. The sword hummed, as if in answer—or in readiness—and I shut out the strange sensation, then whispered, "Did she stop him?"

"She did. According to at least two witnesses, he is afraid of her, or in awe of her, if such a twisted soul can be in awe of anything. Perhaps he can. I always hope there is good in someone somewhere. Anyway, he ceased, and—according to the witnesses, remember—once Xianti retreated, she took your brother's hand in hers and it glowed gold. Then it was reduced to its proper size. It had swollen up, as broken bones do, but the swelling was gone. He even flexed the fingers."

"His eyes? What about his eyes?"

"There is nothing to be done to replace eyes that are..."

"*Don't* say it." Then I stopped myself, trying to remember that the words would not wound me. Nevertheless, they did strike my soul.

"If it helps any, there is said to be less pain than when any other part of the body is gouged out," she said. "You ought to know that from Healer Pai's lessons. But First Great-Grandson will not be writing testaments again. That was the gist of Xianti's taunt."

"And not being able to write would mean the most to him," I muttered, gulped back a sob, and wiped my eyes.

"My sources believe that this incident is the primary motivation behind Koza sending Xianti to command this search."

I forced myself to return to my spot. The sword was quiet. I lay down beside it, and tried to sleep, and tried to sleep, and tried to sleep, until dawn.

TWENTY-THREE

*With the world in turmoil
she was the rock in the rushing river…*

OUR JOURNEY WAS A quiet one, both in lack of trouble and in lack of conversation, except when Granny Ou was in a reminiscent mood, or instructing while we did forms and sparred. More than once I caught Koi's eyes straying toward Sagacious Blade, but I was so uncertain about what ought to be said and what shouldn't that I decided it was safest to say nothing at all.

In the late evenings Granny Ou chatted with Cray, who asked about people I did not know, but whom Cray clearly remembered and cherished.

Two days later we neared the river. Granny Ou told us to find a shady spot and get in some practice with seeds and sparring while she scouted ahead.

We'd toiled hard at seeds each morning, and (with a very critical eye) Granny Ou had overseen more practice when we camped at night. But we obeyed that midday. When we were done, I diligently added attempts at resheathing my sword behind me, frustrating as it was. It still took five, six, eight tries before I'd have to put both hands behind my head to guide the point in. Carrying Sagacious Blade was most comfortable on my back, but I hated having to get it out. Especially returning it.

When we were done, we dropped under the shade of an old parasol tree, chewing water mallow and lotus root as the last of our tastier buns and cakes had been eaten the night before. I turned my head so the soft breeze could reach my sweat-damp neck as well as my face. I understood now why many girls tied up their hair in a topknot or tail, rather than making the unmarried girl's braids: it was cooler.

No one spoke; my heart was still knotted after what I'd learned, and I kept my eyes closed. "When someone says you won't like hearing some news, *listen*," I told myself broodingly. I was grateful that the other two were so quiet. I did not want to make the effort to talk.

"No one remembers old women," Granny Ou said when she rejoined us, puffing slightly from the heat and the uphill climb. "Unless they make themselves memorable. It's always worthwhile to see if there's a transport or even a raft going down to harbor. And even if there isn't, to glean news. As it happens, the gods are smiling on us: we've both. Come along. You three are now apprentice wine makers. This transport is very short on comfort, but it will save us days of crossing some difficult country. I'll tell you the news as we go."

The news that concerned us was the appearance in White Water Harbor of a contingent of the new emperor's minions, who had put up wanted posters for "escaped criminals" depicting old Grand Prince Yiulo, and his grandson, Cousin Yiuti.

The transport was a dilapidated flatboat that required two polers on duty day and night, for the proprietor, a woman even older than Granny Ou, would not tie up at night. "Time is money," she kept saying in a cracked, quavering voice.

She invited Granny Ou to sit with her and reminisce about old times, but we young people were to her as pack animals. It seemed she was in the habit of taking on people like us, free labor for her journeys down-river with her cargo. She sat under the flimsy tent, and we had to smell the spices as she cooked her meals, but we were able to fish, and she let us use her brazier when she was done. The three of us traded poling the transport and sleeping right there on the deck under the stars. At least there was no rain for that succession of balmy days.

We smelled the harbor before the hills cleared, a heady amalgam of horse, brine, and countless spices. The river water became more brackish, the greenery alongside now tufts of seagrass poking up at low tide, and stubby reddish-green seepweed, clumps of mangrove here and there. We had been lifting buckets of water from the river and boiling it for tea, or to drink plain—Granny Ou always traveled with a brick of tea—but for the last leg of the journey we resorted to our flasks in spite of being surrounded by water.

Granny Ou told us to unload the barrels for the proprietor, rather than leaving her to the swingeing prices of the harbor laborers, so we muscled the barrels up a ramp to a quay, and there left her bargaining in a high voice for transport.

Up on the quay, overlooking the rocks that gave the harbor its name, there was a shrine to the God of Soil. Granny Ou bowed three times to it, as did the old proprietor, and other common people coming off the river. A few threw small coins, but everyone else bowed. Though court largely ignored the old gods, I was grateful that we'd had an easy journey without rain or rough weather, and plenty of fresh fish, and gratitude might as well be acknowledged as not: I had no coins, so I followed Cray in bowing three times as we passed. I noticed Koi did the same.

We reached a huge parade court before a three-tiered building that belonged to White Water Harbor's magistrate and to the customs and tax officials. The golden dragon banner flew above, once a sign of order and safety, but no longer.

On a long wall opposite the enormous red drum, there were posted drawings of wanted criminals. As Granny Ou had said, prominent among these were detailed drawings of the grand prince and his grandson. A sketch of my brother accompanied these as well as two of the grand prince's military leaders, but the really big rewards were for Grand Prince Lan Yiulo and his grandson Yiuti. All were depicted with court clothes and hats, and I was glad of my shabby, grimy clothes and my ragged straw hat as I side-eyed those posters.

Granny Ou said, as we threaded through the crowd in the parade court, "I've been considering. I know we discussed finding our way south to Azure Tranquility, but there is an enormous garrison there, which we cannot avoid before taking the road up toward the Falcon village in the mountains. Considering matters on this island, it might be well to take the three of you north to Peaches, where I come from."

Cray uttered a short intake of breath. "Do you think my mother might stop there, if she is returning?"

"I know she will," Granny Ou said. "Though your aunt and cousins came to this island, there is still family in Peaches. If there is going to be trouble, a lot of our wanderers will come home, until we know how matters resolve among those sending armies this way and that. We'll stay at an inn I'm familiar with here, and the three of you can get rid of all your dirt while I poke about for a boat to take us to Peaceable Breezes. While the family silk transports sometimes stop here, we're less likely to find transport north. We'll have more choice at the big harbor."

Peaceable Breezes! The harbor city where my grandfather Gu was governor! Granny Ou had mentioned sailing for Azure Tranquility, where the silk merchant part of the family had an estate that was also used by Falcons, but she had never mentioned which harbor we would leave from, and I had been too upset by what had happened to my family in the prison to dare to ask.

I did now. "Will I be able to visit my grandfather?"

Granny Ou laughed. "Of course we will. My guess is, he's wearing a hole in his terrace as he waits for news. He will welcome you with delight and relief. And you can decide your future from there."

Army men strolled about with spears, their captains with kingfisher feathers in their hats staring at people as they patrolled the prosperous area to either side of the magistrate's building. But farther on, the buildings were less prosperous, the businesses mainly different types of repairs, and the eateries plain benches under awnings, with the kitchen right next to it.

As for those on the successively less repaired streets, the decorated carts and palanquins and people on horseback dwindled, leaving only merchants going about their business. A street or two farther on, clusters of thin, ragged beggars drifted along the shadows. Refugees? I searched through them for familiar faces, realizing that most of these were women, children, and the old. At least, it seemed so, though it was difficult to be certain who was what under those bowed heads and ragged clothes.

"It would be just like Xianti to have swept them off to this side of the imperial island," I muttered under my breath.

"What was that?" Granny Ou said.

"The refugees. I think there aren't any men. Or only one or two, like that one with the crutch, and the stooped one in front of the tea shop back there. All the rest seem to be women and girls, or children and the elderly."

"Yes," Granny Ou said slowly. "So I noticed."

The atmosphere was not precisely tense, but it was not easy, either. The beggars, or refugees, looked to either side and back too often for that. They feared the advent of *someone*.

"Here we go," Granny Ou said, indicating a weatherworn sign depicting two geese flying: Two Geese Inn. I glanced to the left of the door, and scrutinized the stone wall. At first I didn't see the Falcon wing sign for the splashed mud and moss that usually accumulated on walls. But then there it was, obvious once I'd spotted it: an arch with three lines leading down, scratched into the rock. These scratches were so old that moss had grown in the grooves, as it had in cracks and pocks elsewhere in the stone.

Delighted, I turned to see if anyone else rejoiced in the discovery, but Granny Ou—experienced after decades of travel—had already gone inside, Cray right on her heels. Koi trod over the threshold after Cray. I followed through a little courtyard into the building, and stood there looking at my very first inn. The main room was small, with calligraphy painted directly on the walls. Red fish lamps hung overhead. The place smelled of tea and pickled cabbage and braised fish with garlic. My mouth watered, but the rumbling under my belly wasn't all hunger.

"Ah," came Granny Ou's voice, pleased. "They've the attic room free. It has space for our four bedrolls."

Koi said, "I'm going to find the privy." He ducked past me and went outside again.

I said, "So will I." I followed him down the stairs, but faltered in the doorway, wondering if they had privies for men and for women. Or if they were all the same, as in the valley, with screens put up for modesty. Perhaps I ought to ask? I hated the thought of following Koi to find a lot of men staring at me. And while I was at it, I could drop my carryall and harness in the room.

I turned about again and started up the stairs, pausing to glance along the balcony that stretched on three sides above the main room with its tables. Closed doors lined all three sides of this corridor, several with shoes neatly placed beside. A real inn! How many behind those doors were heroes on the wander, with exciting stories to tell?

The stairway narrowed and steepened going up to the attic.

I pulled myself along, and spotted two familiar pairs of shoes outside a flimsy door of slats and oiled paper painted with an arrow of geese on the wing. I was about to unsling my pack and slide off my shoes when Cray's voice rose, "…Mother warned me to expect her to be spoilt rotten, and she *was* spoilt rotten!"

Was she talking about Siarti or Liarti? And how would Cray's mother know the imperial granddaughters?

"Not long after I got there, she flung her comb into Minnow's face. Minnow! She's about as threatening as a bunny…"

A sharp dart of surprise—and indignation—and throat-closing pain—accompanied the unwelcome realization that she was talking about *me!*

I ought to have walked right in, and borne whatever embarrassment resulted, but I froze. Partly in fear, but mainly in intense curiosity.

"…though I will say she never did anything like it again. But her eyes were so far above her head, like them all, that she didn't see Minnow, who worships her the way she worships Madam, nor did she see Perch, or any of us. We were mere furniture, there to serve."

"Surely you knew that she was raised that way? She knew nothing else?"

"Truly, truly, and Madame Gu was quite strict in certain ways. But Great-Aunt, it was *me* she came to when she discovered the sword, and then it spoke to *her*. Was I a tyrant in my past life? I did try to take it, not away from her, just for it to know I was there, but it tried to *cut* me. Me! Who worked so very hard to be worthy of it. I strove and strove, but there it was, speaking to that ignorant *princess*, who didn't even care that she was ignorant—"

"The sword's spirit must have seen this anger in you, child."

Cray choked on a sob. "I'm *not* angry, I'm so *grieved!* I worked so *hard*, but all that really matters is birth, after all. Oh, I don't lay blame on Young Mistress Renti. She does work hard, and tries to be one of us, but she has only to get up and cross a room and everyone stares as though she's a princess in disguise. And Koi, I could slap his face, he makes me so angry. Day after day the three of us sparred in the back court, and he talked as much as Banti, but around *her*, he stands there waiting for orders. As though we'll go back to that life, but we can *never* go back with Banti *gone*—maybe *dead*—"

"My good child," Granny Ou said. "Are you aggrieved over the sword or over Lan Banti?"

Cray began to weep the angry tears of utter injustice.

"There, there, you're just turned seventeen. Life isn't over at seventeen. It's just beginning. And there will be many more charming boys in that future…"

I turned away, sick and shivering and cold at the image of Cray lying next to me, and eating with me, and protecting me, with all that hidden scorn in her heart. And I had not been aware in the slightest.

I slipped down the stairs, for even in shock I glided silently—that despised court walk that I had practiced conscientiously for most of my life—and through the yard into the street. I didn't see any of it. All I saw was Cray's face, as once again, the sun came up on bits of memory, illuminating what I had not perceived before. Those silences. The way she had hidden that drawing of my brother, then rubbed it out. Every realization jabbed mercilessly, the harder because I had been so oblivious. A sob forced its way into my aching chest; the shock hurt worse than Siarti's sudden slap, for at least Siarti had not hidden how much she despised me.

Instinct drove me to put as much distance between Cray and me as I could, and I walked as one in a dream until a vaguely familiar male voice rose above the street noise, "Wait, I know him. Isn't that Prince Banti?"

"That's a girl, idiot—and she's toting a sword."

"But…"

"He's two hand-spans taller. You just want it to be Banti for the reward."

"But I know that face…"

Five insistent fingers closed around my arm, and guided me firmly into the close, pungent atmosphere of a butcher's shop. I began to pull away, glancing at—Koi.

"Run," he said.

As behind me, one of those voices rose, "Wait, wasn't there a girl, too? Missing? Ayah, where did she go?"

We ducked past the protesting butcher, through the back of the shop, where his wife stirred laundry in a steaming half-barrel. We dashed into a tiny yard, scattering clucking chickens, to find ourselves closed in by a fence. I was going to protest when Koi let go of my arm, took two long steps and leaped onto a stack of boxes, then vaulted over the fence.

I ran, jumped, leaped — and landed crouching on the other side.

"Where is she? Stop her!" issued from the butcher's yard, as chickens squawked in protest.

"Which way?"

"Split up!"

Koi dashed past hanging sheets, me right behind him. And so began a chase, during which Koi darted this way and that, overturning baskets, ducking past cloth hanging to dry, over fences and under huge rug looms, until the sounds of pursuit died away.

The pursuit seemed to last forever, though we had run far longer on the obstacle runs in the Falcons' valley. We kept going until we came to a low wall overlooking the crashing waves below. We'd reached a curving promontory, beyond which ships sailed one at a time through a narrow passage, avoiding the sentinel stones surrounded by rushing white water. Other ships sat farther out in the water, their masts inscribing slow circles against the sky.

"What happened?" Koi gasped as we halted to catch our breath. "I saw you come out looking like you saw a ghost. I thought everyone left, but it was just you, and you nearly walked right into that patrol."

"I…" I did not want to answer. As I looked away, urgency reawakened. "Will they search house to house?"

"There is no arrest poster for you, or me," Koi said. "But if they think we know something, they will."

"Yes," I said, remembering the threat of the house to house search at the dyers. My gaze wandered back toward the jumble of small huts in the scattered yards behind the street we'd just left. "How did you get so good at evasion? All I saw were dead ends."

He pulled off his headband to dribble a little water on it from his flask, then wiped his sweaty forehead before tying it on again, blue-black hair damp at his hairline. "A hundred-hundred games of fox and rabbit. First Imperial Prince Lan Xianti was always the fox. That company out there is led by Nua Li, the sword-master's son. One of Lan Xianti's favorite followers. Always a fox as well. We were the rabbits."

"Second Brother never told me about that," I said.

"He'll be giving out our description now," Koi added, avoiding my words. "Tiger Li is what he likes to be called. Loves the hunt. No. Loves the catch. Had inventive ways to beat us up without anything showing, if they caught us out of sight of the imperial guards. We need to..." He paused, looking around as if for a solution.

I was thinking, description: girl in boy's riding tunic of green, with butterflies embroidered on it, tall boy in gray and brown, both with swords—and I remembered one of Xue Two-Sword's stories.

"I think I have an idea," I said, for I'd heard high voices coming from the direction of the street. These were girls' voices, not the pursuit, and when I turned my head I glimpsed a cluster of girls in refugee rags.

I ran toward them, up a narrow alley between what might once have been warehouses, but had been left to the weather. Some had holes in roof and walls, others had fallen down—testament to former days, when this harbor was more prosperous.

The girls stopped, eyeing me warily. I burst out, "Who wants to trade their outer robe for mine? This is a good robe..." I stopped there, my thoughts spiraling out as if I'd fallen off a cliff.

"We just heard them bellowing about two criminals, a boy in gray and a girl in green with butterflies," a sharp-faced girl said, her gaze raking me up and down. Then she shrugged scrawny shoulders. "I'll take it, as we don't look anything like. But you have to give me that bedroll, too, as I'll be facing your danger as you run away."

"Done," I said, finding this reasonable.

I shrugged off my carryall and harness, then slid out of the outer robe, leaving only my undyed under robe. She handed me her grimy, tattered robe whose original color was impossible to descry. It stank so much my throat closed, the amalgam of odors led by many long-ago meals of fried fish. She whirled and darted off as I slowly pulled her robe on.

One of the other girls said, "You'd better run. She'll turn you in."

"No, she won't," answered a taller one. "There's no poster for these two. That means no reward money. Going up to those imperials might get her only a kick in the face, and she knows it."

"We'll go," I assured them as I yanked my harness back on. "I don't want to draw trouble to you."

They nodded, exchanging looks and mutters, but only went a few steps when one turned.

"You should have bargained," the girl said. "Hafi will have already sold that butterfly robe by now. And she never shares."

I resumed my carryall, then pulled on the smelly robe. My eyes watered.

"How'd you get caught? What did you take? Is it that sword? The gem in that hilt would bring a hundred golden—"

"It'd bring death, rock-head," that older girl stated in disgust. "That's a lord's jewel. Any merchant with a brain in his head would know it for stolen, and turn you in faster than breath. We ought to get away from these thieves."

"I didn't take the sword," I said. "It's mine. Would you like the last of my travel food? It isn't much…"

The older girl with the finely sculpted face recoiled slightly, a remainder of a pride nearly eroded entirely away, but the rest crowded eagerly around, and though I only had pickled lotus root chunks left in my pouch, plus some very limp bamboo shoots and fiddlehead ferns we'd picked on the mountainside and washed in streams.

The girls passed these around and crammed them into their mouths. As I tucked my empty pouch back into my carryall, I remembered that I had nothing left now, but there was that inn, and Granny Ou. And Cray. But I'd have to pretend I hadn't heard, for both our sakes—

A small girl pelted up then. "They're taking another fifty of us, but we have to be strong enough to pick strawberries," she shrilled. "Down at the shore." She pointed back toward the wall, where a boat lay in the water, the shore surrounded by detritus.

The girls turned, quick as starlings, and began running, though the older one turned back. "Come, if you like. If there's work, there'll be food."

I started after, but Koi said, "You could probably try selling that sword. It doesn't seem like a Falcon weapon."

"It isn't."

I was going to leave it at that, but as I met his gaze, it occurred to me that he knew very well that it was not a Falcon blade. And yet he was still not asking. That had to be a residue of imperial palace expectations. But if we were to survive, we had to eradicate all those signs from us. However, dared I tell him the truth?

Fast as the wind, memory streamed through my mind of Koi faithfully serving Second Brother. I was learning by bits what that had cost him in Xianti's torments. After that, Koi had risked his life searching for Second Brother. We both wanted to search for Second Brother.

I said, "This is a family sword—of sorts. It...it's charmed, you could say. Actually there's a demon in it who talks to me, though there isn't time now for the entire story. Cray knew about it. She wanted it, but it came to me. I have to learn to use it, and I have to protect it. That means hiding the truth about it."

He dipped his head in a nod. "I will say nothing." And I believed him. He added, "But if we're going to hide ourselves doing whatever work these others are being hired for, we'd better run. First, though... the robe was a good idea. But it's not enough." As he spoke, he was already stripping off his gray one, and pulled from his pack his rumpled, grimy field-laborer blue one, stained from our hot walk. He pulled this on, then said, "We need to change our profiles." He pulled his headband back off and unknotted his hair, letting it fall down his back. He ruffled it hard, then bent and picked up dirt from the ground, rubbing it in until his hair hung in grimy locks, like the hair of most of the refugees. "This is how we slipped Xianti's search net, so many times."

I did the same with shaking fingers.

When we were done, he regretfully set his bedroll down. "It's too bulky to carry, and from the looks of them, none of them had one. It might catch the eye. Pull your harness around front under your clothes..." And when this was done, he picked up a slat of wood from a rotting pile, gave it a whack with his sword so that it came apart in sticks, and selected the longest one. "I'm going to have to fake a bad knee, or they'll sweep me off to wherever they've taken the boys. As for you, I suggest you put a pebble in one shoe."

"But that will slow me up, and hurt," I said.

"Yes. It will also change your walk."

With the harness turned around, Sagacious Blade's hilt was now tucked against the hollow of my shoulder under the noisome robe, the sword's length lying across my stomach to my hip. It poked beyond my thigh, but the horrible robe swung around it. We hobbled our way in the wake of the flight of girls, falling in with another cluster of refugee children. One was hurrying them anxiously, "...or we'll be too late."

"Where do you think this strawberry field is?" I murmured for Koi's ear.

"That boat isn't going far. There's no sail. My guess is, on the other side of that promontory. We can hide among the workers. If the gods grant us luck, the search will die well before they bring us back. We can't go back to the inn just yet in case they do search house to house—inns would be their starting point."

This sounded like a reasonable plan. I fell silent, concentrating on not wincing as I limped along beside him, wishing I'd chosen a smaller pebble. Koi hobbled, back stooped.

The sudden advent of horse hooves caused my heart to bang against my ribs. I moved closer to another girl as Koi dropped back a pace, so that we did not look like we were together, and the riders—a search party, I saw from the back— trotted right past us without so much as a pause, two with nocked arrows, and the rest with one hand on a sword hilt.

We stayed with the children as we passed the last low breakwater, and crossed the shingle to the long boat, where five or six husky rowers sat with their oars in the air, waiting.

The children thinned into a line, the fastest first. The man on the shore was picking and choosing; he shoved aside everyone small, and one clearly frail, shivering soul, boy or girl I could not tell.

When he saw Koi, he blinked in surprise and a sort of glee—the way someone would look at a free beast of burden— then his gaze fell to the stick that Koi had tucked under his armpit. "Bad leg?"

"Yes."

"Eh, you'll do." He gestured to me to follow, after a quick, uninterested scan, then a wrinkled lip, probably at my ripe odor of stale fish dinners.

Another four crowded happily behind us, he waved off the tag end of the children, those too small to run fast, and roared, "Shove off!" as he hopped into the boat.

The burly men used their oars as poles to shove the boat away from the shoreline. We bumped past the rippling waves, then the oarsmen began plying the oars, sending us rolling into deeper water. I laid my head against the rail. My scalp itched terribly from the dirt I'd rubbed into it, and my stomach growled. Also, the need to visit the privy was back, but at least it was a polite reminder rather than blaring insistence. I hoped that the ride would not be long, but it was nice to just relax, and ease my throbbing feet.

In fact, now that I was out of range of the search, I could

get rid of that horrible pebble. Surreptitiously I drew my foot up, felt in it, extracted the rock, and then, with it clutched in my fingers, relaxed. A bit of a rest before whatever work would be required seemed a good idea, especially on an empty stomach.

I thought of my food pouch, now empty. Why had I done that? Was it as Cray said, a way to demonstrate my superiority? But it had been so good to see how those girls, mostly my age, had hungrily fallen on those limp greens as if they were peach tea cakes and date crisps.

But then Cray's voice was back, every word an icicle stabbing my soul. I hadn't paid the maids much attention, but I was told not to. Thus I argued inside my head, though the knot remained tight because there was no shifting the underlying truth: I'd admired Cray for her quick wit, her strength, her skill, and in her heart she had despised me. The worst of it was, it sounded as if she had *tried* to do me justice, but the flaws in me had—

Then a soft voice whispered in my ear, "I don't like this."

My eyes opened, to find Koi's face near mine. He glanced over his shoulder down the length of the boat, to where the man who'd been choosing among us for the boat ride, was going among the hunched, tired, mostly oblivious passengers. It seemed to me most were glad to be sitting in the warm sun, with the sure prospect of a meal at the other end of whatever our destination was.

I caught sight of that older girl, her face drawn, her forehead tight as she watched that man. He wasn't doing much other than walking among the children, but every once in a while, he stopped, and grinned down at someone or other. No, at older girls.

Koi cursed under his breath. It was the first time I'd ever heard him do so, and the hairs on the back of my neck prickled. I looked out over the rail, startled to find the coast a considerable way behind us, the city a jumble except for the triple-tiered roofline of the magisterial building, barely discernible in the haze. We had been carried out to sea on the last of the ebbing tide. The promontory I'd seen was also far behind.

I looked the other way, and discovered that one of the ships I'd scarcely noticed earlier was considerably nearer.

"I think," Koi said, "we've just walked ourselves into a slave-taker."

"What?" I gasped. "But isn't that illegal? Only the government can make criminals into slaves."

"That harbor is under Xianti's followers' command," Koi retorted. "Do you think they'd stop it? In fact, I'll wager anything that they sent for them!"

A girl's voice rose. "Where are we going? This is not harvesting strawberries!"

The rowers laughed.

"I'm not going on that ship!" She sprang up and dived over the side, and began swimming away—something I did not know how to do.

But she hadn't gotten five or six strokes away when one of the rowers picked up a bow, fixed an arrow, and shot her.

Half the passengers cried out. The girl thrashed in the water, dark red spreading around her. We drifted near her, and one of the men reached a long arm and hauled her ungently back aboard. She'd gone limp and pale, water streaming off her—mixed with blood from the wound in the back of her shoulder as she moaned.

"That was a warning. The next shot won't be so kind," the archer roared.

TWENTY-FOUR

…like a beacon to those in darkness…

MURMURS ROSE, HIGH, WORRIED voices, and some of the younger ones began to cry until that same man raised the bow and bellowed, "Shut up!" And, when they did, "Be quiet and cooperative, and we'll all get along fine. You'll get your meals, as promised. What matter if the work is picking strawberries or something else? Work is work, ha ha."

"They don't want to mark the merchandise," Koi whispered.

I knew Koi was pretty good at martial arts, after all that time practicing with Second Brother and all those other princes. And, apparently, Cray. But he wasn't Master Sima the Hero, who had defeated six bandits. I wondered if even Master Sima could defeat these burly men while fighting on a rocking boat, the enemy scattered along its length, each bearing a thick wooden oar twice the length of his sword. Also, the boat was full of captives who'd need to be dodged around.

"Two against seven. And we're nearly in bow range of the ship," Koi said—clearly thinking along the same path as me. "Wait for a better chance."

I did appreciate him saying two against seven rather than one against seven, but we both knew I was worthless in a fight. During the sparring on the mountain, I'd seen both Koi and Cray holding back when I took a turn. Whereas when they sparred, the fights were so much faster, so fast I still had difficulty following. And never had I been able to see even a single move ahead.

Very well. There was no use in scolding myself for what I didn't know. I needed to cultivate my skills, which right now meant considering what I did know. Had I read of any similar situations? Meanwhile, at the other end of the boat, a couple of girls Cray's age had taken charge of the wounded one, pulling the arrow and binding her shoulder with some ripped cloth.

A few more mighty strokes on the part of the oarsmen, and the boat bumped up against the side of a ship. Various ropes and ladders were let down from the rail, and the oarsmen began chivvying the whimpering, frightened children and teenagers toward the ladders. The youngest were grabbed, a rope slung in quick, business-like manner around waists and under armpits, indicating this was a familiar routine. Resentment kindled in me, a useless emotion right now.

"Ladder," Koi said. "Don't let them discover the sword."

I'd just then thought of that, and nodded.

The rope ladder banged me unpleasantly against the side of the ship a time or two as it rocked on the water, then I was up and over, a sailor wrinkling his nose as he grabbed my arm. "Phew, this one really reeks," he commented.

I bit back a "So do you," remembering Mother's advice about enemies who have more power than you: don't ever let them know what you are thinking. If you can, encourage them to underestimate you. Right now, it seemed, I was becoming the Girl Who Stinks. Perhaps I could use that.

The slavers pushed everyone in the direction of the privy (the head, on a ship), and thence below to the holding space. It was a relief to use the privy, and while I did so, I wrestled with my carryall and sword under my clothes, disposing them a bit better. But hiding a sword under clothing is vastly awkward.

Then we were ushered belowdecks. My bruised foot reminded me to alter my walk. I shuffled, trying to copy the girl in front of me.

As soon as we clambered down into the belly of the ship, we discovered that we were not alone. There were at least twice our number below, crowded into various compartments. Koi and the few boys were thrust into one, and then the rest of us in the last and largest, where a number of girls already sat on the bare deck, pressed together fearfully. We were told to sit down, and the slaver who had separated us out said, "Now it's time to speak up if you've any talent or special skill. Life will be much easier if you do."

Some shrilled questions, begged to be let go, and even tried to demand their freedom, as two of the smaller girls began to grizzle.

"Shut those two up," the man snapped, "or I'll shut them up."

Bigger girls shook and coaxed the two into sniffling silence.

"Who can play an instrument? Sing? Dance? Any cooks' apprentices among you?"

But everyone was too intimidated now to speak.

He went among us, pointing at various people. A girl near me got a finger in her face, and she said, "Calligraphy."

"A scribe, is it? How many here know how to write?"

Perhaps ten hands went up. I noted that that older girl, who'd looked out for the little group of refugees, was one. I sat where I was, trying to be as invisible as I could in my awkward pose, with the hilt scraping against the inside of my hip bone as I leaned to one side, the rest of my sword lying along one leg stuck out straight.

But keeping silent had been a mistake, for the man pointed the finger in my face. "You. What can you do?"

"Embroidery," I whimpered, not trying to hide my nerves.

"Embroidery!" His brows shot up a corrugated forehead. "You look, and smell, like you were born in those clothes." He began to turn away, then turned back, eyeing me. "What *have* you got under that reeking robe?" And when I didn't answer, he kicked my leg. His boot toe clacked against Sagacious Blade's sheath.

My heart crowded into my throat. Granny Zim had said nothing, and continued to say nothing as the slaver rapped out, "Whatever that is, give it up. Now. I really don't want to have to frisk that robe and risk my hands rotting, but I will."

With shaking fingers, as everyone watched in silence, I reached into my robe and slowly pulled the sword out.

The man's eyes bulged, and he uttered a laugh. "What is this?" He snatched it from my hand—and the sword lay in his, utterly inert. "Fate is smiling on me now! That stone alone will let me live like a king for a year." He began to draw the blade from the sheath.

I held my breath, but the sword did not cut him. He whistled as the bronze glowed richly in the light of the swinging lamp, the overlapping scales engraved on it shining.

He whistled again, and regarded me with interest. "Where did you get this?"

I remembered the girls' assumption. "Stole it."

"A thief! Ay, you'll not practice on us if you want to keep your hands attached to your arms. What you do once you're sold off is your new owner's problem." He chuckled again, pushing the sword back into the sheath as he turned to point at more of the other captives. "Any of you other girls toting weapons?"

It was plain that those ragged, worn clothes over hunger-thin bodies did not conceal any knives or swords. Most shook their heads, or shrank back.

I stared on shock as he walked away with Sagacious Blade. Sick at heart, I wondered if even the sword had come to despise me, and tears stung my eyes fiercely as the man turned back to his inquiries. "You? What do you know?"

"My family were saddle-makers, before the war..."

"You?"

"We were taking seasoned parasol wood to the instrument makers when the warriors came and took my father and brothers away—"

"You?"

"We sold medicine—"

And so on, until he had gone through all us newcomers. Then he said, "Those who can cook, come along. We need your labor, and you'll get to eat first."

Three girls rose slowly. He took them out into the narrow gangway outside our hold, Sagacious Blade still in his hand. The sound of the thick wooden bolt dropping into place on the outside of the equally thick door made us all jump.

I sat there, utterly defeated. Cray's horrible words came back like carrion birds to pick at my heart. There had been so much truth in them! Was that why the sword stayed silent? Had Granny Zim picked *him* to belong to now?

No. Stop imaging the worst for truth. If she had spoken to that man, he surely would have reacted. For some reason the sword had gone quiet. I must not speculate why. I had to think about escaping this situation. But try as I might, my thoughts arrowed right back to what Cray had said. For a short time I raged against her, but it did not last. I could hear Mother saying calmly, "Did she drive you out?" and, more telling, "Did she know you were there eavesdropping?"

No. Cray hadn't made me run out into the street. I'd done

that. I ought never to have listened at that door, and once I had, I ought to have kept that burden to myself, and right now I'd be on the way to my grandfather...

I drew my knees up, put my head on them, closed my arms around my head, and wept as silently as I could. I was not the only one, which was no comfort whatsoever.

Presently, my head throbbing, I lay down and curled up. Weeping would get me nowhere. I could imagine Mother's voice telling me to use my wits. But my wits seemed to know all the wrong things.

And there I was, back at the sword again. Why hadn't Sagacious Blade cut him, or flown back to me? Granny Ou had said something about the Essence charms fading away. Had they? I could not know. And yet twice it had flown from its trunk to me. Once when I was so sick, and then that terrible night when Xianti had the imperial guards arrest my family, and I called to the sword when Cray told me to try.

Would it come now? But if I called it, and it came, then the enemies would find out that it was charmed, because there was nowhere to hide it in this hold with no furnishings whatever. Ah, was that why Granny Zim had stayed quiet, to hide Sagacious Blade's Essence charm?

All right, if that was so, then I was still alone, but I did have a kind of ally, somewhere at the other end of the ship.

After a time, the tiny air holes high up around the ceiling dimmed, and we were closed in utter darkness. No one spoke except in the softest of whispers, and here and there was muffled weeping. Using the darkness as cover, I undressed, removing Tiger Moth's harness—obviously made to my size, which a thief wouldn't have—and tied it into a ball before shoving it to the bottom of my carryall, under my dirty clothes. Then I pulled on the stenchiferous robe again.

After a time impossible to measure, there came the sounds of footsteps outside the hold, and the bolt was lifted. Lamplight lanced in, held by one of the men as a girl lugged in a bucket of congee. We had to drink it right out of the dipping cup. It was runny, but at least it wasn't burning hot. After the congee, which was not nearly enough, another unhappy-looking girl came around lugging a bucket of water, and again, everyone got a slurp. We were told that we'd be allowed to visit the head twice a day, after meals. Then we were shut into that stuffy hold to sleep.

After a fitful night, the morning went as before. We were

given another dipper of congee, with a chunk of pancake, and more water. This was intended to sustain us for the day. Then we were sent up to visit the head in groups of ten, standing in line at each side of the ship.

I was last in line. I found myself right behind that tall girl, who turned a little. "You aren't really a thief," she murmured, no louder than a breath. "You. And that boy. Martial artists?"

I didn't see a reason to lie. "Only a year, for me," I said. "He's better at it."

"What are you. Thirteen or fourteen?"

"Fourteen."

Her lip lifted in a brief, bleak smile. "A mere child. Thought so. Do you think he will come up with some way to escape?"

"Don't know," I said. "Here's what I do know. None of us can do much alone. Including him. But a lot of us..."

The girl sighed. "What can a lot of twelve-year-olds do besides get themselves killed?"

I couldn't answer that, and anyway, it was her turn to use the head.

We didn't speak as we went back down to the hold. I was returning to the spot I'd slept in, but the girl who'd been next to me muttered, "Can't you go somewhere else? My stomach keeps rising at your smell."

"Can't help that," I said.

"Come over here," spoke up the tall girl. "I'm used to the stink of that robe." And when I reached her, "Why you picked that wretch Hafi to trade with... She deliberately smeared fish guts over herself because she was hoarding food and didn't want to share. And now she's safe in the city, eating well off the proceeds of your pretty robe. I must have killed a king in my last life," she sighed.

"Or she got swept up by the searchers," I pointed out. "While they wouldn't take her to prison as an escaped criminal, they probably *would* take any money she had. They looked like the sorts who would."

The girl sighed again and rested her forehead on her knee, her profile wan and sharp-cut in the weak light. Long-accustomed hunger had taken the curve out of her cheeks, making them hollow. "I don't know if I ought to be glad or sad. I'm sure Hafi once lived a blameless life with her family, her only sins the small ones of a greedy nature. They were rice farmers, until the red-capes swept through like an evil wind."

"What happened?" I asked.

"They said it was war, and they needed the men to defend our prefecture, and the rest of us had to surrender a quarter of our goods as emergency war tax, or our men would starve, and they marched away with our brothers and uncles and fathers. By winter a lot of *us* were starving, when we could not meet the tax demands and still earn enough to eat."

"What did you do?"

"My father ran a school. My brother taught. I'd studied with him, and knew exactly as much, so when he was taken I tried to teach, but the little boys were unruly. They questioned everything I said, and they insisted they lost face being taught by a girl. Every day was the same struggle until one by one their mothers took them away again, using various excuses. The truth was, most couldn't pay the scholarship fee. It was like that all over. Without the work the men did, we struggled, then spring came, but with it that drought..." She shrugged. "When the emperor sent that new magistrate, he drove all of us who could not meet the tax demands out, and we followed everyone else to the capital to petition the emperor. Who was too close to Heaven to see us. It was the temples that fed us, and not very much. Ayoh! This seems to be news to you, and yet your accent is that of the imperial island. And educated." Her voice lowered. "I thought nobles were exempt from the troubles."

I was spared having to answer when the door opened, and one of the men said, "There's a rainstorm coming. Anyone who wants to take advantage of a free bath from the gods, you can come up to the deck."

Since breakfast, the sky had clouded over, the color of the sea a restless gray-green. One clap of loud thunder and the torrent slanted down. I lifted my face to the warm rain, just standing there with my mouth open. Presently I slipped off the sodden robe, and began to stamp on it. Rivulets of grime dribbled on the deck. I kept turning it over and stamping, wringing and stamping, my underclothes squeaking over my skin, until at last it was just water coming off the rags, which turned out to be a very faded eggshell blue.

I emptied out the clothes in my carryall, except for my provisions pouch and my harness. My headband got washed out, too. I even emptied my flask, after tasting the water streaming off the end of a sail. The brine had been washed off by the deluge, so I refilled my flask. Then I lifted my face to the warm rain and let it wash me and my underclothes clean.

All around me, girls scrubbed at scalps, or stamped efficiently. I reflected that most of these girls were long accustomed to washing laundry, probably on the rocks at the riverside, as we'd seen coming down the river with the wine merchant. Many had left on only their thin underclothes, even more ragged than mine, scrawny bare legs mottled with bruises and scrapes as they stamped out their ragged-hemmed under-trousers.

When the storm began to pass, as fast as it had come, it was time to twist hair and cloth alike, wringing them out. It was deceptively peaceful, the slavers either ignoring us or looking on. Most who watched turned their attention toward the rail not far from me, where that tall girl (I soon learned her name was Cygnet) stood, her damp clothes outlining her thin body. Being an older teen, she had the shape of one, though much diminished, but it was her face that truly drew the eye. Clean, she was beautiful, with a perfect heart-shaped face, phoenix eyes, and phoenix-winged brows above. She kept her gaze lowered as if shutting out the world as she finishing wringing out her robe, and then, wet as it was, she pulled it back on rather than spreading it out under the sun the way the rest of us had done.

When the sun began dropping westward, the slavers drove us below again, and locked the hatch on us once more, until the evening congee was brought around.

Time passed. Hunger was a constant companion; though we got the congee twice a day, and every now and then a portion of a pancake or sweet potato, it was never enough food. To pass the time, Cygnet offered to teach anyone who wanted to learn to read, drawing with her finger on the wooden deck when we had light.

I offered to help, and we took turns reciting the Twenty-Five Virtues, though at times her voice was sour with irony, and I knew she was thinking—as I did—how very far we were from the civilization and benevolence exhorted in these. But the girls around us either found it comforting to recite together, or they shrilled the words in challenge, and I remembered that in many parts of the empire commoners were not permitted to read, and even among merchants and persons of wealth, girls were confined to the skills of keeping the home.

I also sensed a bit of challenge in Cygnet, as we traded off reciting the poetry of Ar Laq and the commentaries of Mana Ta on Kanda's works. Her voice was bitter as she flawlessly recited, "For example, all humans feel compassion for the suffering of other humans and animals, at least on some occasions, and this is a manifestation of benevolence. Similarly, every person has some things that he or she would be ashamed to do, or some forms of treatment he or she would disdain to accept, and these are expressions of righteousness." Even with the tone of wormwood tinging the words, her recitation voice was beautifully trained. She added wryly, "I would debate the truth of that."

"But Mana Ta also says that there must be three conditions for civilization and benevolence: an environment that meets the needs of the body, moral and ethical education, and the will to work. Only a few —"

"Monks, nuns, and seers," Cygnet interposed mockingly.

"Only a handful of people, Mana Ta argues, have the strength of character to 'have a constant heart' in the face of physical deprivation," I finished.

"You imply that you've that constant heart?" she rejoined.

"I wish I did," I said, thinking of Mother with her calm, steadfast goodness, now sitting in that prison weighed down by chains. I knew she would greet each day that I did not turn up there with hope and gladness. At least she could not know what had happened to me now. And though I did feel the tug of the bitterness that imbued Cygnet's words, I said firmly, "I do think it's worth striving for."

Cygnet lifted a shoulder, slanting me a look. "I once thought so. Now I'm not so certain."

Our scholars were getting restless, muttering and shifting, one girl of maybe ten years muttering fretfully, "When will the congee come?"

We shifted to poetry then. They liked ballads with a rhythm, especially gallant wanderer ballads. When the girls joined in, we were loud enough that sometimes the same melody and rhythm echoed from the wall between us and the next hold, where the few boys were housed.

That caused a welcome ripple of mirth. Soon gone.

TWENTY-FIVE

…shedding glory all around…

AY! HOW I BROODED while the others slept.

Cray's words about how I'd treated Perch, Minnow, and Eider had burned into my soul. Even though I'd been cautioned repeatedly against the dangers of intimacy with the maids, I understood now how to them I'd merely been aloof. Further, it seemed that Second Brother had never cultivated that "necessary" distance with Koi, and Cray. I found myself wistful at the image of them laughing and talking as they practiced martial arts among the dogs and chickens in the back yard of our palace. How much I would have enjoyed that! But I had worked so hard to emulate the silent serenity of Mother's rooms because it was what I knew. It showed filial respect.

During the daylight hours I listened with close attention, striving not to appear aloof. Between our attempts at making a kind of school, conversation invariably dissolved into complaints about hunger—questions no one could answer—fear and resentment. Some told their stories; most were refugees from the capital, and I began to piece together what had happened to them.

When I did sleep, I was plagued with nightmares.

I woke one morning feeling no more refreshed than when I'd tried to sleep, after a dream in which Cray scolded me, saying that the sword ought to have gone to Second Brother. I kept agreeing with her, louder and louder, but she receded until shafting sunlight struck my face and I woke. The hold was stifling even though it was morning, an oppressive heat that I suspected presaged a storm.

And storm there was. This was no warm, early summer storm, but a demon wind-driven tempest filled with constant purple-white lightning. The thunder reverberated through the ship, more felt than heard, throwing us against one another as we rode up then crested enormous waves. The air holes let in just enough water to make everyone wet and wretched.

Some got miserably sick, adding to the stifling atmosphere, and it was not only the younger ones who wailed in fear. Gradually the steep plunges and rolls subsided, and when at last we were let out, a whoosh of cooler air rushed in. The cook girls went around, one with her nose stuck into her elbow crook, and they came back with two buckets of rainwater for us to clean the deck and the sick ones. "Don't damage the merchandise," Cygnet muttered, but she as well as I and two other older girls helped mop up the younger ones, who were listless and shivering.

The day after that, the little bit of air filtering in smelled different, though when we went up to the heads, there was no bump on the horizon yet.

Cygnet said softly, "Do you smell land?"

"I do."

"And I," a girl named Dinek put in at my shoulder. Short and wiry, she had quick, bright eyes, prominent teeth, and her voice was a high chirp. "We're a day out."

"How can you know that?" I asked, taking another look at the horizon.

"Smell. When we get closer, I might even recognize the harbor, if it's one I've been to." She glanced around to make sure she wasn't being overhead. "We're tea traders."

"The Ou family?" I asked, wondering if I'd just met a cousin.

"No. But I know of that respected clan. They mostly deal in silks, but they've branched into tea bricks, a different part of the trade," Dinek said to me. "I've spent my entire life on ships. Until the cursed day we docked at White Water Harbor, and my brother and I went up a mountain for a picnic, just to get the feel of land again, and those imperial rats took him and handed me off to them." She jerked her chin over her shoulder toward the superstructure where, I presumed, the slavers lived in far more comfort than we did.

We were driven back down to the hold again, and as if to corroborate her guess, the man who came down to lock the door tossed a comb in before saying, "Tomorrow, we want you as tidy as you can make yourselves. We'll be dividing you up by skills and talents before we disembark."

Slam! Thunk! went the bar.

"I wish I could pull out all my hair," a girl muttered loudly. "My parents would forgive me for harming the body they gave me, if they knew I was being sold by these white-eyed rats."

The young ones began to grizzle, but an older girl named Ke picked up the comb, slapped it against her hand, and said with a determined air, "Why whimper and wail? If I'm going to be sold, I intend to smile as nice as I can, in hopes of getting a good madam. Scowling and pouting is sure to land you in the back yard scrubbing the stinkpots and dirty clothes."

That set off discussions—and arguments—about prospective owners.

I shut that out, brooding at my inability to find escape. Sagacious Blade was at the other end of the ship. I could try to call it to me, but what then? I knew I couldn't defeat one of those slavers, much less a ship full of them. They'd only take it away again, or if it decided to cut one, would they try to kill me for it?

If only I could get it to come to me when we went up onto the deck, and I could *fly* away…

And there was Granny Ou in memory, asking if the sword flew.

I didn't believe it. How? Could a person balance on a sword in midair? They did in the gallant wanderer tales, of course. There were entire sects with charmed swords that flew. It was also true that charmed swords were illegal. Maybe before they were collected by various emperors, flying on them had been as common as the stories made out, but of course that skill had to be taught, or the entire world would be in the air, flying between islands.

It was also true that Sagacious Blade had flown straight to me those two times. But there was a substantial difference— the length and breadth of my own body—between a sword flying on its own and one on which I could somehow balance without tumbling to my death.

I shuddered. How I loathed heights! That sensation of my

stomach dropping to my toes, and the almost-vertigo, gripped me even if I leaned out of the upper story of a building and looked straight down. I'd hated promontory watch.

Besides, and here I could hear Mother's voice and see her steady gaze, would I really flee and leave Koi, who had kept me from being caught by that Tiger Li and his company? Would I go off and leave Cygnet and Dinek and Ke and those little girls Rose and Little Star?

But what could I *do?*

I wrestled inwardly as the light faded, and the noise on the deck began to increase. Gradually the occasional bellowing and shouting resolved into singing. It was not the boys next door. These were men's voices, the songs difficult to make out through the thickness of the deck. The songs began to break up into raucous laughter.

"They're getting drunk," a practical fifteen-year-old named MiMi said, crawling past knots of girls either asleep or whispering together. "My aunt can always tell just by the sound of a voice how many they've had—and how many until they pass out snoring."

Cygnet sighed. "Celebrating all the profit they will make off of selling us." She glared my way. Not that I could see. I could tell by the sharpening of her voice. "And *you* believe all that nonsense from Kanda about the good in people. If it wouldn't land in someone's hair, I'd spit."

"If only we could get up there and throw them all overboard," the tea trader girl, Dinek, said in disgust.

"Even if we got out, they must have armed guards on watch," Cygnet retorted. "You were in another boat, Dinek. You didn't see Lei get shot, but the rest of us did."

Lei's wound still troubled her.

"Why would they post a guard?" one of the quieter older girls spoke up. "We're all locked in. We have no weapons. Girls never give anyone trouble, which is probably why they collect us to sell."

No one on guard? If…I shut my eyes, reaching—

And I felt that pulse, the same one I'd felt while I crouched under the bushes while Cray spied on the imperial guard arresting my family. My heart thumped hard once. I drew a deep breath. Think!

I said, "If that was true. And if we could get the door open. What then?"

"Oh," Cygnet drawled, "we'd all pray to the Snow Crane

to sprout us some wings, and fly away."

"No, supposing," I said. "What then?"

Cygnet's hand shot out, and gripped my shoulder, hard. "Do you know something, Ren?"

"I might be able to get the door open. Maybe. I think. If I can, what then? Even if they aren't standing about with weapons to hand, they are roaming about. We can hear them tromping."

The girls fell silent. We turned our faces up, aware of the thud and thump of feet on the deck.

Dinek said, "Can you get the boys out? Can any of them fight? None of us can…"

"The boy I was traveling with can fight, but he's only one. We'd need a better plan than rushing up there right now."

"Like?"

They were listening. "I think it might matter how drunk they get. For example, if the slavers really have drunken themselves insensible, those of us who know the acupoint for freezing muscles could sneak up and lock their meridians long enough to tie them up, so they couldn't attack us."

"That's *true*," spoke up a high voice—one of the twelve-year-olds. "I know six paralyzing acupoints, but I wasn't allowed to use needles, except under the watch of my grandmother."

"You can use your thumbnail and fingernail together, if you strike just right," I said. "It's a martial arts move. Do you think you could do it?"

"I know the exact spot, but I don't know if I'm strong enough that way," came the doubtful response out of the darkness.

"Show me," someone said. "Try on me."

A rustle and a grunt, and a thud. Followed by a slurring, "Ow-w-w."

"I want to learn that meridian thing!"

"Show me!"

"Show me, too!"

"Me, too."

"Me as well," Cygnet put in. "I'm willing to try anything but sit here waiting to be sold off to an entertainment house, which no doubt is to be my fate. No one wants a girl for scribe work, and I saw how those wolves were looking at me during the rainstorm when they let us wash out our clothes. It was like slugs crawling over me. No. Slugs are innocent. They merely act according to their nature, and don't regard people as bags of golden taels."

"Leeches," another girl muttered fiercely.

"Yes," Cygnet said, and her grip hardened on my shoulder. "Ren, I swear I'll slap your face off for getting my hopes up even for an instant if you are merely in one of your cloud-brained speculating moods."

All the while, the singing rose and fell overhead, bawled with increasing raggedness. Were the footsteps fewer? I reached, finding a couple of willing volunteers. I pressed my fingers into the spot between heartbreakingly sharp ribs, but I only pressed until I got a reaction.

"Ow, that feels strange," the girl said. "I went cold. No, numb. Teach me that!"

"Try me…"

For a short time those with the healer training tried to teach others, without much success in the complete darkness. About six seemed to grasp it. The rest poked each other until the general protests caused a cease in that lesson.

Then I felt them turning to me, because I'd first spoken, and people will grasp at the most tenuous of hopes. But I also felt the weight of their hope, their expectation, and with that awareness fountained up the much-copied words from Mana Ta talking about leaders, and the responsibility of leaders. Everyone wants to be safe, to be led away from danger. I wasn't a hero; I wasn't sure of myself at all. But no one else was, either. If I was wrong, would they turn on me?

"We'll have to act quietly. At once," I said, squashing my own doubts. "If they aren't drunk insensible, we come back down here."

"Yes…yes…yes…" came the whispers, and a couple of, "Don't do it. I don't want to get hurt. They'll beat us to death."

"Shut up, you rabbit—"

"*You* shut up," was the fierce response, from someone else. "You don't know what she's lived through—"

"We can't all go," I said, striving to look at this evolving semblance of a plan from all directions. "Those who're afraid, just stay here. If we fail, they won't want to lose all their money. They might hurt us. They surely won't hurt you."

"That's right," Dinek exclaimed. "Stay here. Stay quiet. If we're successful, we'll come and get you. But don't give us away, right?"

"I'm going to pretend I was asleep," someone quavered.

"Me, too."

As they spoke, I felt my way past arms and legs until I reached the door. I stood up, fingering the outline of the door, then turned with my back to it. I held out my hands.

Come, I pleaded in my mind. There was that pulse from within, easier this time, and the sword smacked into my palms with a clatter.

"What was that noise?"

"That sounded like a sword rattling," stated another girl—one who had seldom spoken.

"Everyone quiet," I said.

The hold fell into instant silence, the thick air tense with expectation, as voices rose and fell tunelessly overhead.

I unsheathed Sagacious Blade, and carefully fitted it into the tiny space between the door and the frame. It was not easy. Slowly—slowly—I lifted the bar...

"It worked," I said. "I can open the door."

"It works! Let's go!"

"Not now," MiMi broke in. "My aunt would tell us to hide when brawling customers sounded like they do now. And I'll bet most of them are brawlers. Unless you want to mix with really angry drunks who can still fight, but won't notice if they get hit."

While she spoke, I let the bar gently down, and turned. Now my heart really thundered. There was no alternative: if we landed, we lost what chance we had, for there had to be more of these slavers waiting to receive us.

I said, "Let's firm up our plan. If we run wild, we're sure to get into trouble."

"That's right," several agreed, voices high and nervous. "A plan, a plan."

"Healer girls who know the acupoint, come up here, behind me. Does anyone know how to fight?" I asked, not expecting much of a response.

"I can," offered the girl who'd recognized the sound of a weapon.

The others shuffled aside as she felt her way forward. She said, "Ever since I could walk, I've practiced in the yard with Father and both my brothers. They were in the guard in Apple Blossom prefecture, before the Imperial Prince's company rode in and forced everyone out of the village—"

Cygnet's breath hissed. "That's the village they pushed us into, after forcing us out of the capital!"

"That's right," a younger girl put in, as another chorus bawled raggedly above us. "We walked and walked and walked, and then we were told that we could live in a village. Only there in the houses were other people's clothes, and dishes, and their stores of food, and looms, and things. It was like a village of ghosts."

Cygnet spoke up, sharp with irony. "Then the imperial inspectors came through. Once they were gone, back the guards came, and forced us out again."

"Is that how you ended up at White Water Harbor?" I asked. And when the yeses and noes died down, Cygnet said, "Some were driven over the mountains. Some got put in a village until the inspectors came and went. Then they were forced out. Why does that matter now? We're here, aren't we? Shouldn't we be talking about getting out of here alive?"

"It matters," I said, heated with outrage. "That wicked Cou—Prince Xianti 'solved' the refugee dilemma by trickery, just as..." *First Brother predicted.* The words stopped before my lips could shape them, as did the urge to run and report to Father that I'd found a primary witness. But Father sat in prison.

Meanwhile, in the sudden silence, I sensed uneasy shiftings around me. I had drawn them together, a fragile alliance, but now I was losing that alliance in my quest for justice. No one here was a Censor's daughter. They just wanted to be saved.

I said, "You're right about talking out our plan right now. People who can fight. Someone said..."

"Me. Fan." The girl who knew weapons had waited patiently after being interrupted. "They also took away the guard. After they drove out the begg—ah, the people they'd brought in, took our men, and when we garrison sisters got together a protest party, well, we were arrested and sent to White Water as well, and we found ourselves sold off to these rats. That's why I've kept myself to myself. Speaking up didn't get any of us anywhere."

"Yes, me, too," MiMi said. "I did not want to cook for them."

"Anyway, I can fight," Fan concluded.

"How does this sound?" I'd been recollecting gallant wanderer tales about breaking out of the villains' capture. "While we freeze the muscles of as many as we can, you lead a party to find their weapons. If you can. We don't know where any are, or in what state."

No one argued! It wasn't a good plan. It felt sloppy as soon as I spoke the words, but no one else had anything better. I swallowed in a very dry throat, and tried to sound confident. Sagacious Blade hummed in my hand as I said, "I go first. I let out the boys, and then healers, go to the sleepers, and Fan, you to the weapons. I'll go whichever way I'm needed," I added, aware of my confidence running out like sand from a time piece.

Needed to…? A question I could not answer. But no one asked it. Attention had turned upward, to the silence.

MiMi said, "They'll be head down about now, drooling."

I tried to swallow the boulder in my throat. "Let's go."

TWENTY-SIX

…Under the water-borne moons.

"Yes," a chorus of whispers rose.

I lifted the bar once again, then, holding it high, I pulled the door open before easing the bar down so that it would not thud.

Girls crowded up against my back, smelling of stale congee and sweat and brine, as I felt my way down until my fingertips encountered the next compartment in the hold. I lifted the bar and swung the door open.

"Who's there?" came a teenage boy voice.

"Koi?" I said. "It's Ren."

"Ren?"

"I have my sword. We think they're drunk. We need to disable them and get their weapons—"

The boys crowded us back into the corridor, grunting and shoving, and pushed their way up the ladder before I could get to our plan.

We followed them up the ladder to the hatch, but there the boys halted. The hatch was closed from the outside.

"I'll open it," I said.

They made space. Once again I used Sagacious Blade to work the bar aside. As soon as I did, Koi slipped past me, lifted the hatch, and looked around. After the complete darkness in the hold, the lamp and starlit deck was nearly as bright as day.

A few figures staggered toward the cabin structure without seeing us, but others lay here and there, pungent rice-wine pots beside them, rolling to and fro on the deck.

Then, with a rush, the boys ran in every direction, some yelling.

"Idiots," Koi groaned, rushing out onto the deck.

The healers dispersed and bent over the snoring drinkers, who slumped boneless to the deck.

"Find rope! Find rope!" one girl whispered

"Where?"

"Why are we tying them up?" someone else asked.

Already my plan of silent, swift work had collapsed. A man loomed out of the darkness roaring, "What're you rats about? Get back down..." He swung a stick, which cracked against the back of the girl looking for rope. She gave a cry and fell to the deck, curling up and sobbing as the man stood over her, stick upraised.

Then Koi was on the man from behind, and they crashed to the deck, struggling mightily as I stood there, frozen by indecision. What to do? I'd lost what semblance of control I'd had over this plan.

Koi and his assailant rolled over and over, each grappling hard to subdue the other, as the girl crawled away, still sobbing. I stepped forward, afraid to strike lest I hit Koi. All my martial arts training had fled, leaving me witless, as the man, a head taller and far brawnier than Koi, got Koi down at last, sat astride him and began choking him.

I thumped the sword against his back. "Stop that," I shrilled.

The man swiped a big hand behind him to push me away. I danced back as Koi gasped in a breath, but then that hand returned to its choking. Angrily I pressed the sword against the man's neck. He swerved violently to grab at me, and I ripped the blade free — the edge, honed sharp, slicing cleanly across that bulging vein.

Grandfather Healer had taught us about this vital conduit. I knew how to press it to cause numbness. I knew that cutting it was dangerous, but I was unprepared for the sudden, shocking spray of blood that caused the man to scream invective. The very act of screaming worsened the spray, and he swayed, his hands loosening.

Koi flung the man off and rolled over, gasping and choking as the man collapsed on the deck, the pool of blood widening rapidly.

I stared down, unable to think as he stared back up at me, eyes wide. The world stilled for an eternity, but cannot have lasted longer than two or three beats of the heart as all the anger drained from his face, leaving only the shock, and dismay, and for an instant the bewilderment of the little boy he'd once been. Then his eyes closed and his face slackened as life fled.

I'd killed him.

Twinkling lights obscured my vision, surges of shadow closing in from the sides as Koi lurched to his feet, and swiped up the stick the man had carried. "Breathe, Young Miss," he said urgently to me, then he staggered toward two men swinging weapons, one with a broad, wicked blade, the other with a staff. I sucked in a long, unsteady breath, and the shadows and lights dissipated. I gripped Sagacious Blade in my clammy hand, running after Koi.

The pair of slavers were not moving fast. Their potations had slowed them enough for Fan—appearing from the shadows outside the swinging lamp—and Koi to fend off loose blows. And ram their blades home. Both men tried to fight; Koi reversed the stick and cracked his man behind the ear. That dropped him.

Fan's lay still. She plunged into the darkness, then reappeared before I'd gone ten random steps. "That's the last," she panted.

"All accounted for," Dinek said, coming up to me from the other direction. "You're really good," she said to Fan.

"I should be. I've been thumped into training by two hulking brothers since I could walk—"

Screams ripped the air from the cabins, the high screams of children. I raced toward them, and plunged inside, Fan and Dinek at my heels. Another shock wrung through me when I found a tangle of children in the galley, rolling about fighting each other. Blood ran from scratches as they crashed to and fro, smashing into baskets and barrels of stored food.

"Stop that," I yelled.

Of course they paid not the least heed.

This was not a time for attack, yet I had to get their attention.

Granny Zim had told me that I had a deep lake of potential within me. I'd begun to imagine it somewhere far below, a lake that glowed, as if all the world's fireflies floated there.

I still did not know what constituted potential, but anger and urgency drove me to plunge my will into that light and fling it out as I raised the sword—and we all (including me, I must admit) stared in surprise, shock, and wonder as Sagacious Blade lit up with flame.

I clanged the sword against a big iron pot, which rang like a temple bell. Sparks showered all around us, and the children stilled, chests shuddering. A small boy and a girl sobbed. A bigger boy wiped at the furrowed scratches down the side of his face, blood mixing with smears of berry juice.

"Why are you *destroying food?*" I demanded as they gazed in fear at my sword. I caught the sound of my voice, shrill and angry…I sounded like Cousin Siarti. I gulped, trying to steady myself, to speak as Mother would expect me to. "There's enough in here for us all. Look." I pointed to the bags of rice, strings of onions, and nets of sweet potatoes. "There's enough here for days and days. And we only have to be on this ship until tomorrow."

Slowly their gazes shifted to the bags, the baskets, the strings. "There's enough for everybody," I said, more softly.

"About that," Cygnet's voice floated from behind.

She sauntered up to the door of the galley, several girls following.

"What?" I said.

"What was your idea, O cloud-minded one?" Cygnet's tone was derisive, then she glanced at the sword. And even though the flame was gone, when she spoke again, her tone was slightly less combative. I sensed that even if she did not respect me, she respected Sagacious Blade. "I meant, if we won."

"It seems obvious, isn't it? We turned over the bound slavers to the local magistrates for justice—"

The older girls behind Cygnet whooped in shrill, raucous laughter.

Cygnet's mouth twisted. "Even if they were still alive, do you really believe that there is an honest magistrate in a harbor where a slaver is going to dock during daylight to offload a crowd of children?"

"What do you mean, still alive—"

"We locked up their muscles and slit their throats," Cygnet said. "What else?"

"I didn't mean to *kill* them!"

"They drank themselves into oblivion, and will never wake up. Kinder deaths than any they dealt out, I feel sure. Kinder than yours." Cygnet pointed to Sagacious Blade, still gripped in my hand. "Though it took you long enough. From what I saw, he'd just about strangled that boy he was on top of."

Appalled, I just stared, and another of the older girls hooted in disbelief. "You're upset because we sent a pack of slave-takers to the underworld?" Tall, curly-haired Ke demanded. Her voice was loud and angry but there was a desperation in her wide gaze. "After they've spent their lives making a misery of *how many* innocent lives?"

A ring of teens gazed at me with expressions of scorn, disbelief, anxiety, wariness. Everyone angry.

"Give me that," a scrawny teenage boy almost as tall as Koi said suddenly. He plunged toward me, and ripped Sagacious Blade from my hand.

Or rather, he tried. Weird greenish light crackled around his fingers and he yelped, staggering back, and tripped over a broken stool to sprawl on the deck. He cradled his burned hand against his chest and stared at me. "What *is* that?" His tone was very different.

Koi appeared in the far door. "It's the pangolin sword. She's a pangolin."

"You mean, a demon?" MiMi asked. "It's demons that take the shape of animals and humans."

"Demons are *powerful*," someone whispered.

The ring of teens was still staring at me, but in question. "You never did tell us where you come from," Cygnet said slowly.

"Because it doesn't matter," I responded, keeping my voice level, as Mana Ta whispered the first of the three prerequisites for life, *an environment that meets people's basic physical needs.* I had found my center again, at least for the moment: what mattered was not me in myself, but that I do my best to get order back. Or a semblance of it.

I said, taking care to meet each pair of eyes, "I agree that I was not thinking clearly about magistrates. Though we don't actually know they are corrupt. Right now, though, I'm more concerned about us. On this ship. And these four attacking each other, and wasting food while at it. Also, that boy there attacking me. What were you going to do with my sword if you had it? The enemies are gone. Do you want to fight everyone here? For what?"

The boy cradling his hand flushed, muttering, "Better I have it than an idiot."

One of the younger children still sitting on the deck hiccoughed on a sob. "I'm so hungry," she said. "They were going to keep it *all*." She glared at the boy next to her.

"We were just going to make sure..." he began, then muttered something truculent, and looked away.

I said to him, "Why?" And when his gaze briefly lifted, I said, "Don't you see? There's plenty here for *all* of us. Let us start with the fact that no one will go hungry tonight. Today. And wouldn't you like to be able to sleep safely? That means we stop the fighting right now. We are going to share this food. Everyone will get some. We can rest, all of us. Isn't that better than more fighting and being afraid?"

"Are you going to guard us?" the girl said.

"Yes." I raised Sagacious Blade.

At that, gazes shifted, and Dinek said, "Yes. That is exactly what I want. You might be a cloud-headed scholar's girl, but that's better than another set of villains taking the place of the ones lying out there." She made a demon-warding sign toward the deck, where the dead slavers lay.

"Me, too," MiMi said, wiping her mouth. "I did it. I cut two of their throats after that girl over there froze them. Then I puked. I don't ever want to...do that again."

"One was my brother's age," Fan said, looking away, over the rail. "Maybe his dad made him be a slaver? I don't know." She drew in an audible breath. "I liked the fight just fine when I was in it. I loved winning, though he was so drunk his eyes were rolling. I'll do it again if I have to." She braced her shoulders, chin up. "I just want to get off this cursed ship."

"We'll first have to fix a destination," Dinek stated. "The current is carrying us shoreward, and though we're not in range of what we call a lee shore yet, that will happen before Phoenix moon goes down." She pointed at the horizon.

"You know about ships," I said to her. "Does that mean you can sail one?"

Dinek chuckled, her rabbit teeth gleaming white in the lamplight. "Not by myself. I can navigate, if that's what you're asking. My mother is one of the best navigators on the Trade Route. I can tell you where to point the sails—I've known that since I my first journey when I turned six—and I can direct the rudder, though it'll take several of us to haul it over. Which we need to do soon." She jerked her thumb over her shoulder toward the stern, where the rudder had been tied down so that the crew could all drink.

I turned to the ring of older teens. Everything Mother had said about authority flitted through my mind, and I felt an odd sense, as if authority swelled around me, then receded, like a tide.

Everybody wants safety, I reminded myself.

I said to Cygnet, "You ought to know the writing where Suanek warns us that hanging onto anger is like drinking poison and expecting the other person to die." Her eyes shifted when I mentioned Suanek. "The slavers are dead, and we were successful because we listened to each other. MiMi told us the right moment. Dinek there knows how to operate this ship. Fan and Koi were our best defenders."

"And me," said the surly boy on the deck, still rubbing his hand. "I killed two. With that fish-gutting blade! I'll kill another ten of them if I get a good sword!"

"You just hacked at them," Fan began with disgust, "while they were snoring."

As the boy started up, face crimson, I said quickly, "Dinek needs us to change the direction of the ship. Let's do that. Then we can share ideas about what to do next."

"May as well draw water from a basket," Cygnet muttered, but her glare arrowed at that crimson-faced boy.

"I know nothing about ships," Koi said. "But I know something about kitchens. If you want to point the ship the right way, I'll see that things get cleaned up here, and food started." He pointed at the four children still sitting on the galley deck. "You're going to clean up the mess you made."

Though one or two grumbled, no one refused. Now that the excitement was cooling, what remained were tired, hungry, frightened children, most of them used to obeying their elders.

We followed Dinek out onto the deck. She looked skyward, then in all directions, her feet spread on the deck and her toes wiggling in her straw sandals as if she were sensing movement, then she said, "That one sail is keeping us stable in these light winds. We should raise both of these two, and I need people to help me with the rudder…"

While this was going on, Fan said the boy whose hand Sagacious Blade had struck, "Let's get these dead slavers over the side."

"I'm not touching them," he said.

Fan turned away, muttering.

"What did you say?" the boy asked belligerently, his voice cracking.

"I said, I'm your grandmother," Fan retorted.

The implication that he ought to bow to her set him off, and he advanced on her raising a fist. She stood her ground, blood still splashed from a fight with a slaver across her robe, when Koi stalked out of the galley. "I thought I heard you bleating, Jai," he said to the boy. And to Fan, "We both will help."

Jai regarded Koi, his teeth worrying at a very chapped bottom lip—I could see the cracks in the moonlight—then he jerked a shoulder up. "Why not? Better than letting them start to reek."

Ke and Lei had come out of another door, then stopped at the sound of angry voices. They now advanced with an air of purpose, Lei with one hand up at her shoulder, as though it hurt pretty much constantly.

I addressed Ke. "Do you think they had salve or willow bark or yarrow?"

"We went to look," Ke said. "They have yarrow, but she would only let me smear sting-salve on her."

"It already feels better," Lei said.

And Grandmother Zim said, "She is lying."

I started, but coughed, hiding the reaction. "I think we ought to look at it," I said, trying to sound confident. Though I'd absorbed pages of both Grandfather Healer's book on healing and his herbal, and pretended to care for ills, we'd only wrapped two broken limbs. There had been nothing like an arrow puncture to actually practice on.

"No, please," Lei said breathlessly. "Unless you truly know what a healer does. It already hurts so much. I don't want to be hurt more."

"I know it needs to be clean," I said. "That means boiled water, and then yarrow. I don't have to check your tongue or feel your pulse to know that your body is reacting to infection. I can see it even in the light of this lamp. Cleaning it and yarrow really will take down the infection."

"I'll be fast, I promise," Ke said.

Lei whimpered, but followed her, and, finding myself alone, I whispered, "Granny Zim, do you read minds?"

"No. But years and years of hearing the timbre of voices, and breathing, have taught me enough that you could say I hear the intent behind the words. Including false words, when they know they are lying. There is music in voices—"

"But we're going to be sailing right into that storm,"

someone protested from under one of the sails. "Don't you see those clouds?"

Distracted, fearful, I lifted my gaze to the sky. Phoenix Moon still shone brightly, but far to my left loomed a silent phalanx of cloud like Heaven's advance march.

"I don't smell lightning," Dinek said, rubbing her hands as she strode forward, confident in a matter she knew. "It won't be here before dawn, and then it'll wash down this deck. It will be good rain. You'll see."

I crossed the deck, skirting the black pools of congealing blood where slavers had died. Each of those pools stabbed my spirit. My idea had been to take the ship without the shedding of blood. It could have been done, too. Though Cygnet was probably right about the local magistrate being corrupt.

I needed to know.

I looked down at my sword, which still had a dark smear along the edge. I looked around for something to clean it with, a sudden ache in my chest weighing my spirit. Realization struck, hard: I had taken a life. I didn't know now if that man had been strangling Koi or subduing him, but it had looked as if he wanted to kill Koi. Would Koi have killed him first? Where was the justice here?

They were slavers. But they hadn't wanted to kill us. Not for moral reasons. Far from it: for every life they'd gain money. A dead boy brought them nothing…

"You bear a sword," Granny Zim said, quite kindly. "This is its nature. You don't wield a sword to make, though it can defend. My own life was given to music. It, too, could be a weapon, in the sense of forcing open the door to the deepest emotions, but one did survive the experience."

"You said you heard the music in voices, and that makes you hear truth. Can you teach me about music?" I whispered, squeezing my eyes shut as I tried to fight down that inner debate. "Are you listening all the time? Could you hear me even when you were in the trunk?"

"My awareness is best proximate to the blade, to which I am annealed," she replied. "Mostly I dream, except when emotions crescendo. I dream in the stars' sustained music as they dance in interlocking spirals."

"The stars have music?"

"Everything is music, my young Bu. Everything. You can find a mirror to the stars' vast dance in the tiniest spirals, such as the shells of snails. It is all music, a deliberate count, a pattern, as the augurs would say."

I found her voice soothing. And while the ship began to heel, coming to life, she recited:

> *"Pottery, gourds, and leather,*
> *Wood and stone and metal,*
> *Silken strings, bamboo*
> *Crystal and glass:*
> *From these, the ten timbres.*

We begin with three forms of a seven-toned scale..."

There was more, a great deal more, but I was soon lost, my mind sliding back to voices. What had Granny Zim heard in Cray's voice that decided her not to choose Cray over me? Cray had worked so very hard. Ah, but so had I. Just not in martial arts. Cray valued martial arts the most. Perhaps she had not seen my work as work.

Even now I wonder, what could Granny Zim have heard in my voice besides hope and curiosity when I was so young, unformed clay that I was?

TWENTY-SEVEN

All-round talent the subjects trust;
Do what's given you and gain heavenly
harmony…

BUT THE REVERIE BROKE when Dinek trotted brisky up to me, clapping her hands and rubbing them. "We are heading out toward sea, east by south. Though we will need a destination."

Koi was back. "The others are poking about in the cabins, Young Miss," he muttered, low-voiced.

"Just Ren," I said. "There is no more Young Miss."

I must have sounded more fierce than I meant to because Koi looked down. I'd meant to do away with the remains of court rank, but I saw that I'd brought it back by sounding as if I gave an order, when I only meant to suggest.

An awkward pause ensued, until he said to the tops of his sandals, "The captain has a trunk full of silver boaters, as well as bags of coins. I expect Jai's idea was to get your sword so he can fight off all comers."

"There are the slavers' swords."

"He wants yours, because of the flames. He doesn't know anything about fighting, but he's a brawler." He didn't say how he knew, but I guessed that there had been trouble in the boys' hold. And Koi had won, judging by how Jai had done what Koi asked.

Voices echoed through the three-story cabin structure, and

soon everyone began to gather on the deck. They all avoided the blood as well.

"The deck is clear at the stern," Cygnet said, appearing before me. "And those tending that rudder thing want to hear what is said."

"Let's gather there," I said.

Koi led the way. The rest of the former prisoners gathered in clusters, and most sat down out of habit, looking up expectantly, Cygnet with her arms crossed, her expression skeptical in the light of the swinging lamps.

I said, "What do you want to do next?"

"Go home," a girl shrilled.

"Yes! Yes! Go back home!"

"If we go back to the imperial island, what's going to happen to us?" Cygnet asked. "It'll be another gang of slavers. We were gathered up and the imperial guards were just riding around!"

"Unless we sail to Peaceable Breezes Harbor. I don't believe Governor Gu will sell you," I said.

Cygnet retorted, "If he's not with the new emperor, then they'll be attacking him next."

Dinek nodded. "I don't claim to know naval tactics, but you can't sail the seas in trade and not be aware of what they call formations. Blockades, if they don't want to let anyone into a harbor. I wager anything the new emperor has a formation outside of that harbor, and they check every ship coming in."

"I wish I could somehow rescue my brothers," Fan admitted.

Koi said, "Do you know how to raid an army garrison?"

Fan shook her head. "I was never permitted to go on missions. I'm good in the practice court. That's all."

Voices rose from all sides, then Cygnet stood up, long hair streaming down her back, the breeze toying with her ragged robe. In the moonlight, she looked like a faerie.

She didn't say anything, but people quieted, gazing at her expectantly. It was clear to me that she might not like it, but she was accustomed to being the center of attention. "You all know by now that the cabins are full of silver and gems. I want to take a share of that and go somewhere where the empire isn't attacking." She lifted her chin. "And start a school. For girls."

Jai laughed disparagingly, but his laughter was drowned out when five, then ten girls shouted, "I'll go! I'll be a student! I wasn't allowed to read! Me, too!"

Jai chewed his lip, eyeing me truculently. "Are you going to keep all the silver?"

"No one is keeping all the silver," I said. "At least, my idea is to share it out fairly."

Jai said, "These babies will lose theirs before they go ten steps." He pointed at Little Snow and Rose, sitting together at one side, looking very small and scared. "If you turn them loose, you *know* it'll happen. Why give them what they're going to lose anyway?"

Fan rounded on him. "Why give you any food? You're just going to poop it out anyway."

Some of the little ones, their eyes ringed with exhaustion and hunger, gusted with laughter, the kind of laughter that trembles on the edge of tears.

Much as I was beginning to dislike Jai, he was right about turning ten-year-olds loose in the world, with or without money. They ought to be with their families. But thanks to the troubles around the dragon throne, these families were not living useful lives at home. Their villages had been raided for men and supplies, the rest scattered all over, hungry and afraid.

The usual surge of hatred for Xianti burned through me, but it widened to his uncle, the new emperor, who had let Xianti do what he'd done. Encouraged it, even.

I said to Jai, "I don't know what's right. But you don't have to worry about them. We can put you off somewhere. With your share. As soon as we can."

MiMi came up to me, and whispered behind her hand, "The rice had been soaking for morning, so it cooked fast. But even if we use every cup and bowl and plate, we won't have enough dishes for everyone."

Another problem! Koi spoke from behind me, "Might I suggest something?"

MiMi and I turned his way.

He said, "The little ones are used to getting a dipperful. They can get two dippers if they want. They don't seem to care how it gets inside them, as long as it gets there. Save the plates for the ones who'll make the most trouble." A glance toward Jai and Cygnet.

MiMi looked at me, then nodded. "We can do that." She bustled away.

I turned to him. "I guess they didn't need you in there?"

"I just got those little pests cleaning up. As soon as MiMi

saw that, she took over. She knows which pots to use. How much to put in each. I've been around the palace kitchen ever since I was small, and I watched a lot of the cooking, but she got trained. She brought in a few others. Besides the ones the slavers had doing the work."

"I'm hungry," someone wailed.

"It's coming," I said. "After you eat, everyone ought to rest. You will be safe. We'll make sure of that."

Fan raised the sword she'd been using and tapped it against her hand as she glared under a furrowed brow in the direction of Jai and another boy somewhat younger. "I'm going to help guard."

"Where do we sleep?" Rose quavered.

"I don't want to go back in that hole!" a boy yelled.

"Sleep anywhere you want," Dinek said. "But there's going to be rain before morning."

MiMi came out then, leading several girls lugging buckets with dippers in them.

I knew that the serving of food in imperial court was a matter of the strictest ritual. Where people sat, who was served first, what they were served, on which dishes, all was expressly set out. But I had never considered that there was an art to serving people gathered in the same space who did not know one another.

The girls with the buckets headed straight for the smaller children. And sure enough, they made no fuss about dishes. They sat up like puppies yearning for a treat, as the rest of MiMi's kitchen helpers brought out cups and plates and bowls of congee. As they handed these out to teenagers, I saw that they had added in fried sweet potato chunks, cooked in sesame oil. At the smell wafting off those plates, my stomach ceased its fret, and roared for sustenance.

In court, the higher the rank the quicker one is served. But MiMi left me for last, along with Koi and Fan and Dinek. I took that as a gesture of trust, and my throat ached again, but that did not keep me from slurping down my share as hastily as I could swallow when it did reach me.

As soon as the food entered my stomach, an almost overwhelming lassitude stole over me. Some sort of herb? But there was no strange smell, or sense of an evil thing invading my body. It was reaction, and tiredness, catching up with me.

Though we had not finished talking about the next step, I knew I could not do anything more. When a girl took my licked plate from my hand, I wandered in the direction of the cabins. Others were already there, crowding into each, and lying together on the bunks and on the deck.

When I reached the top floor, where the leader had obviously slept, I found teens and children sprawled everywhere. Jai was one, having claimed the captain's huge bunk. But he must have gone to sleep the moment he lay down, because three small children had crawled up at the foot of that bed, which I would have expected him to object violently to. They were huddled together for comfort. Two of those were clearly sister and brother, with a small friend, judging by how her hand held the sister's, though both sets of fingers had relaxed.

I backed out, walked a few steps, and sank down onto the balcony with my back to the wall, Sagacious Blade across my knees. I'd said they would be safe. I might as well stay awake as long as I could, keeping watch.

A quiet step, and there was Koi, yawning violently as he mounted the steps, a sword in hand. He carried it absently, and correctly, the way a warrior does. I still carried Sagacious Blade like a walking stick. I did not want to sheathe it until it was clean. "I've collected all the weapons except for this sword, and the one Fan wants."

"Oh, good," I said thankfully. "Where are they?"

"Down in the hold where we were. No one seems to want to go there."

"We should throw them into the sea," I said, and then shook my head. "No, that is a waste."

"Very much a waste," Koi said. "We might need them. Though no one is trained except Fan and me. The others know it. May I put a question…Ren?" he asked, and in that pause, I heard the choked-off *Young Miss*.

A bubble of unlikely laughter rose within me, but I was too tired to express it. "You called my brother Banti. Cray told me that. You can think of him as Banti, but I'm 'Young Miss' even after a year among the Falcons?"

He looked away. "It's…different," he said.

"How?" I asked. "I truly want to learn. I don't think of myself as above others in worth, but C—some believe I did think that way. It wasn't merely a matter of proper address between ranks in the imperial court."

He said, "With…your brother, we were together every day. We talked all the time. He cleaned me up after I was beaten bloody by Tiger Li and Xianti, and I cleaned him up. We bathed together. Slept side by side on the mountain, when we had to do fox and hounds overnight. But I rarely saw you. And it was strictly forbidden. Madam made that very clear, we were never to look at you, much less speak. And you…"

"Ay, don't say I swanned about like a grand princess, I truly did not think that way at all."

"No, it was more that you were so like Madam. Everyone admires her so. We did not want to disappoint her."

I sighed, relaxing a little. "That is…ah-h-h." A sudden, violent yawn seized me. "I tried so hard to be like her." I sat upright, rousing when I remembered how we'd gotten here in the first place—which was completely my fault. "I owe you an explanation," I said, deciding to get it over with at once—like poor Lei, letting Ke clean out that arrow wound. "I was going to go to the privy. But I decided to put down my pack first. I heard Cray and Granny Ou in that attic. Cray was talking. About me, mostly. She…said some things that were mostly true. I should not have listened, I know. I ran out, and that's how you found me."

Koi was silent for a moment, then mumbled, "I know she was brought to protect you. She was proud of that. Being chosen, I mean."

"I know. And she did her best."

Koi went on, "I know her pretty well, I think. She has a strong sense of duty. She'll be faulting herself for our disappearance."

"If we could somehow go back, I'd…" *try to give this sword to her.* "Do most anything."

He sent me a look. "Supposing we did go back. What would you do? They're likely to have left as soon as they could find transport, what with Tiger Li and his boys rampaging all over the harbor."

I said, "I'd go to my grandfather, of course. He needs to know what I learned about Mother. Also, he'd know how to properly search for my brother," I added, a pulse of rage waking in spite of the heavy weight of exhaustion over my entire body.

"About your brother. I…" He trailed off, and looked away.

I roused more at that. "Don't you dare stop there. What about my brother?"

Koi studied me, the light from the swinging lamp reflecting in his huge pupils as his gaze searched mine, right eye, left eye, right. Did he see our resemblance in me? "I figured it out," he said finally. "During the journey from the dyers. But I didn't want to say. In front of Cray. However, Banti is your brother, so I think you should know, even if I have no proof in the way First Young Master would be sure to ask. But I know where he went. I'm pretty sure."

I half-rose, ready to demand we turn the ship about. "To?"

"Prince Yiuti," Koi admitted.

No, I wailed inwardly. Yiuti wasn't poisonous like the imperial grandchildren. But he was like fire in a high wind. "Did you find evidence?"

"No. That's just it. There was no evidence of him anywhere. It was as if he disappeared. The only way there would be no evidence is if someone really powerful made him disappear. I don't mean killing him. There would have been evidence of that. My family in the Household would know, even if the imperial palace thought they were hiding his being strangled or poisoned or stabbed, as happened to so many servants. The palace doesn't know how much the Household Department knows."

I thought of Eider. For the first time, it occurred to me that spying might not always be for evil intent. When we don't regard it as evil, we call it scouting.

"If he'd gone to any of his other friends, Gui would have found something. But he found no trace at all."

"Yiuti...better than Xianti finding him," I said, wishing that I could be glad that Second Brother was safe, but I didn't believe he'd be entirely safe with Cousin Yiuti.

Koi gave a small nod. "Cray would hate that." He seemed to consider saying more, then left it at that, giving way to a huge yawn.

I said, "But he's not *her* brother."

"No." His gaze shifted away, then he yawned again. "I'm going to sleep across the doorway where Jai is. I'll wake up if he does, in case he wants to look for trouble." He rose and went away.

I stretched out and fell asleep.

TWENTY-EIGHT

She sought them and taught them:
All creatures, water and air, strive for
benevolence,
Ten-thousand decisions yearn for the best.

I WOKE TO DAYLIGHT, and the sound of bare feet pattering around me. Warm rain spattered my face.

I sat up, overwhelmed by the smells rising off my clothes. The rain was coming, and I desperately needed a bath. Though my head throbbed, I picked up Sagacious Blade and went back down to the galley, where I found lukewarm tea waiting for anyone who wanted it, and half a pot of congee.

For the first time since that terrible illness, I'd slept past dawn. As I stood over the pot of congealing congee, eating from the dipper, Rose appeared, looking less like a pale little ghost. "We divided up," she piped. "The girls get all the back, and the boys have to go to the front, where it's smaller, if they want to wash their clothes in the rain. There's *more* of *us*," she finished triumphantly as if it were a good thing to have far more girls than boys.

"That's a smart idea," I said.

She lowered her head—and I saw the effect of someone, somewhere, admonishing her that girls ought to be modest and humble, but her shoulders betrayed a little wriggle of pride. Then she flitted away, joined by Little Snow and other ten-year-old girls.

I ate three dippers of congee, then found a stack of cups someone had washed out. I poured tea into one and followed Rose out behind the great cabin structure to the stern, where a swarm of little girls in underthings—and a few happily naked—jumped up and down on their clothes, though the rain was barely a spatter. But a low rumble in the distance presaged a gray-blue curtain that approached, then overtook us, banishing the glimpses of sun as rain slanted down.

Squeals of glee rose. I flung off my outer robe, and began to stamp it, then I dropped to my knees and scrubbed at the blood splatters. I don't even know why, but as I scrubbed I said a prayer for the dead, who were not feeling this warm, sweet rain. I hoped they'd come back as something innocent— bunnies, or golden fish, or finches—to wash their souls clean. Then I turned to my task with more vigor than I'd thought I would be able to find within myself. I left on my long undyed under tunic, but took off my underthings, washed those out, and then my hair. The rain came down hard enough to sting, droplets bouncing back up. I opened my mouth to the sky, letting the rain wash out my mouth and the empty teacup both.

Last, I cleaned Sagacious Blade. Little girls, noticing, ran up. "I want to see fire," one stated, black eyes wide and excited. "Make the sword fire, Ren the Pangolin!"

"Make the fire, ple-e-e-ease?"

I reached within—mostly as an experiment. I'd put Essence fire to the sword while desperate. To my considerable relief, I was able to will up a handful of that mysterious light and send it along the blade. Desperation was not a necessary component, then. Though it had motivated me.

The girls laughed and clapped with glee, then flitted away to finish their tasks as they chattered about good demons and pangolins and were they Essence animals, like cranes? No thought to tomorrow, no thought to the rest of the day. And yet, here they were, taking care of themselves the best they knew how. Not their fault they were young. Though I was not that much ahead of them, I scolded myself as I combed out my hair, tugging painfully at snarls. I resented Jai's prediction, but I knew it was probably truer than not. What to do next?

By the time I'd pulled up my hair and fixed it, leaving the comb there for someone else to use, I knew what I wanted: to find out the truth of that island the slavers were taking us to.

That didn't mean I'd get to find out, but the craving to begin somewhere to widen my understanding of our situation galled me.

When the rain lifted, we got a brief, spectacular rainbow, then the sun shone, breathlessly bright, as the clouds fled eastward. The deck began to steam. My things were soon damp, and I dressed again, then entered the galley just as Koi, Dinek, Fan, and Cygnet came looking for me.

Before I could second-guess myself, I explained my thinking.

Fan grunted. "I like your idea of taking a look into that harbor. But we'd have to scout it on the sly. You and I don't look too bad, Dinek, but the rest of these people are in rags. And Ren, you will forgive me for pointing out that robe of yours is the worst of them all, even if it no longer reeks."

"I can fix that, at least," I said. "The cabins are full of silks and fine fabrics. Those slavers seemed fond of fine things. I can make and mend from their clothes, and teach whoever wants to learn."

"I'd take those lessons," Cygnet said. "At home, we had a servant for mending, and there was a shop that I still miss for their beautiful robes, but that life is gone. I hate drab clothes. If I have to make my own, I'll do it. Especially as I saw some beautiful silk in one of those rooms. In fact, I'd better go claim that gorgeous blue robe before those little hoptoads ruin it."

She went off, signaling a general dispersal.

Everyone looked much better for a full meal, but MiMi came up to me a little later and said, low-voiced, "We're going to have to land fairly soon if we don't want to starve again. We've been running through the stores very fast."

Having left that burden with me, MiMi went off. Ayah! I could think as I sewed; that idea unexpectedly brought Cousin Taisa to mind. I hoped she was all right.

I soon finished ripping apart my rag robe for thread, to adapt a moss-green robe I'd found tossed on the floor in one of the rooms. The shape of bamboo leaves had been woven in. Not bright enough for those who liked clothes, I guess, as I glimpsed youngsters running around with crimson silk, purple, deep blue, and even imperial gold trailing behind them. Jeweled hairpins wobbled in inexpert topknots, and sashes and jade belt ornaments fluttered and swung.

I sat under the awning adjacent the galley to commence my sewing, as Dinek and Fan sat with me, soon joined by others,

Cygnet with her summer-sky blue robe. Koi appeared, and leaned against the wall, one hand holding the sword he'd found among the slavers' things.

"My idea is to find someplace safe to land," I said. "We need stores. We've got plenty of silver ingots to buy them. Which leads to my second goal, finding out what we can about the magistrates here."

"And then?" Cygnet asked. "What then?"

"It's primary-witness evidence," I said. "I'd carry it back to Governor Gu."

Dinek said, "It will be troublesome to bring us about, but I've seen worse shores. If we can find a secluded inlet, as long as there are no rocks under the surface, and the tides don't fight us, we could moor this ship and send out the boats."

"And then?" Cygnet said, winged brows raised.

"Plan after that," I said. "I'm only deciding for myself. Ay, and for any of the small ones who don't want to venture into the world alone. Jai was not wrong about what might happen to them. I believe they'd be safe with m—" *my grandfather,* "with the governor in the northern province of the imperial island. Wherever it is."

Dinek said, "As soon as I can land and find my way to a chart, I'll know where we lie."

"I want to find a place for my school," Cygnet stated. "I'll take any of them who want to learn. But I don't know if this island is safe enough. Slavers landing here suggests wolves in the palaces and rats in the temples."

Dinek gave a nod of agreement. "If I can get people to help me let down the smaller boat, I can explore the shore, and report back. I've got three volunteers I trust who can help me with sail and oars."

"Then who will sail this ship if there is danger?" Ke protested.

They turned my way. Were they waiting for someone to argue with?

Koi got up. "Dinek, can you show me how to raise and lower the boats?"

They went off together, solving the problem between them, or so I hoped.

I said, "I'm going to start making over this robe. And I have three needles…"

The rest of that day was divided between sewing, eating, and talking. I remembered what MiMi said, but each time I resolved to deny myself a meal in order to make food last, my stomach would gnaw painfully, and I'd end up eating again. I drank as much tea as I could to suppress my appetite, but food I craved, and from the looks of the others, so did they.

Most of the little ones stayed interested in sewing for about ten breaths, then ran off, as some of the teens poked closely into every box and drawer in all the cabins, now that all the trunks had been explored. A few more venturesome went back down into the hold, which everyone had avoided, with the discovery that the smallest hold, far forward, had a lock.

I set aside my sewing and took Sagacious Blade with me. Dinek used a sailing tool to hammer the lock off. Lamplight revealed spider webs, and under those, extra stores—mostly chickpeas, rice, jugs of oil, and baskets of dried seaweed. At the very back, two more small trunks of actual golden taels, with the imperial stamp. And more weapons.

"That gold," I said, looking into excited faces, "represents great wealth, but also many, many questions. Any of us carrying all that to the coin changers will be like sticking a straw up a tiger's nose." Father had told us about how investigators always began by following the progression of great sums. "This is the kind of wealth that means prison, maybe execution, for anyone but government or military officials or merchants with imperial tallies."

Most of the older teens backed off a step, as if proximity would land them in jail.

Jai chewed his lip.

Koi had listened with a grim face. He would have heard those lessons, too, surely. He said privately to me once we'd brought all the food up to the deck, "We're going to have to decide what to do with Jai. He keeps going off with those three bigger boys who stick to the corners. So far they're too afraid of your sword to act. But it's only a matter of time. And hunger. Also, those two girls who don't talk to anyone else."

"I saw. I'm sure they want to get the weapons and take over the ship," I said, sighing. "And keep all the loot. Just like the Red Hand Gang in the Jong Siang tales of the 110 Outlaw Gallants, when they tried to take over the ship from Jong Siang and Chan the Dancer after *they* took the ship from pirates. What can we do? I don't want to kill them, the way the outlaws did. The Red Hand Gang were bloody assassins. Jai and those others are...like us."

"In ten years they might be the Red Hand Gang," Koi said.

"Unless someone stops them."

"Not by killing. We could put them on the shore," I suggested.

"But we don't know who is on that island. I can see Jai trying to sell word of us to anyone who will listen." Koi scowled down at his hands, then looked up. "But I agree about not killing him for something he might do. I have a sort of idea. Depending on what Dinek says, I could go scout. And use one of those bags of mixed coinage, maybe a couple of the silver boaters, to get provisions."

"Take Jai?"

"That's my idea. Tell him he can learn to scout the way a martial artist does. He says he knows small boats. He's desperate to learn martial arts, under all the swagger and bullying. Maybe it would give him something to do besides lurk around waiting to jump people when their backs are turned. I don't suppose he's thinking much beyond that, jump before he gets jumped. I expect he's been jumped a lot, the way he flinches. Then tries to hide it."

"Good plan," I exclaimed.

Our discussion broke up when not one but two squabbles broke out, girls' shrill voices bringing me to my feet. Koi vanished.

By the time I reached the cabins, Cygnet and Fan had broken up the fights, separating teary, pouting girls. They'd been fighting over some hair clasps from one of the cabin, one etched with ducks.

"We've got to do something about these children," Fan said when we retreated out onto the balcony. "They're bored, and that gets them fretful and riled. They're used to being told what to do, and doing it."

"Perhaps we ought to start Cygnet's school right here?" I suggested. "It worked while we were prisoners."

"That's because there was nothing else to do. Some of us don't want to learn to read and write," Ke stated.

"Why? You want to be ignorant?" Cygnet demanded.

Ke flushed. "Better than having a head stuffed full of useless blather! I saw my aunt struggle with doing other people's laundry and cleaning while my uncle sat about, studying for those cursed imperial examinations year after year. As far as I'm concerned, we do just fine without books, and I'd burn them all if I could."

"Why am I even listening?" Cygnet said, "Talking to you is

more pointless than playing flute to a cow."

The two girls faced one another, and I walked between them, the way Cray had got between Minnow and me so long ago. "Ke, what else can you teach those children?"

She lifted her chin. "I can teach them to dance," she said. "I was training to be a dancer."

The look she leveled at Cygnet brought to mind the many disparaging things that Cygnet had said about entertainment houses, places I had only the haziest idea about. But her context had been the prospect of being sold into one.

"I started learning dancing," I said, drawing their gazes my way. "I'm a mere beginner, but I can help you teach them."

Ke looked at me in surprise. "You did?"

"I did. I didn't get lessons very long before the troubles happened that put me here, but it would feel good to dance."

That raised a chorus: "I want to dance! I want to, too! Show me! Show me! Do we get pretty sleeves?"

We divided up the children between several teachers, and, remembering Cygnet's complaints about unruly boys, I said I'd sit with her students—Sagacious Blade at my side—first. I didn't think Ke would get resistance from the girls who wanted to dance.

"Time for school," I said to the gaggle of tens and elevens. "If you are not learning to cook, or do ship tasks, or dance, you're going to do school."

"Even us?" said a girl.

"Yes," Cygnet declared. "First, sit in rows."

Again I saw that the habit of obedience was there in those who'd had a family to live with, even if they were not taught to recite the Twenty-Five Virtues. We soon had almost everyone except Dinek's ship handlers and MiMi's cooks—who were already busy—doing some kind of lessons. The exception being those five who slunk around out of my sight. But I knew they were there.

I sat at the front. Cygnet was so assured at the front of a class; I already knew from our attempt at lessons in the hold that she remembered all the primary instruction by heart, without recourse to a book or scroll. There was something soothing in the repetitions and recitations, a steadiness that I had never noticed when I was small, because that was just life. But after our recent experiences, it was sublime to sit in rows on the deck, the summer breezes toying with hair and sashes as we recited the rules to a just, orderly, kind world.

Occasional breezes wafted the enticing smells of cooking fresh-caught fish and chickpeas ground into flour and fried crispy in the oil, as if to remind us of the promise of such a world.

Cygnet began with the ancient stories about the dragon who chose the first king, giving his time the name Golden Dragon Dynasty. Then she started them on those first recitations that paired with learning one's characters.

Once they were well established, I went to the stern, where Ke and the girls had begun the first movements. Ke hummed accompaniment. She had a fine voice.

The experiment became expected by the next day, and routine by the third. We had lessons in the mornings, afternoons, and evenings, meals between; by the third day, MiMi was giving me significant glances in the kitchen. We had consumed everything that had been in the galley when we took the ship, and we were rapidly diminishing the locked-up stores.

Troubled—wondering if Koi and Jai had decided to vanish altogether—I lay down in one of the cabins on what had become "my" bed, which was a pad made up of winter blankets. It was too warm for coverlets.

I was asleep when something poked my arm. I jerked awake and reached for the sword, but Granny Zim said nothing, and then Koi whispered, "It's me. We're back."

One of the girls in the room behind me muttered, stirring.

I got up and followed Koi out onto the deck. We were not the only ones awake. MiMi and two of her older kitchen crew were struggling to raise bags and baskets and barrels with the ropes, as Dinek gave low-voiced directions.

"Jai is asleep already," Koi said before I could ask. "I had him bring the boat back to the ship while I slept. He knows sailing, just as he said. His people were fishers."

"You let yourself sleep while he was awake?" I commented.

In the light of Ghost Moon, on its low circle, I saw Koi shrug.

There was expression in that shrug that I could not interpret, and I was not certain if asking would be intrusive. I decided to remain safely with questions concerning the general good. "What happened? You were gone three days."

"And we learned a lot. As well as bringing back all that." He tipped his head behind, where MiMi and one of the boys maneuvered another rice bag over the rail. "Do you want to hear it all, or just a summary?"

"All," I said.

"We sailed toward the harbor, stashed the boat in reeds, and followed a fishers' trail up over a ridge into the city. It's weatherworn, and rundown, even the magistrate's building. But the place was bustling..." He went on to explain that he and Jai had used coins from one of the cabins to buy baskets, which made the two look like messengers rather than loiterers. They bought food from street vendors, and ate while listening to the dock laborers, some of whom speculated about where the *Cattail* might be, and if the big storm had blown it off course.

"Is that the name of our ship?" I asked.

"I think so. But here's what we discovered. Whoever rules in the magistrate building is running the slave auction, twice a year. There are two warehouses full of slaves to be sold, divided out by skills and looks, exactly the way those who took us had said. They're waiting for the last expected ship. Probably ours. Before holding the general auction. All the yachts and boats in the harbor are buyers. They're all housed in the two inns, which must be nicer inside than they look from the outside. We heard music coming out of both, noise, and good smells."

Koi rubbed his hands over his knees, his palms rasping softly on the fabric. "We made our way along to the warehouses. I heard children crying in the big one on the left, before I was chased away. I claimed to be running a message for my master, who wanted to know how long he must wait, and I was cursed and kicked at, as the guard said, *Your master will hear the summons drum, same as everyone else.*"

"That's horrible," I said.

"Yes. We climbed up over the ridge behind the warehouses. It's a crescent island. There's a big island covering most of the horizon straight north, with a lot of dragons' teeth between. Fishing boats," Koi said. "Jai told me they'll come in on the evening tide, and begin salting the take. We found an old cart abandoned behind an empty temple, and we brought it back down and slept under it at nights. Today, we went around buying up supplies. Sima told us that to remain traceless, you don't buy all at one place. You do some here. Some there. Always a different story—wave your hands instead of making up a lot of lies, and then they're more likely to make up a story for you. Fit you into what they expect."

"That's like scouting?" I asked.

"Yes. I think it helped that we're young, and dressed like servants. I showed Jai the proper servant manner, and when he balked, I told him it's a better disguise than masks and black cloaks, because no one knows it's a disguise."

"That's clever," I exclaimed.

A smile flickered on Koi's somber face, then he went on. "I bought as much as I could until I ran out of coins, then we lugged it all to the boat once the sun set. We sailed on the tide, and that's it."

Koi looked down. Rub, rub, rub, then he looked up. "I want to save them."

"Yes."

"In the warehouse."

"I know."

"We could do it."

"How?" Hope flared, then stilled. "You said there are guards. You and Fan are our only fighters. You know how bad I am."

"You're not as bad as you think you are. You, and that sword especially. I would like to hear more about its story, if you will tell me," he added.

"There's a…a person. I don't think she's a demon. Or was one, though who knows, now? She calls herself Granny Zim. I think from her accent and some words, which are the sorts you see in the very old scrolls, that she might have lived long ago. But her way of telling a story is…a spiral." Yes, that was the right image. "Cray knew. I think she knows more about it than I. She kept the secret."

"Ayah, that reminds me. Cray and Granny Ou must be on their way to Peaches. Which we could try to reach, once we're done emptying those warehouses. But is that the name of their Falcon scrape, or a nickname? And on which island, did you ever hear?"

"I didn't. All I ever heard was Peaches. And, north. Not how far north, though."

"There are so many places with 'peach' in the name, for Suanek's immortal peaches." He scowled. "We might find out something about Peaches if we seek that wing sign at inns. But that's for later. What do you say about rescuing those slaves in the warehouses?"

"You mentioned guards, and we got onto the sword. Let's go back to the guards," I said. "Surely those buyers have their own guards, as well."

"True. But there are guards and guards. The ones lounging around the warehouses looked to me like brawlers rather than martial artists. They could be hired from any number of places, for any number of reasons. I never thought about it until we were sailing back, but all those fox and rabbit games Lan Xianti forced on us at the princes' court was training. I can even tell you the names of some of the strategies we used. Like, the fox exploiting the tiger's might," Koi said.

"It sounds very martial. But how does that help us now? We're not being chased."

"When Lan Xianti was the leader, and how very good it is to say his cursed name instead of all his titles, though I want to spit every time I do say it." Koi pushed the air away with both hands. "We had to lose when Lan Xianti led, or he found ways to take it out on everyone. We had to find a way to lose in public sight, so they couldn't half kill us."

"I wish my brother had told me."

"He did not want you to know. What could you do except be concerned? He wanted you to be happy."

I sighed, remembering some other things my brother had said that had puzzled me, but I had not thought to ask. But I will, I promised myself. When I find him. "Go on, how do your strategies evading Lan Xianti help us now?"

"It's not so much strategies as that we learned to notice things that we might never have noticed. Like, evaluating the guards by their stances. The ones favoring Xianti overlooked what he did. The ones trying to keep order watched in a way that meant they were going to report, and Xianti in those days did not dare irritate the emperor, who was favoring Guiza. Anyway, martial artists stand the way Sima the Hero did. They're always alert when on watch. Those guards loafed. Chatted. The ones who noticed us looked at our empty hands and our baskets, and ignored us. Someone who was alert would have questioned us."

"Ay, now I think I see."

"As for strategies, there's another, called saving the turtle by rescuing the rabbit. That's the one I think we could use."

"What does it mean? What would we do?"

"Say a cook fire overturned on one of those fine yachts, one moored close to another fine yacht. With some oil splashed about, those fires will spread fast. While I would not want to burn a ship belonging to fishers or traders, I don't feel that way about the yacht of a slaver."

I considered that, ambivalent about how my heart inclined toward agreement. Did that make my morals suspect? Oh, how I wished for Mother to comb out my tangled thoughts for me!

Koi had gone on. "…if everyone comes down to fight the fires, or to watch—and you know half the town will turn up to watch a good fire—we go to the warehouse. We take out the four guards…"

"How?"

"I thought about that. Because I knew you would object. Four—no, five of us to one guard, get him off balance, then the fifth uses the thumb to freeze them. Your idea of binding and gagging them would suit. We'll only be there moments, if we're not caught."

"Let's not do any more killing, if we can avoid it," I said, with that man's bewildered face before me, drained of all the anger before he died. Who put the anger there? Kanda says we are all born innocent, with good hearts…

I blinked and shook my head. "Whatever happens to them after we leave is up to them. And those who hired them. But if we can, I would rather leave them to that choice rather than make the choice for them."

"The way an emperor does."

"Yes," I said, fervently—misinterpreting his tone completely. "It sounds like a good plan to me. I'm not much of a warrior, but I know the acupoints. Tay and Tiger Moth and I proved that repeatedly." I rubbed my neck.

"Fan and I'll handle any fighting. You deal with the warehouse guards, and getting the prisoners out," Koi said. He smiled grimly. "Then we'll loose Jai and a couple of the wild ones to douse the warehouses with jugs of oil, and burn them to the ground. That ought to cover our retreat."

TWENTY-NINE

In western winds no banners streamed —
No war horse pranced or armor jingled.
Still, in lawless times to heed the law —
She asked, is that not the highest virtue?

MOST OF THE FORMER slaves hailed Koi's idea, and fervently threw themselves into planning for the rescue mission. They looked to Koi and Fan for martial arts training. Or trickery, I ought to say; from the sound of it, most wanted to be taught in one day how to defeat a company of armed guards.

"You can't," Koi said bluntly. "I've been practicing with a sword since I was small, and I still can't defeat a master. Fan and I together wouldn't be able to defeat the master I was training with before I ended up here. But I've learned that several people. Even weak ones. Can bring down an unwary guard. If they take the guard by surprise, and work together. That means no screaming and running wild, which alerts the enemy. We have to be as sneaky as snakes..."

Fan and Koi got them divided up into teams, taught them step by step — distract the guard, get him off balance, everyone pounce, thumb to the acupoint — over and over. They relished this form, especially the parts where they took turns being the "unwary" guard and flipped him around, but whenever anyone laughed, or exclaimed, Koi and Fan both silenced them. "Let's repeat it once more," Fan said. "Silence is success.

Noise is defeat."

"Silence is success. Noise is defeat."

"Once more," Koi said.

"Silence is success. Noise is defeat."

They repeated that each time one of the groups let out a sound. By the end of a watch, they were thoroughly tired of repeating it, and by noon, the only sound attendant on the repetitions of a take-down sequence were grunts and thumps.

All this while we sailed back toward the harbor. By the time the sun went down, and they were released to wait for the evening meal, there was no restless bickering or chasing around. They flopped and sprawled on the stern deck.

The planners and I met in the galley, as had become habit. There was always tea going.

"They need more time," Fan said, wringing one hand, which an over-enthusiastic rescuer had wrenched when Fan served as a guard. "We've got them to stop blabbing and laughing, at least, but they need *training*. They can do the sequence, but it's still a game to them. None of them can actually fight."

Koi nodded. "I know. We don't want it to come to a fight. This plan won't work unless we take the slavers completely by surprise. If we are wily and silent, I think we can do it. You didn't see how lazy they were. They don't seem to think that there could ever be any danger."

"I still worry," I said, and hesitated when the older teens looked at me with impatience or disbelief. Ke rolled her eyes.

Koi said, "Why? You worried about Hali Ye and his followers?"

That was the name of the older boy who kept eyeing Sagacious Blade.

"I am, but it's not entirely them…"

"They won't be able to sell us out because I'm going to keep Hali Ye with me, and if he so much as looks wrong, Jai will jump him. Afterward, who knows, but I'm not worried about them during the time it takes to try our plan. What else?"

"It's related. I'm afraid that if something does happen—even something small—each group will suddenly become five panicked people running around screaming and getting in each other's way, the way they did that night. The groups are good," I said hastily, seeing Fan's brows lower. "I'm just saying that…that they are a lot of children, and yes, I count myself. I can see you're going to remind me that I am merely fourteen, which is the same as four to you seventeen and eighteen-year-olds. But...it's how...they are from such different places, and different families. And different types of learning. So if something goes wrong, they're looking to luck, and demons, and the like. Did you hear Little Snow telling the rest that because this is a Horse year, those born in the Year of the Horse will have extra luck, which they can double by wearing red somewhere on them, with a horse drawn on it? That yelling you heard earlier was them trying to get those born in a Horse year to come into their group."

"They just want strong luck." MiMi looked up from grinding chickpeas, and swiped an errant lock of hair back from her damp forehead with a forearm. "That makes perfect sense to me. We'll need it."

"Except counting on luck rather than a strong right arm is like trying to harness wind imps," Fan said with a laugh.

I hesitated. Mother had explained once that "luck" was the ignorant commoner's name for Essence. But I still did not understand Essence at all.

"I dealt with that," Fan added, yawning. "The groups will stay the way we worked them. We've got at least one stronger one in each group."

"I'm glad," I said, abandoning luck and Essence, as those were not the real problem. "They really impressed me as I went from group to group with the two healers who know the acupoint. But..."

"Ayoh, Ren, *must* you predicting gloom?" Ke snapped. "You might have demon blood, but you never said you're also an augur."

Koi raised a hand. "I think I see what you mean, Ren. It's not like the Falcons. We have not trained together, so we cannot trust one another in a fight the way the Falcons did."

"We don't have any experience with fighting," MiMi said.

"And we don't know one another well enough to trust," Fan added. "That's what practice is for." She thumbed her jaw. "I keep thinking, we're doing everything wrong, that is, not the way I was raised, which was to take years to hone skills. But MiMi, we don't have that time. Those slavers are looking for this ship. If they stop looking, they'll just sell off the people they have now, and we will never have a chance to rescue them."

"I know that, but Ren is still croaking bad luck at us, which is sure to bring it."

"Not bad luck," Dinek said, and snapped her fingers. "I think it's bad luck not to think about these things. Because I know exactly what you're getting at, Ren." She turned to me. "Trade ship crews all consider themselves a second family. Sometimes they *are* a family. If there's trouble in a port, all we have to do is shout 'Reeds!' for the *Five Reeds* tea trader, or 'Pepper!' for *Kanda's Pepper Tree*, and all that crew runs to our aid."

Koi nodded at her. "That's it." And to me, "Ren, you saw that with the Falcons, did you?"

"I saw it in Cray, when she began wearing a blue headband. I saw it with the other masters, who had blue headbands. I didn't ask, because I wasn't sure about questions..." I stopped there.

Koi said, "That's right."

"What questions?" Ke asked.

Koi said, "Most of the Falcon masters are in out the world looking for those who need them. Which is why there weren't many blue headbands."

"What questions?" Ke the dancer persisted, looking from him to me. "If there's a secret, I want to know it. Especially if whatever it is, is putting us in more danger than we're in already."

Koi said, "We were training with the Falcons. They aren't a secret sect, that is, not in the sense of sects of assassins, or Essence cultivators, who are outside the imperial laws. The Falcons don't bind people into the sect with tattoos, or secret rites. The blue headbands are a sign that someone in the group thought that a person made a good rescue. They can give one to beginners, or those in training—it doesn't have to be a master. Which happened to a friend."

"She rescued me," I said.

"Exactly right. What I'm getting at is, when Falcons see a blue headband, they know they can trust that person."

Ke's eyes widened over her snub nose. "I see! I see! If we use our ship name, then we become like a... sect? But even if we call ourselves a sect, or a crew, or a company, what does that actually give us? We still aren't any good at fighting, save you two."

"Nothing," Koi said. "Except a sense of belonging. And we're not a sect. We don't have a martial arts style, or rules for how to live. But we are shipmates, the way Dinek said. Or we could be. If our teams of four all feel they belong to a crew, it might help them work together."

"I think I see it. But we need a new ship name, don't we?" Ke rose to her feet with a graceful swing that I admired all the more because it was unconscious, the opposite of Liarti's pretenses of modest grace. "Or should we be Cattails?"

"No," Cygnet said, entering and making for the tea. "We need another ship name. As Ar Laq would say, *Cattail* is stained by all the tears, and the blood, shed by those kept in those holds. I swear, during thunderstorms I can almost hear the whisper of ghosts down there."

Ke rolled her eyes at the poet's name, but before she could say anything, MiMi clanged a spoon on the small gong hanging nearby. "Food's ready. Why not ask for suggestions for a new name as we go around with the pots and dishes?"

We did. Everyone had an idea. They shouted over one another. Then they gradually divided into those who hated every suggestion, and those who agreed with whatever the last one was.

And that's when Rose shrilled loud enough to be heard on Ghost Moon, "I know! Let's be Pangolins! That sword is *full* of luck!" She turned to me in triumph. "*You* brought us luck!"

I stared, appalled.

"Don't you want to?" Rose asked, her face puckering. "I meant it as an honor."

"Let's be Revengers," Jai said.

"Rescuers!"

"I want to be something *pretty*, that has lakes and rivers of luck. Like Phoenixes!"

"I like Pangolins," someone else said. "There are too many phoenix things. But I've never heard of pangolin things."

"Pangolins are lucky animals because they eat flies and stinging bugs, and those bugs that eat the wood of your house." That was a scholar's boy of thirteen or so, knobby of knees and wrists. He rarely spoke. He raised serious black eyes to me. "That's surely why your ancestors cultivated from pangolins, because they help people."

"That's it!"

"You're very right."

"Pangolins! I want to be a pangolin."

I had no answer that I could express, so I took a walk around the ship, trying to overcome my trepidation and dismay. I knew it was merely a name, a tribute to Sagacious

Blade, and they hoped that the sword that could burst into flame might see us through danger. It even deflected any questions about my actual ancestry.

But that left me with a powerful need to become what they needed. The sword was not "full of luck." It was full of more profound matters than luck, but they did not know that. The fire had come from Essence.

How could I learn about Essence? It was everywhere, in every part of history. Essence and augury. Geomancers used Essence to tame the terrible tremors that could shake entire islands, binding each in place with talismans that eased the violence of the tremors to gentle shakes as the great dragon below the island resettled itself in it millennia-long slumbers. The gallant wanderer tales had been full of Essence masters cultivating their powers—but none of the stories had instructed the reader in how. Only that it was done.

I needed to understand Essence. I had proved to myself that Granny Zim's lake was real, even if my image of floating fireflies was false. But I'd only managed to bring forth fire. As I prowled along the rail, I tried to do what my parents had taught me to do when faced with a problem to solve: go back to the fundamentals. Kanda wrote that the world of Heaven and Earth is good, and that goodness is born into human hearts. The Way taught that Purpose is the stuff of which Essence derives.

How to even begin to understand Purpose?

I halted, and looked out at Phoenix Moon's glowing pathway on the night-dark sea. "Granny Zim, is it true that the stars govern everything?"

"Govern is incorrect, my Bu, in the sense that a net is not governed by its hemp."

"In my studies, I saw many references to the *Book of Wisdom*, The Book of Sticks, some say. Both my parents said I need not read it. It had been forbidden for many dynasties, as it had caused so much trouble. They insisted it was better to leave study of the Heavenly Stems and Earthy Branches to the augurs, who spent lifetimes at it."

We are better employed, Father had repeated, *cultivating Kanda's doctrine, which represents moderation, rectitude, objectivity, sincerity, honesty and propriety. The guiding principle is that one should never act in excess. To grasp it, the student must comprehend all three parts…*

I sighed. "You understand Essence," I pleaded. "You *are*

Essence. Aren't you?"

"My Essence," Granny Zim said, "was understood best through music." And she gave me more of her lessons in the fundamentals of music. But that did not help me in this situation.

Essence was all around me, it seemed. It was *in* me. How could I study it? Even Granny Zim had not the language of Essence scholarship. She spoke in terms of music.

When she had finished her definition, and my steps brought me back to the eating area, Dinek came up to me. "If the wind stays steady, we'll reach that shore before morning."

"Another day of practice," Fan suggested, "and then we go in the boats while we still have light. We can hide in the reeds and then get into places as the sun sets."

"Wait for dinner," MiMi put in. "And even better, if they have dinner with a lot of wine."

The younger ones went off, many yawning, leaving us older ones looking tight-lipped and furrow-browed. I could see that I was not the only one trying to think ahead, into a future we could not predict.

I doubt any of us slept well.

The next morning, we practiced again, but when it was time to leave, there were two who changed their minds.

One was the girl who had taken the terrible blow to her shoulder blade from the man I killed. She decided to stay to help work the ship, which was going to sail around the east end of the island and be ready to receive us before morning, on the north shore. "I sinned," she said earnestly to Fan, Koi, and me. "I ought never to have offered to attack that night. Especially after I stunned two of the sleepers. And did nothing when the others cut their throats with the kitchen knives. I vowed before the Snow Crane before I started healer training I would never harm, only heal. This," she wiggled her shoulder, and winced, "is a reminder of that broken vow."

The boy who stayed back wouldn't face his friends. "What good am I when I can't see at night?" he mumbled.

"You see well enough to find your meals," Hali Ye sneered.

"That's smell."

"Leave it," Koi said to Ye. "It's much better to stay behind now than to turn back after we begin the plan. Everyone else, I've a surprise. I was going to do this later, but I might as well right now. We're going to rescue those people wearing Pangolin headbands." And here, Koi brought out a basket of strips of light brown cloth. I saw that he'd gathered up a lot of the worn fabric that so many had flung off in favor of the slavers' pretty silks. He'd chosen pieces dyed the light brown that so many common clothes are made of, as the dye is everywhere around us in trees' leaves, fruit, seeds, nuts, bark, heartwood and roots.

"Pangolin headbands?" a girl repeated.

"Last night I collected all the pangolin-colored cloth that got flung away," Koi said. "Pangolins are very close to this color. After we come back to the ship, we can hem these, and maybe even figure out how to put a pangolin on them."

He pulled off his old headband, and tied a fray-edged light brown one. With that determined air in his face, still thin and sharp-boned from our long hungry days, he looked like a young warrior.

Everyone — except Hali Ye and his followers — cheered, and tied them on, or turned to have a friend tie theirs. Hali Ye put one on, but his contempt was plain.

I took off my old one, and also tied one on. It felt like a physical representation of the burden of trust those younger ones placed in us, and my vitals roiled with nerves.

Later, after I'd put on my harness once again and slung Sagacious Blade at my back, we climbed down from the ship into the boats. I could see excitement at a fever pitch around me in bright, quick eyes, wide grins, and hear it in strident voices. I could not bear the thought of any of them being hurt. Not coming back.

Dinek's sailors plied their oars. I said inwardly to Granny Zim, "Could I heal with that lake of Essence? Twice, I've heard of the cinnabar princess doing it. Granny Ou seemed to be sure of her prison source. If Essence can be described as internal force, would that not be internal force used only for good purpose?"

Granny Zim said, "My good child! Do you know how much Essence to use? If I choose to play a qin loudly, I know how to bring out resonance. If a warrior decides he wants to play a qin, which he has never done, and uses his strength, he merely breaks the strings. Essence must be balanced, like all things."

Ay! There I was, back to my lack of training.

By the time we reached the shoreline and had gone as close to the shore as we could, the sun was sinking. We got muddy to the thighs going ashore, but at least the air was warm.

Dinek's crew rowed the boats back to the ship, so that they could be hoisted up. We were now completely on our own. I saw the others realize it, too, as many watched the ship in the gathering gloom.

"Let's go," Koi whispered. "We have a long walk ahead."

This almost being Ghost Month, when the two moons' arc is lowest in the sky and they are farthest apart, darkness came on quickly. Ghost Moon was already low, and Phoenix Moon would not be up until very late. The world diminished to a thousand shades of tarnished silver, but Koi and Jai were sure-footed over a narrow trail.

We sped in a long snake line until we arrived at the top of a hill, looking down into the small harbor village. Even in the starlight, everything looked dilapidated, except for the fine boats of various sizes bobbing in the bay. Noise reached us, mostly coming from two large buildings across from each other, windows glowing from lamplight. More lit windows surrounded the bay.

Fan said, "This is where we separate. We'll wait for your first fire," to Koi.

"And we'll join you at the old temple."

Wide pairs of eyes jerked back and forth between Koi and Fan. Koi had explained to me how Sima taught them to repeat plans for nervous beginners. Even so, it reassured me. We knew what we must do. We had to do it.

We separated, and Fan began to lead our warehouse group up and around back of the inns and the surrounding buildings. Hidden branches whapped us; once, someone let out a yip, which caused a nervous giggle. The voices were soft, nearly insubstantial, but Fan jerked around and gave the two girls such a terrible look that they abruptly silenced.

There was no more "Silence is success..."

This was it.

Somehow Fan's look instead of making them repeat the slogan sharpened everyone's focus as we made our way past a cluster of buildings, some with glowing windows, until at last two huge, square buildings appeared. These had to be the warehouses.

"Sit down behind that," Fan whispered, pointing to a crumbling fence. "We'll scout, then come back once we know where all the guards are."

She gestured to me, and I followed her down the hillside, nearly stumbling when my sandaled foot encountered hidden animal holes. Sagacious Blade clattered on my back with a sound that sounded like thunder to my ears. Fan glanced briefly at me. I winced, but neither of us spoke—there was a guard, not twenty-five paces from where we halted behind a clump of mustard. Beyond his silhouette stood another man. Their voices were a murmur in the quiet summer air; in the distance, the buzz of many voices, blobs of swinging lamps going back and forth from the bay to the buildings farther up a gentle slope.

"Don't look at the lights," Fan whispered.

I shifted my gaze away. "I see two guards. Where are the other two?"

"Stay here. I'm going behind the first warehouse to spot the others. I'll be right back."

I stayed where I was, straining to listen as the two men chatted desultorily. From their words, they were complaining about their chief. Both held swords in loose hands. They might have any number of other weapons. I eased myself down to a squat, careful to hold Sagacious Blade's sheath away from scraping the ground.

I counted to fifty three times before there was a quiet step, a shifting shadow, and Fan was back. She breathed a laugh. "This is fun…if only my brothers were here, and not that bunch of babies. But there's no help for it. Be fast, can you, Ren? I'm afraid they'll forget everything we drove into their heads, at the first sign of reaction."

"Me, too," I admitted.

"I'm going to take the farther two guards with my teams. I'll give an owl hoot when I'm in place."

We retrieved the teams, separated, and crept slowly forward. My hearing seemed preternaturally sharp, my two teams breathing hard and fast.

Fan's laugh had been that of someone having fun, but I was sick with apprehension.

It seemed another eternity until a soft owl hoot rose; they were in place. Now what? We were supposed to wait for—

"What's that?" one of the men broke off, his voice louder.

For a terrifying moment I thought he meant Fan's owl hoot, but he pointed down at the bay. From the middle of the mass of winking, bobbing lights, rose a flicker. As I leaned forward, a sudden whoosh brought a sheet of flame up.

Voices rose, clashing.

"Some idiot spilled wine, or dropped a candle," said one of

the men. "Bunch of drunks! Why don't I go down to see if they need a hand?"

He took off, and a moment later was joined by a second guard from out of the inky gloom beyond the nearby warehouse. That was followed by another owl hoot that definitely sounded like a human voice, and I said, "Now."

Heart in my throat, I got up and pelted down toward the remaining guard, the girls—all eight were girls—coming after me.

The man turned as we approached. He straightened up, instantly alert, right hand going to the hilt of the sword, then his posture eased slightly as he saw us, a pack of children. "What are you—"

Three girls hit him from the back, and he stumbled forward, and began cursing. But he did not fall. Though two girls crouched together, ready for him to be pushed backward over them, he planted his feet wide, the sword gleaming coldly. "What are you brats doing? Get out of here!"

One girl whimpered. All faces turned to me, and I knew that they were about to become eight frightened children ready to run away.

Desperately, I ripped Sagacious Blade free, and as it arced over my head, I threw Essence over it and it burst into flame. He backed up a step, then snarled, "The oil on the blade trick is funny once," and brought his blade at me, as if to swat mine away.

It was a slow, casual blow, exactly the speed with which the Falcons had swung to teach us to block and lunge. I blocked and lunged, but as I did, I saw his elbow, and all that practice with Tay and Tiger Moth was back. I turned my wrist, and tapped the blunt edge of my blade to that exact spot on the elbow that ignites fireworks through the meridians.

He shouted, and—exhilarated that it was actually working—I tapped another acupoint as I advanced.

He staggered back a step. And another…and tripped over the crouched girls, his sword flying out of the hand still surely buzzing from the acupoint tap.

I was on him at once, my thumb driving into the chest acupoint, and he stiffened, eyes wide and shocked.

"We did it, we did it," keened one of the girls.

"Who has the ropes?"

"Here."

For ropes, we'd ripped up the worst of the rags—beginning

with the remains of the robe I had traded my butterfly robe for. The tying went fast; they had practiced that over and over, and now that our target was down, we knew what to do. I checked the gag, making sure it was tight, and then I whispered, "Down low… I'm going to check on—"

"Ren," Fan exclaimed hoarsely. "That was brilliant, using your fire! How did you know I needed a distraction?" She clutched her arm, on which a black smear spread.

"You're hurt—"

"Later," she said impatiently. "Let's get the prisoners out."

We separated, and each ran to the doors of the warehouses, both of which were locked. Two strikes with Sagacious Blade, a spray of sparks, and the lock broke.

I opened the door, then stepped back at a huge, hot, moist waft of close-packed humanity. I forced myself back inside, and said, "This is a rescue, as quiet as you can, follow us in a line. No pushing, no pushing, one line! Fast!"

Voices rose, but adult-sized persons turned to hush them with hissing violence, and the prisoners began to stream out, clumping up briefly. Fay's group joined ours, also running silently, some hand in hand with children.

I ran with Sagacious Blade still in hand, as there was no time to fumble it back into the sheath behind me. We skimmed around to the back of the warehouse, and straight north, toward the sinking Phoenix moon. How long must we run? It seemed so long… where was Koi's temple? Had we passed it without knowing it? No, there was the old, abandoned temple, its roof corners turned up toward Heaven.

And as we paused there to let people breathe, for many were quite weak, the sound of pounding footsteps reached me. Fan joined me, raising her sword. I copied her stance—

I made out Koi and Jai leading their team, in the flickering light from behind. They had set fire to the warehouses, which were already engulfed in flames.

"Let's go," Koi said. "I'm afraid if they look up here, they might see our silhouettes."

"I think they've got plenty to occupy them," Fan said, waving at the fires.

Jai crowed hoarsely. "Ha!"

"Let's not test that," Koi retorted, and began to run.

We swarmed through the ruined temple and up over the ridge, looking out. There, as promised, lay another, far wider bay, the western shore dotted with fishing craft pulled into the shallows. The *Pangolin* lay not far from the shore, masts swaying gently.

Our boats had been pulled to the shore, and I could see Dinek with the oar teams. "We have a ship," Fan yelled, and I repeated her words to our group. "We're going to yon island on the horizon. These are our boats."

The rescued people ran to the beach, voices breaking out, fearful, excited, some in tears, others angry as they tried to get into the boats first. When the boats were full, Fan and I both ran along the beach, trying to calm those pushing into the wavelets on the rocky beach, "They will come back! They will come back!"

Some calmed, but—though I didn't immediately notice—a goodly number slunk into the darkness toward the fishing boats. That included Hali Ye and his followers. They stole the fishers' craft and shortly vanished out to sea.

We Pangolins stayed until there were no more strays, then flung ourselves into the boats, which were so heavy the water nearly reached the oarlocks. We helped pull on the oars toward the *Pangolin*.

Dinek was already yelling for the sail teams to raise the sails when the ropes snaked down, and we clambered up. I never even noticed rope burns until later; on deck, we turned to help pull up the boats, as the ship slowly began to sail, the deck absolutely crowded with people everywhere you looked.

For a time everything was noise and confusion, but then some internal group relationship invisible to us prevailed, and the newcomers began to fall silent, group by group, then person by person. Most were girls and young women, with a few boys and one or two young men, one of these a tall, very thin monk with a scarred face, wearing the pale blue of Snow Crane shamans.

The monk finally came forward, put his hands together, and bowed. "May these grateful individuals inquire who you are, and what is your purpose?"

The other Pangolins looked to Koi, to me, to Fan. Jai stood at Koi's shoulder, picking at his gnawed lips.

I recognized by now when Koi was feeling awkward by the way he'd shift from one foot to another, and so I lifted my voice. "We were supposed to be sold with you, but we took over our ship, and came to rescue you. We're proposing to go to that island on the horizon, if it's safe."

A young woman a few years older than Cousin Arati

sobbed, holding two small children close. Then she dropped to her knees before us, tugging her children down. Obediently they dropped down, and all three pressed their foreheads to the deck. At once all the rest bowed to follow suit, even though I'd sprang forward, trying to catch the young woman's hands.

Koi also tried to stop them, his ears as red as fire, but it was Jai's face that caught my attention. He stared at them, mouth ajar, and tears glimmering in his eyes. It was not until later that I understood that in spite of the troubles of the past year, and in spite of our relative ranks, Koi and I had had the balance of those who valued us. This was Jai's first experience with respect.

THIRTY

...sailed through a world of danger...

WE'D SCARCELY CLIMBED ABOARD when Dinek came to find us. She explained that while we were waiting for nightfall, she and her crew had worked the ship around the east end of the island, then slowly sailed north then west as they scanned anxiously for the ruins on the ridge.

As the rescued people milled about on deck, Dinek—as euphoric as we were—tapped a tattered chart that Koi had lifted from one of the yachts. "Look! Look! This chart had the slavers' bay well marked, but it was barely a sketch on *this* side of the island, and all those rocky dragon teeth! The fishers must know this dangerous seabed, but the boats had to row slowly ahead, doing constant soundings with poles before we dared to sail in. As it was, the ship got two scrapes on the underside! But not enough to rend holes into the hull."

While Dinek was explaining the dangers the *Pangolin* had survived in order to meet up with us, MiMi and her cooks passed out all the pancakes that they had been making and piling in baskets while the *Pangolin* crept along. They knew that the rescued people would be as hungry as we'd been when we emerged from the hold.

There was no time to sit down, much less talk. The newcomers milled around, grimy and starved as we'd been; though the deck was crowded, no one was willing to go below into the hold. There were more mothers and aunts than there had been in our group, with a couple of men who had been rejected as potential warriors: the Snow Crane monk, a blind ceramics artisan.

As I worked my way to the galley to get some tea to quench my thirst after that long run, I listened to snatches of fretful conversation as mothers clung tightly to children. It seemed the slavers had separated parents from children between the two warehouses, holding the children's lives hostage against good behavior by the adults. Only a few teens had been included among the children, to keep order.

The sun was already rising; by the time I made it to the galley, MiMi cornered me to whisper that there was probably a day's food left. My eyes burned with tiredness. I'd lost sight of Koi, and Fan. There was nowhere to rest. The cabins were packed with people, entire families crammed into a cabin with a single bunk.

Shafts of early sun lanced along the deck when I finally found Koi with some of our others, gathered along the balcony outside the second-floor cabins.

I was mounting the steps tiredly when one of the younger Pangolins said, "Do you think we got away with it? Or will they chase us?"

Koi turned to the boy. "As soon as the light came up, they must have spotted all our footprints. That was probably about the time the fisher folk charged over the ridge into the harbor town. They'll want to know where the missing fishing boats are."

"Missing? Fishing boats?" Fan asked.

"Some of those we let free ran off," Koi said. "As well as Hali Ye and his group. They tossed down their headbands and followed after some of the prisoners. We couldn't have stopped them."

"Good riddance. Ye was a nasty one," Fan muttered. "Kind who'd smile to your face, and stab you when your back was turned."

"Can't blame the prisoners." Cygnet shrugged. "They didn't know who we are. Anyway, they're gone. They are no longer our problem—"

Good, I thought, looking around wearily for a spot on which to sit down…

"And we have a bigger problem," Dinek said, topping the stairs.

Sick dread jolted me. I saw my reaction in the others as Dinek pointed off toward the enormous line of the northern island jutting across the entire horizon. "Have you noticed we aren't getting any closer?"

I fought against a yawn. "I did notice. But we have wind pushing us, so I thought it was just my impatience to get there."

"These light airs are not nearly strong enough for this wicked current," Dinek said, gripping the balcony rail. "The current is pushing us back toward those dragon teeth. And our being top-heavy counters the airs."

"What can we do?"

Dinek said, "I'm...I haven't..." She rubbed her eyes. "I never thought to command a ship. I'm still *learning*." She dropped her hands, clapping them against her thighs. "I don't know if it will work. But Mother and Grandmother and Aunt Vuasek all say that we maneuver tighter when the hold is full all the way aft. The current is here..." She wiggled her hand in the air. "With sails pulled *this* way, and rudder *here*..." She made violent gestures that clearly confused the others as much as they confused me.

"What must we do?" Koi asked.

"Get everything into the hold. That will put the lug above the surface—so bad for us— down below, where it won't drag so much..." She moved the heel of her hand forward, like an inchworm—a type of movement no ship was capable of making.

The why of it was beyond understanding, but now we could all see those huge, craggy rocks nearing a little with each surge of the waves. From atop one, birds eyed us.

"Let's get the people below," Dinek said, smacking the back of her hand against the other palm. "Now!"

We forced ourselves into action once again, shaking and waking people and pointing to the rocks, while that enormous island remained on the northern horizon. The current seemed to be moving in a slow circle. Assuming we survived the dragon teeth (which was impossible) we'd be deposited back on the shore of the island we'd left.

In the distance, tiny figures could be seen gesticulating on its shore.

"Get down below!" our Pangolins shrilled. "We have to escape the dragon teeth rocks!"

Koi caught up with me. "That's the slavers on that shore."

"They have no boats this side of the island," I said.

"It looks to me as if they are forcing the fishers to surrender the rest of their fishing boats," Koi said as Cygnet shouted, "Didn't you hear? We have to change direction—go below, all the way to the back!"

The newcomers had begun to stir, not liking being roused. They looked exhausted and miserable, but then a woman stopped, her face red with fear and anger. "Oh, no, I don't fall for that trick twice?"

"What?" Dinek said.

"What?" more of the rescued people echoed, looking at one another.

"*They* said I'd be safer below. I paid everything I had! *They* said they'd take me to Hawthorne Island, but they *locked us in,* and took us *prisoner!* To sell as slaves! I'm a respected silk-weaver! I don't know why you let us out, but I'm not going down there again!"

"Nor I!"

"Nor I!"

I could see the shock turn into question, then affront, and anger. And as people pressed together, I could see from the angles of arms and jaws and exchanged glances that there was a good chance we were about to lose the *Pangolin*—right before it crashed into those rocks.

What could I do? I turned my attention to my sword. I laid my hand on the hilt, and sank my awareness into the lake of soft glows, but what use would fire be? We were too closely packed for a gesture. I did not want to risk burning anyone.

I raised my voice. "I'm going below. I'll lead the way."

"I'll go with you," MiMi said, her gaze darting at the circle of people. "It means someone else has to cook, if you want any food *before those rocks tear up the ship.* Come on! We're going below," she called to her crew.

We headed toward the hatch, while behind us, Dinek was trying to explain balance and wind and sails.

The monk came through the tightest part of the crowd, which melted aside. "I will go below," he said, approaching. And with him beside me, we went below to that familiar stuffy space. The people began to follow.

"We're leaving the hatch open," Dinek yelled down. "Ke and Liu are bringing lamps down. Go all the way to the back, as far as you can!"

"Got it," I shouted back, and then turned. "Koi? Are those

fishing boats chasing us?"

But he was back on deck.

Whether the slavers were chasing us or not, there was nothing to be done except to go below, as Dinek needed. I held one of the lamps high, making my way along the scratched hold, the familiar smell making me shiver. I was so tired that my mind seemed to want to slide between Granny Zim's realm, which was quiet and calm, and the mounting dangers of this world. I'd taken my hand from the sword hilt behind my ear in order to carry the lamp, but my inner eye still painted that soft glow over the gloom before me. I handed the lamp off to Ke, who held it high so that people could see.

I turned away from the lamp, blinking at the people around me. The eerie glow swirled slowly, like the drift of dandelion seeds on the wind, coalescing brightly around a baby sleeping in a woman's arms, and over there, around a short, round figure whose features in the gloom reminded me of a pig's rounded cheeks and uptilted nose, a jolly image, pigs being cherished among commoners, I'd read, as symbols of abundance and luck.

"You are seeing those with Essence talent," the monk addressed me as we crowded up in the last hold. "The child has the potential. The other's talent lies in comforting the very young."

The pig woman held two children, both sleeping on her shoulder. Was she a demon? In the flickering light, her pig features shifted to a human's round cheeks and chin as she smiled to reassure those around her.

My weary mind then comprehended what the monk was saying: I was seeing those with Essence talent, but neither the baby nor the pig woman could aid us now.

"Essence talent," I repeated as more people pressed in, then sat down, profiles and silhouettes outlined in circles of light from lamps. We felt the ship shudder as the rudder shifted slowly. Then the ship jolted. The hull scraped with a terrible squeal over something; all heads snapped that way.

Instinctively I abandoned the next question—do I have talent? Do I glow, too?—and looked around me, trying to peer through the hull. Of course I could not see beyond the wood of the hull, and yet for a heartbeat my perception floated above the lake of lights. No, it was the sea, surging with glowing life lights, as individual motes drifted and darted above and around me.

The Snow Crane monk, who had followed me, said quietly, "Now you are seeing the life below the waters."

I turned to him, startled. The light from Ke's lamp struck him from the side, creating stark shadows from every contour. What I'd taken for scars were actually scales, below the surface of his skin—I say "his" because he was completely bald, and very tall as well as very thin, with narrow shoulders. Eel?

I will stay with "his" as he wore the robe of a monk, but I suspect gender was immaterial; as I gazed into those eyes with horizontal pupils, it occurred to me that this monk was very old, whatever form he, she, or it took in order to cultivate.

He smiled. "I took human form to live in the air, and to witness the birth of rain. But in this moment, we must work together to preserve this ship."

Amazed—beyond question—I said, "How?"

"Go back up, and I will show you."

At first I was afraid that my going would stir up trouble and suspicion again, but it seemed the monk had won general trust during their time in the warehouse. Or the jolt had so frightened the rescued people that the threat of imminent crashing into those rocks had replaced their fear that the Pangolins were secretly slavers. People moved aside, and I vaulted up to the weather deck, and to the front. It was then that I saw that the monk had not come with me.

I caught sight of Koi, Jai, and Fan, grimly watching off in one direction. My heart gave a lurch when I remembered the slavers. I risked a glance—yes, they had commandeered the fishing craft and were chasing us, skimming over the water, the rails crowded with men holding weapons.

What to do? I was terrible at fighting! And we had all these people. And threatening rocks! Where was the monk?

I turned to go back, but his voice spoke in that behind-the-ear space that Granny Zim used: "Heed not those fishing vessels. See before you."

I blinked, and there was that eerie glow again, a liminal awareness of the realm of the five senses overlain by the realm of Essence, that is, of Essence-filled lives, some brighter than others in a way that had nothing to do with physical size.

The eel-monk must have sketched signs into the air, for into the Essence Realm glowed a complication of talismans within a vast wheel, corresponding to the Houses of the Heavens. Some talismans glowed different colors. I gazed, bewildered, for it was all far too complicated for me to begin to comprehend, and there was no tine.

"You command fire, and metal. I cannot, for I am a being of water," spoke the monk into my mind. "I give you the rock as target. You send your arrow of fire."

"Arrow?"

"The same way you bring fire to your metal."

He meant Sagacious Blade!

As the ship headed straight for a twisted rock full of sharp edges, the eel-monk said, "Send your fire now."

I raised Sagacious Blade, pointed at the rock, and I drew in a deep breath, scooping from the glowing lake within me and mentally shaping it into the shape of an arrow. Zing! Water surged and boiled, and spray shot skyward, scintillating with tiny bits of rock. The *Pangolin* sailed harmlessly through the churning waters.

A wordless command next, the image of a massive ridge of rock below the surface, and I shouted back to Dinek, "Left, left, left!"

Dinek shrilled something. The masts creaked, the sails clattered, and the ship timbers groaned. We slid by the ridge; as we passed, I saw that this rock was fuzzed with the nests of undersea creatures of all kinds.

I had the pattern. The monk threaded us through the dangerous waters, avoiding those upthrusting rocky spires that were homes to undersea life. I could see that life as countless motes of light busy going about their spire home. When we encountered a rock with no life in or around it, I got the command to send a fire arrow.

"Oh-h-h-h!" I was distantly aware of a growing ring of watchers as water boiled up, and exploded skyward.

"The fishers are getting closer," someone wailed, as the air filled with the sound of hissing arrows. I glanced, distracted, to see the deadly rain falling some fifty paces behind us.

"Here," said the monk, compelling my attention back.

I gripped the rail with one hand, made an effort, and shut out everything except the monk's voice, and Sagacious Blade in my other hand. The new threat was a shadow below the surface. I exploded that rock, sending another fountain skyward to splash around us as we sailed through.

"There."

I send another arrow of flame.

This rock stuck up above the surface. It exploded into dust.

Then, "To the right!"

And Dinek repeated my cry to her crew.

The *Pangolin* creaked. Groaned. Shuddered. Leaned at a slant.

A sudden loud *rap, rap:* two arrows from the slavers slammed into the hull.

The monk said, calmly, "You may send a burst of fire to warn them of the rocks now."

I turned, gasping at how close the fishing vessels had come. Obedient to the monk's directive, I pulled fire from the lake of glowing fireflies, though aware that I was having to dig deeper. I braced myself and slung it over the distance between our ship and the lead fisher. It hissed into the water short of the fisher's bow, but they paid no attention—

And then, with shocking suddenness, that lead fisher stopped short as they struck one of the below-surface columns. Timbers splintered, the sound carrying over the water. The fisher's masts rocked, then toppled slowly to one side. The boat listed, dumping slavers and guards and weapons into the water.

I turned back to the dragon's teeth.

"There," the monk said, and I shouted a command at Dinek, though my voice was losing force. The lake was becoming dimmer, the fire more difficult, and the sword lay so heavy in my hand that it took all my strength to lift it.

Three more explosions, and we were abruptly clear, while behind us, two more fishers had crashed into dragon's teeth.

"The chase is over," someone called from far away.

"Did you hear that?" Koi said, barely audible. "Ren. Renti? Renti?"

"The chase is over," I said, or tried to say, then slid down into a heap as the world gently turned to night.

THIRTY-ONE

*The sagacious one looks back towards the
ancients,
then forward to those yet to come…*

I ROUSED BRIEFLY, BURNING with thirst, as somewhere, a voice spoke: "Give her water as often as she will take it…"
The fire quenched, I sank again into soft darkness.

"…The spirit dwells in the heart. Will and strength form the door. The world enters through the five senses. When the door opens, the spirit perceives, and nothing remains hidden. When the door closes the spirit retires into the heart…"

Interspersed between brief wakings, the voices spoke in memory, one after another. For a time I could not determine whose memories these were, for I floated there in that soft darkness that was neither sky nor sea nor earth, a mote of light without any awareness except as unnamed I.

"…Remember, my good child, the three teachings: there are the matters of Essence, that is, the vitality of life, consisting of charms, formations, and geomancy to help people govern the chaos of the physical world; the rituals that shape civilization; and the lessons of Kanda, teaching that the path to goodness is shaped by moral training and ethical action…"

"...You must never play your guzheng during rain and thunder..."

Noise. Shouts. Creaking masts, then a voice, "No, they are not attacking!"
I knew that voice. That was Koi.
And closer by, "That's right, drink. Drink more water."

"Essence governs the five elements, in both the sun phase — action — and in the moons phase, resting. Light and dark. Without Essence, no object can exist..."

"Ayah! The civilized person will never err in painting the plum, the orchid, the chrysanthemum, or the bamboo: the plum that blooms in winter, promising life to come; the orchid, whose fragrance is never overpowering, symbolizing humility and nobility; the chrysanthemum, which blooms in the cold autumn air, and the bamboo, which yields but does not break..."

Gradually sensory details not my own emerged with the voices, then dwindled again, but not before I caught them: a scent here, the slither of silk there. A sharp scent of pepper, the warmth of the sun on my neck as I strove to master the Eightfold Strike.
But that was not I. His arm wielded Sagacious Blade, not mine, but I lived that memory, over and over...
The last awareness to emerge: identity. I remembered who I was, and what I had done — with the aid of the one who drifted in and out of inner sight, a long glowing silver shape, elegant in its watery element.
I drilled and I recited and I painted the four acceptable subjects for a princess of the lowest rank... That lesson was Mother's voice, and in remembering her, I remembered my duty. I struggled to rouse myself, for it would never do to lie down during lessons!
"There you are," Granny Zim exclaimed. She appeared before my inner eye, a wizened, white-haired woman, smaller than I, wearing musician gray. "Bodies, bodies, bodies! I trust you will forgive us both. We forgot how fragile human bodies are, especially the young. I did give you lessons from each Bu, but it seems you have yet to absorb what I have given you. And our water friend..." Here an image of the eel-monk

flickered before me in that glowing eel form, watching protectively over me, "…is still learning what human forms can and cannot do."

For I was there, too, in image, and so I put my hands together and bowed respectfully.

"You have been pulled out of the world as far as possible without danger, so that you might recover," Granny Zim went on. "And learn. To preserve your life, I am present, a remarkably rejuvenating experience, and yet I know it will have its cost. I remember so much that I had forgotten! The cost needn't be paid now. But you must remember the promise you made to me."

I bowed again. "I have never forgotten that. I must carry you to the mountain when it is time."

"Good child," she said, echoing Mother's voice when she was pleased with me. *Good child…*

And I woke up.

"She's awake!"

"She's awake!"

"Here. Drink some more," a voice murmured close by. That was Ke, the dancer. Her voice was familiar in its proximity, and I realized that she had been tending me since I fell to the deck. When was that? How long…

I opened my eyes to Koi's concerned face. He was keeping a proper distance as Ke held a cup to my lips. It smelled of lotus-seed tea, which I drank down. I looked around, recognizing one of the cabins on the *Pangolin*. Warm air drifted in, carrying sharp voices. Those voices had roused me.

"What's wrong?" my voice came out a croak.

"Here, drink more."

I did, and sat up.

"Are you sure you can sit?"

"I…feel fine," I said, though I was sore all over. But it was the good soreness that I had begun to appreciate while living among the Falcons, learning sword and staff and knife forms each day.

As I sat up, several sets of shoulders eased, and Ke rose from where she sat beside me. "Good," she said briskly. "I don't make a very good nurse. But we didn't want that sword to come after us," she said, smiling.

"Eh?"

"One of the men tried to take it," Koi said from the doorway, where he leaned. "Before I could stop him. The sword cut him quite badly, and burned the cut."

"Oh."

Koi turned his head. "We are nearly at the Snow Crane temple, but the rescues are refusing to leave until the matter of the silver is settled."

I looked up in surprise. "I thought we decided that. Everyone to get a fair share."

"The question concerns the newcomers—"

"*We* rescued *them*," Jai said, from behind Koi. His teeth scraped over those chapped lips as he eyed my sword, which I just in that moment realized lay beside me on the bunk, and he added in a rush, "We did all the work. We ought to keep it, or most of it…"

"It wasn't ours to begin with," I said as I levered myself up. "And won't they need something to start with? Won't we all?"

Koi turned his head, leaning out a little. "She says to share it out equally," he called.

At once a cacophony of voices broke out, but not angry ones. There was a shout of, *Benevolent! Generous!* And then a cheer. Jai's head dropped, but he said nothing as the voices out on deck resolved into the low buzz of people milling around.

Koi turned to Jai. "I told you what she'd say. We'll be all right."

At the word 'we' Jai's head came up again, and the tension went out of his bony, awkward hands.

"Is there a chance of something to eat?" I asked, easing myself up cautiously. Other than the soreness and a sense of light-headedness, I felt good.

Cygnet appeared in the doorway. "Ay!" she exclaimed. "This one is so very relieved to see our Pangolin well, and begs you to grace us with even a brief appearance, while we do what she hath commanded!"

Was this satire? And, what did I command? "What did I command?" I said aloud. "I didn't give any *commands*." I turned to the others, but Ke had already left, Jai stood against the wall, arms crossed, and Koi stepped close.

"You are the chief."

"What? I'm not…"

"We need a chief," he whispered urgently. "They saw what you did." There was question in his searching gaze, but his questions could not possibly outnumber mine.

"Ren?" Cygnet asked—politely, even humbly, from behind Koi.

Behind her, all the Pangolins and the rescued people had crowded around in a mass.

I went to the door of the cabin, aware of my grubby clothes and hair, but at the sight of me, everyone in that crowd dropped to their knees.

"Please rise, please rise," I croaked in the proper form, shivering a little at the memory of the empress and the dowager empress during morning visits in court.

"We are almost at the temple," Dinek shouted through cup-ped hands. "We've figured out how much we have, and divided it by our number, so everyone will get their share." Here Lei shook an upheld abacus so that it rattled like a child's drum.

"Line up if you want yours!"

Koi went over to stand by where she sat at a small table. He held a sword by its sheath. Next to the table waited the trunks of silver, which had been dragged to the deck. Behind Dinek and Lei, the eel-monk stood, smiling with goodwill, as the people shuffled into more or less of a line, and then Lei and Dinek took turns giving out three silver boaters, or the equivalent in various coinages, into each outthrust hand.

Very soon a rhythm was established, as each got their portion and turned away, talking or marveling or clutching it to themselves fearfully. I looked away from the distribution to the rest of the ship, and then beyond it.

We were sailing slowly toward a promontory on which was built a three-tiered temple. It appeared to be quite extensive, with layers of rice terracing gracefully surrounding the temple, and above it, a far older temple, simple in line—a temple to the Sun Goddess, surely. At the lower temple, many small figures could be seen, most in eggshell blue: monks and nuns dedicated to the Snow Crane.

I looked away, out at sea.

At either side of our *Pangolin* sailed large ships flying banners with three wheat spikes, with three florets on each, a lucky nine. These banners were green, the wheat spikes a warm sand color that was not quite imperial gold.

"The Huyun clan," I said, recollecting an old lesson about the primary families in the empire.

The ships had cannon on them, I saw. And at the rails, armed warriors.

"The new governor is Huyun Shandek," he murmured back. "The Huyun guards sounded angry when we told them about the slave auction, and they said there would be a report and an investigation."

"Then we're not prisoners?" I whispered to Koi.

"I don't know what we are," Koi responded. "So far, everything has been very polite and even friendly. Beginning with them telling us they saw the chase, and how you destroyed the rocks, blasting a passage through the dragon teeth. They seem to think that you are an Essence master and we did not dare to deny it. I say we, because that monk came up, to help explain how we had rescued these people." He tipped his chin toward the crowd. "It was he who told the Huyun fleet captain that you, Pangolin Ren, wielding the Pangolin Sword for justice, were our leader."

We need a chief, he'd said before.

I still had questions, but I could see they would have to wait.

The dispersing of the silver was nearly done when Dinek left the table to Lei and moved back to shout orders. The rudder got hauled over, and the sails pulled up so that we lost the wind. On shore, some figures in blue waded out into the rippling waves, as shore birds circled around them, cawing and scolding. They climbed into the boat and began rowing for the *Pangolin*, as the folk we had rescued crowded to the rail, eager to be taken ashore.

Koi saw my question before I asked it. "The Snow Crane monk is taking any who wish to go as pilgrims. They will be aided further from there."

Dinek had finished the orders to lower our longest boat by then, and so, between our boat and that belonging to the temple, the rescues went off in clumps, faces turned toward the temple.

A few first came to me, bowing their thanks; when the first one bowed to me, I wanted to retreat to hide, but Cygnet and Ke and Dinek as well closed in on me from all sides, and so I had to endure this gratitude that I did not truly deserve. I was merely a conduit. One praises the flute-player, seldom the flute when the music is fine, and never the air. The monk had been the flute-player and Sagacious Blade the flute, and I merely the air. But it seemed that in this puzzling situation, I must not say so.

When our boat came back for the last time, and Dinek's crew set about hauling it out of the water, those on shore milled about, guided by blue figures. Some waved to us—and so they passed out of sight.

But not out of our lives, or out of memory. "We did it," one of the younger boys said, crossing the now-empty deck, which seemed vast. He stopped before me, face upraised. "I want to do it again."

"And I!" said Fan, joining us as she rubbed her hands down her grubby robe after hauling the boat to the deck.

"And I"

Fan said, "I have to admit I was scared nearly to pissing myself when we went after those yachts. Everything happened so fast."

"It did!"

"Too fast!"

"But we handled it," Jai said defensively, and turning a mutinous face toward Koi, his voice not quite masking his appeal. "We did!"

"We did," Koi said. "Barely."

"It was an excellent plan," Fan said to him. "It was your plan, and it was excellent."

"It could have gone wrong in so many ways," he said.

"But it didn't," Fan stated, then swiped her hair off her damp forehead. "Ay! Koi, I'm not arguing. I know we've a lot to learn. Dinek says she has a lot to learn about being captain. But we *can* learn it, right?" She turned to me. "Don't you want to rescue people? Do you think the Falcons would take us in?"

"I don't know," I said. "I was only among them a year."

Her eyes widened. "Really? Only a year? And yet you..." She waved back toward the dragon teeth, far to the east of us now. "I thought you were born among them. Who trained you to do that, if it wasn't them?"

I opened my mouth—and halted. Instinct insisted I protect Sagacious Blade. But what kind of lie could I concoct?

Koi said, "Ren is a Talent. But even Talents have to train, yes?" He turned to me.

"I desperately need to reflect," I said.

"A little too humble?" Ke commented, rejoining us. She held out a bowl to me. In it, a scant amount of rice and no more than a smudge of bean paste. "All we have left. They ate *everything*."

"They needed it," Lei said, adding herself to the circle. "And these Huyun ships are taking us into that harbor, so we'll be able to eat soon. Your share of the silver is in the trunks," she added, then turned to me. "Since they didn't know about the little trunk of gold, we kept that hidden, for the ship. We didn't think you would mind, since none of us are keeping it."

There again was that assumption that I had any authority over anyone. It was a false position. I knew that ascribing the authority to my sword was not going to mend the vexing question. Probably the opposite.

I said, "*Pangolin* needs repairs, Dinek?"

"The hull was not breached, but I'm worried about the timbers. Some of those scrapes were bad, and we are shipping too much water down below, where it was tight and dry before. And there is a lot here that could benefit from repair and improvement. Including arms, if we really are going to go after slave takers."

The question lay before us.

"*I* think it's madness," Cygnet said from behind Dinek. "I want to start my school."

"Most of your little ones went with the monk," Ke pointed out. "Can you really start a school with..." She looked around, counting the youngest of the Pangolins, who had stayed aboard. "Five?"

"This untalented scholar's daughter," said Cygnet in a voice anything but humble, "could begin a school with one."

"I want to be in school," Little Snow said, pressing close to Cygnet's side.

"Me, too," Rose added, clutching at Little Snow's hand.

I said, slowly, "We probably need to find out what the Huyun authorities expect from us. I take it we were not permitted to sail away on our own?"

Koi said, "They made it sound like an honor, but they made it clear that we are to have an interview with whoever is in command in the harbor."

I looked around at the tired faces surrounding me. I was the only one who had had any rest. The high spirits of the successful rescue, and the chase, and then dealing with the rescuers were slowly dissipating, leaving tense glances, bitten lips, and a general sense of what happens now?

To a certain extent, it seemed that that had been taken out of our hands. Dinek slipped away to her crew, who were tending the ship as we slanted past the promontory, which hid the temple. Opening before us, a sizable harbor full of ships. Our escort was still on either side and behind us.

I sighed, going to the trunk, where I stooped and took three of the silver boaters lying at the bottom. "At least we'll be able to get ourselves a meal while we wait to see what will happen."

The others used that as a signal to get their share—Cygnet taking the silvers for her future students—until the trunks on deck were empty.

That was when one of the cooks shrilled that the last of the food was ready.

I'd inhaled the little that Ke had brought, and was still very hungry; when had I eaten last? If I'd been asleep for a day and a night, then before we rescued those people, what was my last meal…

I frowned over that until my share was gone—leaving me still hungry, and I gave up trying to remember. Thinking about food was not going to help against hunger. I had to force myself to turn away from Dinek and her crew's share, waiting for them.

I went out to the deck to watch as Dinek's crew brought the *Pangolin* in. From the sharpness of Dinek's tones, and the way her crew were running about, I guessed that it was important to them not to lose face before the Huyun ship escort by making an error. The best thing I could do would be to stay out of their way.

I went back to the cabin to shrug into my harness, since there was no chance of a bath or fresh clothes. When Sagacious Blade was in harness, I went forward. No one was at the prow at the moment, as the rudder and sails were the important parts of the vessel just then. I decided to go back to drilling myself at drawing the blade with one movement—and the much more difficult sheathing the blade behind my head.

The sword nearly leaped out of the sheath. I knew it could move, of course. But had that ease been it—no, *she*—or me? I took up a stance, and swung into the Eightfold Path. My muscles itched, burned a little, and then, within a breath or two, I performed the formation with ease. Remembered ease.

"How did you learn that?"

I turned to find Koi standing behind the mast, standing out of the reach of my swinging blade. We were joined a moment later by Jai, and so I shrugged, and swept the blade up and into the sheath, as though I'd done it ten thousand times before. Which I hadn't. But one of Sagacious Blade's former "Bu" pilgrims had. He had shared with me that memory. To test my theory, I pulled it, and sheathed it again, as easily.

Koi grinned, shook his blade free of its sheath, and said, "A little sparring?"

I needed to integrate those memories with my own body. I nodded, and we set to. Memory—that man's memories—now gave me the ability to make sense of what I saw, but there was still a tiny hesitation before I followed through with the right deflections and counters. And when our blades met, I was still me, a fourteen-year-old girl, and not a man of whatever size. But I had gained considerably, and when we finished, I knew that I needed not only to practice, but to learn to integrate Essence into my practice.

"Hai," a man hailed from one of the escort ships, which I had momentarily forgotten. "Meet us at the dock."

The anchor was down, and Dinek was calling to the crew to lower the boat.

Jai ran off, leaving Koi and me to walk together.

"I understood what you meant before about reflection," Koi said, and glanced my way, as if for permission to go on. Whatever he saw in my face seemed to grant it, for he said, "In your family, reflection was only sometimes a punishment. All of you were in the habit of true reflection."

"It's how we were raised," I said. "You saw that."

"Nobles have the leisure, and the surroundings to reflect. Whether on themselves or on higher matters," Koi observed.

"This is very true! The word I want is cultivate," I said. "Gallant wanderers improve through cultivation. Ay! I am so very glad I read all those stories! To cultivate means to improve, and anyone can do it, common-born or not. I do need to cultivate."

"We all do. What do you think of this idea of forming the Pangolins into rescuers?"

"I like the idea but are we ready for such an endeavor?" I asked. "We've just lost some of our Pangolins. Though I think it a good thing that they followed the Snow Crane monk."

"But you did not choose to," he said, with a curious glance.

"I thought about it," I said. "And I know my first intention might make anyone laugh, but I think you will understand. I have not changed my mind. I want to find my brother if I can, and I was afraid that a temple life, while admirable in so many ways, would make it much more difficult to find him."

Koi did not disagree.

"I don't know how to begin the search, except perhaps to listen to news of the Grand Prince. As for this question, today,

I don't know what to think about the Pangolins' idea. It seems…"

"Absurd?"

"Not that," I said, and the hurt in his face smoothed. "I speak for no one else but myself. I am not equipped in any real sense. What I did was by accident. That monk is… is a shaman," I said, not ready to go into demons and the like, especially as my knowledge was so sparse. "It was the monk who did the Essence formations. All I did was perform my fire trick, until my own vital waters nearly evaporated, I am so very ignorant. You know that I am no Essence master."

Koi said, "I also need to cultivate…not just with this." He lifted his sheathed sword. "But here." He tapped the hilt against his brow. "I can't talk about it with Fan. Not without questions I don't want to answer."

"Is it because of me? My true name and birth," I asked, full of regret for matters I knew I could not help.

"Partly," Koi said. He flexed his hands, looking up and away. "My plan worked, but barely. It was good luck there was only the one fight. I managed to hold that yacht guard off, but he was driving me back when the owner turned up screaming to fight the fire, and he had to let me go. Master Sima once told me I'm good for my age, but I could see I have much more to learn."

"But you were doing martial arts for years and years, with Second Brother."

"Forbidden," Koi said. "Strictly forbidden. This is what I can't say to Fan, not without explaining. As a servant, even with your brother, I knew at all times I had to lose. Though your brother begged me to work harder—to fight harder—I never dared to. I knew what would happen if I put a mark on him. Though I knew he would try to protect me, they'd just pull me out on some excuse, while he was studying, and I'd be lucky to survive the beating. Or worse. The rules are actual laws, that the only weapons in the imperial palace belong to the imperial family, who can do what they want, or to the Imperial Guard."

I remembered what Koi had said earlier, about some of the Imperial Guards not seeing it when Xianti and his followers beat up Second Brother and his friends during their fox and rabbit games. I also remembered that a section of the Imperial Guards had vanished along with the Grand Prince. Perhaps these were sworn loyalties. But I began to comprehend, a very little, how much imperial power rests in the hands of the defenders of the emperor.

"Is that why Mother brought in Cray as a servant? She didn't trust the Imperial Guards?" I asked.

"Yes. Bao is a martial artist. Gui, also. They're Falcons, which I didn't know about until he sent me north with the Watcher. Madam Gu could bring in an outside servant for a daughter, and no one cared, but that's not possible for sons. We were supplied from the Household."

That much I knew.

He said, "I've had two fights, now, where someone wanted to kill me, and I know the difference between sparring to be careful of your opponent, and actually needing to defend your life. But I still have that…I have a lot to learn. I want to learn it. It felt so very good to make a plan, to carry it out, and to see those people set free." His voice lowered to a whisper as he gazed out at sea. "Fan said the same thing. I expect that such a life makes sense to her. After all, she is garrison raised. Jai feels it as well, for his own reasons. I think we all felt it. For me, I know that it was the best thing I have ever done in my life. I want to keep doing it if I can. But I have so much to learn."

His face was still, and I sensed the question that underlay this long explanation. In a sense, he was questioning whether I believed he was entitled to learn, as he was descended from Household servants. And I was hesitant to answer because I sensed that by agreeing I would be giving him permission—which would fortify our relative ranks.

Neither of us had the vocabulary to express the fact that our ranks had altered to a sort of balance.

THIRTY-TWO

Ever looking skyward toward the crowning scarps,
she diligently walked the narrow road…

I HAVE BEEN TO many islands, most of whose capitals are in or near their main harbors, as is customary, but rarely have I seen one as beautiful as Cloud Terrace Harbor, the capital of Mountain Peony Island. The city is cut into the long slopes of the mountain that begins the island's dragon spine, the harbor a generous half-circle full of ships of all kinds.

It is dangerous to speak for everyone—and yes, I am quite aware of the irony in my writing that, considering the vantage from which I sit—but I believe it is safe to say that we were all far too apprehensive to notice the beauty of Cloud Terrace Harbor as we anchored where we had been taken, very near one of the long piers.

Dinek and her crew were the last ones into the boat, swallowing down the last of their cold meal. No one said much as we rowed toward the pier, but I could see Dinek looking back with a troubled glance. She was already attached to the *Pangolin*. These Huyun people could take it away, and we could do nothing.

The rest looked toward shore, the ship pretty much for-gotten. I reflected that even if they liked the idea of Pangolins as rescuers, we were very far from regarding ourselves as a united company. Nor was there at that time a general sense of belonging with respect to the *Pangolin*. To most, it was a mere vessel to get one from one island to the next, one we'd taken from the enemy who'd captured us.

When we reached the dock, there was an escort of Huyun guards in fine military tunics of green and tan, tassels dancing on their swords, with a hatted captain at the head. His broad-brimmed black hat sported the curling kingfisher feather that meant these guards were part of the empire's hierarchy.

They were very careful to use polite language and gestures, but they made certain that none of us strayed as we were led along a street of prosperous shops and tile-roofed buildings, each with heaven-tilted eaves, beautiful designs on walls and window frames, in colors of forest green, crimson, blue, and purple in complementary designs. Though the Year of the Horse was heading toward harvest time, the sayings and charms for prosperity on lintels and door frames were tidy instead of ragged and color-faded, as had been seen in White Water Harbor on the imperial island.

Green was the main theme, especially when we reached the top of a hill which the magistrate's building crowned. Outside, the customary huge drum stood, with a red-wrapped mallet; the drum's skin was marred dull and shiny, which meant that it was often used, or had been. That suggested to me that the locals still believed in justice, which was very different from what we'd seen on the imperial island before the slavers took us without a second glance from Xianti's Tiger Li and company.

As we were led past, I looked for the notice boards. There they were, but I could not see whose faces were on the posters, much less read any of the warnings or decrees. I was afraid to linger, lest that raise scrutiny.

We were taken inside, and directly to a side-chamber, upon which servants better dressed than most of us (well, cleaner), brought in trays of refreshments.

Jai began to lunge out of his chair toward the food, but Koi put his hand on Jai's arm. We all tracked the servants until they exited, closing the door softly behind them. Jai began to lunge again, but Koi's fingers tightened on his arm.

Jai turned a scowl his way, then his eyes widened. "Poison?" he croaked.

Koi glanced at the walls, and I understood at once that he assumed we were being watched from some vantage. That was certainly the imperial palace way.

Fan cleared her throat, then coughed, saying behind the fist that she raised to her lips, "Spies."

One of the boys uttered a soft groan, but we all sat where we were, though most could not take their eyes off the piles of steamed buns on a platter, mooncakes, and dumplings both sweet and savory, from which tempting smells wafted.

I had unconsciously assumed my court manner: back straight, hands crossed over my lap, head lowered, trying to hide the discomfort of my harness twisting as Sagacious Blade was forced to one side behind me by the hard chair. Koi had set his sword down beside his chair. They had not taken it away.

Presently a man entered, his hat bearing a kingfisher feather and a tassel hanging down one side. This was no magistrate (or magisterial secretary) in robe and hat. He was a military man of high rank, though he was not a lot older than First Brother. With him came six guards with long flat staffs—which could be wielded in a fight, or used to beat a prisoner. These six took up a position at the opposite end of the room, facing one another.

The commander surveyed us from a broad face with wide-set eyes. "Welcome to Mountain Peony Island. The individual who has the honor to interview the new arrivals is one Nan," he said politely.

Nan: one of the oldest names in the empire, as old as Tek. So old it had become very common throughout, especially in the south, so in noble circles, the next question would be *which Nan?*, to distinguish between noble and humble birth.

"I received a very interesting report," he said, looking over everyone, his gaze coming back to me. "Conflicting reports, to be more precise." He seemed puzzled as he eyed me; I could almost hear him mentally dismissing me for my youth and decidedly unheroic appearance, and turning to examine the others more closely before bringing his gaze back to Koi. Trying to determine which of us led? He'd decided on Koi, though three of us carried swords. Because he was tallest, and male? Or because he'd kept Jai from diving rudely into the refreshments, which meant we had indeed been observed? "It seems that you outran a pack fleet of stolen fishers by carving a way through Fire Dragon Reef."

The others looked my way, then down. Commander Nan blinked before bringing his gaze back to me.

From long training I did not speak, for I had not been asked a question: in court, that was the expected behavior of the least and lowest. But here?

Commander Nan said generally, "The new governor welcomes all who come to live and to trade. My sole concern, you might say, is piracy."

"Oh! We're certainly not pirates. Not at *all*," Dinek exclaimed, looking more rabbity than ever, in her fear of losing the *Pangolin*. "No, no. We don't even have weapons."

Commander Nan uttered a chuckle. "That's not what I hear."

"I," Cygnet said composedly, "wish only to find an auspicious location in which to establish a school. As Kanda says, food feeds the body, but only education feeds the soul."

Commander Nan did not react to this interruption. I wondered if he'd heard a word Cygnet had said, once he'd really got a good look at her. His gaze was too admiring for words about schools and auspicious locations. Then he seemed to catch himself staring and hastily looked away.

It was that small sign of hastily-recovered politeness that made me begin to feel we were not in immediate danger.

"A school," Commander Nan repeated, as if he'd expected anything but that.

Cygnet flushed, her glowing complexion enhancing her looks even more splendidly. "I am a scholar's daughter," she said crisply. "My great-great-great grandfather won third place in the imperial examination the Dolphin Year during the Era of Abundant Mercies, and we were scholars before then."

Commander Nan glanced down at something, then up at Cygnet. "You claimed to have been taken by slavers?"

"From River's Elbow Village in Four Cranes Prefecture," Cygnet stated. "We were forced to go to the imperial city in order to petition the emperor in his benevolent wisdom to ease our plight before being sent to Apple Blossom Prefecture. Thence to White Water Harbor, where the imperial guard looked on as we were tricked aboard the slave ship."

Commander Nan glanced from his papers to her, then to Koi, then to me, then back again to the papers before saying, "A separate report from East Inlet of Crescent Island claims that they were raided by pirates, who looted bales of silk, cases of tea bricks, cinnabar, salt, and deep-sea pearls before burning the warehouses behind them."

"That's a lie," Fan exclaimed, starting up.

"We took *slaves* away from those warehouses," Jai squawked.

"We burned them because they kept slaves in them," one of the younger boys piped up in a shrill voice.

"These...*we* only took slaves," Koi added, his hand tightening on his sword. He flushed over the beginning, coming out emphatically with the 'we' that servants were forbidden to use. "They stole the fishing craft. And some of the slaves did, as well," he added in a lower voice,

Commander Nan turned toward Fan, who stated, "You can ask anyone. Anyone honest, that is, about Heaven's Serenity Garrison in Apple Blossom prefecture. We of the Zelu family have been garrison guards for at least as many generations as Cygnet's grandfathers were scholars. We were forced out by..." She halted herself there, her gaze going to the uniformed guards standing so still, as if they were carved of wood, and let her voice trail off. "We were taken by slavers, but we took the ship. But that doesn't make us pirates. It was self-defense. We rescued slaves about to be auctioned from those warehouses on Crescent Island. In fact, if you go over to the Snow Crane temple off your eastern promontory, you'll find most of them there, along with the monk who led them."

Commander Nan lifted his hand, saying, "And so the report from the fleet captain points out. I'm merely sharing with you the report I received from Crescent Island itself." His tone was not at all unfriendly. "All these conflicting claims—and then there's the matter of carving your way through a reef that has divided us from Crescent Island for thousands of years. The governor himself is investigating."

Everyone turned to me, and I was about to claim that the Snow Crane monk was actually a shaman, and as such, responsible for that spectacular display of power. I was only a conduit. But what would be the result? Would this commander send people to arrest the monk, who was only doing benevolent things?

I said inwardly, "Granny Zim? Should I tell him that the monk guided me?"

She replied, "I expect that they will not distrust you less."

The pause had turned into a silence; when I didn't speak, Commander Nan went on, "And so, you sailed toward this harbor. Had you a destination in mind? Are you striking out to make names for yourselves?"

On the surface, the question was neutral, even reasonable.

Who does not want to make a name for themselves? But I had seen after reading so many of those gallant wanderer stories that too frequently 'making a name for yourself' meant—in the polite language of the gallant wanderers—seeking duels with other skilled martial artists, to see who is best.

Or, as law-abiding imperial subjects would say: making trouble.

Everyone sidled glances at one another, but I was thinking hard, as I suspected this question was directed at me. In court, I would claim to be an individual of no talent or ambition who only seeks peace. But in the gallant wanderer world, such a humble claim was more likely to be taken as a hint at hidden motives.

Why not resort to plain language, and see what transpired?

I said, "We'd like to rescue others in our plight, but we need training."

The commander blinked at me, then said in a positively cordial voice, "Ayah, I believe I can promise satisfaction there. There are many law-abiding subjects on this island who are part of the, ah, wandering world. Governor Huyun—the *new* governor—handed down specific orders to welcome all willing to abide by the laws, wherever they come from. This island is host to three sects—the Fists of Wood, the Lotus Temple Brethren, and a new one, training marine defenders for the tea traders out of the north. Ki, I believe they call themselves. They registered as a married pair, taking in orphans, boy or girl."

He had not mentioned the Falcons, I noticed.

He went on, "If you register as citizens, you will have the freedom of the island to pursue your cultivation. Or, teach," he added, with a glance at Cygnet, as color rose in his cheeks.

I hesitated, as the others turned to me. Then I remembered that I was Ren the Pangolin. I said, testing, "This Pangolin Ren wishes to abide by all laws that protect harmony and civilization."

"That's exactly what our governor wants," Commander Nan declared, with the fervency of conviction. He'd accepted my new identity without a flicker of disbelief. "Exactly!" His ardor diminished a little as he added, "When the emperor, in his wisdom and mercy…" Here the clasp of hands toward the south. "…withdrew the East Army from these islands five years ago and sent them west, the old governor, before he died, sought to recruit those who would protect our waters as well as the island's subjects. And our new governor carries on his grandfather's legacy—his father having died when First Imperial Grand Prince Lan Miluo beat back the pirates sent by the easterners."

There was a little more history that we pretty much ignored at the time. It was all fine, for to us it meant that we were not about to be thrown into yet another hold, or the land equivalent, while someone else decided how to direct our fates.

A scribe was summoned to register us. The imperial world enclosed us once again as we were exhorted to return on the morrow to report where we were taking up residence—no matter how temporary—and a scribe listed our names, then had us put our thumbprint next to them.

I did suffer somewhat of a qualm as I dipped my thumb into the fragrant vermilion substance and then pressed it to the paper, but I reflected that I was going to do my best to be Pangolin Ren. At any rate, Granny Zim had nothing to say against anything that had happened so far, and so I assumed that I was doing no wrong.

We were then turned loose—that is, all except Dinek, who was kept back to be registered as captain of the *Pangolin*. We were so unused to thinking of ourselves as a company that we wandered out in a clump, no one sure what to do next.

"A place to stay. A bath. Food," I said, more to myself than to the others—though I did speak aloud.

"Good idea," Ke stated, one hand closing over the other arm's pocket sleeve, wherein she'd put her share of the silver. And she set out walking ahead of us, scanning each building.

I began to follow. Ke, it transpired, was looking for the most prosperous entertainment houses, where she might audition as a dancer. But I scrutinized the lefthand side of the doors of inns until I came at last to one called Three Kingfishers that had the Falcon wing sign etched in its wall, between strands of carefully pruned climbing jasmine.

My heart leaped within me, not because I regarded myself as a Falcon so much as because it promised familiarity of a sort. Continuity. I noticed Koi and Jai behind me, and it only occurred then that the Pangolins had dispersed without a thought. Ay, we were too newly a company to regard ourselves as one, I thought as I mounted the steps to go inside. So much for Pangolins!

I halted when I saw that the common room was filled with green tunics having an off-duty meal, playing games, or chatting as they drank tea. But then I recollected that gallant wanderers were welcome on this island, and that the guard actually appeared to be guardians of the peace instead of guardians of tyranny, and so I dared to continue on in.

At the counter a pair of teenage girls Cray's age worked. Both looked from my face to my sword when I sketched the wing sign in the air, and one ran off. Very soon the proprietor came forth from the kitchen, a stout, damp-browed grandmother.

"Falcons?" she said.

"Yes."

I leaned forward. "Do you know of a Peaches Scrape?"

She looked confused. "Peaches?"

"That might be the island name. Granny Ou, a trader, referred to Peaches."

She gave her head a shake. "I don't know all the Falcon scrapes, but sometimes we get those more traveled coming through. You could ask them."

I thanked her, and because I strive for truth in these reminiscences, I admit to being secretly relieved. The sense of familial obligation prompting me to follow Granny Ou had gradually died away over the past days. It seemed years ago since we had last seen them, except the knot in my heart from overhearing Cray's confession still lingered.

I hefted my things and went up the two flights of stairs as Koi and Jai spoke to the innkeeper. We were sent to the attic, which was divided one side for girls and the other for boys. Under the slant of the roof was the usual platform bed shared by all in a row, on the opposite side more shelves for belongings.

Three other girls had claimed shelves. I put my carryall and Sagacious Blade on a fourth, and as I turned away, I caught sight of my reflection in a strip of polished bronze fitted into the door frame. I stared, startled and not pleased: I *looked* like a pirate in my grubby, rumpled green silk with the bamboo shoots worked into the weave. My face was grimy, my hair disheveled. Hot shame burned through me. I knew what Mother would say. But I was expected down there to begin my labors, and also, I reminded myself, I looked no worse than the rest of us.

Two days a week we had to give to the inn if we were staying more than a hand of days. More days would earn one pay. I was promptly put to work. Washing dishes was the first job assigned to those who had no other innkeeping experience.

Hundreds of dishes.

You'd think yourself caught up, but then baskets of dishes came out. My back and arms ached halfway through that first day—and we had not even had to begin at dawn.

Koi was put to carrying trays of fresh food to tables, and then lugging the baskets of dirty dishes to me. Jai had to scrub tables, and sweep every time they turned the sand clock.

We only had one exchange during that long, long day, when Koi said, as he rolled his right shoulder and grimaced, "I guess this work will be good for the arms."

We were let off at sunset, and at last, oh at last, we sat down to a meal that I regarded as princely for its quantity and variety, though it was only four dishes. But after an eternity of watery congee, followed by mere tastes of rice and bean paste, the four dishes of braised whitefish, pickled vegetables, fried plantains, and fresh noodles looked sumptuous.

"Eat slowly," the innkeeper, Ma Shao, said to us. "You youngsters always come in half starved, and if you bolt your food, you end up in the privy losing all my excellent cooking. Don't do that."

It took all my control not to inhale my food, but it was worth the effort. I ended that day in a deeply appreciated bath—the age and prosperity of this city evident in the fact that hot water was brought from the local hot spring to the inn in a conduit, and the taxes paid for its upkeep. There was a sizable bath in the cellar, women on the west side, men on the east.

I slept well that night, and the next morning woke before dawn, as I had for most of my life so far, determined to begin my cultivation.

In the kitchen, a tall, thin woman presided over the tea. She had to be the Falcon Watcher; she said to me in an undertone, "You must have some importance: there are two set to watch here. Don't forget to report to the magistrate."

"When do they open the doors?"

"Phoenix third hour."

It was first hour, so I continued on, determined to begin with self-discipline, after days of no exercise. The innkeeper had pointed us toward a yard behind the fowl pens and outside stove where meat was braised, where one could practice; she'd explained that the Falcon scrape, Mountain-Reflecting-Water, lay on the other side of the mountain and some days' journey east, if we wished to go into training, but for short stays there was this yard.

I went out, hoping to be alone. A couple of others were there, but they paid me no heed, so I took out Sagacious Blade, and consciously put myself through the fundamental seeds to warm up. It was both strange and comforting to be doing these again. How odd it was, the way certain types of movement worked as effectively as scent to throw one back to another place, another life!

The two finished their sparring before I'd finished my seeds, and for a brief time I was alone. I consciously reached for the memory of the sword master. Granny Zim was there, approving me. Perhaps she eased the way, for there was the memory, and I began slowly, working to integrate memory and movement. It was awkward and yet exhilarating, a bit like trying to maneuver a puppet while at the same time feeling as if the puppet was trying to move me. Through it all this unnamed man (for he was merely an unnamed I in his thoughts!) took such joy in the strength of his body, and the smooth glide and arc and strength of the actions. That joy echoed through me.

I worked a single form over and over, until someone else came out. By then the sun was higher in the sky than I expected. No wonder I was hungry—but breakfast had to wait until I'd reported where I was staying.

When I returned, I was surprised to discover several Pangolins sitting at a table off to one side, along with Koi and Jai, their hair wet from the baths, and each in clean silks that I and the other sewers had made.

As I sat down with my steamed buns, I noticed that none of us had congee before us. Then Fan turned to me, her brow furrowed. "I was just telling them that I stayed at the Jolly Pig, where I was told the Fists of Wood Brethren stay when in harbor. When I asked about their training, I was told that no women are allowed, except as cooks and help. Even when I explained my training!"

"Why don't you train with the Falcons?" Koi asked.

Fan said, "You Falcons are fine martial artists, but you train to defend women and children. The Falcon style is too soft. It would be useless against pirates! The Fists style is what I need. I promised Dinek I'd get training against boarders..."

MiMi said, "What about those others that commander mentioned? He said they train for ship fighting."

"A couple," Fan stated, and it seemed that though she

resented her summary rejection by the Fists of Wood, she had doubts about a sect which had a woman as part of its leadership. She moodily chased a last noodle around in her bowl, then sighed. "I can try. Nothing hurt if I try."

"What about the rest of you?" I asked.

"Yes," Ke said, elbowing Dinek. "I happened to see from my window that you rowed back and slept on the *Pangolin*, along with your brats."

"Didn't have to pay," Dinek said with a shrug. "Why not? Also, the Celestial Chart was full, and I didn't want to go to any other inn."

Ke sighed, rolling her eyes. As she thumbed up the last crumbs of her breakfast, she said, "I was hired instantly after my audition, of course."

"But you're in servant brown," MiMi pointed out.

Ke was indeed wearing a robe of dull brown, her hair tied up neatly into two fox ears. She lifted a shoulder as she rose. "I have to begin with the fundamentals, as does everyone, but Madam assured me I'll rise fast, with my talent. I had better go, for there's class, and work, but I did want to see how everyone is doing!"

She flicked her hand as if she held a fan, and swayed away, somehow making that plain robe flutter about her ankles.

Dinek scowled after Ke. "Now that she's gone, I can tell you my plan: I've hired out the *Pangolin* for a tea run." At our confused look, "North, to the tea islands, then back down south to sell it. I'll be on board, along with my crew of 'brats', but I've done a deal with an auntie of the Hat family I met at the Celestial Chart, who will train me for half the take. But I don't want Ke to know that, and I definitely do not want her to know that I want you to guard the gold while we're gone."

"Me?"

"I trust you," Dinek said. "I like Ke, but she is grass on the wall."

A vulgar saying that would have caused my parents to frown. I mentally interpreted that: would grow over anything at any time, given sun and water. In other words, would say, or do, what suited her best.

Fan said, "Yes, she was definite about wanting to buy her own emporium so she could be the madam, instead of working her way up."

"We all have to work our way up," Dinek stated. "Ay! I'm done. I'll go tell the registry that I'm sailing. Ren, I'll be back later tonight, once I've got everything arranged."

Her departure caused a general rising.

Jai ran ahead, and Koi stayed back, saying in a low voice to me, "Are you going to the Falcon scrape with us?"

"I had not thought about it," I said. "Is there a hurry?" I thought immediately of the Watcher and those mysterious two set to observe what I did. Surely if I did nothing out of the ordinary, I would eventually be left alone?

"Jai nearly caused a fight last night, and this morning I caught him about to steal something from the man who heckled him. I think he needs the discipline of the Falcon way. Before he gets himself thrown into jail."

"I agree," I said.

"And so?" Koi asked, looking ahead down the road.

"So?"

"Are you going to travel with us?"

I considered the fact that I was truly free to do what I wanted to do, for the first time since…no, for the first time ever.

"No," I said. "I like it here. Washing dishes all day is horrible, but it's only two days in the week, and Ma Shao said that once I learn some of the other things, I won't have to spend an entire day at it. And I really want to listen for news of my brother. Well, of the Grand Prince, too, in case Second Brother is with him as you guessed."

Koi dipped his head, almost a bow, caught before it completed. "Will you send word if you discover anything?"

"I will," I said. "Ma Shao mentioned that Falcons regularly go between the scrape and the Three Kingfishers."

We said nothing else, for we'd reached the magistrate's building. By the time I'd had my turn to report my new location, the boys were gone, and I walked alone back to the inn, determined to set myself a schedule, and keep to it.

There was no use in seeking an Essence teacher until I actually knew something about Essence. And I had memories to learn from right inside me. I simply had to find a secluded spot somewhere among the tumble of rocks and trees between the terraced streets, to do my cultivation.

That was easily done. Myriad paths led upward from the back yard. I found a secluded grove under some fragrant redbark trees, and once again, without being unconscious or ill, I reached within for a memory.

This former holder of Sagacious Blade felt like a she. A

scholarly sort, relishing the unseen world, but as I sank into the warmth of her memories, there came her deep love for her family. The lessons were there, but also the physical memory of the squeeze of hugs.

Hugs. I sat there on my rock, my arms wrapped around myself as I gazed from beneath the sheltering branches of a parasol tree, out at the sparkling waters of the bay, and the ships peacefully bobbing there. Hugs? It had been long since Mother had hugged me, and of course no one else would offend propriety in such a way.

My arms were empty, and my throat ached, though I could not say why. I had a course of study ahead of me, and I was setting about it properly. I would guard Dinek's gold for the ship. I would find my brother, and help my family. I was trying to be a good person.

THIRTY-THREE

The Jade Countenance looked down in approval as
the young phoenix rose through blue-dark skies,
inspiring those behind cloud-barred windows…

GRANNY ZIM'S ESSENCE-WIELDER, who I began to think of as
Auntie Breeze, taught that Essence governs the five elements in
both the sun phase, or action, and the moons' phase, resting.
The sun sheds light, the moons glide harmoniously in
darkness, revolving through the seasons' circles. Without
Essence, no object can exist, yet it has no shape or shadow.
Everything is made of it; things living and non-living receive
Essence at the moment of their making, which grants them a
form and a nature of their own.

From that soil grows the ideal world that lives in harmony
with both the seen and unseen worlds. The Essence wielder
strives to work to maintain that harmony.

Discovering that Essence studies complemented what I had
been raised to believe buoyed and invigorated me. The next
step — learning to use Essence as I used a writing brush or any
other implement — was relatively easy in that my entire life's
training had prepared me for the discipline necessary. Though
Essence is akin to water in its formlessness, power, and chaotic
nature, I learned quickly how to hold Essence, to command it,
to use it, and to let it go before it could consume me in a
spiritual fire.

I use fire as my image because my attributes, it seemed, were fire and metal. I could as easily have said I would be drowned in it, or buried under an avalanche, or fallen through its winds—this is to underscore that to write about it requires indirection and metaphor, because the language of Essence wielders is so arcane that it is useless to try to define it simply. Let it be said therefore that, with Auntie Breeze's memories as a guide, I rose rapidly through its levels: fire I already knew by instinct, then metal, earth, water, and last was…air.

I'd resolved to never reveal any Essence matters, and so I learned to ward off a small space which would encompass my Essence experiments. Time fled as I cultivated Essence alone, and martial arts both alone, just me and the memories of the stalwart man I named Uncle Rock, and in the yard with other Falcons who lived in or visited the inn.

I found myself fitting into life at the Three Kingfishers before the first snows flew. By the time we scoured, swept, and scrubbed out the last of the horse year to make way for the Year of the Eagle, I began to be entrusted with the cash box, and by the spring of my fifteenth birthday, if Ma Shao was away, I was assigned to disperse the necessary to various vendors, as well as carrying the tax money to the tax office on the first day of the tenth month, with only her daughter Fia (whose eyesight was too weak for close work such as bookkeeping, though she saw quite well at a distance) accompanying me.

I hid my experiments with Essence because of that warning that I was being watched. I didn't resent it. I understood why they would want to keep an eye on a newcomer who could throw fire strong enough to blast ancient rock into dust. They could have imprisoned me, or planted a spy in my proximity, instead of posting someone I never saw. But revealing anything about Essence meant questions about my sword, which I was afraid would lead to my identity, and that I was determined to hide.

Their observers, the local Falcon Watchers told me, had diminished to one by Sky Wishes Day, and before the change of the year, that person only came by once a week or so. By my fifteenth birthday, even that had ended, though I remained wary. I sensed that the entire matter had not ended. It was only suspended.

And one day that spring, when I was on the serving floor, Commander Nan came in alone for a meal.

We recognized one another right away. He said, "So you've settled here, Pangolin Ren! I've been tending to naval matters all morning, and just climbed onto the pier right below the inn here when the noon bell rang. I'm hungry, and the smells coming out this door are tempting."

I had been looking around for an empty table to direct him to, but the place was filled. "You would be most welcome," I began, "however…"

The guards nearest the door had been exchanging glances, and a table of four lower-ranking patrollers got up, bowed to the commander, picked up their plates and cups and squeezed in among cronies at other tables, leaving one free.

"…if your honor will permit thi—ay, me, to wipe it down," I finished in haste, wrenching myself away from old courtly habit when in the presence of someone of rank who could make trouble for me.

I cleaned the table with a few fast swipes, and he sat down, beaming with good will.

I brought him tea, and began to pour it, consciously avoiding the ritual gestures I'd been taught; the first time I was assigned to serve customers, and I'd used proper tea-pouring manners, I'd been laughed at by the family. "Though you do it mighty prettily, we don't try to mimic nobles," Fia told me earnestly. "It might get us some criticism for presumption."

I slopped the tea into the cup. By then, the cook had filled a dish with spiced shrimp and seagrass, which I fetched and put before him. He set to while I flew among the tables, fetching, carrying, clearing, and fetching again. I tried not to look his way. I was not guilty of anything. But I feared my secrets somehow leaking out, and his presence was a reminder of my guise. Quite rightly, I reminded myself as I hefted a tray of six plates of lemon soup. I'd become entirely too comfortable.

Gradually the press began to ease as most returned to duty, leaving those with a free watch sitting over their tea or rice wine or beer among the travelers and gallant wanderers.

When I returned to clear away Commander Nan's empty dish, he sat back, picked up his tea cup and said, "I remember hearing last summer that you accomplished your great deed with a singular sword. I have an interest in swords. May I see yours?"

"I could fetch it later," I said, torn between duty and politeness as I glanced at my tray.

Ma Shao, never far away and always listening, called out,

"I've everything in hand, Young Ren. You may run and fetch it."

I put down the tray at the counter. As I ran up to the attic and down again, I mentally rehearsed the story I'd told the Shao family, and when I returned to the common room, I drew the blade and made a pass, careful not to disturb the other tables.

The nearby customers, a variety of locals, a few guards, sailors, and a party of three dusty-shouldered gallant wanderers, turned appreciatively at the rich ochre flash of sunlight that outlined Sagacious Blade's etched scales, and winked in the great white stone in the hilt.

"Oh, what fine artistry," exclaimed Auntie Gi from the ironmonger's two houses down. "I did not know you had such a blade, Young Ren! You must bring it by so that Peg can look it over. You know he would love to see it."

Everyone agreed.

"You never did explain how you managed to blast your way through the reef," Commander Nan said to me.

"This I have to hear," remarked a grizzled guard from a side table. Now no one was pretending not to listen.

I had learned that self-deprecation was less welcome than a good tale, and that some even took too cryptic a modesty as a kind of insult, even a loss of face, for it implied they had no right to ask. Because everyone paid attention to everyone else's affairs. It seemed to be assumed as a right, perhaps a result of all having to band together during bad times?

"Ay," I said. "Thank you for asking, your honor. I love telling this story, as it's the only time I've ever had the chance to do such a thing!"

As they all listened, I spun out my tale that implied that the Pangolin Blade was a family heirloom with a certain number of fire-blast talismans laid into it by a grateful fox-demon whom a gallant wanderer ancestor had chanced to rescue. I emphasized the tension of the chase by the slavers in their stolen boats, and how scared we were, knowing we could not fight back if they attacked us.

"I don't know how many fire blasts I have left, after that," I said. "I'm afraid to test, and discover that that was the last! But it was in a very good cause."

"That it was," Commander Nan said appreciatively, raising his glass to me. "A toast to you, Young Ren. Did you know that the governor himself went to investigate?"

"No," I said, not wanting to say that I'd thought it prudent to keep my head down. I had not even dared risk looking at the display boards of posters of wanted criminals, lest someone see me doing it and wonder why. Surely the governor had to have discovered the truth about the slavers, or those of us in the harbor would have been hauled in again.

"He did," Commander Nan said. "Those vile serpents had been coming in twice a year to carry out their trade, then slithering away again. The locals were bribed very well to stay quiet. But Governor Huyun settled all, and those locals are still paying restitution for the northside fishers' ruined boats."

"Never slacks, not our Handsome Huyun Shandek," put in he of the grizzled chin. "The best governor ever to bless this island!"

"That's right!"

"A toast to Governor Huyun!" put in another green-wearing guard.

"I'll pay for a house round," roared Grizzled Chin. "Drinks for all!"

"I'll not take a tinny," Ma Shao said instantly, coming out from the kitchen and bowing low to the commander. "I was about to propose that toast myself, for life has never been better since we had the luck of getting our young governor. Though elsewhere in the world I can't say the same, especially these sorry days when even the rats challenge the cats!"

She had to be referring to the recent trouble, when the Upstart Prince Kwai Sheion had tried to invade the island on the eastern side, to be soundly defeated.

Some made signs of warding, and one of the men said, "No inauspicious words."

Ma Shao made a spitting motion three times to the side, then said, "The gods know I'm grateful, and don't I burn luck paper to the kitchen god every morning? I'm not claiming our good fortune as anything *we* did, it's all due to Governor Huyun and his allies, and don't we all know it?"

Everyone hailed this as truth as the other server and I brought out little bottles of warmed rice wine. After the toast, Commander Nan smiled, his face red as an apple, for the house rice wine was both fragrant and strong.

He said to me, "To finish, up on Windward Promontory there was a temple full of witnesses eager to sign any petition testifying to the fact that *they* were not bales of silk, or tea bricks, or baskets of beans, as the criminals had claimed. And so the case was closed. Everyone happy—except the criminals, should they turn up again. They will have a surprise waiting, ha ha!"

The room laughed appreciatively at this sally, there was another toast, and shortly thereafter Commander Nan left to resume his duties, the others also going about their lives.

Once the room was empty, Ma Shao said, "The house can afford to be generous once in a while, when someone of importance is here. Keeps them smiling when they think of us." She turned back. "But not too often, mind."

Fia—as future innkeeper—nodded solemnly, and, tired though I was after a solid day of dashing about, I had to run back up to the attic to store Sagacious Blade. As I toiled up the narrow stairs, once again the impulse gripped me to learn how to send the sword back to its place with a spurt of Essence.

Gripped, but I smothered it. I could never risk using Essence before others, though that was not the real reason I'd been lagging through Auntie Breeze's air lesson memories. I understood the principles now. In my little circle of safety on the cliff a short distance away, I could bend saplings and set leaves whirling into a spiral, then I could disperse them in all directions. My latest lesson was to plant my feet wide and bring Essence up from the earth to lift a boulder and toss it over a cliff, though I found that easier on fire or metal days. I had become so sensitive to the gentle and harmonious rounds of days, moons' cycles, and seasons, that I did not have to think about them in conscious terms any more than my teacher had.

But I hated heights. And I knew that the next lesson after sending objects would be flying myself on my sword.

Instead, as spring ripened, I burrowed back into the lessons in geomancy. Those were useful, after all. Auntie Breeze in her day had wielded Sagacious Blade as a focus for smoothing cracks in the ground when the dragons down deep stirred in their thousand-year sleeps, and she had healed trees that the winds, or small creatures, had weakened. I so loved reviewing her memories—and her deep joy in those accomplishments— that I often dreamed about them.

Those spring days, as I ran up and down the hill from my secluded dell to the inn, I practiced by sending pests from vegetable gardens; there was a mountain full of wild plants for them to eat. I tended trees, restored threatened nests, and performed other small deeds.

All the while, Granny Zim listened, and hummed with approval.

And so, spring ripened to summer, and I learned, and grew, having over winter replaced my inappropriate green silk with a sturdy plain-woven gallant wanderer's robe of green, slit up the sides for riding trousers, though I had never ridden a horse. I had even embroidered a pangolin onto my brown headband, which I wore when I did seeds, formation, and sparring out in the yard with other blue-headbanded Falcons. Pangolin Ren was a gallant wanderer from a line of gallant wanderers, and I had settled thoroughly into that role.

Then one day Shao Apa, Ma Shao's husband, returned from his wanderings, which caused Ma to shut the inn for a night in order to invite all the Shao cousins for a feast. The next day, he called us all outside and put us all through a test of our martial arts.

When it came to my turn, Da Shao, as he insisted we call him, gave Sagacious Blade a long look, eyes narrowed. But he said nothing.

I took my stance, and as had become my habit over the past year, I waited for his attack, and countered for a move or two to assess not only his skill, but his intent: after moving through Uncle Rock's memories of sparring, duels, and twice, actual war, over and over and over again, I had begun to see the possibilities before my mind could even define them.

All so that I could end the fight as quickly as possible.

In this instance, I perceived that Da Shao's skill was so high his moves flowed like air and water, but he was waiting on me. I was never going to take the initiative. I had no desire to fight, but every desire to defend myself. And so, deliberately clenching on the instinct to use Essence to empower my moves, I lunged, deflected, and reached past his defensive line with my free hand to tap two acupoints that—had I put any power in—would have locked his meridians.

He flinched slightly, then gave me a nod. "Very well done."

"This poor beginner won only because Da Shao was not using even half his strength," I said. Which was true.

"And yet you perceived that," he countered. "The Watcher said that you are not a fighter, and I see that it is true, and yet you are quite skilled. Why hide such fine skills? You ought to go up to the scrape, Young Ren."

I bowed, thanking him for his sage advice, and mumbled

something about my friends here; though sometimes I felt the pull, there had been just enough rare gossip drifting in with the ships to keep me firmly in harbor. Such as the fact that my Uncle Torza and his family, including Cousin Oraiti, had apparently vanished before the ferrets arrived to arrest them; Benevolent Winds was now governed by Imperial Crown Prince Xianti's twin, Kianti.

Da Shao did not press; for the remainder of summer he stayed, and he worked us all very hard during that time. Especially me, it seemed. Enough that once in a while I slipped in a little Essence, both to test myself and to give just enough extra sting to the acupoint touches to make anyone want to shake off the feeling and be done with me.

Then one morning he was gone, and Ma Shao and Fia went about their daily routine with a resignation that made it clear this was habit. The most they said was wondering when Tua, Fia's brother, would have liberty long enough to return home.

Chrysanthemums bloomed, then the loquats, and we paid taxes once again, and turned to scrubbing the inn from attic to cellar.

The eagle year gave way to dolphin, and winter began to thaw toward spring. My sixteenth birthday silently dawned and just as silently passed. The only one who would have known was Koi, and though we occasionally sent brief news messages through Falcons passing between the scrape and the harbor, I think it is safe to say that neither of us would have thought to acknowledge such personal matters as birthdays.

Even if I'd known when his was. Servants' birthdays were their own affair, so I'd been raised to believe—and though the entire household celebrated our Lan family birthdays, it was a matter of feast foods and extra drink, but the male servants would never have presumed to do anything more than to bow and wish me or Mother an auspicious year.

Life had thoroughly settled—and of course that was when everything changed.

One spring afternoon, between the midday rush and the evening diners, the door opened, stirring the crimson luck streamers hanging from the overhead lamps, and in walked Dinek!

THIRTY-FOUR

She lifted her eyes to the restless seas,
counting the princes' barbarians in their endless
files,
wildcats and wolves at their head!

IT WAS AN ODD thing I sometimes contemplated as I cultivated Essence and martial arts alone in my grove, how I had tried my best to bridge that mystery of friendship over the past year and a half. I was on greeting terms with many, if not most, along the street. I'd tried to be friendly in ways that did not demand recompense, such as chasing off pests from others' kitchen gardens on the slope behind the row of houses of our street. Perhaps it was my closely-guarded secrets, or perhaps something in my bearing that created an invisible wall around me. For try as I might to move as others did, I still got the occasional comments about my silent step, and the way I poured tea for customers. And I was still not part of any circles among the teenagers I greeted most days.

And yet, when Dinek entered—a person I'd only spent a few days with, during that dreadful slave episode—delight unfurled within me, bright as a lotus when dawn greets it, and I saw in her sudden smile that stretched to a grin that she was genuinely glad to see me, too.

"Ren!" Dinek exclaimed, strutting in, wearing a fine robe of rich brown, and a ship captain's hat. She was still short, and I began to suspect that she was actually a few years older than I, though her round cheeks and rabbit teeth had made her appear younger. "A thousand blessings on you!" She peered at me as her eyes adjusted to the relative dimness of the room after the brightness outside. "Ayah, you've changed."

"*I* have?" I said in surprise. "I've only had to make one set of new clothes."

"Not in girth," she said, squinting. "Ay, yes, a bit. But we were all so starved. I don't know what it is. You are taller, yes?"

"I did have to lengthen my robe two fingers. You're looking fine and stout!"

She smacked one arm. "Stout I am, but you should see Fan. She's even stouter. Ay, those Zelus are apparently all bears. And isn't she proud of it!" Dinek rubbed her hands. "This place smells a thousand times more heavenly than the Jade Palace's kitchen ever could." She sat down at a table, and as I brought over a small warmer and set a pot of ever boiling water on it, she leaned toward me and murmured, "You've still got the gold?"

"Buried safely," I said.

She sank back, her shoulders relaxing. "Good. I've been telling myself for the past year that it wasn't mine to begin with, that if the rest of you had spent it I ought to have nothing to say to it, but I've got a debt as long as your arm."

"Oh?"

"But wait till you see the *Pangolin!*" Her voice was louder now.

I gasped. "That could not be that handsome craft that sailed in on the morning tide?"

Dinek beamed in delight. "You saw *Pangolin?* Did you recognize it?"

"I did not," I admitted. "I watch the ships coming and going, and the goods the traders bring to Cloud Terrace." I would never say to anyone but Koi that I hoped one day a fleet of warships riding in on the tide might belong to the Grand Prince, bringing news about Second Brother. "Especially since Ma Shao began teaching me to order, and to balance the books. This morning I did note a very handsome sea hawk sail in, but it flew no imperial golden dragon."

"*Pangolin* is now every bit as fast as a sea hawk, but with a hold for goods." Dinek blushed red to the ears in pride. "And that's what we need now, a Pangolin banner. I borrowed a Hat trader banner, but we need our own." She slurped tea, then, perhaps thinking she'd been speaking about herself too much, she politely exclaimed, "That's very fine that you're learning bookkeeping! I expect you'll advance fast."

"She's got a talent for it, that girl," Ma Shao said from the kitchen.

I had never told anyone that this was far less a talent than the fact that I had been trained to manage a palace's accounts from the time I could hold an ink brush and an abacus. Ma Shao's "new" lessons were to me reviews of Mother's teaching.

"I am a mere beginner," I said. "But let us leave my small life. Tell me more! It's been well over a year since we last saw one another. You must have had interesting adventures."

"Haven't I just," Dinek declared, her rabbit-tooth grin broad. "Fan and I—she ought to be along in a moment. She went to register our arrival, and maybe try to bribe someone to give us a better berth so we don't have to row halfway to Crescent Island when we return to the ship." She sighed. "This tea is good, but I am as hollow as a reed. Bring me whatever is fastest, would you, Ren?"

"At once."

I was soon back with Ma's famous noodles with pickled parsnips, garlic, and pepper fish. Dinek rubbed her hands, picked up her eating sticks, then said, "Tell me all the local news, and Pangolin news, while I take the edge off my appetite. Or are there any Pangolins left?"

I said, "Some! Local news: there was a battle off the Deep Sea, when the Upstart Prince Kwai Sheion invaded the east coast here."

'Upstart' had preceded the title of the never-met, once-legitimate prince so often that the words came out almost unthinking. Almost. The autumn before, as I'd lain under the attic window breathing in the scent of the loquats blooming on the hills between our street and the one above, I'd recollected First Brother and Father talking about how the ancient and once-admired Kwai family had been abruptly declared criminals, all of them executed except for one or two who had been spirited away. Father leaned toward First Brother, saying, *I want my truth-seeking son to remember that, wrong or right, what happened to the Kwai family can happen to anyone whom the emperor thinks is coveting the dragon throne. Anyone.*

First Brother had said, *This stupid son of no talent dares to ask if Honored Father implies that justice is irrelevant?*

Not for us, Father had said. *Never for us. Every truth that we prove, every correct judgment, is our contribution to civilization.*

Did that prince, who still claimed his title, believe he was pursuing justice?

Dinek waved her eating sticks. "Ayah, that battle was noised all over the Inner Islands," she mumbled around a mouthful. Swallowed. Blinked, then added, "All that anyone speaks of these days are the Wars of the Princes. War is everywhere. Or threatened everywhere, as they sail about trying to snatch or defend the richest islands. Traders have to dodge them all. Tell me about the Pangolins."

"I've seen Cygnet once only. She started a school up near the Morningstar God's temple."

"She did get her school, then? I thought she'd marry a rich man by the end of the first week."

"Not Cygnet." I told Dinek what I knew of Cygnet's school, which permitted girls as well as boys. Followers of the beautiful Morningstar God, who had both male and female aspects, traditionally had no trouble with a scholar-teacher who was not a man. "I see Ke fairly often, as she's frequently on door fan duty."

"Door fan duty?" Dinek pulled over the dish of crispy fried plantains.

"The greeters outside the Rose Parasol, to attract custom. They wave around perfumed fans as they chat with passers-by."

"Rose Parasol? I thought she was at The Lotus Pool."

"Not anymore," I said.

"Oh? Did she get herself booted out?"

"I don't know what happened."

"Ayah, that girl is a cat. She'll always land on four feet, however fate flips her," Dinek said, spearing the last plantain.

"As for others, Koi and Jai are studying martial arts. We exchange news—about our progress," I amended, lest Dinek think to ask what kind of news. "MiMi was lately hired over to the kitchens at the garrison. She took all her crew with her, which is why she was promoted, I think. You'd be surprised at the stories about kitchen wars," I added.

Dinek poured out more tea. "No, I wouldn't. Think about it. The higher the rank of the household, the heavier the burden. And it's not like finishing a voyage, then having a few days on land. As soon as they finish preparing one meal, it's right on to the next. That doesn't count snacks. If a governor wants a snack, I'm sure he doesn't eat lychee nuts or candied haws, but must have nine plates to choose from."

"You must be right," I said. "But MiMi grew up in an inn, and she says she is very happy there." She was also a steady source of news. "Lei is doing embroidery for the dressmaker down the street that way." I pointed westward. "She's trying to build her custom so that she can open her own shop. That's all I know. The rest hired aboard ships, or got work that took them away. How about your crew?"

"We lost two," she said, adding hastily, "not their lives." She made a hasty sign warding evil. "I meant, we just lost them to the land, in the case of little Mek. He decided after another of those dragon tempests that he was done with the sea. And Biu found kin over at Benevolent Winds, when we chanced to meet one at the customs building. His aunties and uncles had thought him lost forever, and claimed him back with tears and smiles. But I've got new hires, every one of them dedicated to the Pangolin idea." Her brow wrinkled. "I wonder where Fan is? It surely does not take that long to go and come back."

Right about then arguing voices rose outside the door.

"…no, don't trouble her!"

"Trouble? Who said anything about trouble? You'd keep me from greeting an old friend?" Ke swayed in, glancing over her shoulder at Fan, who strode on her heels.

Fan was taller than I remembered Koi being, her face sun-browned, broad, and merry. She wore her hair in a man's topknot, but her impressive bosom, set off by a broad leather belt decorated with linked steel rings, emphasized her stout lineaments.

Ke shrugged, saying, "Besides, it never hurts just to ask."

And she turned to sweep us with her quick, assessing gaze. The truth was, I knew why she'd left The Lotus Pool, the most expensive entertainment house in the entire city. Which only catered to men. Her training got her hired at the lowest level, but subsequently, she told me frankly, she learned that no matter how hard she worked at her dancing, despite that curly mane black as a crow's wing, she wasn't pretty, so she would never get beyond the background. She was better off at the Rose Parasol. Most of their custom came to see plays, and hear music; it was not unknown to see parties of shopgirls come in to watch the male players and dancers, and even families came to see the traditional plays offered at festival days.

"Ask what?" Dinek said, crossing her arms. "What plot are you concocting now?"

"No plot," Ke retorted, and crossed *her* arms. "It's a rescue I need done."

"A rescue?"

"I distinctly remember…" Ke began in her share-everything-with-everyone voice, but then she was interrupted by a smiling Ma Shao.

"Why don't you gossip upstairs, girls? You would not wish to disturb the quiet enjoyed by our *paying patrons*." She rolled her eyes toward a pair of green-clad guards who were busy throwing dice.

Upstairs we went to a room with a low table around which four could sit comfortably. I brought Dinek's tea, set it down, and said, "I'll get another pot."

"Never mind that," Fan said, and added meaningly, "We're going to leave in a moment."

"Spit it out," Dinek said to Ke. "Rescue whom?"

Ke leaned forward. "Aku Orchid, niece of my madam, Aku Ni. Madam Aku has not been able to eat or sleep. She never married, you see, and this niece is everything to her."

Dinek waved a hand. "My heart is not a guqin. Stop plucking at it. Speak plainly."

"Aku Orchid was snatched by Ji Jiang of Tiger Island."

Dinek shut her eyes, her forehead furrowing. "Tiger Islands, off the east coast of this island, bordering the Great Sea. Ji Jiang began with an independent fleet, some used to say pirate, others say he fought pirates and took their loot, until he allied with the Grand Prince to defeat the Easterners. Settled on one of the Tiger Islands as a base. Allied with this island last summer when the Upstart Prince tried to invade, promoted to governor of the Tiger Islands."

"All that is irrelevant," Ke stated impatiently. "Does that make her any less snatched?"

I said, "Why doesn't Madam Aku take this matter to the Huyun magistrate?"

"They can't do anything."

"Why not?"

"Ji Jiang, commander of the Tiger Island Fleet and now governor, saw Orchid in her garden at the palace in Dawn's Placid Sea Harbor, at the east end of this island, while they laid plans. He admired her, and so her father, Aku Pan—brother to my madam—had to offer her as a consort, though she's his only child. He's a palace steward, with middling rank. She was not asked, of course. All she cares about is gardens. Her garden is famous." She made a pretty gesture, waving the subject of gardens away. "Madam will pay anything to anyone who will go to the Tiger Islands and snatch her back." And when these words were met with silence, Ke said indignantly, "This is rescuing a girl! Or was all that talk on board the slave ship about rescuing women mere donkey brayings?"

Dinek said slowly, "If this girl truly wants to escape, we could. But how do you know she'd want to? Was she snatched by force?"

"No, Madam says she went because it was her duty, but she was pale as death, and her maid met one of the old palace maids over winter, and said she's desperately unhappy, and that Ji Jiang's harem is a like a prison."

Dinek scowled, then turned to Fan. "What do you think?"

Fan sighed, studying the ceiling. Then she dropped her head. Scowled at Ke. Then she said reluctantly, "It's one person. That's good. But we don't know what kind of defenses they have."

Dinek turned to me. "Ren?"

My thoughts had gone immediately to poor Cousin Arati. And how we had been helpless to interfere.

And I knew what Father would say.

"I would like to agree," I told her, hating every word. "It grieves me, every time I hear of such doings. But first, we have only the maid's testimony. How do we know that is the way Aku Orchid feels? Second. If we were to go there to snatch her away, would we not have to sail as independents?"

"You mean pirates," Fan said sourly. "Because we'd be outside the law."

Dinek's eyes narrowed. "Go on."

"If the Huyun magistrates won't act, then they must have agreed to whatever that Ji Jiang wanted. After all, she's just a girl, the daughter of a mere steward. Which means that our action on her behalf would be breaking the law."

Dinek scowled at the table, slumping back on her heels. "You're right. We'd never be able to come back here."

Fan scowled at Ke.

Ke scowled at me.

Dinek turned her scowl to me. "Do you see a way around it?"

"Perhaps we ought to investigate first. You have to

remember that selling daughters is legal, it's a traditional solution to rescuing a family from dire circumstances."

"Not just daughters," Fan muttered. "That brat Jai, his mother was sold by his father because they were starving one year when the fishing was bad. Though Jai said it was to pay a gambling debt."

Ke said, "But this is just one person, who means everything to her family. That Ji Jiang isn't going to go to war if—"

Dinek threw up a hand. "Wait. Let me think. Auntie Hat Anek pointed out to me a year ago that in some places, what we did to rescue ourselves could have gotten us beheaded." She looked up at me. "I'm correct?"

"Yes," I had to admit. "This is why laws are debated, and why there is a necessity for the censors," I added, greatly daring, but it felt good to say it. "Justice is a loom of never-ending weave."

"Very well, then. To begin with, right now, there's the matter of registry. If we ever expect to return to this harbor, when we sail, we have to have a purpose. Other than stealing a consort from a legal marriage."

Ke shrugged. "That's easy enough. You add on a purpose—trading for tea—but don't mention rescuing a girl who was handed off like a bag of gold."

"I could ask Ma Shao for a purpose. She was born on the eastern shore."

"Tell her?" Ke repeated.

If they'd forgotten that this was a Falcon inn, I decided not to remind them. The Falcons were not precisely secret, but they did not proclaim their sect or purpose, as some did. I said, "I want to be able to come back, too. That means I need to tell Ma Shao, but she will favor rescues, especially of women."

Dinek sat upright. "It won't take long to sail to the east end. We can debate as we go, and yes, we definitely want to have another reason to sail. Even if it's just training. If we do this," she said, turning from me to Ke, "your madam has to accept that there are no promises. We'll investigate first. Then plan."

Ke bit her lip. "It's better than nothing."

"There's no telling anyone else *anything* but that we're sailing to train," Dinek warned. "Outside of your innkeeper," she added to me. "And any legitimate trade we might arrange."

"Eeee," Ke squeaked in triumph, and flounced to the door,

pausing to say to me, "You know where to find me, Ren. Because of course I'm coming, too. You are *not* getting all the credit!" That said to Fan and Dinek, then she was gone.

Fan thumbed her chin. "I don't know why she'd care so much about a girl she's never met. Doesn't seem like the Ke I remember."

"I expect she's looking to climb in her madam's regard," Dinek said shrewdly. "But she also has a soft heart beneath the grasping."

Fan said, "Do I track down the crew, then?" She sighed. "I'll no doubt be searching every single teahouse and gambling den in the city to dig out On."

"On?" I asked.

Dinek turned to Fan. "How to explain On?"

"Does On have another name?" I asked.

"He insists he's simply On," Fan stated. "Especially when he's spouting poetry, or lines from his plays. But he's a terrific warrior." That was given in a tone of finality.

Dinek raised a hand. "It'll take most of the two days to reprovision, and I want to talk to this Madam Aku. All this might be Ke's imagination. Though I doubt it. Find the crew, Fan. Let them know we're preparing to sail."

Fan gave a grunt of assent and left.

I ran down to the kitchen. Ma Shao looked up from chopping parsnips, and I decided to tell her everything. If I could not trust her, I might as well live on a mountaintop. She beckoned me to the yard, where our voices would not be overheard, and I repeated the entire conversation. Then I had to tell her about the *Pangolin*'s history.

At the end, she said, "Ay, that explains the boy you have been sending messages to."

Of course she would know that, though I'd taken care to speak quietly to Falcons departing for the scrape. But who knew what was said at the other end?

She then took me by surprise. "You'll want him to join you, I'm thinking."

"I *wish* we could have Koi with us! But how far away is Mountain-Reflecting-Water Scrape? A month's journey, if one is fast? It'll take weeks to get a message to him, and weeks for him to travel."

"That's by foot," she said. "But for messages such as this, we use Fia's pigeons."

The pigeons had a perch on top of the kitchen, tended by

Fia and the two Watchers who traded off their duties.

"Are not those reserved solely for Falcon matters?" I asked.

Ma Shao smiled briefly. "What is more a Falcon matter than rescuing a girl of sixteen? You are correct in keeping this matter from the Huyun greens. Let's send a message to your Koi."

"But he's still a month of travel away, when our ship journey is a week or ten days."

"You're thinking of the journey from here. However, from the scrape, there is a mere two-day journey down the mountain, and then two or three days more down the river to the east coast. He could watch and listen on the way. Invaluable."

She went inside to fetch the inkstone, paper, and a brush. By the time the note had been written, the sun was setting. "Always fly the pigeons at night," she said to me. "If ever your life comes to the necessity. As I suspect it will."

She did not explain that; the pigeon took off with a batting of wings.

THIRTY-FIVE

The phoenix banner unfurls, shaking off the sky;
Like cavalry horses' feathered hooves treading
upon beams of light.

IN THE TWO DAYS before we sailed, Dinek, Fan, and I ran about madly, executing a very long list of necessities. Ma Shao had told me how long it usually took for the pigeons to fly to the Falcon scrape and return, but I found myself hoping for a miracle, bringing a message from Koi. This sense of urgency seemed practical to me—that is, I defined it as practical. Though I knew that Dinek and Fan had between them brought in a new, experienced, and trusted crew, I had come to rely on Koi during our adventures before coming to this island. Even more important, he was the only one who knew my true goal—and shared it.

We required a legitimate reason to be sailing to the eastern end of the island. This Dinek found when we lugged the buried gold into the Celestial Chart, where it turned out quite a lot of trade business was conducted over tea and meals. Here, Dinek was able to pay off her creditors, or agents of creditors, in particular the Hat clan, who largely traded in northern waters.

It caused me to reflect not only on myself, but on those around me, how that small, heavy chest of richly gleaming metal could spark such a variety of emotions. In me, a strong sense of relief at the end of my responsibility for it. And distaste for the history of the gold, though I knew the gold was just inert metal, and had no desire in itself. To these others, the sight brought sudden smiles all around. I could see their satisfaction in brief bursts of Essence light motes—the motes that every living thing gives off when intense emotions occur. It was not just the anticipated possession, though that was there, it was also a sense of a promise kept. Dinek's reputation was established that day, among those people, and the result was friendliness, and plenty of news shared, instead of mere politesse.

The result? We were carrying a precious cargo of silkworms to someone who had decided to bring the Jade Islands sericulture to this northern island, and trade had been greatly disrupted after the recent invasion attempt. We had to get the silkworms to the Tiger Isles before spring ripened, or they would not hatch. The worms were packed in airy steam baskets and secured down in the hold, where it was dark, clean, dry, and still cold as the current swept down from the icy north and bent eastward.

The last item on the long list was our banner. There had been no possibility of making a suitable one in a mere two days. The only things fluttering in the wind on high were the renewed charms against wind-borne demons and other dangers of the sea; Dinek had returned the borrowed Hat family banner.

Making a banner fell to me, since I was no cook, and equally ignorant as a sailor. The Huyun patrols knew us, so there was no inquiry about a lack of banner. Ke helped me to purchase the fabric, as she was used to the thrifty ways of dancers who needed a variety of costumes that looked good, but were not expensive.

Thus, on the morning of departure, several of the crew carried the banner canvas to the boat. I lugged a heavy satchel containing the pangolin fabric, along with Sagacious Blade and my carryall containing two outfits, which I now considered real riches.

I was the last one aboard. I stepped aboard the *Pangolin* and looked around in amazement. It was scarcely recognizable from the neglected craft that we had taken over. Our *Pangolin* had probably never been cleaned except for the rain-swept, wind-scoured deck and masts and sails. MiMi and her crew of kitchen-trained helpers had scrubbed the galley, but the cabins had been dusty and brine-lined.

There was no speck of dust on the *Pangolin* now. I paused to admire the length of the gleaming deck, until the soft plunk of a lychee peel in the water behind me caused me to glance to the top of the roof of the superstructure, where someone sat, legs dangling over the eave. Though I only saw a silhouette against the sun, those shoulders, the line of neck had to belong to a youth perhaps Second Brother's age.

The sight of this new person, so very much at home, brought to me the fact that the ship had developed its own life. Those I was about to meet had lived aboard it for far longer than I had.

"On!" Dinek called. "Take the helm while I show Pangolin Ren around."

The youth popped the peeled lychee into his mouth, then he leaped out from the roof, causing me to gasp in horror. He caught a rope and swung around the mast with ease, trailing motes of Essence.

He landed before us, a young man about my height or at most a finger's breadth taller, and at first I caught an overlay of fox features, and the ruddy gleam of tails. It was the same sort of flickering image I'd seen when I met the eel-monk, but far briefer, evanescent. I blinked, and the face before me was long, with a curving, sardonic mouth, and thick eyebrows above crinkling eyes—no foxlike features, or far less foxlike than those of the imperial grandchildren.

He executing a mocking bow, intoning, "Welcome O honored and august Pangolin Ren, Owner and—"

Fan rounded the mast, and aimed a boot at his backside. "You're not going to trouble Ren with that nonsense. Unless you'd like a week of night watch?"

On turned quickly, aiming a slap at Fan. Up shot her arm in a block, and for a few heartbeats they exchanged light blows, until Fan uttered a bark of a laugh and clapped her hands. "You heard Dinek!"

On bowed extravagantly to Fan, saying, "To hear is to obey!" He ran off, laughing as he quoted a snatch of poetry about the slow turtle and the quick rabbit.

"If you ignore him," Dinek said to me, "even On gets tired of playing guqin to a wall."

"So that was nonsense, about my being the owner?" I asked.

"I thought we were agreed about that before we first

landed," Dinek said to me in surprise. "We called the ship the *Pangolin* after your name, after all. Fan and I thought it a good idea, because out of all of us, you looked the oldest. We were afraid there might be questions about our being under age, so when we registered, and traded in harbors, we put our hair up, and referred to our elder, the Owner Pangolin."

"*I* look the oldest?" I repeated.

She peered at me. "My close vision isn't the best, but yes. How old are you?"

"I turned sixteen this year."

"Really!" Dinek shook her head. "By rights you ought to be calling *me* elder sister, not the other way around. But we ought to keep things as they are. You've got the sword, the name, and as I said, we all agreed, your manner is very much an owner's manner. I'm not saying that you've been growing eyes above your head," she added in haste. "You never made the least pretense of rank, or any of that. It's just...how you move about. It's..."

I was blushing in deep chagrin. So much for my imagining I'd finally trained myself to fit in without notice.

She must have sensed my embarrassment and regret, for she changed the subject to the ship, and conducted me all along it, pointing out the changes she'd made during her tea run. So much of it was highly specialized terminology that my attention began to wander, swinging back when she made brief mentions to weathering storms, avoiding pirates, and one of the Hat brothers she'd taken on as crew stubbornly insisting that he'd seen a kraken one night while he was at the helm on the night watch.

I heard enough to feel that a year and a half had made this ship's crew into a company. The Pangolins outside the ship were still very much an idea. And that included me. I was the newcomer, and over the next stretch of days I was reminded of that often.

Fan and Dinek shared the captain's great cabin at the top, but they had traded away all the silken cushions and other pirate-like luxury stuff for more practical things a ship needs to run well. Below that, the cabins had been scoured out and changed, with those on the lower level containing sleeping platforms for crew, men on the right, women at left. I had a cabin to myself on the second level, as nominal owner. I was glad of it, because it meant I could cultivate Essence without disturbing anyone, or being disturbed.

Not counting Ke, *Pangolin* had twenty residents. That did include me—and Koi and Jai. Dinek had not forgotten them. Whether my message got through, and they traveled to Dawn's Placid Sea Harbor or not, there were two bed spaces waiting for them on the men's side, just as there'd been this cabin for me.

The ship's routine was divided into watches, for we sailed at night now as well as during the day, unlike those early days when we anchored at night. Some of the crew were older, such as the wizened, one-eyed Ayep Vu. A spare man no taller than I, he was scarred all down one side of his face. It was he who handled the cannon and gunpowder, which now had its own compartment in the hold. He had three grandsons under him, all around our age.

Dinek valued him greatly, he and three Hats, who formed part of the sailing crew. Fan was in charge of defending the ship, and she had, besides the Ayeps, some fighters, such as that strutting, poetry-spouting On. But everyone was expected to serve if the ship required it, and likewise defend it. There was fighting practice in the space before the "House" or superstructure every day.

Other than that, I was free to work on that banner. I took to sitting out on the balcony overlooking the ship, with the fabric hanging down over the rail, except for the portion I worked on. Sometimes Ke helped me, but I knew better than to rely on her.

On the third day out, a heavy storm rumbled over us, full of wind-spirits and a water dragon diving in and out of the clouds, leaving lightning trails and thunderclaps in its wake. I peered from a crack in my door, observing how very different Dinek's ship-handling was now than it had been with a handful of inexperienced children as crew. She strode back and forth, a thick woven rain-covering over her shoulders, her face calm in the brief swings of lantern-light. Gone was the rabbit fear from her countenance, though she would always have those distinctive teeth. I thought they gave her face character.

When the storm began to pass, revealing the pale blue of dawn, I emerged from my cabin to shake out the banner and drape it preparatory to working, as soon as the yawing of the ship eased somewhat. Blotches of rain spread along the heavy fabric, intensifying the spring green to jade-like brightness. We had not really chosen green so much as settled for it, green being the predominant color for the Huyun family, and therefore Mount Peony Island. It was a common color, much in demand, and thus reasonable of cost. The flag-maker had admitted that this particular dye, an experiment, was fine to look at but had proved to be a disappointment, fading quickly in sun and rain. That was fine with us, as we were independents; it was the brown pangolin whose dye I'd chosen for fastness.

I pulled out the pangolin that I'd carefully cut out on the floor of the attic room in Three Kingfishers before I packed up to leave. Having finished hemming the edges of the pangolin—a task that took three days, as the pangolin was roughly the length of two grown men, and one man's length for the width—I was about to begin applying it to the green cloth when there was a thump, and On landed next to me, hair a wet tangle about his ears, for he affected the scholar's long loose back hair, the front part bound up high with a ribbon.

"I've never been so close to a divine." He turned up his face, eyes closed. "Shed on me your wisdom, O Holy Owner."

"What?" I exclaimed, so surprised that I forgot Dinek's warning.

"You." He put his hands together in a mockery of a devout one in supplication for a blessing. "They can't stop talking about how you didn't touch a tinny of the ship gold."

I sighed, and turned to my task, setting the thick, sturdy thread into the heavy needle—so very different from the slim needles and delicate silk I'd handled every day without thought, when living in the palace.

I began stitching, but On didn't move. I was trying to be the wall, but he was also a wall. Very well then. I let my hand tend to a well-remembered task, closed my eyes, and sifted for that inner sense. Not that I was very good yet, but I did perceive that his aura was a complexity of colors, the jonquil of curiosity foremost. I also perceived that his attributes were primarily air, then water, which were oppositional to my fire and metal. It would be easy to make an enemy of such a person if I did not tread a careful path, but water and air were more often the components of an affable nature.

I was unaware that the pause had lengthened to a silence until he spoke:

> *"The ephemeral fly bursts from its hole,*
> *With gauzy wings of brown;*
> *So quick the rise, so quick the fall,*
> *Of the greats 'for we bow down!..."*

I almost groaned. I had copied that "Admonition about Frivolous Pursuits" by Kanda so many times as a child!

I retorted, "*I grieve! Would you but go away/Forth would you wiser be*." It was a twist on the refrain, a clumsy one at that.

But he laughed, and clapped in a semblance of delight. No, it was a kind of delight, though shot through with challenge. I realized that my wall had formed a window, and he was trying to peek in.

Now come the nosy questions, I thought, resigned. I'd invited them by responding.

But he got up, and lightly vaulted over the balcony to the deck below, apparently content with having won a response. A brief spur of Essence trailed behind him. Was he even conscious that he had an Essence talent, however small? I was not going to ask.

Ke appeared then, bearing two bowls of noodles and broth with bits of grilled fish. "Zuyan Bi sent me with this, at Dinek's request. She also told me to help you sew. Do you really need me?" She set down the bowl on the spot where On had been, wrinkling her lip as she gazed at the banner.

In that brief time, I'd rounded the snout. "Not sure. Right now, no. Two of us can't work on the head without jostling one another. But when I get to the body, yes."

She nodded, then peered down at the deck. "That boy is a hideous flirt."

"Oh?" I said.

"Just a warning," Ke retorted, arms crossed under her breasts. "As if I'd give a second glance at anyone wearing old clothes and shoes, who obviously doesn't have two tinnies to rub together."

I shrugged, uninterested, and she, who loved gossip, gave an exasperated sigh. "You are *no* fun, Ren." She took her bowl and vanished with a swish of her pink robe in search of more entertaining company, leaving me to contemplate how gossip and speculation might be considered fun. Maybe this was one of those parts of human interaction right behind the horizon? I'd sometimes felt it, during this past year in particular, when an especially handsome young guard or sailor or especially a gallant wanderer would come into the Three Kingfishers. A trick of the eye, the clean line of jaw, of shoulder, the rise and fall of a musical tenor voice would prompt me to linger and to look or listen. But if the young man—it was always young men, so far—looked back, I'd get that unpleasant tingle all over, as if I'd had too much high-summer sun, and beat a retreat.

How was that fun? Maybe by next year I'd answer that.

In the meantime, I worked on the banner, and did my practice, trying as unobtrusively as possible to avoid encounters with On. But that meant I was aware of him. So I noticed things. Anomalies. Such as the fact that he betrayed the training of a noble, though he — like me — worked to hide it. He spoke with the common accents, he wore sloppy, worn clothes, but at a meal one night, after everyone had shared out some rice wine, I noticed him handling his sleeves with the deft, trained movement I'd only seen at the imperial palace.

I could scarcely fault him for keeping his identity a secret, when I was doing exactly the same. However, it seemed prudent to keep a distance when we were all on deck at Fan's practice. His preferred weapons were double knives, which apparently were favored for the close combat of decks, but he occasionally practiced sword and staff and archery with the others. As I stuck with my sword, it was easy enough to avoid him. As he was among the best, he mostly practiced with Fan and the other dedicated fighters as they honed their skills.

Sailing night and day sped us along on the last of the winter current and favorable winds. We'd reached the southeastern corner of Mountain Peony Island before I was ready. Dinek commandeered Ke and a couple of the Hats to aid me.

The ship hauled wind for the north when I began on the pangolin's tail, as the others worked at the feet. I was aware of nerves. The mission was simple enough: deliver the silkworms, sail to Tiger Eye Bay, the capital of the Tiger Islands, find a way to meet Aku Orchid, and winnow her away without anyone the wiser about how she vanished.

How?

We often debated the details of the plan we'd concocted with Madam Aku — a plot stolen from one of their favorite plays — as others crowded onto the balcony to help stitch. Plans from the wild to the absurd got aired, to huge entertainment among those who sought adventure.

I knew that Dinek was looking to me to find a way. She was still remembering the fortuitous chapter of accidents that had led to our bursting out of the slavers' holds below our feet, and taking the ship. Yes, it had been my idea, but not my execution. The freeing of the slaves on Crescent Island had been Koi's and Fan's plan.

This made me terribly anxious.

Late one afternoon, under cloud-patched skies, we sailed into Dawn's Placid Sea Harbor on the tide. We'd reached the extreme opposite end of the island from Cloud Terrace Harbor. I found myself anxious, and I tried to scold myself. And yet I began scanning the quay as soon as we drew near enough to make out the lineaments of individuals from the throng.

Koi (and Jai, I must not forget him) had become a Falcon, that much I was certain of, or he would have chosen one of the other sects and gone to them. But was he a Pangolin? At that time I could not even define what a Pangolin was, outside of someone on board the ship, except that it implied a company. A "we" separate from all the other "them"s in the world.

"How will we find them?" I hadn't realized I'd spoken aloud until Fan spoke up beside me.

"There'll be a hiring platform. Gallant wanderers and fighting sects hire out for traders wanting defenders."

She pointed toward one end of the quay, where a number of traders seemed to be headed. As we drifted in toward where harbor officials in their little boats pointed their bright red flags, I began to make out individuals. I scrutinized them. There was a tall one, bearing a staff—no, she was a woman, with another woman beside her, shorter and broader, with a pair of throwing axes at her back. Gallant wanderers! They began talking to a merchant in rich hues of crimson and blue, then they were lost as a string of guards in Huyun green passed by on patrol.

Our ship drew nearer, and I pressed against the rail, leaning out as if that would bring me closer. Older man, balding man, an entire family, more men…

My eyes passed a pair of tall young men as too old, then snapped back as my eyes registered a familiarity about the line of one's ear, the shape of a shoulder before my mind did. Crow's-wing black hair, brown headband… Could that be Koi, that one with the staff? He looked…*old*. Old as in a young man instead of the skinny boy who'd trudged beside me down the mountain to the river into White Waters Harbor, who'd chewed his thumb nervously all the while we waited for dark on Crescent Island, before separating to our tasks.

At that moment he lifted his face and peered out at the bay, then stilled. I could swear our eyes met, though I could barely make out his face, then the taller one next to him nudged him and pointed at our ship.

They turned as one, and vanished into the crowd, then emerged again on the pier to climb into one of the boats for hire that took people around to different ships anchored in the bay.

THIRTY-SIX

Unresting, the phoenix sped in her flight,
Ascending, then sweeping down from the height,
Toward the roosts on the oaks. The phoenix
commanded
That justice be done with diligent hand…

IN THE TIME IT took for Koi and Jai to reach us, Zuyan Bi had finished haggling with one of the vendors with broad, low-lying craft full of vegetables, eggs, rice flour, and other fresh commodities that ships were always in need of after a voyage. Zuyan Bi leaned precariously over the rail as buckets bumped the hull up and down, three silver nuggets traded for a bucket of eggs, more greens, onions, garlic, parsnips, and chilis.

Some noise, and the two clambered up and vaulted over the rail. "Koi?"

The word escaped me. That *was* Koi! I'd know those eyes anywhere. His ears reddened as he swallowed visibly, then croaked, "Ren." His voice had deepened.

"Miss me?" Jai elbowed Koi aside with the familiarity of a brother. He was huge. Much bigger even than Fan, who until now had been the tallest and largest person on the *Pangolin*. His voice was still cracking. "Nothing to say?"

It was my turn to swallow in a very dry throat. "It's just that—you're so different. Both of you, I mean." My eyes had gone back to Koi, whose face was still smooth, but the planes of it had changed, losing those round cheeks.

"So've you," Jai said, and, eyeing my body, "you've got—"

Koi flushed bright red and clapped a hand over Jai's mouth. "Don't finish that sentence."

Jai shoved Koi's hand aside, protesting, "But it's *good!* I mean she looks—"

"That sentence," Koi muttered, "is going nowhere good."

Jai, though taller and bigger than Koi, who was lean as a panther, sighed. "Aw..." And he used the diminutive for 'elder brother.' "The sisters don't mind..."

Dinek charged forward. "Koi! Jai? That *is* Jai! Ayoh! Where did you get all that muscle? Make a deal with a demon?"

Jai chortled proudly, as Koi said, "Beware, he eats like three demons. The first day we got to Mountain Reflecting Water, he ate ten pancakes. One right after the other. They named him Pig Gut."

Jai's braying laugh was still that of a teenage boy, though he was larger than most men. "You can call me that if you like. Everybody did at the scrape."

Dinek tipped her head back as she eyed him. "I'm not calling anybody Pig Gut. But you'd better get used to calling *me* Captain."

Fan appeared then, giving the two an assessing rake with her gaze. "If you can fight half as well as you look, we're in excellent shape. We'll be putting in some practice soon's we set sail." She rubbed her hands, chuckling. "Come along. I'll show you where to stow your gear. What was the scrape like?"

"Excellent," Koi said. "A Falcon master named Master Sima, who Ren and I knew from where we were before the slavers took us, was there. He's an expert in Ze Bek form—"

"Ren's form," Fan said. "The best! Only I've yet to find a master in it. Though Ren's somehow gotten faster and better without one, while she was stuck on land..."

They went off, talking easily, while I stood there thinking that all Koi had had for me was a single word: my name. Bewildered, I was going to follow when Dinek came to me. "We can raise the banner now, right?"

I'd finished the last of the tail that morning, some of the stitches hastier than they ought to have been. But we could always pull it down again and repair it, I thought, and said, "We can."

Dinek's eyes brightened and there was the full happy rabbit grin.

By the time we'd raised the banner, which hung limply in the soft breeze, Zuyan Bi and his helpers had stowed their fresh comestibles and finished up a nice pepper-fish soup with cabbage cooked until tender, and dumplings stuffed with carrots and parsnips and onion. Koi and Jai were drawn from the men's side of the House to the delicious smell, and crowded into the kitchen, as we had in the early days.

Zuyan Bi promptly shooed them out. Because Koi had not spoken to me except that one word, I was feeling uncertain about approaching him, especially as Jai seemed to be attached to his side.

They joined us in the cabin off the galley that housed the galley crew at night, and during the day, served as our gathering place for meals. By habit, the two genders sat on their respective sides. My accustomed spot was between Ke and the one girl among the Hat cousins, Dove. Dove was quiet, except when her brothers got up games, then she was as loud as anyone. At meals she kept her attention entirely on her food, but Ke talked enough for all three of us.

"Well, I'd always expected that Koi might turn out well, but I never expected anything of that Jai," Ke said to us as she sat cross-legged beside us on the platform. "Ay! Except for those ears, Koi is sleek as a leopard. But he won't say a word. What is it with some boys, are they going to charge a tael every time they open their mouths? I'm so glad Cygnet is gone. She'd be flipping her sleeves at him, jug ears or no jug ears…"

She went on in that manner as I ate my dumplings, and when Dove said nothing—as usual—and I emulated Dove, she gave a shoulder twitch, then her expression turned serious. "We'll reach Tiger Eye Bay by tomorrow night at the latest, Dinek thinks. Then it's up to you and me, Ren." She sighed. "I begged and pleaded, and I've been counting every day, but now that we're about to do it, my heart is nothing but a knot. You?"

I took a deep breath. "We'll do just as we planned. Quiet, modest, unassuming. At the first sign of distrust, or question, we retreat and figure out another way."

When the meal was over, the tide began to flow out to sea again, the *Pangolin* with it, along with a host of other ships. We now proudly flew a banner, like other respectable traders, even if our ship more resembled a sea hawk, or even a modest yacht, than most lumbering traders.

Fan banged the gong to summon us to martial practice. As

we assembled, everyone looked with interest at the newcomers, some with challenge—On, of course, in the lead. But Fan insisted we gather in lines and do seed forms first, to properly warm our bodies. I—always preferring the back row—was thus able to watch Koi, and Jai. Both flowed through the forms like whitewater rushing toward the sea. To be expected, if they'd been training with Sima the Hero.

Then came what everyone was waiting for: the sparring.

That air-demon fox On went for Jai first, the biggest and most eager. Fan and Koi paired off, both tentative, testing, and then they went at it with clear enjoyment; Fan chose the staff, to match Koi, and the crack of wood and the snap of the whipping folds of their martial robes filled the air, counterpoint to the endless whish-slap of the water against the hull as we plunged toward the cluster of small islands in the distance.

On defeated Jai fairly quickly, and I wondered if Jai's size was getting in his way. That is, if he was still adjusting to how fast he'd grown; at any rate, On's lightning-fast, wickedly flashing blades, and his constant stream of insults and bits of poesy caught Jai off-guard. Jai scowled when his blade shot sparks in the air after a very hard block—just to find On's second blade poised at the artery in his neck.

"Ow-yah," Fan shouted, dropping her staff and wringing her right hand. "Very well, very well, Koi, I see I need more practice with the wood. But wait till we match with the sword."

All the while I fought my bouts, sometimes to a draw, other times I lost.

Koi beat Fan with the sword, too, but she made him work for it, and Jai's scowl turned to a grin as he thrashed his way through the younger fighters. At the watch change, we took a water and tea break, and those with duty stowed their weapons and went to it.

I retreated to get tea, aware of Koi wherever he moved. Or, so I thought. I was just deciding that it was time to try talking to him, when his voice startled me, "You've improved vastly, Ren, but you're holding back."

I turned, nearly spilling my tea. "True," I said, and just like that, we were back to where we were. Or almost. "I hate fighting. I can't seem to get past that. I want to end it as fast as I can."

"You don't win bouts."

He'd been watching me as well as fighting. Well, that was what the masters did. They were supposed to be aware of everything, including the enemy before them. And clearly Koi was intent on mastery.

"I win them internally," I said. "That is, when I can see in one or two moves, three at most, how to defeat my opponent, it's a win for me. But they don't like it when I do that. No one said anything, but I could see it. So I match their skills as much as I can, or I try my best against those better than me, until the inevitable defeat."

He was looking down at the deck. I risked an inward glimpse. His aura was mostly the gray-blue of calm waters, though with the glint of sun on metal. Water and metal, those were his attributes, though there was wood as well. Complex, unexpectedly so, for someone with no Essence talent. But not alone in that. Our cook, Zuyan Bi, was another with complex attributes.

"Do you try the other weapons?" Koi asked. "Or is it always…your sword."

I sensed him about to name Sagacious Blade. So he remembered that quick explanation as we stood beside the warehouse, I wearing that reeking robe, before we tumbled unknowing into the slavers' maw. He remembered, and he was cautious.

"I do when asked to, but I'm worse with them. I've practiced the most with the sword."

"Your form is quite good. I think even Master Sima would approve. It's as if you've trained with a specific master."

"Would the experts see that?" I asked.

He nodded. "Maybe not if you use Essence." He lowered his voice. "Have you trained in that? You never said anything in your notes."

"I did."

"Ah." His glance, which as yet had not met my eyes, strayed in the direction of the sword, still in my other hand. "Ah." A breath, then, "What can you tell me about the mission?"

"Come with me while I put the sword away, and I'll tell you what I know."

He sat with me on the balcony, which had become my place when I wasn't required to be elsewhere, though I no longer had a banner to make. It was comfortable to be falling into the old pattern of talking over a plan, though my other senses—eyes, scent, hearing, touch—remained very aware of his proximity. Perhaps adjusting to almost two years of change, I thought as I finished up, "…and so Ke and I will find out which stores serve Ji Jiang's harem, and we'll try to be delivery persons in order to meet her."

Koi nodded, his profile sober as he watched On and Jai below, Jai determinedly going at On with two knives. Strong he was—I could see it from where I sat—but not nearly as fast as On. There was the old Jai, in how much he hated to lose.

"Interesting crew they gathered, Dinek and Fan," he said. "What do they intend once this mission is done?"

"Probably a tea run, as a spoken goal. Like gallant wanderers. Unspoken, same as the Falcons, rescuing those who need us. On wants to try our skills at a contest somewhere. So do some of the others."

"And you?" Koi asked, at last turned to face me.

"I listened in Cloud Terrace Harbor for news. So far, rumors put the grand prince in the north, or the west. Sometimes they were said to be sneaking into the imperial island." I drew a breath. "And sometimes I wonder if I ought to talk Dinek and Fan into seeking them, but then I'd have to say why. Perhaps I ought to leave, and seek on my own."

Koi gave a nod, then said, "I'd do that with you. Either way."

I looked at him in surprise. Eyes met eyes, those familiar eyes, reassuring and honest. True metal, the phrase came to me. "Don't you want to continue training?" I asked.

He twitched a shoulder. "I could, but Master Sima told me that I'm already better than most of whom I'd face, including the imperial guard. That was my first goal. More training would put me up with the masters who mostly seek each other. That seems a pointless life. For me. I don't speak for others. I guess there is something to be said for anyone who wants to reach the pinnacle of their art. Cooking. Painting. Flute-playing. Dance. Martial skills."

It was a long speech, for him.

I said, "This first mission should be fairly simple. It's to find a single person, whose location we know. If I manage well, then perhaps it's time to go seeking…you-know-who. If I don't succeed with this simple mission, then maybe I'm the one who needs more training."

He gave a slow nod, then said, "Master Sima did tell me that at some point the most effective training is experience."

"Ah," I said. "Da Shao said something like that as well."

"Da Shao?"

I told him about my stay at the Three Kingfishers, after which he told me a bit more about the Falcon scrape, where it was pretty much martial training all the time. Including tracking, and scouting. It seemed that they wanted him to become a Watcher if he had the inclination.

"You ought to come to Mountain Reflecting Water," he said suddenly. "I think you would truly like it there. It's beautiful."

"A Falcon scrape?"

He looked away. "It's like the name, chosen for its balance between sky, air, and water, earth, stone, wood, I was told. It used to be a palace, handed down through the governor's mother. Whose grandmother was a princess of the previous dynasty. I was told that the duchess—who never uses that title, just like the governor prefers governor over duke—was once saved by Falcons, back when it was only women, and so she made the palace over to the Falcons."

"Did you meet her?" I asked.

"No. They said she sometimes visits, but only when she needs tranquility. She's not a martial artist. Anyway, it is beautiful in a way I think you might like."

"Tell me about it," I said.

He started on that, and then went to training, and Falcon history as told by some of the elder masters—women all. Before we knew it, dark had fallen, and we had talked the entire afternoon away. It was time to gather for the last meal of the day.

We rejoined the others. As I went to my usual seat, Ke said, "You two seemed to go right back to your old talk, talk, talk."

"A year and a half is a lot to catch up on," I said, but inwardly I smiled. Everything seemed to have settled to the old, comfortable ways. How steadying!

And I needed steadying, because morning brought with a light rain the strange sight of Tiger's Eye Island. Or more correctly its bay, which was nearly a perfect semi-circle, as if a celestial ball had dropped out of the sky and carved that perfect half-circle out of the middle of a long, thin island with the usual spine of mountains.

As we sailed in, I pointed out to Koi the different types of ships we were seeing—he'd not seen a single ship, of course, while living in that mountain scrape. "The most I've seen were the traders being built in the river two days below the scrape," he told me. "We had to make a detour to avoid them, as they are always hungry for able workers, we were warned. The pay is all right, but they have to promise a year, and the work is from dawn to dusk, as the governor wants the ships on the water fast. Making his investment back, I should think. That many traders would be expensive."

"A year is a long time," I agreed.

We'd spotted masts in inlets along the island, indicating that this was a populous place for so small an island cluster. Must be the inlets all had excellent deepwater access.

There was a mix of traders and Tiger Island warships, to be expected after the troubles the year previous. Many more along the coast, with no banners, which meant repairs. Must have been a great deal of destruction in the aftermath of that battle.

We were signaled to stop far out, again no surprise considering how crowded the bay was. Dinek had our boat lowered, and Ke and I climbed down after the boat crew, Ke looking unwontedly serious. My own heart was thumping.

As the crew picked up their oars, Koi leaped down, jarring the boat.

Dinek appeared at the rail. "Koi? They're not going to get into trouble. They'll be returning at the first sign of any question. That's why Ren doesn't have her Pangolin blade."

"I know," Koi said.

"And even if there was trouble, you don't have your staff. Or your sword," Fan called down from beside Dinek, question in voice and countenance.

"I just want to scout around," he called up. "You lot have been sailing for nearly two years. I've been stuck on a mountain. I'll bring back any news," he added.

The pair's faces cleared, and the oars dipped into the water.

It took a while to navigate between the various military ships, from some of which came the rap of hammers and the whine of saws. I knew without speaking that Koi was going to scout for news of the grand prince; when we pulled up at the wharf, he leaped out and slipped into the milling crowd before the boat was tied off.

Ke and I hefted our baskets, which contained the exquisite gifts that Madam Aku had supplied as our bait. I suffered a brief worry that this might be primarily a military base, but we almost immediately found a street full of luxuries off the double-tiered magistrate's building. We split up. Our plan was predicated on Madam Aku's assurance that a man who can afford a harem can usually afford luxuries. I found a shop that dealt in fine jewelry and hairpins, and Ke a shop that specialized in embroidered shoes, almost at the same time.

We met in the street, armed now with the names of the stores, and Ke whispered, "Let's get this over with. My knees are knocking so hard that I can scarcely stand up."

I dipped my head in a nod.

We had been supplied with different maid's outfits from the costume trunks at Madam Aku's. The colors were brown and dull blue, the most common hues for servants, and we'd twisted up our hair in servants' knobs. "They don't wear aprons at the jewelry store," I said, bundling mine into the basket before I handed it off to Ke, who wore a somewhat similar blue to the jewelry shop workers.

She handed her basket to me. My brown robe was not like the tan of the shoe place, but the brown was dull, at least. I'd try anyway, in hopes that no one paid much attention to servants making deliveries.

The palace was easily visible, dominating the entire city from a hill at the apex of the semi-circle.

After a few false tries, we got to the correct door for deliveries to the harem, and the door guard, after each of us mentioned Aku Orchid, sent a page off to fetch someone.

Our hope was that she could be desperate enough—or even curious enough—to come herself, but if a maid came, we'd debated what kind of message might suffice in luring her out.

It was a maid who appeared, but before disappointment could knot my heart even more, she said, "Come with me."

She led us along a corridor with the high walls common to harems, and then inside a gate to a little garden. There in a gazebo sat a girl perhaps a year older than I, porcelain dishes the color of jade before her: teapot, cup, and a plate of some delicate cakes that looked untouched. She was round of face, her coloring blotchy. She wore silk in several layers, her sleeves rippling to the floor as she clutched her forearms against her middle.

She dismissed the maid with a nod, and then turned a puckered brow to us. "I ordered nothing."

Ke burst out, "Your aunt sent me! We can get you away. All we have to do is, one of us can swap clothes with you, and—"

Orchid raised a hand. She closed her eyes, raised a fist to her lips, and drew in a shuddering breath before she sipped from the beautiful celadon cup before her. Then she said, low, "If you'd come when I first was told, I would have gone. Though I would never be able to go home again."

"Your aunt will take you in. Hide you. Or send you anywhere..."

"I wanted my garden," Orchid said, raising tear-puffy eyes to us. "But when does a girl ever get what she wants? I knew that someone or other was going to make an offer for me, for I was always hearing about my looks and the 'luck' they would bring. I didn't want a man of nearly forty, but as it turns out, a man of forty is in some ways better than a younger one."

"What?" Ke gasped.

Another fist to the lips. I noted a jade ring on one finger. "He gave me time. The sisters are kind. And I've discovered this week that I am in child," she finished on a breath. "What would happen to my child if I were to run? How could I begin its life with the curse of no family, no father?"

"Your aunt—" Ke began.

"She has no man of her own," Orchid interrupted. "Don't you see? I thank you, and I will pray for the both of you for your kindness, but don't you see it, this world belongs to men. This is not the life I wanted, but neither was it for most of the sisters here. And yet it's not so bad. Soon I'll have a child. Maybe two. I'd like that. And this garden is now mine. I can make a better one, because I'm a consort, not the mere daughter of a humble steward. I can now order what I want, instead of begging and wheedling."

"But—" Ke began.

I touched her arm. "She said what she wants. And I think she's not well...?"

Orchid uttered a watery laugh. "Ay, you've no idea how wretched I feel. But the physician says it's to be expected, and it will go off in two or three Phoenix moons. The ginger tea makes it bearable. But oh, I do want to lie down."

Tears ran down Ke's face, as I said, "Orchid, please take these shoes and the hairpin anyway. Your aunt chose them for you. They were to be our bait, but you may as well have them, as she had you in mind."

At that, tears sprang to Orchid's eyes, and I dragged Ke up from the carved bench she'd plopped on, though servants never sit in the presence of those they serve. But we were alone, and Orchid had never been raised to the expectations of a great lady.

We retrieved our baskets and left.

The maid waited at the door to the garden. In silence she conducted us to the outer door. When we reached the street, Ke muttered, "Well, that was bad." She was silently weeping.

I suspected then, and also suspect now, that she was far more disappointed at losing the chance to be a heroine than she was at Orchid's refusal. Me? I was angry, so very angry. I had to get hold of myself. "Ke, why don't you go back to the boat? I'll find Koi, and then we'll return to the *Pangolin*."

She hiccupped on a sob, and sped away, basket banging against her side.

I headed up the street, dodging around clusters of men. Loud, noisy men, who moved down the middle of the road as if they owned it, the few woman weaving around them. "The world belongs to men." I could not blame Orchid for that observation. Even as a child, I had known the truth of it. But why should it be so? It was such injustice, perhaps *the* supreme injustice, that half the people of the world must bend their necks to the other half simply because of their physical form.

What would Father say if I brought that to him as a topic for debate? How could I find quotations to support my conviction, when most of what is handed down as wisdom is written by men?

I became aware of eyes on me, which jolted me out of my reverie a moment before Koi appeared out of nowhere, and yanked me almost off my feet as he stepped behind a tea seller's wooden sign.

I opened my mouth to protest at his uncompromising grip—I was so very angry at everything male—when his free hand flashed in a sign that I had not seen for ten years. But I remembered it instantly. First Brother—Second Brother—the gardener—the language of hands for those unhearing. Of course I had not taught my maids, diligent in keeping my distance, but equally certain was Second Brother having ignored the distinctions of rank and taught Koi.

That sign was: silence! Danger!

I looked up, and then at a flick of a gaze from him, at the street. A group of men marched through the crowd, vigilant, in step. It was a military formation. An honor guard, I realized belatedly.

Confused, I glanced at Koi in question, for honor guards only surrounded people of rank, and if people of rank were parading about, that meant horns and gongs sending commoners to the ground to bow. But these men, hands to the hilts of their swords, merely scoured each passing person with mordant gazes.

Koi drew me aside, and we turned our backs, but not before I spotted the figure they guarded, wearing armor worked in gold, partly hidden by a cloak of red. And above those, the familiar bony features of Lan Xianti, now Imperial Crown Prince.

THIRTY-SEVEN

Riding the skies, rushing like lightning,
Climbing the clouds, she wrings justice from
chaos…

SHOCK RANG THROUGH ME, making me shiver, though the air was merely cool, with the occasional spatter of rain.

We turned our backs, gazing sightlessly at the displays of tea on shelves. I could feel Xianti strutting by; perhaps that was imagination at first, but when I concentrated in that other realm, I had to clutch the edge of the wooden sign at the sudden onslaught of colors and sheer noise that came not through ears but through mind.

I learned two things in that instant: first, it was useless for me to try listening or scanning that way when in crowds. I had no way to shut out unwanted distractions. Secondly, Xianti's attributes were metal and fire, same as mine.

That was a very unsettling blow. Though I could not speak to her with my sword at the ship, I knew what Granny Zim would say, that such things did not make up the whole of us, any more than any other single characteristic did. "We are each a clay made up of so many different elements, and then life experience fashions that clay into our present selves," she had said once.

But I took that discovery not as a sign of kinship, for I felt none in spite of our shared dynastic origin five generations ago. I took it into myself as a warning. I had learned that that combination was rare, at least to the degree that we both possessed. Perhaps it was a family attribute? There were many volatile combinations, but that one in particular was akin to a fire-mountain that spouts steel. In others words, dangerous to all around them.

I already knew that about Xianti. I must guard against those tendencies in myself.

All this passed in a few heartbeats. When I opened my eyes, I became aware of Koi so close I could feel his breath on the top of my head, and his warmth at my shoulder. He stepped away at once, murmuring, "You swayed, and your eyes closed—I was afraid you were going to faint or fall."

"I was listening in that other realm, the Essence realm. But I learned little except that I can't do that in crowds."

"Did you know he was going to be here?"

"No! I would not have come if there'd been *any* chance of seeing *him*. What could he be doing here? And without the usual parade? He never went about without a parade in the imperial city."

Koi nicked his chin down. "He's dressed like a general."

We both turned to the street to peer cautiously out. We needed to get back to the boat, and safely aboard the *Pangolin*. And away as fast as possible, because one thing for certain, wherever Lan Xianti went, grief was sure to follow.

When we reached the boat, Ke said, "There you are! What? You both look as though you've seen a ghost."

"Worse," I said under my breath, my neck aching, for during the endless walk back to the wharf, I'd shuffled, hunched over. Even so I felt horribly exposed, as if spying eyes from the imperial island would pluck me from that crowd.

The Hat brothers' and Ke's ire faded to interest, especially when Koi said, "More when we get out into the bay."

What to say without exposing my origins? When we were halfway to the *Pangolin*, with no boats around us, Koi spoke first. "I used to be a servant on the imperial island before we got captured by slavers. I recognized the new crown prince. He's here. Dressed as a general."

"A disguise?" Ke asked with interest.

"Don't know. As the Tiger Islands are allied with Mountain Peony," Koi said, pointing back toward the large island, still visible to the southwest, "and that's an imperial island, you'd think there's no need to be in disguise."

One of the Hat brothers commented, "Maybe he wants to go about inconspicuous, for the festival. You hear of rankers dressing like anyone else so as to avoid notice."

Dressing in golden armor with a red cloak was scarcely inconspicuous, I was thinking, as Koi said, "That was never his habit when I was on the imperial island. Anyway, if he's here, we should not be here."

"I would like to meet a prince," Ke sighed under her breath.

"Not that one," I said, and when she turned to me, lips parted to unloose a stream of questions, I added, "Remember, he's the one who appointed those imperial guards who stood by as we were all scooped up by the slavers. Right off the imperial island," I added, outraged afresh.

The Hat brothers put their backs into their oars, and we continued to plunge and bucket our way through the choppy waves in the rising wind. The *Pangolin* was at quite a distance, beyond all those military ships. My attention shifted between the *Pangolin*, as I longed to get there faster, and our surroundings. There really were a lot of military vessels of various sorts. I'd learned to identify them by listening to the chatting Huyun guards at the Three Kingfishers. Far more ships than I'd ever seen at any one time in Cloud Terrace Harbor, which was the island's primary harbor. But then so many of these were bannerless, the sounds of hammering and sawing floating over the water—the visible result of the aftermath of fierce battle.

As we wove our way through the lines, my gaze snagged on a golden banner that flapped, revealing and concealing its central image: a crimson firedragon.

A crimson firedragon against gold: that was the banner that Grand Prince Yiulo had put up, in defiance of the nephew now claiming the imperial throne under the Lan Dynasty's golden dragon against a crimson background.

I turned to Koi at the same moment he turned to me, my shock mirrored in his face. Then we both turned back to peer at it as the yacht bearing the firedragon banner plunged toward the inner bay. Above the firedragon, a smaller white banner flew, meaning an envoy sent under truce.

My nerves chilled as I strained to see who was in that boat. It was too distant, the figures indistinguishable, and as sense overcame the shock of reaction, I knew that this would be a mere messenger, an envoy. Second Brother would not be there any more than the grand prince himself, or his grandson.

Even so, everything had now changed.

I was startled when our boat thudded against the *Pangolin*'s hull. We climbed up, helped to raise the boat, and as the Hat brothers and Ke headed straight for the galley to get something to eat, I said to Koi, "We must find that envoy."

"I know. But Xianti is also on that island."

"What are you two talking about?" Fan crossed the deck toward us. "Your meal is waiting. Then it's time for sparring."

Koi glanced my way, then said, "While I was scouting, I chanced to see Imperial Crown Prince Xianti on the main street. In semi-disguise."

Fan's eyebrows shot upward. "You know him by sight?"

"I—we—used to live on the south side of the imperial island, before the slavers got us," Koi said, with a gesture toward me.

"I wondered how you two knew each other."

Koi said, "I was a servant. At the imperial palace. I ran away right around the time the new emperor took the throne."

"I heard a lot of people ran," Fan said, shrugging. "Isn't that the usual situation? What has an imperial prince to do with us?"

I said—reluctantly—"I believe we need to warn the local authorities, so that they can pass the news on to the governor. It cannot be a good thing if Xianti's lurking around here."

"Ji Jiang? He's half a pirate himself, from what I've heard," Fan said. "In any case, that's all imperial politics. Nothing to do with us."

I said, "I was thinking more of the local Huyun magistrate, so that they can pass the word to Governor Huyun—"

"But he's here," Koi said.

"Who's here?" Fan asked.

"Governor Huyun. Not here." Koi pointed at the inner bay. "He's there in Dawn's Placid Sea, a day away. Didn't you see all the Huyun family banners all over when you entered the harbor to get Jai and me? He's there to celebrate Kraken Boat Festival. The palace on the hill was lit up both days we were there waiting for you. We could hear the music. They're putting on a great celebration for him."

Kraken Boat Festival, on the fifth day of the fifth month. It had been considered a festival for common folk, little celebrated in the imperial palace. The Journey to the Clouds took place then, and I wondered if Emperor Koza had gone. If so, why Xianti wasn't there with his imperial uncle.

I shook away those unanswerables. "Then I think even more urgent is the necessity to warn Governor Huyun, or at least find a way to get word to him. This island has been good to us. I think it's a duty to make sure he knows. He can then decide what to do about it."

Fan looked uncertain, until Dinek joined us, taking her place at Fan's side. "I agree. I hate the thought of the Celestial Chart being under attack, if that crown prince is planning to usurp all of Governor Huyun Shandek's men and supplies next. Though I don't see a host of imperial flags, but this imperial prince is unlikely to be lurking around without an attack fleet just over the horizon."

"There's an attack fleet here now." That was On. I had not heard him approach.

He stood next to Koi, slim where Koi was lean. He lounged against the rail, his long hair a dark waterfall down his back.

"What do you mean?" Fan said.

"They've got a sizable attack fleet right here," On repeated. "Look. Right off near the coast there, a centipede ship."

"But all these bannerless ships are under repair," Dinek said.

"They're seaworthy," On said. "Same with the tower ships on the other side of the harbor. Take down the scaffolding around the masts, put up sails. Scarcely more than an hour's work. I'm not saying it's going to happen. But it's possible."

"But those are Ji Jiang's," Dinek said. "Those are the ships taken when the Upstart Prince was defeated. And Ji Jiang was allied with Grand Prince Yiulo back when the empire fought off the Easterners. Do you think he lured in the imperial crown prince, just to attack him?"

"Who cares?" Fan shrugged. "That imperial crown prince is the one who yanked all the men from every prefecture around, ending up with us on the streets begging. Before he had his guards let us get snaffled by the slavers. Far's I'm concerned, if Ji Jiang is going to use all these ships to swoop in and capture him, I'd stand by and cheer them on. I say, let's get out of here, so we don't get swept up in someone else's battle."

"I want to stay," Koi said suddenly. "Beat the trees to see if any dates fall."

With an inward jolt, I remembered the envoy ship—the speculation about Xianti had distracted me.

Koi said to Dinek, "If you have another mission to sail to, leave me behind. I can catch a trader going to the big island, and retrace my steps to the scrape. Meet up with you again in Cloud Terrace in a month or so, unless your mission takes you longer."

"I'm also staying," I said. "First, I ought to warn the governor's people. I could meet up with Koi and travel over land with him." There was no chance I was going to miss even this slight chance to find out news of my brother.

Dinek looked from Koi to me. "Strictly speaking, this is your ship," she said in that ruminative tone that I'd learned meant she was calculating tides and stars and weather and any number of other ship things. "You *are* Pangolin."

I said quickly, "But we all know that I'm not the real owner."

"Yes, and no. Here's what is important to me. I have a duty to you, as you saved this ship, and us, with the Pangolin sword. Right now I've no plans beyond returning to Cloud Terrace, to find out the news at the Celestial Chart," Dinek said. "We're sailing now, and the current will take us right past the edge of the big island. Ren, if you want to go ashore to warn the governor's people, we could dock at Dawn's Placid Sea, and enjoy the festival for one tide, as we did when we gathered in Koi and Jai. Then we'll sail away."

I thanked her, and Koi went to get his pack, and emerged with it and Jai, who said stubbornly, "If brother goes, I go."

It was easy to see that Dinek was just as happy to see Jai leave, but he stuck so close that there was no opportunity for private converse with Koi, who said to me, "I'll give it a week. Then meet you in Dawn's Placid Sea, at the hiring platform, noon."

I had to agree. Between the two of us, there was far greater chance of Xianti, or his inner guard, spotting me—a single female among the throngs of sailors, and apparently instantly recognizable by family features, than there was at his recognizing Koi, a mere servant.

"You should probably alter your dress," I said.

He dipped his head in that not-quite-a-bow. "I know. I won't be a gallant wander by horse first hour."

The Hat brothers, who had boat duty that watch, sighed at the prospect of the long row to shore again, as we all helped lower the boat back down.

Dinek said to Koi, "I can give you two silvers."

Jai stuck out his hand, but Koi shook his head. "I'll earn my keep somewhere. That's how you get the best news."

Jai grumbled under his breath, but followed Koi over the side and down into the boat. They rowed away.

There were many speculative glances cast my way that day, but no one said anything. The prospect of getting to enjoy a festival brightened everyone's mood, especially when Dinek said that of course everyone would get their two silvers.

The hilarity diminished somewhat when we approached the harbor the next morning, to discover that it was absolutely packed with ships, all firmly directed to remain in the outer waters, as the inner bay was reserved for the festival boat parade. That meant that we'd be rowing quite a distance in; the crew who would be on first duty watch was especially grouchy.

The group chose for liberty by the drawing of casting sticks set out under rainy skies. They clutched their two silvers. (I'd refused mine, as I knew how very slim our resources were as yet, having gone with Dinek when she'd paid off her debts and then provisioned the ship). I had my earnings from the Three Kingfishers, so I felt quite wealthy.

We found a slip to leave our boat at, way off at the extreme end of the harbor, and then clambered up—all except On, who leaped from boat to wharf with one light spring.

And then, unexpectedly, he began walking with me. "Have you ever been here before?" he asked.

"No. Have you?" If he was about to show me the way, I'd welcome his company, but—

"Neither have I," he said cheerfully. "I've never set foot on this island before the *Pangolin* docked at Cloud Terrace." He spoke with a slight emphasis as he peered upward through the rain toward the grand three-tiered palace on the rise, mandarin-duck tiles gleaming as a shaft of sun pierced briefly between the clouds. "I expect most inns will be crowded; I'll have to sing for my supper, as usual."

Was this an invitation to ask? I remained silent, Mother's prudent answer to uncertainty.

We ducked back as a bright green and blue kraken danced by, legs kicking and dancing underneath the great body, and extending out, tentacles weaving over and under by expert dancers, then unweaving again. It had to be a hundred paces long, and was followed by a crowd of children, many with krakens dangling on sticks, seaweed tentacles jouncing, others with krakens made out of spun sugar. No one paid the least heed to the rain. At least the air was cool, not cold.

On chattered without cease, punctuated by snatches of his favorite songs, as I threaded my way through the umbrella-bearing crowds toward the magistrate's building below the palace. I said nothing until I reached the front, and eyed the drum doubtfully.

"Shall I bang it for you?" On asked, grinning with clear enjoyment.

"I'm not certain my task concerns present injustice so much as potential injustice. In any case, it does not pertain to me. I only offer information. No, no drum, though I'm certain it would get me before the magistrate faster. But that might be deemed a misuse of the law."

I mounted the steps, and he stayed by my side. I tried to think of a way to separate off without either of us losing face, then mentally accepted the situation. It didn't matter. No doubt I'd be sent away at once, or else passed from one functionary to another up the ranks, between long waits. In which case he'd likely get bored and vanish on his own.

The outer hall was just as crowded as I'd feared it would be, smelling of wet humanity, with traces of incense, straw, and cabbage. On continued to chatter about gambling games and poetry contests as we shuffled forward slowly, me hitching my harness up every once in a while. After a year and a half of living in one place, I'd completely gotten out of the habit of wearing it, and was now unused to the weight of Sagacious Blade and the carryall.

At last I looked into the tired, exasperated face of a young clerk. "Matter?" he barked.

"A message for the governor," I said.

He looked down, reaching for his ink brush, then up again, startled. Until now, from what I had heard around me, most of the "matters" were complaints about a vendor who overcharged for badly repaired shoes, a petition for posters to be put up for a missing donkey, a complaint about the beds at an inn, and the like. Matters important to the petitioners, but nothing aspiring toward those in lofty places.

"The governor?" the clerk repeated, putting down his brush and eyeing me with his head tilted to one side. "If you're hoping to honey-tongue your way into being his companion, you can hire yourself over at the Lotus Blossom—"

Irritation flashed through me at his contemptuous

assumption, and I leaned toward him, so that Sagacious Blade's hilt was visible at my back. "Does it look like I want to offer companionship?" I said in my most courtly tone.

Behind me, On smothered a laugh.

The clerk at the next table, who had begun ignoring his long line in order to listen, also began to snicker, but when I turned my glare to him, he cut it short. I stared at him until he recollected himself and returned to duty.

The clerk before me turned his head. "Page!"

A boy of about twelve ran out from a back room.

The clerk said, "Fetch Secretary Olek." And to me, in a flat voice, barely polite, "If you will step this way…"

The moment I did, he barked at the person behind me, "Matter?"

I went to a side alcove where I'd been pointed. There was a tiny table with nothing on it, not even hot water, though cups had been stacked, but the window had been pushed out far enough to make an awning under which we could look out at the bay.

I sat on the cushion, rolling my shoulders to ease them. Sagacious Blade poked the wall behind me, so I shifted her alongside me as On helped himself to the other cushion. He sat cross-legged, his elbows on the table as he stared at me. "You are better than a stage play. *How* do you do that?"

His tone invited me to ask what he meant by 'that,' but I was in no mood to comply. Already I was regretting this self-appointed errand. Then I got that peripheral sense of someone looking at me. But when I turned my head, I saw only the crowded main room, no one's attention on me.

I peered out the window. A host of small ships was at that moment parading around the bay with decorated sails, banners, and streamers, Huyun green dominating. Several flew great kites depicting sea creatures and water dragons, and of course krakens.

Another page appeared, this one older, and wearing green edging to his gray robe, came to me, gave me a short bow, and said, "Please follow me." And to On, who got up, "Or are you the petitioner?"

On inclined his head toward me, gesturing with a flourish. Yes, he was used at one time to wearing very long sleeves, though the ones now were modestly narrow, and decidedly frayed at the edges. Like many a student who's been studying for the examination year after years, existing on writing letters for those who could not read, and handouts from relatives or friends.

"It is I," I said distinctly, irritated at the page's assumption that On would be the person in question, though that clerk surely had not said "man."

"*'Who can command the banners and the drums?'*" On quoted softly, waving in a parody of a sad farewell, as he sat back down.

I followed the page through a warren of narrow corridors, and then up equally narrow and steep stairs, to a floor with much wider rooms. Again I was left in an alcove at a table with a window behind it. This time there was a finer pot on its warmer, cleaner-looking teacups waiting, and a plate of tea eggs and sticky-rice dumplings, eating sticks enameled in green and blue. Only for this festival.

I helped myself to both tea and refreshments, sure that whichever Important Personage was coming next would keep me waiting for a suitable time. I will never do that if I ever return to court, I promised myself idly. Then laughed at the absurdity.

"Is there a humorous kite out there? Or is it the kraken?" A man sat down opposite me.

He was very handsome, wearing layers of fine silk, his outer robe a soft silvery gray with coral and water weeds embroidered over it in graceful lines. Long tassels hung from the points of his sleeves and from the jade ornament at his belt. His hair clasp was studded with pearls, contrasting pleasingly with his glossy dark hair.

He opened a fan painted with peonies. "I am one Huyun Shandek. I chanced to be here this week, for the festival. Your message?"

I was looking at the governor himself.

My body, long trained, reacted before I could remember my gallant wanderer guise. I rose to perform the proper court bow to a rank above mine, as a fifth-level princess to a governor of noble birth.

The fan closed as he acknowledged my bow; when I saw sharpened interest in his gaze, my mind caught up with my error. "You are?" he added.

"This, ah, *I* am Pangolin Ren," I said, thoroughly rattled, as I had been expecting yet another in the rank-ladder of secretaries, the last of whom would perhaps consent to carry my warning to this man before me now.

Speak and get out, I told myself. "I used to live in the south of the imperial island, and I saw Imperial Crown Prince Lan Xianti often enough to recognize him. Here. That is, not in this harbor, but in Tiger's Eye Bay. He seems to be dressed as a general. Anonymous, or…" I let him think the word *disguise* on his own if he so chose.

The governor regarded me, waiting, as if for more disclosures. There was no surprise in his smiling face.

I fumbled awkwardly, "I thought only of the great trouble he has caused in the imperial island. I did not think it just to stay silent if there was a chance he was bringing trouble here, to this prosperous and most excellently governed island." I bowed again—in gallant wanderer style.

"Pangolin Ren," the governor repeated. "Are you not the one who blasted a path through Fire Dragon Reef a year or two ago?"

"That was a family charm," I said. "It only worked because there was a Snow Crane shaman who used Essence skills to guide me."

"Yes, so some of the witnesses maintained that you explained at the time. Though they only saw, and admired, your actions. Remembering the unfortunate reason why you were on that ship in the first place, I asked Commander Nan to send investigators out to find the rest of your family for you, as a reward for your merits that benefitted us all, but Nan's people reported that they could not find anything."

"He's lying about the reward," Granny Zim said abruptly in my inner ear, speaking for the first time in a year.

"I'm lying about the family charm to him," I responded to her inwardly.

"You must not think them incompetent or lacking in zeal for the task," Huyun Shandek went on. "There is regrettable disruption in the ordinary way of trade and travel, alas. They had to abandon the search."

"We are a small family," I said. *A family of one.*

"So it seems. Nevertheless, I am grateful that you brought your concern to me. As it happens, I am aware of his presence, as is Governor Ji Jiang. I believe the imperial crown prince is traveling anonymously, in order to quietly enjoy the festival, and to participate in a peace conference in the process that the governor is hosting. But I have nothing to do with that."

"Now he's lying, right to your face."

Granny Zim had never been that blunt. By now I had

myself thoroughly in hand, having retreated to court mode, and so I knew that nothing showed on my fac, or in my voice as I said, "Peace is to the benefit of all!"

"Indeed, indeed, you are very right. In fact, I would offer you a toast in agreement, and in thanks for your concern, but I see that the festival has rather strained the resources of these poor facilities, for which I apologize." Now *he* was in full court mode. "But at least I can offer amends for this lack. Please, if you will grace this unworthy house by remaining here with these refreshments, inadequate as they are, so that I may summon my attendants, I would like to invite you to stay for the festivities up in the palace. I venture to suggest that so discerning a person might find the entertainments not too contemptible."

He rose and went to the door, and out.

Before I could so much as catch a breath, On poked his head in the window—which was two stories from the ground. "Are you going to take that offer up?"

"No," I said. "He's lying, and I was about to find a way to get out of here without raising an alarm."

"Easily done," he said, and reached his hand out.

I took it, and stepped onto the tiled roof, my head immediately reeling. "I hate heights," I muttered.

"Shut your eyes," On retorted on a laugh, and a moment before the door opened again in that room, On closed his arms around me and leaped.

THIRTY-EIGHT

Ah! the coiled banners shifted,
Seen by none but the phoenix from towering
clouds,
She alone spoke from the sword pavilion:
"To govern these times requires virtue…"

WE LANDED AS EASILY as if we'd merely descended a step. Essence lights whirled briefly around us and vanished. He let go instantly when I shrugged him off, but stepped back under the awning. I followed, lest whoever had opened that door upstairs chance to look out and spot us.

"You were listening," I remarked.

"I was. I think, all things considered, we ought to remove ourselves to another location."

In the time since we'd first gone inside the rain had ended. The clouds scudded on their way east, leaving the buildings and fences scrubbed and a fresh scent to the air. We passed the huge drum, rounded the corner, and ducked up an alley.

Behind there was a shout, "Clear the way," and the rhythmic tramp of feet.

"That might not have anything to do with us. Want to chance it?" On asked.

"No."

He'd been looking around. The alley was crossed by another alley, high walls on all sides. This was clearly an area of palaces. He took hold of me once again, grunted, and leaped to the top of one of the walls, which was three times the height of a tall man. He glanced inside, and said, "This will do," and took us inside.

Not two heartbeats after we landed, the sound of running footsteps echoed up the stones of the alley on the other side of the wall that we pressed against. We waited in silence until they faded away, then looked around.

We'd trespassed into a private garden. The palace itself, at least, was obscured by ornamental shrubs, flowers, trees, and rocks, but... "Ay," I whispered, pointing to a narrow canal artfully meandering around the flowers and boulders. "The wine stream is running, which means they will be out here soon. They must have only stepped inside to outwait the rain."

We both glanced toward the top of a pavilion, visible not far away. A hop over the little canal, a quick jog in the opposite direction from the pavilion, taking care not to create a trail by trampling fragile orchids or smashing through the many varieties of peonies, and we halted under the shelter of an umbrella tree as another cloud obscured the sun, sending down a brief spray of raindrops. The cloud passed, and over to the west a rainbow gleamed into existence.

He said:

> *"The morning brings a rainbow in the west,*
> *The rain spring brings is sweet..."*

He stopped there, bending with hands to knees to peer at a bronze-golden tiger-face lily, very rare at least on the imperial island. I admired the lily, but my mind supplied the last lines of that poem that begins so innocently.

> *When a family parts, the home is empty,*
> *Who will see the rainbow?*

He straightened up as the rainbow dissolved before a bigger, darker cloud, bringing a heavy shower. "You said wine stream," he commented, holding out a hand to catch rain in his palm. "It looked like water to me."

I sighed. "I'm not about to ask you any questions about your past, so why pretend ignorance?"

His thin brows twitched together. "What do you mean? I thought it was an honest question. You said, 'wine stream.' There's no wine here that I can smell. Unless that's some gardening term?"

I said with extreme skepticism, "You're scholar trained, and you're saying you don't know what a wine stream is?"

"What has my being a scholar—an assumption for which I thank you—to do with wine streams?"

I humored him by defining the obvious. "A wine stream is a winding canal in a palace garden, where the host floats filled wine cups. Wherever the cup bumps up against the edge, the guest nearest must drink the wine and compose a poem to entertain the company. A fashion that..." *Father.* "...I was told is at least two generations old, among scholars. Rich or poor. In fact, the poor ones made most of their meals at gatherings where this game was played."

I'd been glaring at him during this caustic speech, disgusted at what I considered a totally unnecessary pretense, given that we both knew we were hiding our origins. But he wasn't looking at me at all. He gazed down at the canal with such unhidden yearning in his expression that my petty mood dissolved as surely as had the rainbow.

"*How* I should like to do that," he breathed, still staring down at the canal. Then he looked up at me, and reddened a little. "It's true. Enough. About birth. But I was only taught martial matters. There was a garden, but I was only in it with the sword master." He shrugged. "And now I'm in a garden without a sword master! I'd love to stay here and listen to them, but I think our welcome is too uncertain for that."

I'd been poised to run with or without him, but how would I get over the walls?

"Let's go," he suggested, and I fervently assented.

The gray cloud was passing, the rain diminishing. Once again we set out, and threaded our way until the garden gave way to a practical kitchen garden. Here the outbuildings served to shelter us as an army of servants in mauve and yellow bustled back and forth. Eventually there was enough of a break for us to cross a courtyard, and then hop another fence, to another palace.

We again crossed a yard, hopped another fence, and ran on, working our way toward a more modest part of the harbor city. This gave onto a twisting warren of narrow streets.

We finally stopped, both of us breathing heavily, in the enclosed yard of a modest eatery full of ordinary workers gathered around tables, celebrating the festival day. We sat down at a tiny side table, and when the aproned innkeeper came around, I made the sign for two of whatever they were offering. This established us as uninteresting, I knew from my time at the Three Kingfishers. Besides, I was hungry.

"They're looking for you," On said, "but there's a half-chance the first clerk will remember me. We had better change our appearance in case Huyun Shandek dispatches a general search."

"I don't know why he would," I said, but I had already unslung my carryall. I put it down beside me and rummaged in it for another robe to exchange for my favorite green. On top was that maid's robe of brown.

On was busy winding his hair up into a knot on his head, which he fixed with a plain wooden hairpin that he pulled from his own carryall. Then he shrugged out of his faded yellow robe, folded it carefully, and pulled out a wrinkled one of dull gray. He'd just finished pulling it over his under tunic when the food arrived. He hastily sashed the robe, and we both attacked the bowls of noodles cooked in oyster sauce with a fried egg on top.

"I don't know why he would either, unless he thinks you've discovered something he doesn't want discovered," On said around devouring noodles. "Which is interesting because all he said was that he had a peace conference planned for the festival day."

As I inhaled my meal, I considered the conversation. Both Huyun Shandek and I had been lying to the other, me simply to conceal my identity. He, to… what? Granny Zim could tell me when she detected lies, but she could not tell me what he lied about. Though so far, On had proved to be an ally in this instance, he was hiding his own identity—and his motives. I was not going to tell him how I knew that the governor was lying. I had to figure out on my own what he was lying about. Beginning with why he would want me to be safely "entertained" in that palace farther up the hill. That meant he did not want me…back in Tiger Eye Bay?

"He doesn't want you wandering back to Tiger Eye, at least for now. The Island a little over a night's or day's sail away," On said. "Which makes me think that whatever's going on is going to happen tomorrow. But we can't get there anyway, as half the crew is scattered all over the city. It'd take all day to find them. And then what?"

And then what had something to do with that envoy under the white flag. Who Koi was at this moment trying to learn about, I was very certain.

I wanted to find out what Koi knew. But On was right. Before I could even think about gathering the crew, I'd have to get rowed back out to the *Pangolin*, far out in the bay. Assuming I could do that unnoticed (would the governor really have his guards searching for me in the middle of this festival crowd?) it would take at least an hour. Then an hour rowing back, then who knows how many hours searching…

On had gone back to eating. I'd taken the edge off my hunger, and toyed with my spoon as I considered what I knew. "He said peace conference, but did not say with whom. I didn't mention the grand prince's envoy, so I don't know if he's concerned, but if there is really to be a peace conference, why would he want to lock me up? He might be worried that if I talked to others, word might spread, endangering the crown prince and whoever the grand prince sends…"

"Who would endanger them? A lot of laborers and children with kraken toys, against nine sea hawks flying the golden dragon banner, and Ji Jiang's ships? Anyway, he was gloating," On said, and slurped up his last noodle. "Not concerned. Are you going to finish that?"

I pushed my bowl toward him. He promptly attacked it.

"Gloating why? This is maddening."

"Why do you care?"

"I don't. Not about Lan Xianti. As far as he's concerned, if there's a plot against him, I'd say it was justice. But Huyun Shandek is under imperial command. It's more likely he and Xianti are plotting against the grand prince. That's what I would expect of Lan Xianti. As for the grand prince, I don't care about him, either, but I think my brother might have been conscripted into his army."

On's eyes widened, and he repeated, "Brother." Not in the tone of interrogation, it was more an inadvertent expression of regret.

His gaze shifted away, then he said, "There are several alternatives here. The governor is conspiring with the crown prince, against the grand prince."

"Likely," I muttered.

"Two. The governor is conspiring with the grand prince against the crown prince."

"If that was it, I'd be glad to help!"

"And third, the governor is conspiring against them both."

I sat back. "That seems unlikely. What makes you think that?"

"It's a possibility," he said. "I don't pretend to any military expertise, except what was beaten into my head, but it seems to me that whoever commands all those warships in Tiger Eye Bay can do what he wants against the others. As it stands now."

"But those are all captures from the Upstart Prince's war," I said. "Don't they belong to Ji Jiang?"

"Except that Ji Jiang is under the command of Huyun Shandek," On replied, and picked up the bowl to get at the last of the noodles. "Everything does seem to come back to him."

"If there's a plot," I said, "might it be Ji Jiang's? I wish I could talk to Orchid again. As well as Koi."

On shrugged again, drank off the last of the broth, and set the bowl down with a thump. "You can talk to them both, but it'll be after whatever happens."

Unless I could get there first.

"You know what to do," Granny Zim said.

My spoon dropped out of my fingers.

Oh, I knew. I *hate* heights, I wanted to whine. To which my own inner voice whispered, "What if it's Second Brother they send?" Because wily Grand Prince Yiulo would send him if there was any possibility of danger to himself or to his precious grandson Cousin Yiuti, I was very sure.

Yes, I had to know. I didn't know what I could do, but I had to know. Further, I knew I had the means to get there. Sagacious Blade lay against my side, inescapable evidence.

I had the knowledge to fly my sword. I had the Essence. I just had to force myself to do it. And that meant practice first. I would not go before sundown, as I'd be visible to anyone looking up. That meant I had the rest of horse hours and the beginning of dragon to learn. Especially as the day was not ideal for me, being a water day with rain. Water, and air.

I turned my attention to On, who had leaned back, arms crossed. "What are you contemplating?" And when I didn't answer, "Look, I understand keeping your secrets. We all have them. But some of yours aren't much of a secret, specifically that sword. Some may believe that your very obscure family just happens to have inherited a charmed sword, but I'll wager both my silvers—because you get to pay for this meal, O Wealthy Owner—that you have a lot more than a single charm on that thing. I've heard about how it *flew through walls* to come to your hand when you led the Pangolins to take the ship from the slavers."

"All right," I said, relieved. "Say I do know light skills. Or, that I've been taught, but I actually haven't done it. Because I really, really, really *hate* heights. I get dizzy in an instant. How did you manage learning your light skills? How far can you go?"

"I can't fly," he said with obvious regret. "When I was small, I discovered that I could jump not only from trees without getting hurt, I could jump into them. And I took to light skills like a north-born horse favors a north wind. My…guardian had already put me in military training for his own purposes, so I didn't tell him. I learned to lie, hiding it, and I practiced on my own. But I didn't get any training other than what I found out for myself, so I don't know anything about Essence, just what comes by nature. You'll have to do that part. But I can tell you what to do once you've made your talismans or chanted your charms, or whatever it is you do."."

I sighed.

"Come on. Let's find another garden, one without a wine party, and you can practice a little. I will supply audience and commentary.

> *Far off I watch the waterfall plunge to the long river,*
> *Flying waters descending three thousand feet down,*
> *Till I think the Star-lit Path has tumbled from the ninth*
> *height of Heaven…"*

"That," I said with real annoyance, "is not *at all* helpful."

"Sure it is. Reflect on the fact that you will not be flying any three thousand feet," he said with foxlike insouciance.

He kept up the encouragement mostly by teasing as I paid and we left. We wound our way toward the wilder end of the harbor, climbing the hillside where wild willows grew in abundance. The noise of the festival was barely discernable in the distance, mostly the pop of firecrackers now and then. Here and there music and singing.

I drew Sagacious Blade, laid her on the new spring grass, and stepped on the scaled blade. I drew Essence from the sun now peering down, and used it to lift the sword…and I promptly lost my balance.

I tumbled down, rolling to my feet again from long-trained habit. Which made me think of Cray. Who would have loved to be flying a sword at this very time. But it had chosen me.

"Very fine recovery," On said with justifiable humor. "But that won't get you anywhere. I's simple: look at where you want to go. Not up in a tree, or somewhere high up. Try an arm's length from where you are now. Look at that spot. Don't look away. Then…"

I glowered at a small weed, eased Essence beneath me…and the sword lifted and set me down gently as if I'd stepped there.

"That's it! Now, you repeat it a few thousand times," he said with heartless cheer. "Or, so I had to do when I was five years old."

"Ha ha," I retorted.

"You'll be faster, because you know what to do, which a five-year-old doesn't. You just have to train your eyes to target, same as tossing pitch pot. You already have balance from your martial arts. I've seen you do forms. You never wobble. Put that balance to work now."

I picked another weed, lifted the short distance, and so on, until On said, "Now to the top of that boulder."

I did the gaze fixing, but crouched down with one knee on the blade—and the lift glided smoothly and easily. I practiced that way for a time, until the sun vanished behind a cloud, and I sensed that I was using too much Essence. It had been hours.

"I need to stop," I said. "But I don't know how to manage this when I must go to Tiger Eye Bay. Which I can't see."

"You've been there," he said. "Just remember a spot you were standing at. Keep that in mind."

We ate again, watching our surroundings warily. But there were no parties of searching guards, just celebrants enjoying the constant parades, the music, and the dancers who came out to lure custom to their places of entertainment.

I dared not look at On when I left. I'd decided to fix on Koi, whose image was so clear in mind. On quoted another bombastic old poem about flying dragons and demons as I knelt. The sword rose, and wind buffeted my face and clothes.

I slid through the air. It really was like sliding, though I rose higher and higher. I kept my eyes looking rigidly forward into the darkness, my mind firmly fixed on Koi. Gradually the wind increased, but it was never a storm force. I was peripherally aware of the northern coast sliding away behind me, and the lightless bumps of small islands moving smoothly below me as the starlit sea gleamed in moonslight.

Faster and faster I flew, Granny Zim once again humming with approval in my inner ear, until I sensed a sprinkling of golden lights slipping into view below, as the stars glittered above. The sword came down with a clatter and a stumble on my part. I leaped behind a well, scanning the tiny court I'd landed in. Then I recognized Koi bent over a barrel, washing dishes.

"Koi," I whispered as loudly as I dared.

He straightened up, looking about wildly, then stilled when he saw me. He set a dish down and crossed the small yard, wiping his hands on his apron. "Ren? How did you get here?"

I picked up Sagacious Blade, and slid her into the sheath. He regarded the blade, and me, with widened eyes as I asked, "What have you learned?"

"Just what's generally known on the street. They're all talking about it here." He nodded to the restaurant. "Jai and I right away got hired to clear tables and wash dishes. The harbor is so crowded with people coming down from the mountains for the festival, and the added numbers of all these military, that jobs go begging."

"Anything about Xianti?"

"According to rumor, there's to be a peace conference, hosted by Ji Jiang, the commander whose additional ships helped beat the Upstart Prince. The truce is between the crown prince and the grand prince, terms to be discussed. No war for a year…shared conscripts…territories…it's all rumor."

"Ji Jiang," I repeated. If he was behind this plan, why had Huyun Shandek been so ready to lock me up—that after sharing no details?

In a rush of words, I told Koi about what had happened, ending with, "Why wouldn't he want to brag about a peace conference, which surely everyone would consider meritorious?"

"I don't know."

"Here's my fear. They won't treat with anyone not of suitable rank. You just know that Grand Prince Yiulo won't risk his precious grandson. Our fear that if Second Brother is with Yiuti, they will send him in their stead, seems more likely every time I think about it."

Koi said, "Agreed. But still I've heard nothing specific. The envoy was taken to the palace, that's all I know. And of course there was no getting in *there*."

I walked around in a small circle. "Specifics. I've got to talk to Orchid. Poor thing, she's vilely ill from being in child, but from the sound of it, she's the new favorite, and surely she's heard something. I have to try."

Koi's lips parted, then he said, "I'll wait here for you, then."

"What place is this?"

"Toreg's Seagrass."

At that moment, someone called from the door, "Where are those dishes?"

"Coming," Koi shouted.

He turned back to heft a heavy tray, and I laid out Sagacious Blade.

This time it was easier. I pictured the harem gazebo that Orchid had met Ke and me in, and the blade lofted me high above the palace walls. I only realized that I was guiding it by instinct when I saw a familiar figure scurrying along a zig-zag path and the Sagacious Blade jinked sideways, and flew down to confront that maid.

She staggered back, and almost dropped the lamp that she carried on a stick. As it was, it swung violently, throwing wild shadows up and down the surrounding walls until I said, "It's just me. I need to speak to Madam Aku Orchid." When the maid hesitated, eyes wide and frightened, I dug in my carryall and pulled out a silver piece. "Here. For your trouble. It's about the safety of the island," I added.

"I'll see what I can do," she said softly and scurried away, clutching the silver coin.

I waited where I was. And waited. And waited. Every heartbeat seemed like a hundred. I reminded myself that Orchid was ill. That she probably had a long walk. I was deciding she would not come and I had better leave when a lamp bobbed along the pillared corridors again, this time with two people, the second clutching a silk cloak about her.

"Thank you for coming," I said to Orchid, relief washing through me. "I'm sorry to bring you out of bed—"

"It is not as bad at night, for some reason," Orchid murmured. "Leili said something about the safety of the island? Was this some sort of ruse, or her exaggeration?"

"That's what she said, Sixth Madam," Leili whispered.

"I did say it, and I wish it was a ruse. That is, I'm not certain. I might be wrong. Do you know anything about this peace conference? What has Governor Je said about it?"

"Only that it is happening," Orchid replied uneasily. "Why?"

"Is he…was this his idea?"

"I don't know. *You* should know that women are not involved in governing matters. You sound court-raised."

I thought of Mother and Father going over testaments together, but the court did not know that. How many women secretly gave their best advice from behind silken screens?

Orchid said slowly, "I do know that he's been concerned, but I know no details—"

A rush of footsteps, and here came more bobbing lamps, this time before tall figures. We were instantly surrounded by graywing guards, led by a balding man in flowing layers of silk.

He put his arm protectively around Orchid. "You ought not to be running about in the night airs, my lovely Orchid." He turned a frown on me. "Who are you? Why are you disturbing my household?"

I bowed. "A person of no importance, who begs to put one question to you: is it you who commands those bannerless ships out there in the bay?"

His bushy eyebrows shot upward. "What kind of question is—here, this is ridiculous, to stand about out here. Come inside."

I knew my danger would be higher, but I had Sagacious Blade with me. I was willing to risk it.

He led the way to a small room decorated in shades of crimson, green, and gold, with a nine-fold screen depicting qilin on the wing above cloudy mountaintops. He sat in the primary chair, indicating chairs to the side.

I sat on the edge of one as the silent graywings stood behind our chairs. "You are a young one," Ji Jiang commented. "You can't be any older than my Orchid here. What are you doing running around at night, asking questions about affairs you have no business sticking your nose in?"

I said politely, but distinctly, "If it is you commanding those bannerless ships, I will admit that I am wrong, apologize with three bows, and take myself away."

"Very sure of yourself, for one so young," he retorted, his tone mitigating somewhat. "Because I am in a benevolent mood, and this is a festival day, I will indulge you: the bannerless ships are bannerless because they are under repair. No one is commanding them at present, in any military sense. And they have nothing to do with the negotiations currently being held between persons of rank above you *and* me."

I confess I was momentarily defeated, but my discussion

with On returned to me, and I said, "May I put it another way? Who supplied the laborers aboard those ships?"

Ji Jiang uttered a laugh. "If you knew the population of these small islands, you would realize how foolish that question is! There are only three islands with any significant villages. The rest are filled mostly with birds, except for the occasional fisher, some hermits, and a shaman who speaks to undersea creatures, and harms no one. Whereas Governor Huyun, who has fifty times the resources of these poor islands, generously offered to provide the labor to restore those ships."

"Those seaworthy ships," I said. "Honored Governor Ji, permit this poor, ignorant one a last question: are you certain that those are laborers, and not mariners? Especially fighting mariners?"

Ji Jiang uttered another laugh, but this one was less certain. He eyed me for a time, as a water clock dripped somewhere, and a quiet maid brought in a censer, and set it near Orchid, who remained utterly silent.

"Who are you?" Ji Jiang asked. "Who sent you?"

"I am no one of importance. I came myself. However, my concern is for one of the aides close to Prince Yiuti. My brother. And I'm afraid of what might happen if, ah, this peace conference has another purpose."

"Clear the room," Ji Jiang said abruptly, without looking away from me. He leaned over and patted Orchid's hand. "My dear, I am concerned for your health. I request you to return and rest."

Orchid stood, curtseyed to him, gave me a slight, questioning nod, and went out, her maid following. The graywings filed out and closed the door.

Ji Jiang frowned at me, then said slowly, "The truth is, even if those ships are stiff with warriors, I can do nothing. I've only recently been restored to this island, which belonged to my family for generations. The former emperor drove off my father over matters I will not go into now, but the Imperial Grand Prince Yiulo took hands with me to defeat the Easterners when they tried to cut these islands out with an invasion."

"That I know."

"So I hoped that there would be a way to heal the breach in the imperial family, when the young governor suggested a peace conference here while everyone enjoyed the festival." He scowled at his fists on his knees, then said, "The Tiger Islands have always been subordinate to the Ti Family on the larger island. That did not change when the Huyuns took over. Huyun Shandek is young, but he's an able governor. And it seemed a boon from heaven when he generously provided for the repair of that fleet, from his unlimited funds. But it is true, what you say about seaworthiness. I asked repeatedly for those ships to be sailed to Dawn Harbor over there across the strait, which could more easily accommodate them. It's a strain on our treasury to feed and supply those laborers…" He frowned and waved a hand. "As I said, whether this is to be a historical moment of peace, or something else, I can do nothing. The two princes have each agreed to be limited to nine warships, no larger than sea hawks. You can see the imperial banner on nine out there now. The firedragon banner will be seen tomorrow, as agreed."

"Where is the firedragon envoy, may I ask?"

"On his way back to wherever the grand prince is waiting, probably somewhere just into the Great Sea. Not far, as they are expected on the morrow."

"And Governor Huyun's part in all this?"

"He is merely a witness of suitable rank for the treaty the two Lan princes are expected to make."

"So if something goes amiss, it is…"

"I will be held responsible," Ji Jiang said, and eyed me. "How old *are* you?"

"Old enough to want to prevent something terrible if I can."

"Such as…"

"Such as all those bannerless ships converging on a mere eighteen sea hawks, and both princes being captured. Or worse."

Another silence, during which the water clock dripped. It took no great guesses to imagine Ji Jiang's thoughts now: if anything went wrong, the emperor would be summoning him to explain. And either he went to court, and risked beheading, or he refused, which meant returning to his exile and existence as a mercenary or pirate.

"Why?" he asked. Then he rubbed his eyes with thumb and forefinger. "No. I'm not asking a girl barely of marriageable age."

I rose. "Then this girl will depart, thanking the governor for his forbearance with her foolish questions."

"Not foolish at all," he said with a breathless bark of a

laugh. "That is what disturbs me." He lifted his voice. "Let her go."

The door opened, the graywings let me pass, and I wended my way through the harem's garden until I was sure I was alone, then I took to the air again, for Toreg's Seagrass.

THIRTY-NINE

Mothers, is this what you want for your sons?
In land and in sea, new ghosts complain and old
ghosts drift.
Under the thundering sky, their voices wail in the
rain.

KOI WAS WAITING FOR me, sitting on a bench with his hands gripping his knees. His shoulders sagged in relief when I landed with a little more of a jolt than I'd expected. I did not recognize until then that so much expenditure of Essence, especially at night, surrounded by water, was tiring. But I was also fiercely awake, my mind racing.

I sheathed the sword as I approached Koi. "You did not need to wait for me."

"My shift was over. I thought I may as well be ready for you or for a party of guards," he said with a slight smile. "Glad it's you and not the guards. It's been a long day, mostly of washing dishes. I do have one bit of news: the envoy sailed out of the bay at the beginning of dragon hour. I missed it as that was the busiest time."

"I know," I said, and told him everything that had happened.

At the end, he said, "I was wondering about those ships after what you told me earlier. Though we don't have direct evidence, there's enough circumstantial evidence to convince me that Huyun Shandek is not expecting any kind of peace conference. Everything would be run differently if he was."

"I agree." I sank down beside him on the bench. "And I agree about circumstantial evidence. I played Circle long enough with Second Brother for me to try imagining all these bits we've learned placed on a board."

"What does that suggest to you?"

"It might be wrong, because the important parts are all in the heads of the players, rather than positioned in black and white stones. But...the way I used to play...ay! My Circle board has always made sense in terms of supply, need, support..."

"Logistics," he said.

"That's the word. Second Brother did try to get me to see the game as military movement, but I found that so tedious. It was far more fun for me to think of it as finding ways to deny and provide — ay! What I meant to say is, even though Ji Jiang referred to Huyun Shendak's island as large, which it is in comparison with the Tiger Islands, it's not the size of the imperial island, nor as populous. So where is the governor getting his unlimited funding?"

"Generations of family treasure?"

"But that would go fast when you think of what's going on just in this island alone. Ji Jiang complained about having to feed all the people on those bannerless ships — whether workers or warriors — but the supplies for the actual building had to come from somewhere. And didn't you tell me he's also got an army of people building sea vessels somewhere upriver?"

"Traders," Koi said. "Jai and I had to sneak around the lake where that's going on."

"Traders," I repeated, an image of the *Pangolin* in my eye. "Did you see them?"

"Only a glimpse from the mountain path, before we took the detour route."

"Did they look like traders to you?"

"They looked like the skeletons of ships," Koi said, shrugging. "I can't tell one from another. You have to remember I haven't been seeing nearly as many ships as you."

"I did learn a lot about ships, watching the harbor every day, and listening to the talk in the Three Kingfishers. I learned that the skeleton of a trader is pretty much the same as that of a sea hawk. Think of what Dinek has done to the *Pangolin*."

Koi whistled under his breath. After a pause, as we sat there trying to mentally assemble a puzzle with so many disparate pieces, he said slowly, "If he's secretly building a fleet of warships, even with unlimited treasure, it has to be to a purpose."

Chill gripped me. "That aside, let's look at this situation: countless manned, seaworthy bannerless ships against eighteen sea hawks. If Huyun Shandek really dares to kill the princes—Xianti and whichever prince is sent by Great-Uncle Lan Yiulo, if he doesn't send my brother—the emperor really will blame Ji Jiang."

"Meanwhile, with no crown prince, and one of the fighting dragons gone, that leaves a clear path..." Koi began.

"To the dragon throne," we said together.

Koi looked at me. I looked back.

"We have to get word to the grand prince not to come," I said.

"And?" Koi prompted.

I was fighting an inner battle then. Because I knew what must immediately be done, but the matter of my family brought the familiar surge of fury, of a yearning for justice, the bloodier the better.

Which is, I knew, exactly the path that Lan Xianti always took.

I forced out the words, though they tasted of ash and aloe, "We have to warn Xianti."

Koi's mouth thinned. But he jerked his head in a nod. "If we want to prevent this island from suffering imperial wrath, yes. If the princes die here, the emperor will lay everything to waste." He spread his hands to include the entire bay.

Tiredness hit me then, like a deluge of slushy snow, leaving me shivering. How I hated this task. But it had to be done. "Do you know where he is?"

"Everyone knows where he is," Koi said. "He's got the top floor of the finest inn that overlooks the bay."

Which would be expected of a 'general' of very high rank. "Let's go."

Koi reached behind a barrel, where he'd stashed his carryall and sword. "Let me fetch Jai."

Jai was still inside, finishing an enormous meal now that their shift was over. Koi went in, and came out with Jai, who whispered a stream of questions. "We're really going to attack that inn? Really? I thought Xianti was a white-eyed wolf. Why are we rescuing him? It is a rescue, right?"

Koi cut into the flow. "He is definitely a white-eyed wolf, but if we don't, this island will suffer if he dies. Ren? Plan?"

"How does this sound? Jai, you hold the door, so to speak. Koi, you and I take out any guards around him. We know there will be plenty. No killing," I added. "Each of those men has a family. They're doing their job." It was their commander I loathed, and I did not want to kill a lot of people just to warn a viper who might not even listen.

"More of an insult if we knock 'em out and tie 'em up," Jai gloated. "Like we could have killed them but didn't. Won't he hate that? Ha ha, I love thinking about how he'll hate that, such a slap in the face, ha ha."

He kept that up as we let ourselves out the back gate into a narrow alley, and Koi led the way toward the three-tiered inn towering over its neighbors. Tiredness pulled at my limbs and burned my eyes, but my nerves sang.

"Ay," Granny Zim said to me, "the tree hopes for calm but the wind never stops. Carry on, my Bu."

We reached the inn, and did a quick scan. "Five, six, seven guards on the ground level," Koi counted.

"They look half asleep," Jai jeered.

"They'll wake fast enough if we raise a noise. Let's split them between us, and quiet as we can. Jai, we've practiced this."

"I know, reach from the back, choke hold, neck press, ease them down."

Koi turned to me. "Ren, I know you don't like the prospect of fighting..."

"I can do it," I said. "If I'm fast, there won't be a real fight. I can use Essence to freeze muscles."

Koi nodded, and we advanced.

I took my time, my stomach trembling with nerves. I did know what to do. I'd trained and trained, but the actual doing is still terrifying the first time.

As the man turned, mouth opening, I slammed my finger into the correct acupoint, sending a blast of fear-driven Essence that would probably keep him paralyzed until dawn—but I was slow. In that time, Koi took down four of the guards, slipping from one to the next like a shadow, and Jai took care of two.

We were committed.

Leaving Jai in the shadows by the door, we pried open a

window, slipped inside the empty common room, and then eased up the stairs. One, two, three guards more for me. I found it easier each time I had to attack and disable them, though Koi took out the most, easing them soundlessly to the floor.

One did get out a short exclamation, which alerted the last two, but Koi was a whirl of constant action, reminding me of Master Sima when he'd sparred with another expert martial artist at the Falcon valley. I dispatched the last one with a touch of Sagacious Blade to the breastbone acupoint and another blast of Essence.

We were left looking at one another outside a pair of red-enameled doors painted with cranes in flight. I was so tempted to shove the confrontation onto Koi, but I knew that Xianti would never listen to a servant. Also, I wanted to protect Koi's identity if I could. I had vowed to face Xianti someday, and get justice for my family. This confrontation was simply earlier than I'd expected.

I entered the enormous bedchamber. It smelled of incense and the scents of human endeavor; there were two long lumps in the bed. The one on the outside, with the covers half pulled away, had feminine lineaments—of course Xianti would put his own comfort first, hogging the bedcovers, leaving his companion to shiver.

Her eyes sprang open when I touched her on the shoulder. Her gaze widened, going from the sword gleaming in my hand from the light of Ghost Moon in the widow, to me. I held out a coin and put my finger to my lips. She slipped out of the bed, grabbing up her silk robe and taking the coin in the same movement. Then she ran barefoot out the door, without a look back in a way that I took as disdain for Xianti. She certainly was not the least worried for him.

I regarded him there. He lay on his side, back turned toward his former companion. The moonlight sharply etched cheekbone and eye socket, those familiar features that I'd always regarded as evil. The old fear and dread threatened to overwhelm me, but I consciously dismissed that, gripping Sagacious Blade. I was not helpless now.

I poked him, hard, with the sword.

He startled, and sat up, bewildered, naked except for his hair hanging down around him. He looked ludicrous, and my fear dissolved.

He froze when he saw the sword. I must have been a

silhouette, for he started when I said, "You can yell, but no one will hear you. I took down all your guards."

"A *girl?*" he exclaimed.

"I'd love to slit your throat," I said, with all the venom I could not suppress, "you worthless rat."

"How dare—"

"Shut your mouth," I snapped, and struggled to stem the acid tide of hatred. Anger begets anger, I reminded myself. Not justice. "I'm here to warn you. Huyun Shandek is planning to kill you and whoever Great-Uncle Yiulo sends."

"Great-Uncle...who *are* you? I want my robe." He reached slowly for the robe lying carelessly over the elaborate bed frame, and slowly thrust his arms into the flowing sleeves as I spoke.

"If you don't want to end up with a face full of dust—richly deserved as it would be—you've got the rest of this night to get out of here, put your noisome self onto one of those nine ships, and sail out of this bay before the firedragon ships arrive."

"You're mad. Huyun has nothing whatsoever in this bay..."

As he spoke, he had been working one hand under the pillow. He whipped out a dagger, and lunged up at me.

But I was ready. I blocked his blow, though barely. He was fast and strong, after all those years of bullying guards and cousins in the princes' court. I threw a surge of Essence-fire down my blade, shocking him, and tapped the acupoint that froze him.

As I did so, I must have moved into weak blue light from the window, for he made a great effort of will, gargling in sheer disbelief, "R-r-r-e-n-n-n-t-i?"

"I do not want to hear my name in your filthy mouth," I retorted and again struggled with a firestorm of anger. It took all the effort I had in me, but I evened out my voice. "Did you see those bannerless ships? How many were there, fifty? More like a hundred fifty, including the scouts and sea hawks. Are you sure they're full of laborers, and not trained mariners, those cannon not loaded and ready to fire?"

He stared, and I sensed his uncertainty.

"What do you think they can they do against nine? Or eighteen, for that matter? Your nine-ship honor guard is merely a bite at the feast."

"Unghnnn!"

"Believe me or don't believe me. I don't care if you end up

dead. Your life is worth less than those servants out there, much less. At least they provide necessary work. But you? Nothing you do is good, *nothing*. If you were capable of even a mouse's dropping of wisdom or mercy, I wouldn't regret the warning as much. As it is, I will *never* forgive you for what you did to my family."

I walked out and shut the door, to find Koi leaning there, sword in hand, one foot propped against the wall behind him. "Feel better?"

"No." I listened. No shouting. "You didn't do anything to his companion?"

"I just said to keep quiet as she fled by me, and I haven't heard a sound."

"Good. Let's go before these guards begin to rouse."

When we got to the street, Jai joined us. "That was fun. But short. Are we doing it again?"

I sighed, my neck aching. "We've the hardest task ahead of us: how to get a warning to the grand prince, when we don't know where he is, and we haven't the *Pangolin* in order to wait outside the bay to intercept him. But we've got to try. We need a sailboat — if either of you know how to sail one."

"Jai can."

"I can," Jai muttered. "But it's a lot of work, and I've been doing dishes..."

"We both have," Koi reminded him mildly.

Jai brightened. "We can always steal one. That would be fun." And when Koi and I frowned at him, he sighed. "It's in a good cause, isn't it?"

"Steal, no. We'd just be chased. But commandeer?" I said.

"From that crown prince?" Jai asked, eyes round.

"No. You don't ask a tiger for its skin. Even if you might have fed the tiger with a warning," Koi said.

"That it might ignore," I added. "But maybe Ji Jiang's people...Let's go to the wharf."

To our surprise, Ji Jiang had obviously been considering matters. When we approached the guard tower before the military wharf, a sentry came forward with a lamp, peered at us, and said, "Girl with fox ear hair twists. White stone in sword hilt. I'm to say that there is a ship ready." He indicated a scout craft, floating right there at the wharf a short distance away, sailors looking up expectantly.

Jai started toward the wharf, but I held up a hand. "Is there a small sailboat no one is using?"

The man did not hide his surprise. "The governor did say to give you what you needed."

"Please convey our grateful thanks. A small sail craft will do. I don't know if we can return it."

As he went off to confer with a couple of other silhouettes, Jai muttered, "What's the use in us having to sweat the sailing if we don't have to?"

"Because we'll be alone," Koi said. "Instead of surrounded by a lot of people who might have orders to arrest us as soon as we finish."

"Oh."

We were soon in a slim sailboat much like one of those aboard the *Pangolin*. Jai handled it well, as we rode in light airs out into the bay.

I settled back, pillowing my aching head on one arm. "Is the scout craft following us?" I asked presently.

"It is," Koi said.

"Why chase us, if we're doing a good thing?" Jai asked as he leaned into the rope, tautening the clattering sail.

"Because Ji Jiang will be able to assure whoever asks that he tried to catch us. I'm very certain that scout craft has orders to watch whatever we do, but fail to catch up," I said, with my eyes shut. That was a common ruse in the gallant wanderer tales, and from what I'd learned of Ji Jiang, it seemed likely.

"Why do you get to nap?" Jai muttered. "You got to sail around on a sword while *we* spent a thousand years doing dishes."

I opened my eyes. "What you're doing, with the ropes? I have to do that in the sky. Or I'll fall right down."

"Oh."

Koi smothered a smile—I could see it in pale Ghost Moon's light. He said, "My suggestion is, Ren gets first nap. When Ghost Moon is two fingers above the sea, we'll trade off, two awake to make sure no one falls asleep. And at dawn, last one gets the longest nap, until we spot something."

"I'll take the last watch," Jai said quickly.

I laughed to myself. There was probably less than a year's difference in our ages, but sometimes I felt like I was ten years older. Ten years older in terrible experience? Except I knew that bad things had happened to him, too. We all follow our own paths, as Mana Ta said.

I sank into slumber, waking when Koi touched my shoulder. It was my turn to stay awake with Jai while Koi got a brief sleep. He laid his head on his pack, and three breaths later he was out.

The sky was still clear from horizon to the receding silhouette of the island behind us. Jai was humming softly, so softly it was barely discernable over the sounds of the sea. In retrospect, I'd heard him while I slept, a pleasant sound. And a very good way to keep oneself awake.

We did not speak, lest we waken Koi, but to me it felt like a companionable silence, as the stars wheeled incrementally overhead. I let my mind sink into Essence studies, feeling the inexorable pull of the stars, and of Ghost Moon slowly sliding toward the horizon, Phoenix moon now cresting one of the islands in the north on its way up.

The east had begun to shade toward blue when Jai yawned hugely, and then a second time. I held out my hand for the ropes. In silence we traded places, and he stretched out his long length beside Koi, dropping immediately into sleep. I was supposed to waken Koi in order for him to keep me awake, but I knew I would not sleep. Koi looked so peaceful there, his shoulder unconsciously leaning against my calf.

No sooner had I thought that than he stirred, opened his eyes, and sat up. "You were supposed to wake me."

"I didn't want to disturb either of you."

In answer, he glanced down at Jai, who lay flat on his back in the bottom of the sailboat, mouth open as he snored.

I suppressed a tremor of laughter, until I met Koi's eyes. "I've traveled with him enough to know that once he falls asleep, he's going to stay that way until he either gets enough sleep, or you shake him violently and shout in his ear," he said.

Sure enough, Jai did not stir.

Koi looked around, as did I. Then he said, "I know you've been on the run since yesterday, except for that nap. So you might not have had a chance to think ahead very far. Whereas I spent the entire day washing dishes. You get a chance to think, washing dishes."

He paused, and I said, "Go on."

"Might be counting on rain at the first breath of wind, but..." He looked briefly at me. "If we find your brother. Have you thought past that?"

"What's there to think about?" I asked. "We get him away. I feel sure he'd love the *Pangolin*. He used to talk about climbing aboard a ship to see the world. And if he doesn't like ships after all, there's the freedom of the gallant wanderer life on some other island, as we try to figure out how to save our family."

We both looked about, but there was no sign of Xianti's nine ships flying the imperial banner. He might have sailed, or not. Unless we had the extreme bad luck to be in the same waters, we would not know.

Satisfied we were alone, I said, "I might be too stupid to think of a way to rescue my family on my own, though I've tried. Many nights, I've lain awake thinking of nothing else. But with Second Brother joining us, I believe everything will be so much better."

Koi remained silent.

"Don't you?" I asked.

"I think it depends what he has been learning," Koi said slowly.

"Surely he's learning just as we are," I protested. "It might be within the imperial teachings, but that will aid us if there is a way within imperial law to at least get my family out of the prison."

Koi said, "That is a good point."

"That has to be part of his intention, if he stayed with the grand prince," I said.

Koi slowly nodded. "I believe he'd think that way."

We wasted time trying to guess at how that might be done, but we were aware that we did not know enough about imperial law. For that, alas, we would need Father. Still, I was willing to talk about suppositions, however wild, because it brought my family nearer, in a sense.

After a time, my throat was dry, and I remembered that we'd brought no water. And here we were in the middle of the ocean. But I could not think about that now.

I did another sweep — then rubbed my eyes. Either that was a notch on the western horizon, or I was still too tired to see well.

I pointed, and Koi slewed around to stare. Rub his eyes, too, and keep staring.

We kept our gazes on the spot, which wavered, vanished, then was back again. It was a notch. A ship! But from the wrong direction. Alarm chased away the lassitude when it occurred to me that it could be the leader of a pack of ships. Xianti's? A fleet from Huyun Shandek would scarcely be better. Ji Jiang's scout would surely stay well north of us...

The sails appeared. Familiar lines — but then sails are pretty much alike. Surely, surely that could not be…

But it was the *Pangolin*, moving east by south. I did not know if it could see us, so small against the dim light, so I gathered some Essence from that imminent sun I could feel below the horizon and threw it skyward as a fireball.

The sails angled with jerks, and whoever was tending the helm threw it over. The *Pangolin* began an arc toward us. Koi took over navigating our sailboat, and the two soon converged. In the strengthening light, I made out a row of faces looking down at us.

"How did you find us?" I screeched up at them, at the same time that Fan bellowed in her field voice, "How did you get stranded out here?"

Dinek appeared at Fan's side, On leaning next to her, grinning.

"I found Dinek," On called. "She knew where everyone was, and called us in. I figured you'd do something mad like this, and here we are."

"Do you want to come up?" Dinek called.

"I do," Jai said, then turned to us in question.

"Go ahead," I said.

Koi nodded. "We'll be all right."

"Dinek, we're going to sail back and forth right here, across the mouth of the bay, for if the grand prince comes, he must come this way—"

"Sail ho," one of Ayep Vu's gunners called from up on the mast.

"Don't let them catch you," I called quickly. "Go beyond the horizon. Wait for us. If it takes until night, would you put lamps on the deck, so the sailboat can find you?"

"I will," Dinek called, as a rope was thrown over the side, and Jai clambered up the hull. Then he turned to look unhappily down, as if he had second thoughts.

Dinek called, "I left Dove Hat in the harbor to do some investigating. She's a good crew member, but she's a brilliant mole. I think I told you she saved us two or three times last year by digging and digging for the truth."

I could hear question in her voice, as if I might object to her taking the initiative like that. Too tired to figure it all out, I called up as space widened between the sailboat and the *Pangolin*, "Wonderful idea! Thank you!"

"Want a third?" On then called.

"I want an army," I called back. "But since I don't have

one, the two of us will do. There's someone we're hoping to find news of. Maybe we'll be offered news in trade for the warning."

The *Pangolin* was soon out of range, tacking away into the gloom of the west.

Straight east, exactly where I'd figured, a tower ship plunged the waves, the dragon on its banner looking black in the weak blue light of pre-dawn.

That had to be Grand Prince Yiulo.

Koi's profile was grim. But he faced forward, and I knew without a word that with him it was the same as it was with me: sometimes the logic of the heart supersedes that of the mind. We were going to try, and try, and try, until the net was broken and the fish were dead.

FORTY

Her lone voice rose over sea and mountain,
as sun's rays warmed the green pines
and water rilled in the fire-steaming pool
where she tamed poison dragons…

KOI SAID ABRUPTLY, "EVEN if Banti's not here, we should not assume he's dead."

I looked at him, but he gazed straight ahead.

I said, "But he could not have avoided the imperials on his own. I'd hoped he could back then, because I was so ignorant. The more I've learned about their methods, and martial methods in general, the slimmer my hopes. It has to be Yiuti."

"There's…another possibility."

My heart knotted painfully. "What? Why haven't you told me before this?"

"Because it's a secret I swore to protect. I've been thinking about this secret for the past year, at least. All things considered, including the fact that I know you can be trusted with secrets, I feel I ought to tell you."

"I promise to keep it."

"You remember what happened to Cedar?"

"Cedar?" I repeated, then my memory catapulted me back to the palace: the younger generation of graywings, who had tree names. Graywings lost their birth names (if they had any) when they became graywings. "He's the one Xianti burned with firecrackers, and Princess Vaha healed."

"She always insisted that it was the Morningstar God who healed him, but ever since I learned about the healing she did in the dungeon, I suspect it might be something like what happened to you, when you burned the reef, with the help of that strange monk who tended to go invisible."

"Invisible? But I always saw—no, no, we're nearing that ship. Please. Tell me."

"Simply this, Graywing Cedar is part of a kind of resistance. Among the graywings. Some servants. My aunt is one, a cousin another. I ran errands for them, once in a while. It's a very slow resistance, of course, as they have no weapons save their wits, and other covert means that must remain undetectable. They managed to save several servants from the imperial princesses especially, who ordered maids to be strangled at whim, until the empress scolded them for putting her to the trouble of interviewing new servants and getting them trained. Banti knows about it, as we were friends with some of the younger graywings—playing Circle and the like—through my cousin."

Koi paused, looking up at the ship sending waves out for our sailboat to bump over. "So if he's not here, and these firedragon Lans know nothing, I'm going to believe that Cedar got him away safely," Koi said under his breath.

We were hailed from the ship, and I shouted up that I had a message for the grand prince.

"Who sent you?" someone shouted down to us.

"I come myself," I called. And, louder, "I am Lan Renti, daughter of Chief Censor Lan Kaiza."

I knew it was a risk, not only naming myself, but offering Father's title when he had been stripped of his rank. But that had been done by the grand prince's rival.

We had drifted quite close, and Koi kept the sailboat from crashing against the hull as voices rose up on board, then the shouter was abruptly shoved aside, and there was Second Brother's dear face peering down. "Renti? It is you? Ay, you've grown up!"

I found myself laughing and weeping at once, in my tiredness and tension and joyful surprise. "So have you," I cried, tears dripping down onto my badly rumpled tunic.

A shout, and a stir, and Banti called, "Should we send

down some sort of bench or chair? I don't think we have a proper one for girls…"

"No need," I shouted, getting hold of myself. "Rope ladders will do."

Koi deferred, so I went first; he was slipping back into servant mode. He'd even pulled off his headband. Mine was already stuffed in my carryall, as I'd assumed the guise of a maid once again, to get into Ji Jiang's harem.

As soon as we stepped on deck, the sailors dipped their heads in the short bow for a fifth rank princess, and the imperial world closed around me again, leaving me self-conscious in my grubby clothes, my hair twisted in the maid's fox ears, and of course my carryall and…

"You've got a sword?" Second Brother exclaimed in surprise as he extended his hands.

Mother had taught us that physical displays were at all times frowned on in public, and absolutely forbidden between the sexes unless one was married. But I walked into his arms anyway, so glad to see him that I trembled all over, fighting back another cascade of tears.

Those gathered around laughed and cheered as he crushed me in a hug; I peered past Banti's shoulder, which came to the level of my eyes, to find Yiuti grinning at me, his gaze avid. He, too, had grown, all the roundness in his cheeks gone. He had always been short and chunky as a boy, shorter even than I, though he was Second Brother's age. He was somewhat taller—we were now eye to eye—and very broad in the chest and arms.

Far friendlier was Cousin Oraiti's happy smile. I remembered then that he and his father—governor of the very important island Benevolent Winds—had barely escaped ahead of the emperor's forces. Now, Xianti's twin Kianti was the governor there.

Banti let me go, and exclaimed, "Whew! I don't know what's stronger, the sweat or the brine."

I shrugged that off, saying, "You'll understand once you hear my message. Speaking of…" I halted on the verge of telling them to avoid the bay. Imperial order meant imperial manners, and I was no longer a gallant wanderer, equal to all other gallant wanderers, but a fifth, or lowest, rank princess, and a mere girl.

Banti then turned to Koi, his entire face brightening in

welcome. "Thank you," he murmured.

At the same time, I bowed to Yiuti, saying, "This lament-able wretch begs forgiveness for offending Cousin Yiuti's eyes with my squalid self, but my message is very urgent. If it is possible for this one's message to be conveyed to his imperial highness the grand prince..."

"Imperial Grandfather is back at our base," Yiuti said. "He sent us."

Second Brother added, "We've been arguing about which of us is to face Xianti. I think I ought to go, but Yiuti wants—never mind that. Is this some kind of ruse?"

Yiuti elbowed him. "Let's take this into my quarters." He waved a dismissive hand, and the other noble-born young men standing around us instantly bowed and effaced themselves. The sailors had already gone back to their stations.

"If this undeserving younger sister may offer a sugg-estion," I said as I followed Banti, who followed Yiuti, "if these ships would prefer not to encounter Xianti and his nine sea hawks, perhaps it might be prudent to choose any direction but north toward Tiger Eye Bay."

"He's on his way out of the bay?" Yiuti said over his shoulder, and uttered an anticipatory laugh. "I'd *love* to take him on. But Grandfather did make me promise..." And he shouted an order to reverse direction.

We entered the superstructure, and climbed up to the second floor, which apparently was a huge suite entirely for the two princes. A crimson firedragon romped across the nine folds of a screen of golden silk, with mountains and cascades, eagles in flight, lotus pools, and other emblems of power or prosperity sketched in shades of silver, gray, and white against the gold.

Servants silently glided forward with steaming tea pots and beautiful porcelain cups as well as trays of food, all of which Yiuti waved off with a cursory hand. "We're not hungry. Go away."

He sat in the principal chair, as I suppressed hunger and thirst—so very like those old days in court!—and chose the one below Banti.

Yiuti leaned forward. "Now, what's all this? Why are you carrying a sword?"

"This ignorant sister has been trying to learn to defend herself," I began. "But her story is of the least importance—"

"Yes, yes," Yiuti said. "Never mind that. I know you ran off before Xianti's hounds could get you." He blinked, squinting slightly at Koi. "Isn't that your Fish, Banti? Of course he'd take care of your sister. Good, good, good. But what's this about Xianti? We wouldn't have come at all, except that I did want to meet Ji Jiang, who allied with Grandfather years ago, when the Easterners tried to invade. And who spearheaded the attack on the Upstart Prince's upstart uncle. And, because his message came through Huyun Shandek, whose family has always been loyal to the throne."

During my childhood in the imperial palace, I was in speaking distance of the princes' male servants so seldom that I had forgotten that Yiuti had found it hugely entertaining to address them all—including female servants—as "Fish." Their generation of servants being named for creatures of lake, river, and sea. His referring to Koi as Fish pulled me further into the constraints of imperial manners.

Instinctively I hesitated a heartbeat or two, endeavoring to reframe my message in a way that excluded me as much as possible, and I said, "If this ignorant one may put a question to your highness—"

"My *imperial* highness." Yiuti grinned. "I'm insisting on the full title only because that serpent Xianti got his worthless uncle to try to strip us of our rank."

"—your imperial highness, did the envoy on his return report on what he saw in the bay?"

Yiuti flung his long sleeves back as he leaned toward me, one hand tossing his jade belt ornament on his palm. "He did. Filled with ships taken from the Upstart. Still hammering and sawing repairs. That must have been a wild fight! I was really looking forward to hearing the details." He looked at me expectantly.

"It is considered to be very likely," I began cautiously, "that those bannerless ships were in fact full of warriors, ready to sail both against you, your honor guard of nine ships, and the crown prince and his. And that they are under the command of Governor Huyun Shandek."

"Really!" Yiuti exclaimed, elbows now on knees. "And Ji Jiang is in on this plot? He's turned on my grandfather?"

"According to his own testimony, he did not know. It is his sailboat that was provided to send this lowly one and her companion, Koi," (I laid emphasis on his name) "to warn you."

"Ayah!" Yiuti exclaimed, and turned to Banti. "That's more like it. If this is true, then you were right, BanBan." A nice-sounding, brotherly nickname, except I noticed that Second Brother had not been given permission to call him YiuYiu. "You did think it was a plot all along. Only you were wrong about whose plot it was. Now I want us to go face down Xianti, just to see who comes out alive."

"It'll be you, no doubt about that," Second Brother said easily. "But is it worth losing a ship, maybe more, to Xianti's treachery when his imperial highness Grand-Uncle Yiulo specifically forbade you to risk the ships?"

Yiuti kicked the table in front of him, making the porcelain on it rattle and ring. "Ay! So he did. So he did. So he did. Promised him we'll let him decide when we take the battle to those rats. Choose the ground, choose the ground."

He turned his head. "Carp! Where's the midday meal?"

He rose, heaved a sigh as if he was about to descend into a brimstone mine with his own shovel, and muttered, "I'd better get them to find a suitable room for a girl. Who ever thought we'd have a girl on a warship? But you're my cousin, Renti. We can't have you looking like that. Though we can't offer you better clothes, we can at least give you a civilized chamber." He walked off in a rippling of silk, his train hissing behind him, light glimmering over the plum branches embroidered over the back of his robe. "Stay here, BanBan. Visit with your sister until we can find a cabin to put her in. Can't have my cousin out on the deck, being stared at by those lowborn conscript-hounds — we'll all lose face."

The door shut behind him.

Second Brother sat back, thumbing his eyes. "I can't believe it's you, Little Sister." He smiled at me, his expression bright again. "Learning the sword — how? Where?" He looked up at Koi, who had taken his place as silent servant behind Second Brother's chair. "Thank you for protecting her, Koi. I should have known that you would." He glanced at the door, then leaned over and patted the chair next to him. "Sit down, sit down."

Koi gave his head a shake. "I'd better not, Second Young Master."

Second Brother sighed, and turned to me. I leaned toward him. "When can we leave?"

"Leave?" Second Brother repeated. "Leave where?"

"This ship. *We* have a ship," I said. "It's waiting for us behind the horizon. Now that I've found you, and you're safe, we can figure out how to rescue the rest of our family. While they are still alive."

"They aren't under immediate threat," Second Brother said. "There's an impasse. Xianti doesn't dare move against them, since Vaha has been visiting them. In fact, she's made over their cells into a palace room as much as she can. Also Grandfather Gu made it plain to Uncle Koza that if anything happens to Mother, he's closing his harbor to imperial trade, and coming over the mountain with an army. Uncle Koza is spread so thin, trying to hunt *us* down, that he dares not risk it."

"But they are still in prison," I said.

"Yes. And that's why I've stayed with Uncle Yiulo. He promised me that his first command when he secures the dragon throne is to free our family and reinstate Father as Chief Censor. And elevate him to Grand Prince. His second will restore Uncle Torza to Benevolent Winds."

"I want to find my own way to rescue Father and Mother," I said. "Surely, two different approaches would achieve our wishes faster?"

"How, Little Sister?" he asked mildly. "If you have a plan, tell me. I'll talk to Yiuti. Who can talk to his grandfather, who has the wherewithal." He glanced at the door, and added, in a low voice, "I don't think he'll permit you to go. No, don't frown, please don't. Can't you see? He's thinking of the family. Half of Grand-Uncle Yiulo's strongest support comes from those boys out there, second or third or fifth sons all, except for Cousin Oraiti, who was stripped of rank. Like us. Most with fathers as ministers, who would be appalled if you were not taken in and protected. They hate Uncle Koza every bit as much as we do. You probably don't know how many purges among the ministers Uncle Koza instituted. Everyone who didn't instantly hit forehead to the floor after he killed his brother and claimed the throne."

I could see myself being drawn back into the power duels—and gently ushered to the side, to sit, watch indirectly, and wait for my fate to be decided. I swallowed in an aching throat.

A servant entered, bowed, and said, "This lowly one begs forgiveness for the interruption, but his highness summons all to the dining chamber."

"Tell him we're coming," Second Brother said easily.

The servant bowed and went out.

Second Brother turned to me. "Come, Little Sister," he said sympathetically. Affectionately. "You've done so very well, heroically well. You can be easy now. You're among friends again. You're protected."

I hated how my voice quivered as I said. "Brother, I can't forget that it was Cousin Yiuti who got you arrested in the first place, taking that military token. You *and* our family."

Second Brother waved that away, his beautiful lavender robe glistening in the shafting sunlight through the open windows. It was carved with airy symbols—so like him, air being his principal attribute. Air and wood, the latter a living symbol unlike metal, stone, air, and fire. Trees bend with the wind, they root strong. They are symbols of loyalty. "He's apologized for that. Punished himself by drinking three times three cups before all the company, once we were safely out of the imperial capital, and promptly fell flat on his face. Grand-Uncle Yiulo points out that that was merely a convenient excuse for Xianti, who was going to find some way to get at First Brother anyway. Preferably through the family, because using Kanda's words about bad fathers making bad sons would be so much more painful for First Brother." His expression saddened as he rose and extended his hand to me.

What could I do? Not sit there, certainly. Besides, I was desperately hungry and thirsty.

Second Brother took me by the privy first, where I refreshed myself, and, using the waiting jug of fresh water for pouring over the hands, dipped an end of my robe and scrubbed hard over as much skin as I could reach. Then I pulled the fox ears from my hair, shook it out, and braided it properly, pulling it up on my head and securing it with the single, plain hairpin that one of the girls at the Falcon Valley had given to me.

There was nothing to be done about my robe, but I expected that Yiuti would want to claim all the attention, and I would be expected to sit silently, as unmarried girls of low rank had been trained to do. When I left the privy and found Koi waiting, I fell into the old posture, tiny steps, head modestly bent, hands crossed right over left in front of me.

"I'm to take the carryall and sword to Second Young

Master's chamber," Koi said.

I was going to protest, then gave a mental shrug. It wasn't as if I was in danger.

I handed the carryall and Sagacious Blade over to Koi, feeling no lighter, because my heart had knotted into stone. I could not figure out why. I'd found not just news of Second Brother, but I'd found *him!* I knew that my family was still alive, and in relative comfort. I ought to be rejoicing!

Perhaps it was merely the tiredness dragging at my limbs, and the gnawing hunger I'd been ignoring since nightfall. It seemed more like a week since I'd eaten half a bowl of noodles with On. Who, at least, had believed me enough to take action in parallel to my movements, bringing *Pangolin* out to sea. That lifted my spirits enough for me to straighten my spine and walk like a princess next to Second Brother as we entered the far chamber, a long, narrow room with little tables down both sides below a bigger table carved with tiger legs. It sat on a platform, like a throne. Yiuti settled there in a welter of silks.

Second Brother's place was at his right hand, I discovered. And, as I'm sure was meant as an honor, the table next to him, instead of behind him, had been set for me. Since there were no other women present, I did not have to sit by myself on the other side, behind a gauze curtain to screen my unwed self from male eyes.

A long line of servants brought in plates and plates of dishes. Because I'd been trained this past year in such things, I noticed that the rejected refreshments of earlier had been recooked, or rearranged in the case of cakes, which relieved my sense of outrage at potential waste. Ma Shao would approve!

Yiuti stood and offered a toast to me, "Who dared the ocean with only a servant as protection, in order to bring us a warning that the treachery that I'd expected from that serpent Xianti was indeed true."

He drank, the nobles stood and drank, then they sat down and promptly ignored me. Except for covert glances now and then, and a friendly smile from cousin Oraiti. But when I chanced to meet any other eyes, they looked away in haste.

I was able to make an excellent meal, of delicacies I had not tasted for nearly two years, as I watched and listened in my old court mode. There was no poetry. No scholarly allusions. This was largely a military gathering, as if I could not have guessed Yiuti's preferences by the elaborate sword rack against the back wall, armor on a stand at another wall, and all the screens depicting battle scenes: heroes fighting demons, heroes fighting krakens, and heroes with dragons on their chest armor fighting shadowy enemies with distorted faces and red hair. I noticed that on one ancient, painted screen, the golden dragons had been repainted crimson, the color fresh and new unlike the rest of the screen.

The conversation was military, and all centered around Yiuti. Though it had been Huyun Shandek who had concocted the plot to betray both princes—and he did come in for his share of abuse—it was mainly Xianti against whom Yiuti pronounced curses and insults. Twice he proposed wild plans for catching up with Xianti's ships in order to annihilate all nine, and it was Second Brother who dissuaded him, both times after first loading at least as many compliments on Yiuti for his prowess, his heroism, his martial strength, as Yiuti had loaded insults onto the unwitting Xianti.

The second time, as Yiuti's flushed face and sharp, barked words made it clear he was steadily getting drunker, the other boys glanced to Second Brother for clues about what to say.

Then Yiuti started all over again.

It had gotten quite dark when at last Yiuti could no longer hold a cup, and Second Brother signaled with a glance to the silent servants standing behind Yiuti. They tenderly picked up the prince and began to walk-carry him off as he mumbled.

Before he got to the door, he made an effort to straighten, looked back, and said, "BanBan...find place...sister. Nice place. Messenger...Loyal... Good girl, your s-shishturr..."

Second Brother gave me a look, and I stood up, bowed, and uttered suitable thanks. Yiuti turned a surprisingly sweet smile my way, and out he was carried, back to promising retribution on that white-eyed rat Xianti.

The boys had stood as well, and all bowed respectfully to Yiuti's back. When he was gone, Second Brother flicked a look at Cousin Oraiti, who said to these nobles, some of whom appeared to be barely fifteen, others a few years older than Second Brother and Yiuti, "Shall we have some games?"

Everyone got up and filed out, talking among themselves. A few looked back at me, puzzled, as if they tried to fit me into an expected role.

Second Brother waited until they were gone, then said,

"I'm not certain what to do," he admitted. "You ought not to be with us, especially without a maid, but it seems unfair to confine you to the cabin I'm supposed to find for you. I think you can have the cubby off my room, if Koi doesn't mind staying in with me."

"I can sleep on the floor," Koi said.

"Thank you, Koi," Second Brother said—and it was sincere. He had been restored to the old rank in the eyes of the Firedragon Lans, but he had not changed in essentials. He had grown. Had he been that much of a leader, however casual, when we lived in the imperial palace? I'd seen all those boys, even the older ones, turning to him.

How long before Yiuti saw that?

I said to Second Brother, "I'm serious about you coming with me. Please have them lower the sailboat again, would you? I'm glad Cousin Yiuti and Grand-Uncle Yiulo have promised to free our parents, but I would feel much better working at it ourselves. We could do it together."

"We can do it together from the grand prince's base. He has great plans, Little Sister. Ay, he won't like this setback about Huyun Shandek, but he'll figure a way around it. He's had friendly messages back from Prince Ran, which means the west could be his…"

I put out a hand to interrupt. "When you say *we*, how serious is that?"

He stopped talking and turned to me, and now he seemed puzzled.

"Second Brother, how much will either of them listen to me? It seems to me that Cousin Yiuti, at least, wishes to stuff me right back into a kind of one-cabin harem, out of sight. And out of mind, except to come out at banquets, where I will be expected to sit in silence."

Second Brother sighed. "I see. And I feel obliged to point out that that is not meant as a slight on you. It's customary. Generations of custom. Women don't go to war." He thumbed his eyes. "For which I thank all the gods," he added on a breath. "It's bad enough as it is. Renti, surely you can see I'm trying to curtail Yiuti's wilder notions. Oraiti, too. Grand Uncle Yiulo *depends* on that. We are not like the Upstart Prince and his uncle—"

"I don't understand," I said. "How do they relate to our problem now? I thought they went to war against this island,

and were defeated and killed at Tiger Island when they tried to invade the big island by sneaking through the smaller ones."

Second Brother raised his hand. "No. The *uncle* went to war in his *nephew*'s name. He was the last of the Kwai family. The uncle, Ing Moa, was from the mother's family, the Ings. Noble, but not princes. He could not save the older boy, and I guess did not try to save the sisters. He only saved the younger Kwai son. Who vanished. Some say Kwai Sheion wasn't even in the battle at all, but ran off well before. That's what I meant—Yiuti is the wild one, determined to restore the family to the dragon throne on his grandfather's behalf. Grand Prince Yiulo is more cautious. Unlike the Upstart Prince's uncle."

I waited impatiently for him to take a breath, and then said, "They all sound alike to me: war for war's sake. Please, Second Brother. Please come with me. Let's find a way to get Mother, Father, and First Brother away. We don't have to fight to restore titles. There is an entire world out there for us to explore, and make good lives..." I saw his pensive expression, which reminded me of Koi's equally pensive expression when we were talking in the sailboat, and I was telling him about my plan if we found Second Brother. My wonderful plan of reunion, of finding a way together to rescue our family.

Second Brother's way was right here. He might not like war, but it was clear to me that he had chosen this path. Even though he knew Yiuti was a wildfire waiting to combust. Even though he knew that Grand Uncle Yiulo's "caution" was still making promises contingent on a lot of bloody conquering before he could keep them. It was the only method that he could see, because that was the method outlined by history.

How many decent men have reluctantly made that choice?

I am going to change that if I can, I vowed then.

"Let me talk to the staff," Second Brother said gently. "I promise, I'll get them to make that cubby as comfortable as possible, and you'll have the run of my room when I'm on the deck. We're outside a lot. We have martial exercise for half of every fine day. When I can get free, we can play Circle, as we used to. And when I can't, Oraiti is good company, you already know that. We'll reach Grand Uncle's retreat in ten days' time, then you can get proper clothes, and the finer chamber that you deserve."

He left me there, and walked out.

I turned to Koi, my eyes aching. "Where are my things?

Let's see if we can talk them into lowering the…"

That same look was in his face.

"No," I breathed. "You're not abandoning my family, too?"

Koi would not meet my eyes. "He is not abandoning them. But he feels other demands are equally urgent."

"What could be more urgent than rescuing our family?"

"Keeping Crown Prince Xianti from the dragon throne, which will cause untold misery. That's one."

I paused, knowing it was true. I added bitterly, "But it seems the conflict is no hard choice for him."

Koi made a negating motion. "I think…"

"Tell me, Koi. I'm still Pangolin Ren, though I stand on this imperial ship."

His sober gaze met mine. "He sees himself as filial. But…you know the saying that the worm and the bird see the tree differently?"

"So?"

He groped, his gaze sliding away. "When the dragon fire fever took the household. While you had Madam's anxious face at your bedside, all he saw was the back of her head."

This struck me, hard.

He hastened to add, "This is in no way a slander of Madam. Who is admirable in all the ways possible, but no one can be in two places at once."

I remembered then that Second Brother had made some references to Mother, and I had not understood his tone or countenance, except that there was no anger. But grief, a little? Because we were both sick, but she had stayed at my bedside.

"I think I see," I said, and now the grief was mine. Because it was true, I had absorbed so much of Mother's attention, believing it my right, without once thinking that what I had, my brothers would lack. Not that First Brother would even notice, for he had absorbed all of Father's attention that Father could spare from duty.

I had to think about that. But later. I turned back to Koi. "Another thing. *You* don't believe Yiuti's promises, do you? Didn't you see how those boys look to my brother? How long before Yiuti sees that?"

"That's why I have to stay," Koi said, barely audible. "Someone has to protect him."

Agonized, I found a thousand protests rising from my heart to my lips, but none of them reached the air.

The pines and bamboo on the mountain slopes
alone hear my zither.
If I play till the strings break,
who else will hear?
It will not be in vain,
If they send back their peace.

On would know that poem about the silent, peaceful, loyal, living woods. If I could dissuade Koi from what he thought was right, would I miss him as much as I did now, though we stood face to face? Another agonizing dilemma, one I was in no mood to debate. All I knew then was that it hurt with surprising sharpness to see him reduced to servant place once more. I knew I could not bear to see him bowing before me, and referring to himself as lowly one as he called me Young Miss, when we had been free and equal. But he was sacrificing that freedom because loyalty was greater.

I forced out the words, "I understand. You're going to protect him."

"Yes! That's why I have to stay," Koi said. "I will try to send word to you through the Falcons once we arrive at Whale Haven. Though it might take months, unless I'm very lucky and meet Falcons who might send a pigeon. But I can't count on that. They only send them for dire circumstances."

"I know."

"I'll have to obscure names, in case the imperial prince has spies intercepting letters. They can do anything if they have a dragon token. So I'll use the numeral two for your brother. Fox for Yiuti—he'd like that—and fox elder for his grandfather. I guess a real letter is impossible, but at least I can let you know we're safe, though I won't mention where we are."

"Whale Haven Island: I'll remember. And I'd like that."

Koi's answering smile was the briefest flicker, but it was there, then he turned away, groped behind a trunk, and brought out my carryall and Sagacious Blade, which was quiescent in his hands. "If you go now, I can tell them, oh, that a lover sailed up in a charmed boat and took you away. They'll have to believe it, for they won't think of a sword that flies. If you don't mind such an explanation muddying your reputation."

"Why should I?" I said, with the careless ease of ignorance, and then scowled. "As far as I'm concerned, why should men get a reputation as a dashing hero when they collect lovers, and women are muddied? I think I'll go start collecting some lovers right now, and *dare* anyone to call me mud."

"I expect you'll find it very easy, when you do decide to." Koi's gaze slid away, then he opened a side door, which led to the companionway alongside the cabins. The ship's rail was three steps away.

Night again, and I was tired, but grief gave me strength, and I remembered that I'd asked for lamps to be lit to guide the sailboat to the *Pangolin*. These could also guide me from the air.

Before either of us could speak further, we heard the door open back in Second Brother's chamber. I drew Sagacious Blade, knelt on it, and rose softly into the air; the sailors all looked out to sea, and not upward.

I flew away, weeping salt tears into the ocean, until at last I spied the *Pangolin*'s golden lights.

END OF BOOK ONE

ABOUT THE AUTHOR

Sherwood Smith writes fantasy, science fiction, and historical fiction. Her full bibliography can be found on her website at https://www.sherwoodsmith.net.

About Book View Cafe

Book View Café is an author-owned cooperative of professional writers, publishing in a variety of genres including fantasy, science fiction, romance, mystery, and more.

Its authors include New York Times and USA Today bestsellers as well as winners and nominees of many prestigious awards such as the Agatha Award, Hugo Award, Lambda Literary Award, Locus Award, Nebula Award, RITA Award, Philip K. Dick Award, World Fantasy Award, and many others.

Since its debut in 2008, Book View Café has gained a reputation for producing high quality books in both print and electronic form. BVC's e-books are DRM-free and distributed around the world.

Book View Café's monthly newsletter includes new releases, specials, author news, and event announcements. To sign up, visit https://www.bookviewcafe.com/bookstore/newsletter/